LADY TREMAINE

LADY TREMAINE

A Novel

Rachel Hochhauser

ST. MARTIN'S PRESS
NEW YORK

First published in the United States by St. Martin's Press, an imprint of St. Martin's Publishing Group

EU Representative: Macmillan Publishers Ireland Ltd, 1st Floor, The Liffey Trust Centre, 117–126 Sheriff Street Upper, Dublin 1, DO1 YC43

www.stmartins.com

Designed by Jen Edwards

The Library of Congress Cataloging-in-Publication Data is available upon request.

ISBN 978-1-250-39634-1 (hardcover)
ISBN 978-1-250-44254-3 (Canadian & international, sold outside the U.S., subject to rights availability)
ISBN 978-1-250-39635-8 (ebook)

Our books may be purchased in bulk for specialty retail/wholesale, literacy, corporate/premium, educational, and subscription box use. Please contact MacmillanSpecialMarkets@macmillan.com.

First Edition: 2026

10 9 8 7 6 5 4 3 2 1

For Bea. And for Isabel.

LADY
TREMAINE

CHAPTER ONE

I'VE BEEN WARNED TO BE WARY OF STRANGERS IN THE WOODS SINCE I was a little girl. A person, alone, unfamiliar, hidden in the dappled darkness, is not to be trusted. And, certainly, the woods can hide the sorts of people you'd rather not encounter. Outlaws and outcasts. Gruesomely mutilated pariahs—those with fingers taken for thieving, lips and tongues cut out for lying, flesh rotting for submission to disease. But just as shadows serve to hide and disguise, they also provide privacy and solitude, and, if you look carefully, beauty. The darkness of the woods offers a break from watchful eyes and rules to follow and stiffened skirts and the never-ending etiquette of being a woman in the world. For a few short hours of the day, I've always considered it a fair trade: darkness for freedom.

But when I first heard the twig snap and saw the man ahead of me, I was scared. I saw beard and sword and steel. Year after year of warnings—to stay in the light, to travel in pairs, to avoid complicity in your fate—surfaced with one shallow breath.

That morning, it was early, and I had been somewhere I was not supposed to be. No matter if the stranger intended no harm. Fear makes people dangerous. And you see: To him, I, too, was a stranger in the woods.

I HAD STARTED MY DAY AS USUAL. FEET OUT OF THE BEDCOVERS BE-fore dawn, searching for slippers on the cold floor. The hurried application of smock and kirtle, frost riming the obsidian windowpanes. I shoved my hand into a leather glove and gently roused Lucy, who slept beneath the velvet folds of her own wing.

Keeping a peregrine in my bedchambers was unusual, but it was my only means of indulging her. All else with a falcon was measured, calculated, managed, tied down. She was trussed to her perch. Flew only when allowed. Weighed near daily on a brass scale. I could not help but offer a small bit of nocturnal warmth.

She sat on my gauntlet, bound by her jesses to my very body, and we went out into the dark hallway. I held the bird aloft ahead of me, arm extended as if she were a lantern, feeling my way along the wall. Past Rosamund's door. Past Mathilde's. Past the steps that led up to Elin. Feet soft on the worn tread of the carpet.

A sound emerged from the shadows behind me. I turned back to see my eldest framed by the slender crack of her doorway, face lit by the stub of a flickering candle. "Do not say *not today*," Mathilde whispered.

I frowned. "I will meet you at breakfast."

"No one will see us," she protested. "I can help you."

Lucy's talons tightened on the glove and I pulled her closer. "Back to bed." The candle was not so dim that I missed the shadow of dissatisfaction on Mathilde's face. She shut her door without speaking, leaving me near blind in the semidarkness. It made no difference, I told myself. Soon the world and its sleeping daughters would turn their faces toward the light.

IN THE KITCHEN, WENTHELEN, STURDY AND RED-FACED, STOOD OVER a pot gurgling on the hearth. Small piles of ash collected beneath rush-lights. The room smelled of cooking vegetables.

"Taste this." She plucked her spoon from the pot.

"I'm sure it's—" The wooden instrument was inserted into my mouth. Wenthelen, a good cook who required the compliments of a great chef, rummaged with the utensil for several long moments.

"Satisfactory," I said, when I was able to. In truth, the broth needed salt and the savory flavor of meat, but I couldn't say so—I'd insisted that we buy a pound of sugar instead of a flank of beef.

Wenthelen took a step closer. The spoon twitched in her hand.

"It is nothing short of delectable!" I cried, stepping backward, into Alice, our only other household staff, who had just entered behind me. "Did I detect a hint of spice? You've elevated the humble parsnip to a veritable triumph!"

"Leak's worse," Alice announced placidly.

I turned to our housekeeper—gray eyes and gray hair, pulled into a bun so tight it left her forehead expressionless—and frowned at her. "You always say so on the day after rain."

"And it rains a lot." Alice frowned back, as unflustered as Wenthelen was perturbed. "We made a tidy sum on Rosie's embroidery bits."

"Those pennies are to go to the haberdasher."

She crossed her arms. "Write the thatcher."

"The girls need lace sleeves."

"Lace sleeves." Wenthelen tutted from the edge of the hearth. Seeing the look on my face, she added: "Ma'am."

"Everyone is wearing blond flounces this year." I'd seen the fine needle and bobbin meshwork peeking out of necklines and gathered in diaphanous ruffles at elbows. "And the world is unkind to those who don't follow its rules."

Alice lifted my old cloak from the peg and shook it out, tucking a twist of cloth into one of the pockets. "And yet, you go out each morning dressed like a swineherd."

I snatched at the cloak. "I can hardly hunt in silk."

Alice glanced at the dark windows. "You might have better luck in the afternoon."

"Better luck would be if I were hunting for sport."

Wenthelen stuck the spoon back into the pot and gave its contents a hearty stir. "We could buy meat if you did not insist on buying sugar."

"We could not have guests if I could not serve confections."

Wenthelen only sighed and clucked at my falcon—"Go on, then, Lucy, get us something for supper"—before turning to face Alice: "Try the stew."

"Needs salt—" Alice started to say.

I hurried away.

ACCORDING TO A MAP, I OWN A PIECE OF LAND. BUT A MAP IS A SYM-bol. It has no real connection to the soil—it serves as an artifact or an echo. A map is made and then the land changes and the map does not change with it. And yet we respect maps as if they are the law, treating their boundaries as finite, allowing them to determine *yours, mine, ours, theirs, his*. Rarely *hers*.

But the map says: I do own some land. An aberration in the system: A man—my husband—died with no male heirs. *His* became *hers*. The map now draws a line around what is mine: a property that sits next to, but does not touch, a stream. On paper, it is a snaking blue line, thin and nearly invisible.

Because that snaking blue line does not cross my property, it is not good hunting land. The quail and the grouse and the pheasants stay closer to the streams and rivers that branch and fracture the landscape. So, for the purposes of my morning routine, I often choose to be liberal with the boundaries of the map.

Technically, this is illegal.

THE HUNT DID NOT START WELL. BY THE TIME THE SUN HOVERED ON the horizon, we'd still had no luck. No movement or missed chances. Lucy sat, high on a branch above me, waiting, and I moved slowly beneath her, poking at the brambles with a stick, hoping to flush a pheasant. The ground was soft and sucking. I watched the brambles and Lucy watched it all: the curls of water in the stream, the leaves quivering on the branches, the fog moving like breath along the forest floor.

Peregrines need room to hunt; they start high and dive low. Sky and space and speed are their best tools. Across the stream, the growth thinned, and the forest's canopy gave way to large pockets of sky; the land had the open air that would yield us game. But the crossing of the water was as symbolic as water itself. On one side: dubiously legal hunting. On the other: punishable poaching on royal land.

As if sensing my intentions, Lucy pulled her feathers in tight, her body going slick.

"It's fine," I assured her.

She blinked slowly, hiding her eyes from me for half a moment.

"Quail and grouse do not abide by the rules of a map. Three hops and we'll be back on the right side."

I bent over, gathered my skirts in my hands, and tied a practiced knot between my legs. There were no logs or rocks to use, so, after a running start, I leapt across the water and landed in the soft mud on the other side. The jump soaked my hem and splattered my shins with black slurry. I looked around. The forest has eyes but cannot speak. It had no way of telling on me.

I did not believe in magic, nor did I think members of royalty were divine, but there was something to be said for their land. Working my way through the underbrush, I used the stick to poke and prod the growth. Blackthorn and ferns and holly. Tangled thickets of vine and clusters of orange-red hawthorn haws and the young green of early rose hips. The air was quiet, and I went still, inhaling. Here, with a little bit more space and a little bit of sun, the odor of damp—of decay and of turning leaves—had a life of its own, a quiet, dark fertility that calmed me. I squinted up at a patch of white sky as Lucy took flight and rose above.

A falcon is a murderous creature. There is destruction in its bones. Its body hums, faster than the fastest clock, priming itself for that quick moment. *Tick.* The click of an eyelid. *Tick.* The silent swivel of a head. *Tick.* A stoop so fast it is but a gray streak in your eye. Time runs out. The bird gives over all that is regal and becomes what it was meant to be, what it was born to be, and the hum becomes a roar. The sound of Lucy's bell told me she had moved before I saw, and then she was in front of me, closed wings, head down, legs back, diving faster than I could watch her. A vicious entry into the brush, twigs breaking, wings flapping: The rabbit was dead before I'd known it was alive, the unpleasantness done in less than two heartbeats.

"A rabbit, Lucy!" I cried. Peregrines hunt other birds—pigeons and partridges and teal. A coney was a coup for a falcon of her size. "See?" I said to her, gesturing at the stream. "You only needed a bit more space."

I went to her side. Plenty has been said about the dignity of a hunt, but it's what comes after the kill that you must make peace with. Lucy had her talons buried in the bloody bowels of the mammal. It was not feminine. It was not pristine. But we needed the animal for supper— the very world in its essence.

A hungry raptor cannot resist blood, but there is a trick that will part a bird from its quarry. I removed a gizzard from the twist of cloth in my pocket and, kneeling, offered it to Lucy. Her eyes followed my fingers, distracted by the giblets. With my other hand, I gathered great fistfuls of wet leaves and piled them over the dead coney. When Lucy glanced back down to her kill, she saw only mulch from the forest floor. Up again, and there was the gizzard. She willingly went to my glove to eat it. And, after tying her jesses, I fastened the rabbit to my belt where she would not see it.

BACK ON THE RIGHT SIDE OF THE STREAM, I FOUND THE UNEVEN PATH
once more. "I'd wager the girls are still asleep," I told Lucy, who ignored
me, per her custom. As we moved forward, the trees began to thin, and
the rutted road was visible in the distance. "Snug in their warm beds."
And I could see it: Rosamund's and Mathilde's dark hair fanned around
their heads, in separate side-by-side rooms. Elin, upstairs. Wenthelen
and Alice in the kitchens down below. Our small collection of bodies
a last stand against nature's takeover of the house. Sleeping or awake
made no difference: Time was marching us forward, every day a new
mishap, a brick that loosened or a wall that cracked. Slender wrists
trying to uphold a falling roof.

Wrists that would have lace.

Alice might fuss and Wenthelen might stamp, but lace and sugar—
and the maintenance of a proper carriage and a good set of gloves and
so many other details—were necessities. One had to have a shell, or at
least the projection of one, for protection. For the sake of presentability,
all our lives were a performance. Our dresses as pleated and heavy as
the curtains on a grand stage. Respectability was a lifeboat that would
float the girls along the gentle tides of stability, straight onto the secure
banks of marriage. A leaking roof would not be a bother if they lived
beneath a new one.

Lucy blinked and then rapidly straightened, swiveling her head,
leaning forward, the quick movement a warning to me. Her weight
shifted on my fist. She knew just before it would happen and then it
did: A crack—the sound you look out for, unmistakable, the snap of a
twig, a boot in the brittle brush—came from ahead.

I stilled, hoping for cover in the shadows. In front of us on the path,
alongside the stream, a dark-haired man stood, facing the road.

There was a reason I hunted at dawn. The hour was typically one
of solitude. While the road ahead was used by many, few had any purpose to come down to the stream when the sky had not yet rid itself
of night. There were never witnesses to connect the bedraggled huntress to the lady of the nearby estate. I was less alarmed by the bodily

threat of a strange man than I was by his capability to identify me. My circumstances—mud-spattered with a petulant bird on my arm and a dead rabbit tied to my belt—were not only ill fitting for a woman of my station; it would reflect poorly on everyone in my household.

He had not yet seen me. To my side, there was the stream, which, surely, I could no longer cross. To the other, a steep rise covered in thick vegetation. I could go forward along the path, or backward in the opposite direction, trapped between the imaginary dividing line of royal land and a briar-covered embankment. Real thorns, royal thorns, a stranger, or the wrong direction. But Lucy destroyed any chance of stealth. Attuned to my fear, she bated—leaping off the glove, a motion of fury and panic—molting into an explosion of feathers. The jesses kept her tethered and her bells rang.

Peregrine falcons are ruthless birds. Athletic and fast. Black heads and orange-ringed eyes and a body the color of armor. With Lucy on my arm, an unfamiliar person might have thought I had a weapon, or at least an ally. I had certainly encountered people who thought I could command her to attack, to dive for their throats, and the soft bits of their bodies. But, while Lucy was indeed designed to kill, her violence was only a steppingstone to her survival. If someone were to think she might have helped me when I was in danger, I would have to correct them: Lucy would eat my eyeballs if she needed to.

Carefully, I withdrew her hood from my pocket and slipped it over her head, touching, ever so briefly, her tiny skull. Unable to see, she quieted. When I looked up again, the stranger was watching us.

"Good morrow." I nodded.

"Good morrow," he replied, though his tone did not suggest it. My concern dissipated a little; he had an accent, which was not common in our small kingdom. He was unlikely to recognize me.

I looked at him: black hair, dark eyes. He wore the rough handspun cloth of a peasant and had a longsword—indistinct, with little markings—at his waist. The clothing of a commoner. Still, I steeled myself: His boots were fine enough that he might have stolen them and his undecorated sword, though not fashionable, looked to be well used and worn.

He took us in, in turn: the woman with the bird and the cottontail. "You caught a rabbit here." He paused, extending a finger toward Lucy. "With that?"

"She caught the rabbit," I corrected. On my arm, in her plumed hood, Lucy looked like a decorated warrior in miniature.

"You trained her?"

I nodded, but was suddenly wary that he might want the bird. "She answers only to me."

"Rabbits are plentiful here?"

I said: "Rabbits are plentiful by their nature." But game was *not* plentiful in these woods and certainly not on the wrong side of the stream.

He glanced down at my skirts, which were still tied in a knot. "You're familiar with these woods." A statement intended as a question.

I was not accustomed to being interrogated. "Nature is free for any to explore."

"Not when it's not your land."

I lifted my chin to stare at him. His eyes were unreadable. "This isn't anyone's land. And I did not know that there was anyone appointed as guardian of the woods."

The man scowled. "If you caught that rabbit on that side of the river"—he pointed—"it's king's land."

"Well, quite fortunate for me the rabbit was on this side of the stream."

"This side," he repeated, looking down pointedly at my hem, which was wet.

But I didn't respond because I had caught sight of what was happening on the road far behind him.

Ahead through the trees, a carriage was stuck in the mud. Four horses strained to pull the rig forward. My heart quickened and gut tightened, for though its body was small, the coach's windows were glass, and the doors had a golden coat of arms. The equipage was unmistakably royal.

The byway that passes my home is well traveled. But I had heard the whispers in recent weeks and knew the carriage was not likely to move past our gate. When it reached our iron arches, it would turn off the well-worn path and head up our overgrown drive, stopping in the gravel at the front entrance.

And I—Lady of the Dead Rabbit, Lady of the Mud—was meant to throw open the door and welcome its passengers. (Surely I was not a quarter of a mile away from my hall, covered in sludge, trading insults with a stranger.) But more than keeping up with expectations, it was, if the rumors were true, of the utmost importance that I be home to receive the carriage and welcome the message it bore. Our futures—the women of the slender wrists and the heavy roof—might depend on it.

"I must be going." I tried to keep the urgency from my voice.

"You're unaccompanied," the man observed. "What are you doing out here alone?"

In the distance, a footman had gotten out of the carriage and was inspecting the wheel. I gathered myself, returning my gaze to the stranger's. "I would think that's self-evident." I needed to hurry and if the man was going to rob me, or worse, he would have done it already. "I've been alone in the woods plenty of times without incident."

"Arrogance is a dangerous companion."

I ran out of patience. "Sir, the candidate for dangerous companion is yourself. If you'd step aside, I must be along."

He cocked his head and stared at me. "Don't let me get in your way."

When I was a few paces along, he called out again: "You shouldn't be alone in the woods."

I couldn't tell if the words were a threat or a warning. The world loved a woman alone in the woods. Whatever happened to these women—outcomes we lamented—there was also a sense of relief. They had ignored the warnings. The path they chose, neither well trodden nor well lit, allowed us to emotionally divest. These women broke the rules. Issued an invitation. Created an opening for unkindness. Our own daughters, sisters, mothers—studious rule-followers, virtuous listeners—would be fine.

Up ahead, the footman was sliding branches beneath the wheel. Despite the golden insignias on the side of the carriage, there was no retinue, no guards surrounding the rig—an indication that only a messenger would be riding inside. But messages could be life-changing. Especially if they bore an invitation to a royal ball.

I crept along the hillside, further muddying myself, until I was far enough along to stay out of sight. Climbing up through the vines, I slipped across the road and through a concealed hole in the laurel hedge, the rabbit knocking against my hip bone.

It went without saying: My daughters were never allowed in the woods.

CHAPTER TWO

B EFORE THERE WERE HALF-MOONS OF DIRT BENEATH MY NAILS, there were jewels on my fingers. And before there were lines on my face, there was joy. But all of that was long ago. I've sold most of my jewels. There is, alas, no price on joy. But if joy were a commodity, I'd trade all I have—all that's left of it—for my daughters. Rosie. Mathilde. (Here a few images come to mind: Twin braids. A freckle on a calf. Mathilde's scar. The long shadows cast by a child's eyelashes. Minute details that come to represent a whole being.)

My name is Lady Etheldreda Verity Isolde Tremaine Bramley. The man in the woods thought I, mud-spattered and soiled, was a peasant. I have been familiar with the loam of the earth since I was a girl, but he was wrong.

My father was a brewer—a respectable trade that was still far from gentility. Brewers make enough money that their daughters, and their dowries, might be considered for marriage with the landed class. But our village was small, with few gentlemen, and we socialized with the yeomanry and gentry alike, caught somewhere between the two worlds, capable in both, fully accepted by neither.

Our family manor was on the outskirts of the king's territory, far from most of the nobility and the day-to-day machinations of court, its customs and norms. I grew up with little knowledge of those formalities, in a household of men. I passed most of my time in the kitchen, stealing rolls and tarts and apples; in the stables, feeding the same rolls and tarts and apples to the livestock; or outside, assisting the boys and the men.

As a brewer, my father spent his days busied by every manner of task—boiling wort, cleaning barrels, keeping records. He and my brother often involved themselves in the needs of the house and our land, stepping in to smith or woodwork. Both at the brewery and at home, I was allowed to observe or, less frequently, help. If something were to break or go wrong, instead of calling for a specialist, my father would first turn to his hands. Always, he said, you start with the tools you have. Through him, I learned how to manage a home and a cellar: how to salt or smoke a successful hunt's bounty; how to prune a cherry tree; how to rack barrels without breaking your back; how to mix clay, soil, straw, and dung into daub and apply it across the stable's wattles. When I wasn't trailing after my father, I explored the woods around our home, put my hands and feet in the river, and made tiny pretend creatures from twigs and leaves. The days of my girlhood were dusty, dirty, sooty, and sweaty. Above all, they were happy.

On my twelfth birthday, a tutor named Agatha—a severe woman with pox scars and beautiful red hair who covered her smell of sour milk with a pungent lilac water—was hired to oversee my education: namely, to instill me with knowledge of the manners and etiquette that would be necessary for marriage. It was through Agatha, a bit belatedly, that I was taught the formalities and customs of genteel women, a counterbalance to my years spent shadowing my father.

I was also taught how many raps a knuckle can take before it bleeds. How fingers held too firmly on an arm, or a neck, will leave marks of a sickly yellow. How a forcefully articulated dressing-down—or an afternoon of forced repetition—could hurt the mind more than any pinch or punishment. But Agatha's methods were effective, and I also learned how to hold and manipulate a fan to send messages, how to walk with a ladylike gait, and how to properly wield a spoon (scoop the food away from your body). I learned how to create and repair linens and manage a household and lead a dinner prayer. I learned to eat slowly, with small, refined bites, and to listen politely, and to lift my chin, and to speak softly. Because this was not part of my life from the very beginning, to this day, being a woman with a title can feel like a carapace that I inhabit.

I resisted the switch—from long days outdoors in the sun or the mist to long hours in the great hall learning table manners and the art of the curtsy—not because I feared Agatha or feared marriage, but because I missed the freedom of unplanned afternoons. I didn't know to fear marriage: Marriage was just assumed. A duty and an inevitable future.

If I had paid close attention, I might have seen some of the warnings. Rosy-cheeked girls who wed and watched their skin turn gray. Women in our village who married men so far away we never saw them again. Swollen lips and bruised eyes—echoes of violence, as ancient as man himself—that made themselves known at the market and local taverns.

But the stories we passed on and murmured about were what happened to the girls who had *not* married. There were women who fell into ruin. Spinsters who lived at the mercy of unknown relatives. In my hamlet, an unwed maidservant was once discovered to be with child, and then, later, beaten to death by an unknown hand—purple at the belly, a thrashing meant to induce miscarriage—so that she could not, would not, name the father. A different year, a pregnant woman had wandered into our township. Alone and in labor. She could not walk. She crawled in the dirt. And no one helped her, for to help her would be to assume responsibility. The constable threw her convulsing body over the back of a horse and carted her to county lines. I'd once heard a story of a widow whose deceased husband left her and her daughter nothing but the choice of prostitution. Both of their bodies were later found in the shallow stream where people did their washing, limbs bloody, faces forgotten, except where the daughter's forehead had been branded with a hot iron. Each telling gruesome. Whispered about. But without a sense of surprise or horror: These instances were recounted and incanted as warning.

We women were born and bred to expect marriage, and it all happened when we were too young to know better. Fifteen, sixteen, seventeen: so young a girl's first breath was still a part of the earth's atmosphere. So young you pinched your cheeks to make them pink, you strung flowers in your hair, you denuded daisies whispering of love, you believed in the power of the moon and in the twinkling of the stars as if all of nature and its tidal pulls would take care of you, so blind to the truth of what lay ahead.

I later came to realize: Nature was a system, not a nurturer. For every life, there was death; for every bit of laughter, there were tears. For every anguish, there was joy. For the broken bones and crushed eggshells, there were small miracles. For the predators, there was prey. For the herbivores, there were plants, and for the carnivores, there was meat, and every meal for every being caused some other living thing harm. Nature was balance.

The only being that defied the ancient standard—the standard of *me first, me only, I, I, me*—was a mother. A mother, in the bones of her bones, was not in balance. She gave, without ending. She thought not as an *I* but as a *we* and more often it was *you, you, you, my darling, you.* A mother protected, tipping scales, weighing odds, defying the system. And I did not have one.

I do not know if my parents had a happy marriage. My father did not like to talk about my mother, for talking about her brought pain, and he saw little purpose in discomfort. The pain, at least, told me he had loved her, though love, too, was something my father did not like to talk about.

I had three siblings. The first was a stillbirth. Two of us had survived to adulthood. My mother died delivering the last of us, my younger brother, Joseph, who died himself before his first birthday. (Four children, two survive: Balance can be cruel.)

I was three when she passed, and sometimes I think I can remember her. Long fingers, holding my face, humming, dark hair, memories as shapeless as a dream itself. Is this so different from the twin braids, the freckle, the scar, the shadow of an eyelash that, when held together, represent my own children? I was never certain if I confused the recollections with the details I begged my older brother for, somehow twining his remembering with my own. My only tangible evidence was a necklace my mother had left behind—a cameo carved into shell that depicted her countenance. It felt fitting that all I had was her outline, as if her details were not meant for me. The little I knew about my mother was that she *was* a mother, and it wasn't until I had children of my own that I could understand and inhabit this, or truly feel any connection between the two of us.

I have wondered at the immeasurable ways my life would be different if she had lived longer. Perhaps I would have known more, when knowing would have been useful. Perhaps I would have expected some of the pain, some of the blood, that goes in hand with living. Perhaps what is hard in me, what can be cruel, would be softer. But I think, above all else, she might have stopped me from marrying so young. Or at least better prepared me.

A marriage can be violent, even if a man is not. By the time my daughters were grown, there were no men left in my house. Though we were not starving, we needed food. Though we lived in a grand hall, we were not well off. The scant means we did have—what I'd gotten from selling off furniture piece by piece, stripping the walls painting by painting, trading necklaces and brooches jewel by jewel—went toward maintaining the upright charade Agatha had drilled into me through bloodied knuckles and bruised arms: the appearance that all was well.

❦

ONCE THROUGH THE HEDGE, I COULD SEE THE HOUSE, THE ORCHARD, the air itself was still asleep, as if I had imagined the morning—the death of the rabbit, the approaching carriage, the stranger in the wood. Frost covered the sundial at the center of the garden, and the outbuildings— the cellar and smokehouse—were half disguised in the fog. Approaching the grand and slumping hall from the back, the upper half-timbered floors looked gray in the weak sunlight. More whitewash was needed. My whole life had become a ruse like the house we lived in: grand and ornate on the exterior and crumbling, brick by brick, inside.

The first time I came to Bramley Hall, I had been stunned by the beautiful gate out front: intricate ironwork covered in curls and gold that emulated the delicate tendrils of a climbing vine. We went up along the gravel drive, through an orchard of fruit trees, and the house had come into sight: massive and pleasant, with exposed timbers in a diamond pattern. Multiple gables and intricately carved bargeboards. The main entrance—metal studded and carved—was so ornate that even the door's hinges were decorative.

But the years had passed and what had felt luxurious and ornamental had become onerous and decrepit. The front gate had broken (rusted, permanently, to stay open) and the timbers were rotting. The roof leaked in three places. But the trees along the gravel were pruned (a skill I had thanks to my father) and the weeds were at bay (here, an image of Rosamund frowning at me, hands swimming in work gloves) and the chandeliers in the great hall gleamed (Mathilde, standing precariously on a stool). What skills we had were all applied to maintaining anywhere a guest might see.

Just as a scab protects a wound, I came to understand Agatha's manners and lessons as layers of armor. They developed and hardened around me, holding me upright. I was constantly aware of the world's expectations. They were the rules I lived by. Fitting in was survival.

So, I hid our circumstances from the world. The facade that all was well—that we had means, that we followed the rules, that we were well heeled and well mannered—offered a chance at a future for my daughters. One that didn't involve searching for game at sunrise or re-pairing stockings until they were composed of only repairs or shivering our way through winter for lack of wood. Marriage could be violent, but marrying them well was the only chance I had to spirit the girls up and away from what life had dealt us. It was the lesson from my father: You use the tools you have.

I stared up at the house, its mullioned windows opaque in the morn-ing light, listening for the sounds of the carriage. There was no time to return Lucy to her mews. And I couldn't answer the door with a bird on my arm.

"Will you wait for me?" I asked Lucy, removing her hood and ges-turing to the oversized oak that grew in the middle of our lawn. She stared at me with a critical eye. You cannot abandon a raptor to the wild. Even the most well-trained falcon, imprinted since birth, might leave you.

But not if they were hungry. Not if they had a need for you to pro-vide food. And, though Lucy had eaten, she didn't feel as heavy as when her belly was full. Leaving her unattended was a risk I'd have to take if I wanted to see my daughters established. I already rose each morning to search for supper so we could use our little money for sugar and silk, and our tables could be laden with pastries and sweetmeats, and we could smile from behind clouds of sherbet-colored cloth whenever guests came over. One day, if I was successful, we could all be done with the risks and the pretending. With my whole soul, I wanted my family to find some stability in the world.

Nature keeps the world in balance. Security is not a probability. But my daughters had what I did not: a mother. The carriage was a tipping point. And I was determined to tip all in their favor.

With no time to take Lucy to the mews, I cast her feathered body toward the tree, murmuring instructions to stay until I could retrieve her. Then, she was gliding away, and there was nothing left to do but hurry inside.

CHAPTER THREE

I
T WAS NOT JUST ANY BALL.

The speculation was that the prince was looking for a wife. An engagement to a woman in another kingdom had fallen through. Or the king's health was failing and there was a pressing need for legitimate heirs. Or the royal family wanted a celebration to instill goodwill with the people. It changed with each telling. The talk was plentiful.

But here is where the rumor found its thrust: Across the kingdom, all the noble households with young women had begun to receive invitations—a chance to brush against the possibility of something greater. It was easy to understand the excitement this caused. The flurry. The hopes and dreams of girls flapped their wings and took flight, dizzying them at the prospect of rescue from an unknown future.

I didn't mislead myself. Any woman could look at the numbers, the odds, the means, without getting too far ahead: There was but one prince and a kingdom full of women. It was the ball I'd set my sights on. There was no better place to introduce a daughter—no better marker of her deservedness, her gentility—than an invitation. It could offer just enough sheen to make up for the lack of a dowry.

Despite my eagerness, I felt a sense of apprehension. I had not known if the rumors were true. I lacked confidence that my daughters were prepared. I wasn't certain I was ready to let them into the world. The related expenses would be monumental. And I feared that the ghosts of my past might make themselves known.

But—the carriage was already in the drive.

I ENTERED THROUGH THE SAME DOOR THROUGH WHICH I HAD LEFT in darkness two hours before.

"Get up," I cried, seeing Wenthelen on a kitchen stool.

She turned slowly to look at me, raising an eyebrow.

"A carriage." I realized I was out of breath and tried to slow down. "With the king's coat of arms." I unfastened the rabbit and slung it onto the wooden table at the center of the room.

Wenthelen's eyes widened, and she stood. "What will you have me do?"

"Find an apron," I said. "Tuck up your hair. I'm going to get the girls."

"I've never seen anyone royal before." She shook herself.

"No one royal is inside that carriage. There are not enough guards." I rushed across the room, toward the back stairs. "Tidy the entry and prepare some cider. And whatever we have to serve with it. As quickly as you can."

"I haven't done the baking."

"Find something."

"The rabbit?"

"You cannot serve a bloody rabbit."

As if just realizing what she'd seen, she repeated herself: "A rabbit! Well done, Lucy."

"Hurry up," I said.

"Yes, m'lady."

"For the hundredth time, you don't need to call me that." I paused at the doorway. "Except you should. Today, you should."

"Yes, m'lady," she said again, lip tugging upward.

❦

DESPITE ALL THE YEARS THAT HAD PASSED, I STILL HEARD AGATHA'S voice, her lessons. *Back straight. Shoulders relaxed. Small and dainty steps.* I heard her as I raced down the hall, taking two stairs at a time. I heard her—*avoid clumsy movements*—as I barged through Rosamund's door.

She was still asleep, her dark hair carefully braided and laid out beside her on the pillow. Gray morning light filled the windows.

"Rosie," I said gently, looking around her chambers. A good portion of the room was dedicated to a dressing area walled off by two paneled screens. Dresses were thrown over the panels and across the furniture: enormous blooms of lace and silk and velvet that had deflated and landed on the chaise longue, across the foot of the bed, and on the back of a chair.

Of all the tasks we had, Rosamund was the best with needle and thread, and she put the skill to good use: She could bead and smock and pleat, and it was thanks to her fingers that the rest of us ever looked half presentable. She could take a decades-old dress, break it down into pieces, and design a new pattern that fit the same swaths of cloth. She spent twice as much time on her own clothing, preening and fussing with embroidery and ribbons, dressing carefully even on the days we never left the house. If you stood in the center of her room, you could see yourself in three mirrors, reflecting back and forth into infinity. The rug on that spot was well worn.

Her attention to sartorial detail did not extend to other areas of her chamber: On a plate on the nightstand, there were crumbs that I did not doubt had been there for longer than I wanted to know. A layer of film covered an old basin of wash water. Half-dead flowers withered in a vase on the sill. Ignoring the squalor, I went to the window, looking out in hopes of catching sight of Lucy, but the oak tree was too far. "Rosie," I said more firmly. "You must wake up."

I walked to the bed. When I placed a hand on her forehead, her eyes fluttered open. "You must get up now and put on a good dress. As good as you can muster, as quickly as possible. A coach from the palace is here, and we'll need to greet it in a few minutes."

She sat up straight, her face falling. "Mother!"

"I know, dearest."

She glanced frantically around the room: upturned dresses and discarded, half-finished embroidery projects and, on the floor, near the bed, a pair of stockings, inside out. "I have nothing ready—I can't possibly be ready."

"They're already here." I went back over to the window. The carriage was making slow progress. The only advantage of an estate that hadn't been well maintained was that our potholes would buy us a few precious minutes. Still, I felt my breath hitch. "I need to go wake your sister. Hurry."

She let out a chirp of despair.

UNLIKE HER SISTER, MATHILDE SLEPT WITH THE CURTAINS PULLED shut, each beam of errant light unwelcome. I strode straight to the windows and pulled back the thick drapes, coughing from the dust.

"Please get up." I nearly tripped on a potted fern. "My goodness, you keep it so dark." I peered around in the dim light: The silk-covered walls had begun to peel in the corners. A small table where Mathilde did her letters was piled with books. In bed, beside her, I saw there were more—volumes placed at haphazard angles. "I don't even know how you can see in here."

"It helps me sleep." She stared at me from the bed, eyes alert. "I heard the carriage."

"Then you know to hurry," I urged, because she still hadn't moved. *Avoid raising your voice unnecessarily*, Agatha said.

"Mama—" my daughter called. I paused at the door, turning back. Mathilde gestured toward my ankles and mud-covered boots.

"Oh, by God's bones." I sighed. "Wake Elin if you have time, but only if you have time. I want you in the hall when they knock on the door."

⚘

IN THE END, I COULDN'T CHANGE MY BOOTS, OR WASH OFF THE MUD, but I did put on a new skirt, one that puddled on the floor and covered my mess. If I had peered into a looking glass, I was certain I would have seen a disheveled sight: hair escaping in pieces, chest flushed from running. My extra minutes had been devoted to my girls, and when they assembled behind me on the stairwell, I was relieved to see them dressed and ready, in contrasting gray and yellow silk.

At first glance, my daughters looked alike—tall and big-limbed with long dark hair. Mathilde was more beautiful. She had gray eyes and a dusting of freckles and an imperious nature that lent itself to a sense of mystery—or at least an ingrained sense of hierarchy. If she lacked warmth, I told myself it was because she was older, and had seen more, and her nature was to observe and absorb. She was more helpful to me, able to see what needed to be said or done and do it without my bidding. But there was a hardness in her that I assumed had come from a hardness in me, as if she had been carved out of the same material I was made of when she'd formed herself in the womb.

Rosie had her father's aquiline nose, and a broadness to her face that she balanced with elaborate updos and extra rouge. But if she lacked her sister's natural graces, she more than made up for it with charm. She was happy and flirtatious and embraced all the frippery that Mathilde resisted. She had perfected the art of being a woman. My father would not have recognized her tools, but she wielded them with prowess.

Any mother who tells you she loves all her children—or appraises them—equally is lying. There is no way to measure or balance love. Love is an animal of its own bidding and inclination; it prowls and pounces and feels; it grows and it hurts and it withers. My love for the girls was ranging and reaching. It assessed them because assessment was a part of protection. It saw their differences, because to ignore them would be to love them less. The love of a mother does away with scales and measurement altogether; it envelops and understands and embraces what is cracked along with what is beautiful.

We arranged ourselves in the entry hall. Alice—as angular and tall and thin as a board—came in and stood beside Wenthelen. I was relieved to see that she, too, had put on a clean apron and covered her hair. I waited on the middle stair and Mathilde and Rosie stood behind me in birth order. I could feel their breathless bodies when the knock came.

Our front door was tall and wide and heavy. The hinges screamed when Wenthelen swung the giant panel open. The royal messenger stood on the other side of the threshold, and behind him, a page. The footman, muddy from his exertions, remained beside the carriage.

"Lady Bramley," Alice announced, and stepped aside.

"Good day," the messenger said, and I returned the greeting.

"I bid you welcome." I gestured for him to come inside. He stepped up and over the stone at our doorstep and looked around the entry hall.

When our home was built, however many years before—and it had been built at various intervals, so each part of the house dated to a different time, like an ever-growing creature that, across decades, sprouted new appendages—the entry hall had been given the greatest attention. Above the beams that crossed over our heads, there was an intricate, if now faded, mural. The walls were covered with tapestries that started at the roofline and touched the floor—showpieces that we were able to maintain, thanks to Rosie's prowess. At one time, the room would have been filled with a house of people standing in order. What we lacked now in staff, we made up for with candlesticks and rugs; we'd emptied other rooms of the house so that the entry could remain opulent.

The messenger cleared his throat. "I am a messenger of His Royal Highness, the king."

"We are humbled by the honor of your visit," I replied.

The page—a petite boy of no more than twelve—raised a small horn and blew it, the noise shrill and echoing in the hall. From inside his tunic, the messenger withdrew a scroll and spent a moment picking at the reluctant knot.

Rosie tried to stifle a nervous snigger behind me, and the messenger looked up sharply. She bit her lip and we waited in silence until he loosened the ribbon and undid the tie. Before reading, he looked around, eyes sliding over Wenthelen and Alice, pausing on me and then on each daughter, before continuing around the room, taking inventory.

Finally, he held out his scroll, though he spoke without looking at it. "On behalf of His Royal Highness, I come to your home this day to invite you to attend a celebration of the prince's name day. Festivities will begin at sundown on the twenty-seventh day of this month." He loosely rebound the paper, indicating he'd finished.

I nodded, feeling echoes of the same relief and apprehension that the carriage had stirred earlier. "We thank you kindly." Behind me, my daughters dipped and curtsied, echoing my platitude. "The roads are hard, and the day is long. May we offer a moment of respite?" I swept my hand behind me, toward the hall, as if there were a table of tiered platters of food, cakes, and candies on display, just past the doorway. Wenthelen froze, at the edge of the entry, terrified the messenger would call my bluff. We had cider. We had oat biscuits. A stew fit for a peasant. A dead rabbit. That was all we had. I steadied my breath.

The messenger replaced the scroll back in his tunic and shook his head. "There are many households to visit."

I worked to keep the relief from my face. "May your journey continue safely."

But the uniformed man then pulled a different paper from his pocket and consulted it. "The invitation is extended to the honorable Elin of Bramley and her guardian, Lady Etheldreda Bramley."

Behind me, I heard Rosamund and Mathilde suck in air. *A steady and even tempo,* said Agatha in my head. *Remain calm, keep the chin high.* "I can confirm that the invitation has reached the home of Elin of Bramley," I said. "But we have more than one woman of age in the household."

He checked his list again. "The invitation specifies only Miss Elin and her chaperone."

Respectful demeanor and delicate gestures. "All the young women in this home are of eligible birth and age."

"Madam," the messenger said, with increasing irritation, "the only names invited at the household are those that I have already shared."

"Surely," I said with vehemence, forgetting Agatha and the long-ago lessons, "that is a mistake."

"Mother," Mathilde whispered behind me, as a warning.

"Mother," Rosamund begged, as a plea.

"I can assure you," the messenger said with finality, "the king does not make mistakes."

It was not a point I dared to argue. I felt my heart racing, heard my girls murmuring as we went through the rote motions—the *thank-you*s and *bid thee well*s and *safe journey*s—before Alice closed the door. All stood still and silent as we listened to the crunch of wheels on gravel and the rattle of the departing carriage.

I looked back toward the girls, my gray and yellow flowers, on the stairs. But when I turned, I saw that Elin—so pale I had half a mind to outline her in ink—also stood at the top of the steps, hand hovering above the banister.

I rubbed my temple, which had begun to throb. "When did you get here?"

In front of her, Rosamund collapsed in a heap of silk and tears. "Why," she wailed, "have we not been invited?"

"I have not a clue," I said stiffly, looking away from Elin. But it wasn't true. I knew why.

And it had everything to do with Henry.

CHAPTER FOUR

I'D KNOWN OF HENRY'S FAMILY SINCE I CAN REMEMBER. GROWING up, the Tremaines were recognized in our township for their pack of boys—large—and their hunting lodge—larger—and above all else, their fortune (largest). Merchants made wealthy across generations, they spent most of their time in their primary manor hall, in the central part of the kingdom. But during the hunting season, they traveled to the territory I called home to pursue the waterfowl and game birds that proliferated on our lakes and moorlands. The Tremaines' arrival—with a litany of carriages and horses and livestock, servants and staff, maids and cooks and luggage and barrels of wine and ale—was met with fascination, watched from fenceposts and through windows, and gossiped about at the market and in kitchens.

The people in my hamlet were not accustomed to fanfare. Most were thin and hungry. Meager crops had to be coaxed from windswept patches of dirt. Our land was pine filled and hilly and rock strewn. The Tremaines traveled with a decorative tent used for roadside lunches.

Besides the tent, and other whispered details of opulence—that their buttons were made from jewels, that their caravan traveled carrying glass windows with them because the old lodge was only fitted with parchment—they were also known for their birds. Each family member had a falcon. The raptors came in travel cases and compartments, and in a special carriage designed for their transport, covered in nets and screens.

Hawking demands equipment, money, time, and land. It wasn't familiar to most of the people in our township. But when the falcons were flying high, we all knew: The Tremaines were home.

THE FIRST TIME HENRY AND I SPOKE, I WAS TWELVE AND OUT GATH-ering berries. I was wandering through the briars when a voice came from up high: "There's more on the other side!"

Startled, I looked up, into the sky, and then at the branches of the tree. I could barely see through the sunlight, but there he was, sleeves rolled up, shinnying down along the trunk: a young boy, skinny and sandy-haired and brown-eyed, with a scraped elbow that indicated he had climbed plenty of trees before this, to varying degrees of success.

I recognized him right away as one of the Tremaine brothers. Henry—the tall one. A year older than I and the third of seven sons. Less lucky in his birth order but lucky in birth, for he had been born feet first and both he and his mother survived to tell it.

"I'll show you," he said, dropping the last several feet to the ground. "This way."

I was not supposed to be alone with boys, but I followed behind him.

"Another few weeks and the bushes will be filled." He held a branch back for me. "You don't talk much, do you?"

I considered the question and then considered not answering. I said instead: "Only when I have something good to say," which felt like a violation of the statement. I realized I was a little nervous—we were not only unchaperoned, but he was from an elevated social tier. "Or bad," I added, confusing even myself.

He grinned indulgently. "What about everything that's in between?"

I thought carefully. "There's no point."

He looked back over his shoulder as we continued onward. "Well, what's your name?"

"Etheldreda Verity Isolde—"

"Etheldreda," he repeated. "Is that good or bad?"

I took the question to mean: Did I like my name? No one had ever asked me that before. "Both," I decided. "I was named for my mother."

"Is she the good part or the bad part?"

"She's dead," I said simply, as if death trumped character evaluation. But in truth, I hadn't known her well enough to determine. I was old enough to know that death wasn't always bad, and mothers weren't always good.

He waited for me to explain further and, when I didn't, said: "I'll call you Ethel. You can call me Henry."

"Thank you," I said, mildly surprised. "Your family has the big hall. My father knows yours—he's the brewer."

I studied him as he walked in front of me—looking at his undershirt sticking out of his collar, the way his hair curled a bit at the nape of his neck, and his gangling, energetic stride. He showed me a trove of berries, thicker and bigger and riper, growing much closer to the water's edge. I marveled at the size of them, hurrying to fill my basket, pausing only to push the bursting fruit into my mouth.

The encounter might have been forgettable, except that as we stood there, me purple-fingered and purple-mouthed, he had shushed me, stilled me, reaching out a hand to stop my movement. He pointed up.

Above us, in the sky, there were two wild hawks, both with wings spread. They flew together, in a dance, their bodies alternately fat and thick or like a blade. The air, solid, then liquid, did their bidding. They'd float side by side and then one would tilt, the flourish of a wrist, and slide beneath the other. A feathered roll and a swift follow and both soared once more. They moved like water on the surface of a stream, like a trill of music, like the sensation of your stomach dropping to your groin.

Thus, my first memory of Henry: the taste of berries, his hand tight on my wrist, both of us looking upward, with reverence.

❦

THE NEXT FEW YEARS, WHEN HENRY SAW ME IN THE VILLAGE OR AT the market, he would say hello, and call me Ethel.

Hello, Ethel: Once when I was picking up extra cheese from the stall. I'd hardly turned around in time to say hello back. *Hello, Ethel*: A year later, and him a bit taller, when we passed one another at a harvest celebration, the food heaped in piles and the fires smoking. And then, another year passed, and a *Hello, Ethel*, when I stumbled upon him alone with his bird.

Stumbled upon is perhaps not accurate. Alongside all of Henry's *Hello, Ethels*—each instance remembered and held close—I had spied and catalogued the comings and goings of his family. More specifically, I had observed what they did with their birds.

From the inside of a broom shrub, surrounded by yellow flowers, I watched the mews at the edge of the Tremaine property. Each bird had its own compartment, with a perch on a raised platform and a large screened window. The falconers cleaned these compartments along with the equipment they housed, exercised the hawks in the yard, and took copious notes in various books and ledgers. Before feeding the birds, they weighed them on a brass scale unlike any I'd seen. They trained the birds with bait on lines and I watched from the scratchy confines of the shrub as the raptors flew away and returned again, their bodies alternating between a forceful clumsiness—the flap and cluster of wings, the abrupt grip of the talons, the mash of meat in a tendoned fist—and an incredible, weightless grace.

And from behind rocks and trees at the edges of various fields and forest clearings, I watched the Tremaines themselves: exercising the birds, walking them—the falcons like soft gargoyles hulking on gloved fists—feeding them, talking to them, discussing them. I heard a new vocabulary—*wingover, imping, cadge, trounce*—words I would not

define until later but remembered all the same. I heard words I knew—
weathering, haggard, rouse, bate—used in ways I didn't recognize. The
foreign language both excluded and beckoned to me.

Falconry, at its core, is taking a creature that is primordial, instinc-
tive, beautifully primitive, and fundamentally selfish and teaching it
obedience, order, and fidelity. Watching the birds and their handlers,
fresh out of daily lessons for comportment and fan signals and feminine restraint, is it any wonder I was enthralled? It was not enough to
listen to and observe the falconers in their weathered mews yard, to spy
on the Tremaines from a distance; I wanted to be closer to the birds,
as close as they'd let me. I wanted to know what it would feel like to
have a falcon land on my outstretched arm, to look into its eyes and
understand its wisdom.

I couldn't do that hiding in a bush.

I might have revealed myself. Or it might have been an accident.
Either way, one day, Henry caught me.

HE WAS MANNING HIS BIRD—I WOULD LEARN LATER THAT IT WAS A
merlin, small and agile—and I was watching from behind a large slab
of granite. Instead of flushing the prey, Henry stood waiting for mur-
murations of smaller birds. When these unnatural clouds appeared, undulating to rhythms of some unseen force, he would release his merlin
from the glove, both of us witnessing its aerial pursuit. Each time a
small bird was caught, there was a flurry of activity: the hawk morph-
ing into a fearsome creature, an explosion of feathers, Henry procuring
a piece of meat to urge his bird to release its quarry. But the minutes
between these pursuits were long. I grew tired of watching the real
clouds form and dissipate and form again in the sky above. So much
of falconry is patience. Sitting behind the rock that day, I did not have
any. I kicked some pebbles.

Without turning to face my hiding spot, Henry called: "Hello,
Ethel."

I stepped out from behind the rock, too eager to feel embarrassed. "How does it know to come back to you?"

"It's nice to see you out here."

"And why does it give you the little birds and not eat them?"

He looked at me, amused. "The food I give her is much easier than eating a bird. She's happy to swap."

I frowned. "She's killing them for no reason?" We both looked down at the bag at Henry's feet, inside of which were two dead birds.

"The starlings eat the crops and there are thousands more of them than there should be. And Miriam will eat them later besides." He held up his glove, lifting his bird a few inches. "This is Miriam. Would you like to hold her?"

I hesitated, not because I didn't want to, but because I wanted to so badly, I thought the moment deserved ceremony.

"Come on, then," Henry said. He cast his merlin upward, and she flew onto a low branch of a nearby tree. When she had settled, he removed the glove.

Wordlessly, I went over and accepted the gauntlet. The weight and stiffness of it surprised me, but I slid my hand in, small in the large mouth. Unlike the jeweled buttons and embroidered tents, the glove was simple and crudely crafted: a string in place of laces, and the fingers, reinforced with extra padding, were bulky and unsightly. The thick leather extended past my elbow.

Henry nodded his encouragement. "Now hold out your arm. She will fly down and perch on it. No sudden movements; stay steady and calm."

He moved us to the center of the clearing and showed me the angle to hold my arm and how to position my fingers, my thumb making a platform. Then, he let out a shrill three-note whistle—low–high–low— and with a few flaps, Miriam thrust herself off her branch. Wings wide, she swooped down, inches from the ground, before rising once more to come up onto my fist. I was surprised by the strength of her grip, the heft of her body.

"Hello, Miriam," I whispered. She had opaque obsidian eyes and a yellow beak that faded to gray at the tip. She was not human at all. I was amazed that this ancient thing perched on my fist—an alien knot of sinew and feather and lethal tendons and claws, furred and pulsing with restrained strength—was the same graceful creature that could float on air.

"Why doesn't she fly away?" I kept my voice quiet. My fist might have been a tree. Her magnificence had turned me into scenery.

Henry reached out and stroked her chest with the back of his finger. "She's trained."

"As one does with a hound?"

Henry shook his head. "When you train a falcon, they imprint—they come to view a falconer as a provider. Or a parent. There's a sense of trust and dependence. I—we, the falconers—are a source of food. But if the bird gets too high, it might fly away."

I looked up into the sky, which, though above us, felt bottomless. "How high?"

"*High* means heavy." Henry paused and helped me cast Miriam off once more. She flew back to the branch—the same movements as before, in reverse. "Fat. If a bird is overfed, then it doesn't have a need to come back."

"So, you starve them?" Already I was Miriam's advocate.

He laughed. "There is nothing more pampered than a captive hawk. A starving bird doesn't have any energy to fly. We weigh them every day to ensure they're *keen*. It's the repeated promise of food, and our follow-through on that promise, that keeps them coming back." He cocked his head and looked at me. "You're very curious."

If only in my mind, Agatha inserted herself just then, to tell me that being curious was not a virtue. So, instead of asking another question, I nodded toward Miriam and just said, "She's lovely."

"That she is," Henry agreed, looking at her on the branch.

"So very lovely," I burst out with more feeling.

He glanced at my face, then to the bird, and back again. "You're interested in the falcons."

I nodded, pressing my lips together.

"You see those little leather anklets, there, on her legs? They always stay on. They are used to connect to her jesses—which are those leather straps hanging from her feet. Those connect her to the glove, which is called a gauntlet, or to her perch, back in her mews."

I tried to memorize each word.

Watching my face, he continued: "There's a brass bell on her, attached with a bewit, which is another kind of leather strap, so she can be found easily when we're hunting."

I settled back, leaning against a tree, waiting for more. And Henry indulged me: *Eyases* were young birds and *passagers* were older ones. *Hoods* were the small helmets that covered the bird's eyes. Hawks did not defecate, they *muted*. A *stoop* was a headlong dive in pursuit of prey. I said nothing, consuming every detail in greedy silence.

Such was my first lesson in falconry.

In secret, Henry continued to teach me about the raptors. Because the best times for bringing out a falcon were early in the morning and late in the afternoon, I was able to complete my midday lessons with Agatha—*never be alone in the company of a man without a chaperone, never introduce yourself first, never, never, never*—and then blatantly disregard them in a field with a boy and a bird without rousing any suspicion.

My family would not have wanted me to be around Henry unchaperoned. And his would not have wanted him spending time with the brewer's daughter. He had just had his seventeenth birthday and they had started treating him like a man, assigning a new set of duties and expectations, pulling him into long council sessions that he sat through in a stiff-backed chair. But he, still savoring the vestigial taste of freedom, wanted to pass his mornings in misty inlets and his afternoons with a bird on his arm.

If anyone knew we were spending so much time together, our lessons would have come to a swift end. (Here, an echo of all the stories of unwed women—the various brutalities and shames.) But I did not feel I was doing anything wrong with Henry. I was accustomed to spending time around men. I revealed to him the best places for collecting nettles and elderberries and mullein. I took him to the largest rock with footholds that had been worn into it centuries before. I demonstrated how to spy on his own family members and explained where I had hidden to observe their mews.

It was this last revelation that piqued his interest, and one day, later in the season, he asked me to show him. I took him the back way up to his own property, along the boulder-strewn creek, past the penned sheep, through a copse of hazel trees, to the exact spot where I had furtively watched the falconers in their daily ministrations and careful attentiveness to the birds.

"Here?" Henry gestured to a large shrub that provided some cover.

I nodded. "Yes, right here, or over there"—I pointed to a thicket of gorse—"where you have a better view of the yard."

"And it wasn't boring?"

I pursed my lips. "No more boring than sewing even stitches in a hall."

He looked amused. "Did you ever watch me here?"

"No," I lied. "But—"

"Shhh," he shushed me. Then, in a murmur: "They're coming!"

"Who?"

"Darius and Stephen." He pointed over toward the mews. "Our falconers."

"They're your falconers; you don't have to hide."

But I did. Henry joined me in the gorse, putting a finger to his lips and raising his eyebrows. It was easy for him to make a game of these things; it was not his honor that might be called into question. Crouching in the dirt next to me, he whispered: "Perchance we'll apprehend them relieving themselves."

Fear of being caught aside, it was a delight to talk in such a way. I laughed. "Or picking their noses."

We quieted, waiting.

Kneeling next to Henry, I grew ever so aware of my body. Hip to hip, we were closer than we had ever been, our heads leaning toward one another. He smelled of mint, which he had a habit of chewing. My stomach twisted in a way entirely unfamiliar.

"Look," he whispered, because the two men had paused in the center of the mews, right in front of us, thirty feet away. I was sure that, if they glanced over, they would see us, heads bobbing above the waxy gorse leaf. The men were talking, quietly, and we could not hear the words. "They're arguing," I said, feeling, intrinsically, that we shouldn't be there. That they would see us.

"No, I think—"

But he stopped talking. One of the falconers had reached out and cupped the other man's cheek in the palm of his hand, a tenderhearted gesture, recognizable and familiar in its sentiment. It echoed what those who denuded daisies wished for, what I imagined my parents had had, a frisson of what I felt crouched in the mud beside Henry; it echoed love.

We both stilled and stopped breathing. Quietly, quietly, we crawled backward, on our hands, like two crabs, until we were far enough away to stand, and Henry took my hand and pulled me up, and then we were running, crashing through the pine needles, pebbles flying, shocked and breathless.

When we finally stopped, we were both panting. We locked eyes and said nothing. It was implicit: We agreed to tell no one, not for what it might mean for Darius and Stephen, not for the trill of power and control it might have provided, not now, not ever. We realized we were still holding hands and let go, abruptly.

I wish I had understood it better then: The whole world was filled with people keeping secrets.

CHAPTER FIVE

AFTER THE MESSENGER LEFT, THE ENTRYWAY DEFLATED AROUND us, then inflated, and then deflated, the tapestries on the walls moving ever so slightly. The house was breathing. Or it was us, heartbeats in our throats. All the girls and I, posed on the staircase, gray and yellow and brown. And there, at the top, was Elin.

"Did you hear?" I looked her over. I had thought my daughters had presented appropriately, but Elin had hooked and secured herself into a chaste dress of the softest pink, each loop of lace in place, every tiny button carefully nestled through its fastening. Tow-colored hair curled and styled. Waist cinched tight. The picture of composure. In her hands, she held a small, worn booklet.

She nodded. "A ball." Looking at the door as if it might swing open again, she added, in wonder: "And they invited me."

"I don't care what the messenger said." I turned back to my daughters. "There was a mistake."

"Ma*ma*—" Mathilde began, emphasizing the second syllable, but I held up a finger, insisting she stop.

"Let me think."

Rosamund cried into her hands. "Why would she be invited and not the two of us? Mathilde has more years to her name."

"All three of you are of genteel birth," I agreed. "And not one of you is yet introduced to society."

"Perhaps," Elin ventured, allowing herself a modest smile, "it's because the girls weren't born in the house and don't share my last name." She, who had never encountered a merit she did not like to expatiate on, held up the thin volume in her hands—a book on female virtue that rarely left her side. "If there were a mistake, let us take some solace, for mistakes can be stepping stones to wisdom."

We ignored her. "It has to be an accident," Rosamund cried.

"Perhaps a clerical error—" Mathilde continued.

"Or they do not have proper records," Rosamund interrupted.

"Which is what *clerical error* means."

"An error is different than not having the records in the first place," Rosamund countered.

"Let me think," I repeated.

"You could write a letter," Elin suggested. "One penned with grace and care—"

"A letter?" Mathilde laughed. "To the king?"

"If I could, I would gladly share my invitation," Elin offered, "for the greatest treasures are those we share with others."

"We can't take your place." Mathilde scowled at her. "They have your name."

"And there's two of us and one of you," Rosamund cried.

"Girls—" I said.

Elin came down one step, looking back and forth at each of her stepsisters. "Gilded edges can be found on even the darkest of clouds—"

Rosamund shrieked: "That solves nothing!"

Elin began to quote her well-worn source, which she held aloft before her: "'Despair is a common trap—'"

Mathilde twirled to face Elin, her movement quick with exasperation. "Elin, please—"

"'For every vine with thorns there are roses—'"

"If you spout one more inconsequential maxim," Mathilde erupted, "I will rip out your tongue and turn it into a pâté!"

We all stilled, watching Elin, who had a habit of fainting under pressure. When she did not wobble, I clapped my hands. "Girls, be quiet."

All three of them were already silent.

I looked at Rosie and Mathilde. "Go and make yourselves useful. Ready the press for apples. Or . . ." I waved my hands, wordless with aggravation. "Mend something!"

When they had left—long-faced, feet quickened by frustration— I lifted my skirts and began to climb the stairs toward my stepdaughter. "Elin—"

"Heavens!" She covered her mouth, looking down at my muddied feet.

I eyed her stonily.

"Your boots." She spoke through her fingers. "Why, they're soiled!"

"There was no time to change."

"Our visitors might have seen." The upper uncovered half of her face was a mask of concern—for her own propriety or mine, it was unclear.

"And they did not," I stated sharply, losing patience.

Her brow furrowed. "But you yourself would say that comportment is the bedrock upon which one builds—"

I interrupted her, covering my shoes with a hasty flourish of my petticoat. "We do not all have the leisure of hours spent readying at the looking glass. It would do you well to consider that the semblance of virtue can prove as potent as its earnest practice."

Her hand lowered. She opened her mouth, but before any words came out, I clucked and reached forward to finger her dress. "And all that effort for naught. I do not think the color suits you. You're looking a little pink at the eyes."

Her eyelashes fluttered. Clasping her book, clutching a bit too tightly, Elin nodded.

"Go on," I instructed, jutting my chin toward the steps to her room.

After she'd gone upstairs, I felt, briefly, some regret for my tone. It quickly dissipated. When a girl's innocence outlives its lifespan, it is only a burden to herself and those around her.

Outside, I moved hurriedly across the grass, toward the place I had left Lucy. Rosie's angst had been on the surface, but mine was thrumming through me, a kind of poison in my body. I was offered one relief, at least: My falcon was in the oak at the back of the house, perched on an upper branch. I put my hands on my hips and smiled at her. "Come down, Luce," I called. I tried our low-high-low whistle— a reverberance from my past.

She roused, raising her feathers, but did not move from the branch.

There are several ways to get a falcon down from a tree. Special whistles and commands, a lure—meat or food—waved in a circular motion to catch her attention, or, if desperate, I could borrow another bird, one whose presence would compel movement. But I welcomed a few minutes alone to turn over all that had happened that morning. I would wait.

I had no sooner settled on the idea when the back door opened and Alice emerged. She made her way across the grass determinedly, stooping a bit as she chose her footing. She carried a large bowl. Her body— tall and thin as a sapling—never looked like it could support her tasks, but like a tree that bends in the wind, she was never broken by them.

When she was close enough to be heard, she called: "You've lost your head for letting her stay up there alone."

"I didn't have a choice." I was used to the housekeeper's impertinence. I did not pay Alice or Wenthelen. They shared living quarters—an echo of one man's palm on another's cheek; an arrangement that would not be tolerated by most households—and rather than taking one of the small dormer rooms intended for staff, they resided in a high-ceilinged chamber on the second floor. Wenthelen decided what to cook and took pleasure in telling us what to do in the kitchen. They often dined beside us. Given our peculiar understanding, they typically shared their sentiments unchecked. I added: "She'll come down on her own time."

"She doesn't own your time, and we've got plenty to do." Alice's mien usually landed somewhere between pragmatic and severe. Just then, she was frowning at me.

"Do you own my time?"

"The apples aren't going to pick themselves."

If there was abundance of anything in our life, it was apples. Someone had long ago planted Bramley's grounds with hundreds of trees. The initiative had become our folly: For a season of each year, we were wealthy in fruit. We baked apples whole and into tarts and pies. We turned them into sauce and cooked them into porridge. We fermented them into the acidic cider that we drank through all the other seasons of the year. But I was in no mood to think about the fruit—the many bushels that needed picking, then washing, then pressing, then more. I kicked at the dirt. "Damn the apples."

"M'lady," Alice admonished.

"Damn the damn apples." I turned away from the tree to look at the house again. "For once it would be nice to let them rot."

"Then you won't have my help come spring when the land is nothing but wasp-filled mush." Alice saddled the bowl against her hip and used her free hand to point to Lucy. "Wenthelen said she caught a rabbit." Raising her voice, she called: "Well done, Lucy!"

"I flushed it," I said, mildly.

"Your toil was evenly distributed, then?"

"No less so than all our other work." I nodded up at the tower keep, where Elin kept her chambers. "Even now, she's up there with her feet raised when I've been asking her for days to help pick the fruit."

"She pinks after even a single minute in the sun." Alice's sigh went soft. "Besides, her feet aren't up. More likely she's running herself ragged practicing her penmanship."

I stared at Alice, incredulous. The woman worked inside and out.

She helped with our meager menagerie—a skinny horse named Arno and Lucy. Wenthelen ran the kitchen and a small kitchen garden, in which we grew carrots and onions and herbs. In the spring, we had beans and peas, and in the summer, there was lettuce and purslane. Mathilde managed our accounts and books. Rosamund had a tiny flock of scrubby chickens and gathered their eggs in the afternoon. She applied herself to countless embroidery pieces—textiles Wenthelen would store and bring to the market to barter and sell for all we needed: wheat and milled grains and spices. And sugar.

Elin—well, that was my predicament.

Dedication to useless truisms had done little to prepare her for the lifelong reality of keeping oneself well fed, well shod, and warm through all the seasons of the year. When all our lives had taken a turn, my daughters had learned to tie their skirts and roll up their sleeves. But Elin—raised as a lady, both fawned over and buffered from the world—had been unwilling. It wasn't quite lassitude; she shirked chores to apply herself with diligence to the achievements that would mark her as accomplished. Instead of adapting to her new circumstances, she had spent years waiting for them to change. Dedicating herself to the markers of gentility: Instruments and language and translations. Posture and poise and art. That bed linens also had to be washed and floors swept and wicks dipped into candle wax was of little matter. My efforts to mold Elin from a child into a young woman in our situation had been like attempting to mold air.

"It is such salt," I nearly spat, "that she is the one to go to the ball! Will she have Rosie make her a dress? Mathilde fashion her hair?"

Alice chose to ignore me and instead held out the bowl for my inspection. "For Lucy. She's the one that caught the rabbit, after all." She tilted the basin toward me. No part of the animal would go to waste.

"Come on, Lucy!" Alice called. To me, she said: "You can't both be so stubborn."

There was a flapping of wings and Lucy, not gently, not gracefully, came down to the bowl.

Alice, taking hold of the jesses, looked at me, eyebrow raised in triumph. "The little ladies may be invited yet."

I shook my head. There were many reasons my daughters might not have received an invitation to the ball. All manner of missteps, oversights, and accidents that could lead to a girl's name being left off a list. But there was one reason—linked to a memory of gristle and blood and the musty smell of horse tack—that I knew, in the bone of my bones, was the cause.

CHAPTER SIX

AFTER HENRY SPENT A SUMMER TEACHING ME ABOUT THE hawks, another year passed before I saw him again. Encouraged by sporadic letters, I waited for the day I'd see the Tremaine birds and flags once more. But the morning the Tremaines finally came, I missed the caravan marking their arrival. The birds were up, and the flags were out, but I'd spent hours struggling to finish my lessons, eyes returning and then returning again to the window in hopes of seeing a faraway falcon stooping in a high-speed dive.

Agatha watched over my shoulder as I repaired a set of my father's stockings. Under normal circumstances, I could sew tiny and capable stitches. But I could not focus, distracted by the agony of the moment: the scratch of wool, the heat of the fire on a too-hot day, the prick of a needle, and the sense of time moving slowly, there, inside the hall, and quickly, outside, just beyond my reach, as the day slipped away. When I made mistakes, Agatha, back straight, would task me with ripping out my stitches and starting over, her own sewing needle hovering threateningly above my skin.

When we finished at long last, I rushed outside, sucking in the warm, clean air and the smell of wild sage. Henry and I had agreed, via letter, to meet behind the mews whenever the Tremaines did arrive. I hurried along the back path, moving as fast as I could in my skirts. I was perspiring and out of breath.

But when I arrived, I saw he was not waiting for me as we had planned. I stood, uncertain. And I might have sat awhile, except I could hear his laughter. So I did what I had not done before, and ventured farther onto the grounds.

I saw him first. In our year apart, he had grown a whole head taller, widened across the shoulders, and, though it was unmistakably Henry, he was another person entirely. More than decorum stopped me short. At his side, there was a girl. Besides the gamekeepers, who were herding the animals into their pens, they were alone.

I often think it inaccurate when blond people are described as yellow-haired, but the girl's braids were truly gold, like a drawing of what a young maiden was supposed to look like. She sat, perched on the stone wall of an empty pigpen, her boots hidden beneath the hem of her formal dress. Here is the picture I still return to: yellow against blue (her hair, the sky), red against white (her mouth, her teeth), bone against bone (my molars, grinding and clenched).

"Ethel!" Henry saw me. "You're here!"

I stepped forward. "Indeed." I did not have yellow hair, but I was now seventeen—with all the bodily changes that entailed—and I hoped he would notice.

The yellow-haired girl took note of me. Henry, trotting over, looked pleased, and I saw the yellow-haired girl take note of this, too.

He turned back to look at her, though he addressed me. "Ethel, may I have the honor of introducing Miss Sigrid Camelia White, daughter of Sir Harris White, and our guest at the lodge."

I dropped into a curtsy, gathering the folds of my skirt in one hand and bending the other arm slightly at the elbow, just as Agatha had taught me. When I finished, I thought I saw the faintest hint of a smirk on Miss Sigrid Camelia White's face, but then it was gone.

Henry continued: "Sigrid, this is Ethel, the brewer's daughter. She lives over that hill."

A pause. "A treat to make your acquaintance," Sigrid chirped, and waited for Henry to offer a hand so she could climb off the short wall. She gave me the slightest approximation of a curtsy. I could feel her taking in my dress—a simple, everyday garment, distinctly different from the patterned brocade on her own bodice. Perhaps my first lesson that women have their own kind of armor.

She said: "So you live here, for all the seasons?"

I nodded. "Every one since I was born."

"Ethel knows her way around better than any," Henry offered.

"Do tell me, then"—Sigrid widened her eyes—"what there is to do? The men have their hunting, of course . . . but I'll be here all season and . . ." She gestured out expansively to the world around us and offered me a brilliant smile.

Sigrid had a manner of smiling after saying something offensive— a toothy visage that convincingly went all the way to her eyebrows, her whole face transforming, eyes going clear, demanding forgiveness before you realized you'd been insulted. She was beautiful. It was a beautiful smile. And I would come to regard it as her dancing bear: distracting and not without a hint of danger.

"The same things people do anywhere," I said.

She looked out, toward an imaginary horizon, for her view was blocked by a wall of the barn. "I imagine it gets lonely."

No sisters. No mother. I had kept a rabbit as a girl, until it ran off. I stopped myself from looking down and met Sigrid's eyes instead. "Only if you're someone who requires constant companionship."

"Well, I'm certain there is plenty to amuse us all," Henry interjected. "Ethel and I like to take Miriam, my merlin, out in the afternoons. You might join us, Sigrid."

Henry pointed down toward the mews. Sigrid nodded, twisting a lock of her hair around one of her fingers. Neither of them looked at me, so I did not have to conceal my distress.

✿

FOR THE FOLLOWING WEEKS, SIGRID JOINED US FOR EVERY ONE OF OUR
outings, appearing each day in clothing unsuitable for our excursions:
silk shoes that could not walk through the frost-tipped grass and fine
gowns that collected nettles and brambles and a large sun hat and veil
that distracted Miriam. But, other than offering herself up as a distraction, Sigrid did not interest herself in the falconry.

Dutifully, Henry continued to teach me. And Sigrid, wholly indif-
ferent, would perch on a log or rock. Because of my physical proximity
to Henry, and because we were the ones with a shared interest, I did
not feel as threatened by Sigrid during these daytime lessons. But, each
evening, when suppertime neared, I would have to say goodbye and the
two of them would leave together, returning to the hunting lodge for a
formal supper with their families.

I imagined these meals, creating pictures in my mind of braised
meat and gravies, Sigrid's smile lit by the candles, Henry's eyes tracing
her pale fingers and painted lips as she ate elaborate pastries and suc-
culent desserts. I imagined that, for the briefest of moments, she would
knock his knee beneath the table, and blush, as though it had been an
accident. I'd think about these scenes in my own family's hall, sitting in
candlelit darkness with my father and brother and a plate of salted beef.

Despite my jealousy, Sigrid's arrival shifted one thing for the better:
With a third, I could see Henry without subterfuge, and our daily
meetings were now made known to our families. It was for this reason
that, a few weeks after their arrival, I—via an invitation issued to my
entire family—was finally welcomed to sup at the Tremaines' lodge.

My social position straddled the line between well born and the
working class. As a landowner and successful tradesman, my father was
respected. But he was not a gentleman. And, though Agatha had tried
everything in her arsenal to prepare me, I strained not to reveal that it
was my first dinner in an opulent hall. We ate partridge and lettuces
and vegetables and cheese. *Wait for the head of the table to start*, Agatha's

voice reminded me. Between my father and brother, Henry's father and six brothers, and Sigrid's own family, the room was overwhelmed with men. Their rows of eyes ignored us. We women—myself, the mothers, Sigrid, and her sister—receded. And neither Sigrid nor I was seated close enough to knock knees with Henry.

Over the course of the meal, it became clearer why she chose to spend her time in the fields with the frost and brambles and sunlight. While there were plenty of options for companionship, Henry was— I saw it—the best of the group. His eldest brother, Edmund, the heir, was supercilious and had a perpetual drop of liquid hanging from the tip of his nose. The one who followed, Eben, was resentful and haughty. In one meal alone, he did not hesitate to dress down two different ser- vants. The fourth, the one after Henry, a man named Eyvin, was born different from everyone else, and, though kind, was unable to have long conversations, or converse in any intelligible manner at all. And the remaining brothers were still young, the youngest not even included at the meal and still dining with his nursemaids. As for the women, Sig- rid's sister, Mary, was modest to the point of apologizing for speaking, and it was obvious within minutes that Sigrid and her mother disliked each other's company. Henry, by contrast, was handsome and kind and warm. Both Sigrid and I tittered at each of his jests.

"It is most interesting," his father, a silver-haired and clean-shaven man named Errol, said, after one of our peals of laughter, "to see such a friendship blossom between you three." Both Sigrid and I quieted immediately, understanding the careful edge in his statement. *Do not draw attention to yourself*, warned Agatha. But the assertion helped me understand that my presence in our trio had the inverse effect of enabling Sigrid to spend time with Henry as well. I wondered, with a small amount of concern, whether that was the purpose I played in Henry's family's eyes.

"Do not stop your laughter," his father continued, addressing only Sigrid, "for its melody brightens our gathering."

My concern increased.

✿

AFTER THE MEAL, THE WOMEN WENT INTO THE DRAWING ROOM, AND I was separated from Henry and my family. The two mothers took up a game of piquet at a table in the corner, and Sigrid's sister, Mary, brought out her needlepoint. Sigrid reclined on a chaise, intending, it appeared, to do nothing. For lack of a purpose, I went over to the window to take in the view.

Through the pane—glass, not parchment—the landscape was dark. I could make out the reflection of the room behind me better than the world outside, so I was able to see when Sigrid's mother motioned that Sigrid should go over to me as an act, it seemed, of charity. Sigrid flung her fan aside and stood.

"Hello," I said. I didn't turn to greet her when she came up beside me, for I could see her face fine in the rippled glass.

"I am stuffed as full as a roast pig at a feast." She placed a flat hand against her waist.

"A delicious meal."

We stood in silence for several moments unable to make conversation. Finally, she suggested: "Shall we take a turn around the room?"

Reluctantly, I allowed her to take my arm and pull me away from the window. We passed Mary, squinting over her hoop. Sigrid whispered: "My sister is to be married—a third cousin of the king. But she has always been uninteresting and I doubt it will improve her much in that regard."

I glanced backward to ensure we had not been overheard. Mary was using a fingernail to scratch her chin. Satisfied, I looked over at Sigrid, who employed one of her brilliant smiles. "I," she continued, "have had six proposals already. One of them I suppose does not count, for he died before he could actually propose. But I am told it was his intention."

"How awful—"

"Yes," she agreed. "Awful."

I felt we might have different meanings. "It seems you have many opportunities for happiness."

"One of the offers came in a letter. There is talk of my beauty even in faraway kingdoms." She laid her other hand on my arm. "I mean that modestly, of course. One cannot control their looks any more than they can choose which way they come out of the womb."

We had reached the end of the room and had to turn to reverse direction. "Very contrary to personality, which can be shaped and molded with effort."

"Yes, and we must be thankful for that," she said, missing my point. "Mary has never met her betrothed. We both sat for portraits so hers could be sent ahead. Hers was, I'm afraid, a bit overdone. Sir William, to whom she is promised, may be surprised when he sees her. And somehow, in mine, the artist did not quite manage to render me justly."

"It is a challenge to accurately capture a person's likeness."

She looked over at me. "You are quite good-looking."

I paused before saying: "You do me a kindness." Whatever tier she had placed me on, it was, in her estimation, beneath her own, and so the compliment could be given with warmth and generosity.

"You have thick hair and sharp cheekbones and big eyes. But you'd benefit from lighter skin. Have you tried paint? I'll tell you my secrets." She held out her fingers, as she listed them. "Curl papers at night. Rouge in the morning. Always use two maidservants to pull the strings of your undergarments—don't settle for the strength of one. Raw eggs for complexion. A beer-based hair tonic. When in a pinch, you can use a drop of belladonna to dilate your pupils." She narrowed her eyes, looking at me. "You might try a veil in the sun, and gloves. And I don't mean that old falconry one."

"I fear if I incorporated those steps into my morning routine, I'd only manage to finish as the sun sets."

"Do you mean to say you do nothing? Why, it's remarkable you look as you do!"

"I suppose I am happy with being a bit remarkable," I mused. "It is better than the opposite."

"Oh," she said with a chuckle. "You have given me a laugh."

I laughed with her. But in that moment, Sigrid became a mirror: What was I compared to her? She was blond and I brunette. She was blue-eyed and I brown. She grew up surrounded by women and nursemaids and governesses and knew how to do artistic stitches and make velvet roses and play the harp and sing songs in a golden voice that felt like drowning in intolerable honey. (This, she had demonstrated to Henry and I, earlier in the clearing. Her voice, I acknowledged, was quite pretty, and had served an unintended purpose of flushing out the birds for Miriam.)

"Ethel," she admonished. "You must not think me vapid. Countenance impacts marriage and marriage is freedom. Before I came here, I thought: *I'll marry the eldest one.* And get an heir! But it turned out the eldest is Edmund. And, well—you've seen him. And I would be stuck coming to *this* place every year." One of her smiles. "Not to mention I fancy one of his brothers. Much better looking. You always end up wanting what you shouldn't have." She mouthed, noiselessly: *Henry.*

I didn't respond. The men began to enter the drawing room. The doors opened and they streamed forth, in pairs and trios, and then, alone, there was Henry, watched carefully by our two sets of eyes from across the room.

It had been clear, during our days together, that Sigrid had wanted Henry to pay attention to her. But she expected the world to conform to her whims and I had assumed, or hoped, that Henry was just a part of that. The idea of them marrying curdled my stomach—casting each glance and approving nod from their parents all throughout supper in a new light.

In all the talk of men and marriage—the matchmaking and trading of women, the planning of lineage and futures and dowries—there had been nothing to prepare me for wanting Henry. Desire was not a determinant in the outcomes of women. But I had felt it the past weeks, every gesture of his threaded to mine, every flick of his eyebrow, turn of his wrist. (His wrists! Which I had only just noticed, the hair on the backs golden, the skin nutty and roasted, and surely tasting of salt. I had licked my own in the privacy of my room, imagining.)

I had started to piece together the parts of him that I had been watching, unknowingly, all along. He was kind, to others and to animals. (He had, that very day, fished a drowning bumblebee from a barrel of water.) He was patient, waiting for hours for the birds, or sitting at gatherings with his father while the men droned on about trade and taxation and the state of the coffers. He was always ready to laugh—delighted in turn by the littlest things around him. And, above all, he was interested—in the world, and in me, and in all that I had to say. He asked for my thoughts. He responded in turn. That he did the same with Sigrid, I had been willing and ready to ignore.

"And you?" Sigrid asked, as we neared the men. "Are you promised to some village local?"

"Something like that," I said, without taking my eyes off Henry. I didn't just want to lick his wrists, I wanted to eat them, to make him a part of me, forever.

That night, I drank a raw egg, straight from the shell.

A FEW DAYS LATER, WE WERE OUT, ONCE MORE, WITH THE BIRDS. Henry had let me take a well-trained tiercel from the mews, and we exercised both falcons in a scrubby thicket of pine. Sigrid sat on a small rock and watched us, bored.

"Henry," she called. "You have a wonderful walk."

"Excuse me?" he said, over his shoulder.

"Your gait—it's well done."

Henry paused, confused.

"Oh, don't stop!" she cried.

He looked to me for help. I complied. "You see, we ladies are taught how to walk." I made a great show of demonstrating. "Small steps, gliding, gliding. You cannot appear to move when you move."

He laughed. "And here I was, believing you all floated above the ground so naturally. If I had only realized a walk could be studied and scrutinized, I would have taken up the sport earlier."

"Oh yes." I grinned. "It's quite studied. Just as a scholar studies text and a gardener tends to their blossoms, an excellent walker is most often the result of dutiful consideration."

"But that contradicts my point entirely," Sigrid said. "Henry's walk is the result of no studying at all. It is quite natural."

"I am very lucky, then, that such a natural act comes naturally," he said.

Certainly, I wanted to confirm, complimenting a man's walk could not actually endear a man to the flatterer. But Henry appeared pleased and was walking across the glade with bravado.

I whistled and called the tiercel back to my glove. I saw, in Sigrid's eyes, a quick fear of the movement.

"There's nothing to be afraid of," I said to her, loudly enough to ensure Henry could hear me.

He paused his marching and went to Sigrid. "Are you sure you do not want to try holding one?"

In his question, I heard an echo of our meeting the year before. The tiercel, I was sure, felt rage, too, for he went slick and tight on my glove. But Sigrid shook her head, emphatically. "I can admire better from here."

"Look." I held out my gauntlet. "They're harmless." If I hadn't been wearing the gloves, the talons would have pierced my skin.

"Not to the mice and the grouse." Sigrid pursed her lips.

Henry shrugged, quickly losing interest, and turned back to me to discuss how I was doing with the male falcon. But I gave him only half my attention, for I had realized where I might have an advantage.

"You seem uninspired by hawking," I called to Sigrid.

Her gaze lingered on the bird on my hand before she looked away. "Hawking is a fine sport."

"But not one that stirs your passions."

She looked at me shrewdly. "I do not find hunting to be a . . . delicate . . . activity."

"We have been very unfair to tax you so!" I could feel Henry watching us, back and forth, and continued: "We'll have to do something different tomorrow." Resolving to spend more time in places that framed Sigrid's character unfavorably, I turned to Henry. "Perhaps a walk through the gorge? It's quite steep and rugged, but I am certain we are all up to the task."

He shook his head. "Best avoided in the rainy season. It gets slippery."

"We could take a rowboat out on the lake," I suggested.

He frowned. "Too precarious." After a moment's pause, he proposed: "Perhaps we could go for a ride?"

Sigrid stood from her rock and dusted her hands. "I am an accomplished rider."

"Of course you are," I responded, quiet enough so no one could hear.

WE MET THE FOLLOWING DAY IN THE TREMAINES' STABLES. I HAD brought my own mare and Henry's stood outside, saddled and waiting. We walked along the stalls, looking to pick a horse for Sigrid.

She stopped in front of a black stallion, twice as tall as she was. "How about this one?"

Henry shook his head. "That is Cedric, and he belongs to one of my father's men-at-arms. I do not think he would take kindly to him being borrowed." He moved forward to the next stall. "Here, this one is Old Bess. She's friendly."

"No one wants to ride a horse named Old Bess." Sigrid wrinkled her nose. The stable smelled of hay and animals: mud and old leather and the distinct ammonia of horse urine.

I patted Bess on the nose, conciliatory, and took a step forward to the next stall, where a horse was snorting and switching its tail, a roiling energy trapped beneath his chestnut coat.

"Not that one," Henry said. "That's Lawrence."

"Lawrence?" I repeated.

"I know a Sir Lawrence," Sigrid exclaimed. "What a funny name for a horse."

"Lawrence is a devil," Henry warned.

"It sounds like this one is suited only for more accomplished riders," I said, and Henry nodded at me appreciatively, extending a hand and squeezing my shoulder. His grasp was light but not insignificant. Unable to help myself, I turned back to Sigrid, eyes ablaze. "Certainly, Sigrid, you might feel better suited for Old Bess?"

She lifted her chin, eyes lingering where Henry's hand had been a moment before. "I have been well tutored in the equestrian arts since I was practically a babe."

"One of the mares would be a fine choice," Henry said, gesturing forward. "Lawrence is new and skittish."

"Henry." I turned to him. "Do not question Sigrid's absolute mastery over our equine friends."

"Indeed." She drew herself upward. "I have spent many a pleasant afternoon on the backs of all sorts of horses, and I am sure Lawrence will be no different."

Henry looked concerned. "You do not know the terrain."

"The terrain here is dirt and rocks, just as it is elsewhere," I reasoned. My shoulder still felt warm.

"Come," Sigrid said to him. "You must let us have our fun where we can!"

She and I regarded one another. We each had our schemes and, for the briefest of moments, they had intersected. It almost felt like friendship. We both had to look away.

Contrary to my desires, Sigrid did prove to be a satisfactory rider. The three of us trotted out and into the woods, supplied with a small picnic prepared by the Tremaine kitchens. Henry rode ahead.

Sigrid and I, slowed by our side-sitting saddles, rode alongside one another.

My lesson with Agatha had been suspended for the day. Spending time with suitable men in suitable company was the one permissible excuse for missed instruction. (This was logical, for the entire point of the instruction was to support me in interactions with suitable men in suitable company.) It was freeing and wonderful to be outdoors in the exact middle of the day, when the sun was highest in the sky and the frost had melted from the grass. Caught up in the moment, I was startled when Sigrid started talking. If I had paid attention, her smile might have warned me.

"It is precious, your little infatuation," she said.

"I beg your pardon?"

"With Henry! It makes one feel a kind of . . ." She searched for the right word. "Delight."

I watched her, ever so aware of Henry, just paces ahead.

"And I want you to know," she continued, "that there is no ill will between us. Regardless of how I do choose to proceed. You see, I haven't made up my mind. But it has been very instructive to observe the desires of others. How could I be certain Henry is truly covetable if I did not see him coveted by another? That is, after all, how we determine value, isn't it? A jewel is only worth as much as people are willing to pay."

Her speech had provided me an opportunity to recover. "One might argue a jewel has intrinsic value and beauty in its own right."

"No matter the difference, it is the highest bidder that secures the jewel in the end." A large smile. One of her best.

I watched Henry's back, up ahead and out of earshot. "Yes, and it must be paid for with the most appropriate currency."

"In my experience, the type of currency matters a great deal less than the quantity. And if we understand each other clearly, I do not believe a tally would yield you any favors." Sigrid, sideways on her horse, was already facing me, and she leaned over, as if to suggest our closeness.

"I mean this as a kindness, naturally. A message from a friend. It does not do one good to get too far ahead of oneself. It results only in disappointment."

I could look at her no longer and turned my attention ahead. I did not want Sigrid to have what she desired. No matter myself in the equation: I wanted her life to put a check on her expectations.

WE STOPPED FOR OUR MEAL MIDAFTERNOON. HENRY UNFOLDED A quilted coverlet and we perched upon it: Henry with his legs stretched in front of him, and Sigrid and I on either side, our dresses spread.

"Why, you look just like a mushroom," Sigrid exclaimed, gesturing to the way my dress had billowed around me.

Watching her snicker and flirt with Henry, my own food turned tasteless. Sigrid had every advantage. She was accomplished and educated. She had the right family and the right manners and the right looks. She bathed her hair in beer and kept her skin as pale as the day she was born. Even then, she sat in gloves and her ridiculous hat—a wide-brimmed, silk-lined topper made from grass woven together in a pattern as intricate and delicate as lace.

She had thwarted all my attempts to cast her unfavorably. I could not rid myself of her buzzing laughter. She was like an insect that returned to one's meal again and again. But, watching her pinch tiny bites of sweet pudding into her mouth, the action reminded me: Sigrid had been raised to keep her hunger bridled. Women, in her world, were not meant to express desire or thirst or appetite. Women were not meant to *express*. But I had always sat at a table of men who ate with their fingers, ripped flesh from bone, laughing as the fat glinted on their lips and chins. And it was only recently I had understood I was supposed to be different.

When Sigrid complained of the warmth of the sun, adjusting her brim to better shade her complexion, I suggested we take a different, quicker route home. Leading our small caravan, I devised my plan. As

Henry had boasted weeks before, I knew every part of our little township, each river and stream, the worst bits of the bog, the oversized
beehives and hidden hollows and unkempt hedgerows. I knew, also,
how challenging the steep, rocky trail I had selected could be.

My mare was sure-footed and I set a fast pace. Henry, whose geld-
ing was solid and slow, fell behind. Sigrid's horse was ignoring her
directions, but, oblivious, she kept close behind me, prattling on about
a variety of subjects—fine linen as sun protection, an incident where a
cook had tried to pass off a cheat bread that was not made with white
flour, a silver girandole her mother believed had been stolen—unaware
of my rancor.

I was stewing, urging my horse to go faster than I should have,
wishing I could at least observe some uncertainty in Sigrid, when I saw
the ground-nesting wasps ahead. I didn't slow—the quickest flash of
a decision. The horse's hooves made sharp noises on the stones. It was
only when I was nearly upon them—Sigrid pondering aloud which
spices would be best to chew for fresh breath—that I wondered if I
was making a mistake. Doubt settled heavily into my chest. The option
to call out and warn her presented itself, hanging in the air. I felt, suddenly, cold certainty, and a sense of wrongness. I directed my mare to
the side, around the nest, and said nothing. When I passed, I turned
back, to watch.

Unaware of the danger, Sigrid kept her horse in the middle of the
path. Lawrence stepped into the nest, then abruptly lifted his hoof
from the ground and stomped, swishing his tail. His ears pricked.

"Look out," I said, half-heartedly. I had created the situation and
was now powerless to stop it.

Sigrid, confused, gathered her reins tighter. The horse, agitated, still
held his hoof—stung—limply above the ground, and started to dance,
to one side then the other. I pulled off the path, backing my mare up,
whispering calm breath into her ears.

Next to Sigrid, the insects began to emerge, growing in numbers.
She let out a scream. "They're on me, they're on me—get them off!"

"Sigrid," I called out, backing away, afraid my own horse would spook. "Keep your calm. You must keep your calm."

She didn't listen or couldn't hear, and I continued, loudly: "Stop shrieking. Your horse. Sigrid! Your *horse!*" I was shouting myself now, for Lawrence was panicking, bucking up. The wasps attacked them both— Sigrid and the animal were covered in stings. The insects continued to dive, subjecting girl and horse alike, again and again, to their brutal assaults. I heard Henry shouting from behind us.

"Grab the reins," I called. "You *must* calm down!"

The horse reared once more and lost his footing. His frame toppled sideways, away from her, and I watched it happen, terrified, aware of each hoof and the weight of the animal's body. She landed on top, but cried out in fear or pain. I dismounted, and Henry was rushing toward us, and as quickly as we could both manage, we were at Sigrid's side, attempting to remove her from the ground and from the wasps, which were stinging indiscriminately.

"We need to get you up," I said.

"Yes, you idiot!" she cried. "My hand is trapped!"

"Here," Henry said, trying to maneuver her. We worked to free her as the horse writhed. I felt a wasp sting my forearm, and then another my neck. Sigrid and the horse were both heaving in pain. We managed to pull her off just a moment before Lawrence sprang up and dashed for the bushes.

It was then that we could see Sigrid's hand and she started screaming anew. It was a different scream and one I recognized. Unmistakable, chilling: It was the cry of an animal that fears it will die.

Henry and I brought her back to the hunting lodge. She was too afraid to climb on his horse, and so he carried her, her hand dripping blood down his side. She was pale and gray, and her hand, when I could bear to look at it, was filled with wrong-angled fingers, pulverized in places, a mash of meat and tendons. Sigrid's screams were met with her mother's. A doctor was called for. There were breathless long moments and a sense of urgency—a pulsing energy of injury that made me feel both a desire to be close and the need to get far, far away—until Henry and I were sent outside for our uselessness.

We were both badly shaken. I was shaking. Without discussion, we went to the mews, which were empty.

Henry paced back and forth, and finally—I had been waiting for him to speak first—said: "Horrible. Truly horrible."

"Henry, I—"

"I should have been closer. I could have tried to grab the reins or—"

I held up a hand, insisting he quiet. "Henry, I could have stopped it. I should have."

"You can't stop a horse from spooking."

"Well, then, neither could you. But you're not understanding me. I picked the route. We were quarreling and—"

"You were quarreling?"

"It was an awful decision. If I'd known what would happen—"

"You were quarreling?" he repeated.

"The poor horse—will he be all right? Will he come home?" I deeply regretted what I had done to that horse.

"Ethel," Henry said, severely. "What were you quarreling about?"

I paused my hand-wringing. "You," I said, in surprise. We locked eyes. "Of course," I added.

He strode over to me and took my face between two firm hands and kissed me, hard.

"Forgive me," he said, taking a step back. "But what is there to quarrel about?"

CHAPTER SEVEN

WENTHELEN WAS IN THE GARDEN, CRUSHING APPLES WITH our small hand-cranked mill. "Alice is putting Lucy in her mews," I told her, nodding at the basket of fruit by her feet. "Are those the ones we picked last week?"

Cider apples must mellow for several days to develop their sugars. Picking one, I took a bite to check its sweetness. Throughout the season we'd be mashing them into pomace, pressing the grinds over clean straw, and then filtering the juice into barrels for fermentation. Wenthelen, who had overseen enough presses to ignore my question, didn't respond. She paused the revolution of the mill to lay a hand on her chest. "Poor girls, missing the party. But—Elin!—can you imagine—one of ours, married to a prince?"

I took another bite of apple. "No one is marrying anyone."

"A popular thought," she replied, snorting.

Then I heard it: loud, racking sobs—muffled but distinct. I looked up, peering at the open windows of the hall. "Rosamund."

Wenthelen nodded, not quite meeting my eye.

I sighed, wiping sticky juice from my chin. "Has she been at it this whole time?"

"Might want to let her lose a little steam." Wenthelen resumed her cranking. "The girl has nothing to think about but bows and balls. If you'd let her come to the market with me, take some commissions—"

"I do not think that wise."

"She's so talented," she insisted.

"No—"

"And she wants to come—"

"She is not a tradeswoman!" I exclaimed, harshly. Softening, I added: "She cannot appear to be one."

Wenthelen stopped milling for a short moment, and then began again with renewed vigor. "I tried to bring Elin some oat cake. But she refused."

I sighed. "Does no one have the ability to pull themselves upright?"

"She's so slight."

"I can't force the girl to eat."

"She needs a bit of color in her cheeks! She's upset."

"About getting invited to a ball?"

I had once heard a sculptor compare his children to marble. He said, like stone, their future shape lingers inside of them, waiting to be revealed. But I believed that children were paintings as much as they were sculptures. You shepherded them along from blank canvas: guiding and cajoling and teaching and begging and reprimanding and instructing and demanding, pushing and prodding the finished art into a picture of your own making. A stone is just a stone until someone appears with a chisel. I felt all of Rosie's and Mathilde's mistakes and missteps, their faults and flaws, as if they were my own.

Elin's, though, were another matter altogether.

If she didn't want to eat, that was her decision. I didn't feel inclined to serve her warm biscuits on a silver platter and stand by to ensure she chewed and swallowed.

But Wenthelen—who had known the girl since she was born— swelled, readying her arguments.

"I'll talk to her." I sighed, and tossed the rest of my apple into the mill.

✿

By her own choice, Elin's personal chambers were in the tower keep, the oldest part of the house where the walls were three feet thick and years of wear had polished the sloped stone floor shiny and smooth. The staircase, which turned around on itself, had a low ceiling that forced me to hunch. Elin was shorter than the rest of us, but I am sure there were other reasons she chose to sleep in that room; the tight, round turret was designed to be a last defense in a siege. It is challenging to fight your way up a set of steps; a person could retreat there in hopes of defending themselves.

I had not come up in some time. "Elin?" I called out as I rounded the corner.

She—no longer in pink, but every bit as fastened and cinched as a trussed tenderloin—sat at a small table, translating poems. In front of her, one of the deep-set windows framed clouds and sky. What her room might have lacked in light and ambience, it gained in view: It was the only place in the house where, on a clear day, you could see the castle in the distance, the pinpricks of its towers rising above the canopy of trees that surrounded us.

"May I come in?" Without waiting for a response, I went across to her bed and perched on its edge.

"You scared them away," she said, motioning toward her window, which was open. She had scattered bits of seed and crumbs across the deep sill, and there were bird and mouse droppings across the stone.

"You know I like birds," I said, carefully, not mentioning what we both thought: Lucy dined on little sparrows for supper. I gestured to the crumbs. "But we work so hard to keep the mice away, and here you are with welcome gifts."

Elin saved the runts. The birds with the broken legs and the spiders in the corner. The injured and the left behind. But where she felt affinity or duty, I saw only patience for weakness. She might fuss over a bird with a bent wing, but she'd never deign to wring the neck or pluck the feathers from the capon she liked to eat for supper.

"I take it from my portion." Settling her quill back into the inkpot, she nodded toward the picked-apart remains of the oat cake that sat beside her bed.

"Wenthelen wants you to eat your portion." I waved a hand, dismissing her concern. "And if it were you that had made the oat cakes, perhaps you would not be so quick to share them with the rodents." I had not come upstairs to talk to Elin about her creatures and critters, but it was often difficult not to get sidetracked by a worldview that felt so different from my own. Every chore Elin couldn't manage to complete, by ineptitude or lassitude, was a yoke to be borne by another. As if reading my thoughts, Elin tucked her unblemished fingers—long, slender, and completely unfamiliar with the quern stone we used to turn grain to flour—into her lap. I glanced around at her chambers: Here she spent her morning thinking of poetry, practicing her penmanship, participating in the specific labor of being a lady, when, if I listened carefully, I could still hear the crank of Wenthelen's mill.

I smoothed her bedsheet with a flat palm. "I came to talk to you about the ball."

"Oh, yes." She smiled, then hid her mouth behind a lifted hand. "The ball. It is a duty to partake in social gatherings from time to time, as it strengthens the bonds of community."

"You might just say you'd like to go." I snatched the sheet tight, trying to imagine her, innocent and senseless, navigating the rapidly changing social landscape that surrounded the palace. "Though I do not think you'd enjoy life in the court."

She reached for her small booklet—the compendium of good behavior for young woman—as if it might offer some protection. The volume had once belonged to her mother and now seemed to perform the duty of an absent parent. "I would never imagine that the prince would be interested in me," she said, modestly. Her finger agitated one of the pages.

"There will be plenty of eligible connections present besides the prince."

Hope lit her features. "Then you will chaperone me?"

"If you go," I said slowly, hoping she would understand, "then it will signal that you are ready to be an adult in the world. And if you are an adult in the world, then you will need to be one in this household." I gathered myself. "Your attendance requires a dress with a train and feathers for your hair. I will ensure you have what you need, but I expect you to contribute to the expense—the considerable expense—of your going."

Her nose wrinkled in distaste at the discussion of financial affairs. "Once I am married, I will have the means."

"I cannot wait until then," I exclaimed. "You'll need to contribute—to participate—in the work it will entail in this household." I wanted to speak with complete clarity, to ensure she understood, so I enunciated each word: "To help pay, you will collect the ashes from the fireplaces every morning and sell them to the rag-and-bone man, who will use them to make lye."

Elin, already pale, blanched. The action was beneath our household, and, even in our squalor, beneath her station. "The ashes?" she echoed, faintly, drawing her feet inward.

"There are few places left to find extra coin."

She fixed me with her blue eyes. "I cannot be perceived as a lady without truly embodying one." She looked down at her thin hands, still placed delicately in her lap, as if they were already speckled with soot. "If I allow myself to coarsen, who would have me?"

I stiffened, preventing my own back from twisting on her behalf. "And if you do not collect the ashes, how will you get to the ball? I will advance you the fabric, and everything else, but you must do these things. For the sake of contribution and for the sake of this household." I nodded to her little book. "You must find virtue in humility."

She waited a moment, weighing, I think, all her desires. To go to the ball, to be a lady, to escape the life we all lived together, she would have to stoop to do the things she had thus far considered herself above. "All right," she said with a nod that confirmed something to herself more than to me.

"Good," I replied—satisfied, but not pleased, for already I knew that pennies from ashes would not be enough to cover the added expense. "I'll see to getting you cloth and trimmings. You can finish in time if you apply yourself diligently."

It was difficult not to add more *ifs*. *If* you had ever learned to sew practical items instead of the samplers meant to demonstrate a young girl's prowess. *If* you were able to finish a useful project instead of just the useless litany of accomplishments meant to mark your own refinement. *If* your father hadn't needlessly spoiled you.

Elin widened her eyes as if she could hear my thoughts and turned to look out the window. The palace's turrets were barely visible in the distance. "I used to dream about going to the castle. When I was little, my mother would go to balls. She'd be gone for days at a time."

"Dreams do not bear the fruits of utility." I made little effort to soften the edge in my voice. "You'd best focus on your work and figuring out that dress."

But it wasn't true. Dreams were what kept one alive. It was only that mine had already come true—and then disintegrated.

CHAPTER EIGHT

A FTER HENRY KISSED ME, MY DAYS DID NOT FEEL EXPANSIVE
enough to contain all that I felt. If I had been eager to get outside to see him previously, the distraction—the pull—reached new
heights. I could barely sleep. We rushed to meet one another as often
as we were able, taking less care with our subterfuge. The proximity to
having something I wanted only made me want it all the more.

Sigrid, convalescing, was easily forgotten. Any guilt I might have
had about what had happened to her was overshadowed by my bliss
with Henry. But a handful of days after the accident, we visited her.

Laid up on a daybed in her chambers, she sat propped against a pile
of pillows. On her hand, she'd wrapped her stained bandage with a lace
ribbon. Sigrid was not an easy patient. Covered in wasp stings, puffed
and red and itching, she reprimanded her maidservants at every turn.

Made uncomfortable by such blatant snarking, I took a step closer
to Henry. And Sigrid, asinine in some ways, but shrewd in all others,
quickly saw that something had shifted between the two of us.

"You two are . . ." she observed. For a moment, there was no malice
on her face, only surprise. I still take satisfaction in that surprise. She

did not see me as a threat, or even someone to think about, until that moment. She soon recovered and offered one of her signature smiles. "I see you've made great use of my convalescence."

"You might join us again in the afternoons," Henry offered. "When you're well enough."

"We are to head back home." She sniffed. "My mother does not trust these country healers. Besides"—she again turned to face me—"I am sure you much prefer your time together. After all, it's likely limited."

It was satisfying, then, to take Henry's hand in my own, and squeeze it with all the strength of my healthy fingers.

Shortly after seeing Sigrid, knowing we had little time left for secrecy, Henry went to his father, and then my own. I wasn't present for those conversations and spent that day trying to manage the twin needles of hope and anxiety that pierced my thoughts again, and again, and yet again. Hindsight makes it easy to dismiss the tension of waiting, but I will never forget those long minutes when Henry was in my father's study with the door closed.

My father, of course, agreed. It was Henry's family that made their dissatisfaction known. But, unlike me, Henry had a say over his future. He told his parents he would marry me, with or without their involvement. And who could imagine a life without Henry? The Tremaines, too, knew he was the best in the room.

Was it foolish that I took Henry's insistence, his devotion, for granted? I knew nothing else. We were two cups, nestled. A hook and an eye, a latch and a clasp, as fitted and natural as a tree and its own bark.

Customarily, when a young woman was married, her family provided a trousseau: a few good dresses, chemises, petticoats, stays, soft linens for the table and bed, hand-embroidered handkerchiefs and napkins—a set large enough for whatever household she was about to oversee—and, the finest item of all, her wedding dress. I did not have sisters, or a mother, to fuss over these details. And my engagement to Henry was sudden, so I did not have time to prepare a set of napkins, or to worry over the perfumes and toiletries a new bride might have felt entitled to. But from the very first suggestion of betrothal, Agatha and I had worked on the dress.

Up to that point, every sartorial item in my life had been picked for practicality. My velvets were mockado—made with wool—to ensure their warmth. My shoes were buskins—outdoor boots—for mules and heels got lost in the sandy, boggy heath. My hems were shorter than fashionable to avoid the winter mud. Fabrics were brown, or gray, or burgundy, for they showed little dirt and required less dye. So, the choice of a blue organza, so pale it looked like the edge of the sky, so delicate it felt imbued with nobility, was momentous.

Agatha helped me with every step: the cutting of the cloth against the pattern, the measuring of the train, the pinning, the many fittings, the countless stitches, the adding of embellishments and buttons and ribbons. It was the first time we were working together, toward the same goal. She may have believed she had finally tamed me, or that her job was done. But I felt, in the adding of each stitch, in the repetition of the needle diving in and out of that blue cloth, in the pulling of the thread, that I was building a pathway to my own future.

I had already learned clothing was armor. Now I was experiencing it as a totem of mobility. And on the day of the wedding itself, it became an artifact: the dress that saw me leave my childhood home. The sleeve that wiped my tears when I said goodbye to my father. The stays that squeezed my waist in the carriage ride back to Henry's lodge.

That first evening alone with Henry, we went to our room early. The wedding had been in the morning, followed by a very long dinner, and later a lighter supper, and hours of conversing and celebrating, and a candle dance—the dancers holding a taper, lighting one another's wicks as they passed—that had rubbed blisters into my feet. We were departing in the morning, first thing. We were alone for the first time that day.

"That was the longest day of my life," Henry said, falling into a chair.

"I think my feet would like to quit my body." I looked at myself in the looking glass. Bare shoulders. Pearls woven into my hair. "And I've stained my dress," I said, dismayed, fingering my sleeve.

A maid knocked. She had come to help undo my buttons. Seeing a look of fear on my face, Henry sent her away. "I'll help you with your buttons," he said, and came over to meet me in front of the mirror.

My heart was in my throat. Gently, he turned me, and looked down my back. "I have never seen so many buttons." He spun me around, to face him, once more. "I'm quite serious. You are sprouting them. You have buttons from the base of your skull all the way down to the floor."

"I know," I told him, pulling my hair aside so he could access the silk-covered fasteners. "I sewed them on myself."

"Why would one ever do such a thing?" He began to help me, undoing the buttons carefully, moving down my spine.

"To dispel unwanted suitors."

We smirked at one another in the mirror. I could feel the night's air on my neck, then my shoulders, then the small of my back. His fingers traced my spine. They were warm.

"I think, alas, we have run out of buttons," he said, into the nape of my neck.

"Then I do not think I can stall much longer." I tilted back to look at him. His steady, reassuring eyes. The dress slid from my shoulders, and down toward the floor.

It remained in a pile by the mirror overnight. In the morning, the maid folded it into paper, and tucked the bundle into my trunk. And we began the six-day journey in a wagon and on horseback to Henry's family's manor hall.

I loved Henry and I was cautious with fear. I was sore and miserable from the time in the claustrophobic wagon, and unused to riding a horse for so long—my legs were stiff and my head hurt each time the carriage went over a rut or a bump. Most of the time we had spent together had been in the woods, with the birds, but now we were surrounded by people and men and horses and hoofbeats and dust. In the evenings, we would stop at inns and other estates, following the well-worn path the Tremaines took each year. But to me it was all new: each house, each host, each meal. I had never traveled far, and now I was breaking bread and making conversation with all manner of people.

When we finally arrived, I was stunned by the sight of the Tremaines' home: stone columns and baroque carvings surrounded by verdant, unending gardens. I understood, in the ensuing hours, all that I'd gained through my marriage, and why the alliance, even to a third-born, had overwhelmed my small village. There were more people working at the estate than lived in my entire hamlet: They moved about carrying straw and bales of cloth, piling firewood, leading livestock, warming themselves at small fires, herding children and animals. The hunting lodge—the pinnacle of wealth in my village—was rustic in comparison.

Henry was employed by his father. Though my husband traveled often, we were set up to reside on a small, leased country home not far from his parents. It was there that I learned, via letter, that both my father and brother had died of the same plague. My family had passed within months of my leaving while I had been dining on currants and stuffed pheasants in the Tremaines' great hall.

Death was no stranger to me or those that I knew—it was part and parcel with being alive. (I had heard the squeal of an animal that knew it would be slaughtered. I had seen men hung in the town square. I had seen, also, people crushed to death in the rabid crowd at one of the same executions. I had heard the stories of the women—the fevers that come after birth, the bodies in the stream, the promise behind the purpled eyes.) So, it wasn't the death, but rather the loss, that I had to make sense of. The letter said that my father's estate had been divided to pay his debts. But it did not say what had become of my family's belongings and I could not stop thinking about Father's canvas-and-serge apron, the garment that had covered his chest as reliably as a second layer of skin. The idea that it had been burned or discarded was almost as unbearable as the loss of his life itself.

I learned: A whole world of sorrow could be delivered in the news of one letter.

For a time, I was unmoored by the loneliness of what had happened. I found myself unable to fulfill household duties, unwilling to join feasts at the Tremaines' hall. The hours were gray. And then, I learned I was pregnant.

When I told Henry, his brown eyes went browner, bigger, wider. I felt a surge of feeling as he took my fingers in his and squeezed. The hope and fear on his face were familiar. They were the same opposing forces—push and pull, hot and cold—driving my own beating heart.

MY DAUGHTERS WERE BORN TWELVE MONTHS APART, ALMOST TO THE day. If time were your only consideration, you might consider them close enough to be twins. Bathed together, raised together, hair braided together. But the girls turned out to be nothing alike.

Mathilde came first—and early. She nearly wrecked me.

Even now, I don't like to recall the days after. The smell of iron and the stupor. You are so tethered, so madly in love, so trapped. I lived in an echo chamber of insanity. In the chaos that followed the birth, the blood and piss and vomit, the touch-and-go and near goodbye of it all, she was unnamed. I didn't want to name her, and refused, for days, for what must have been weeks. She was sickly and small and certain not to make it. I kept her on my chest, on my body, refusing the wet nurse, refusing to leave her. Her limbs were afterthoughts. Bones in skin. The whole of her balanced in my palm. I wanted to give her my very breath.

Live, live, live, live, live, I told her. It was the message in my every heartbeat. Mathilde means mighty in battle. She is named for those days, for the instructions she ultimately followed. She is the victor of a tiny war, of my womb; she still, to this day, gives me life.

The year that followed passed unconsciously. Henry's face, looking at me, always. Filled with questions. What had happened? Where had I gone? I was too anxious to leave the baby and angry to be so unfree. Too exhausted to sleep, too in love to relax, completely thrown and consumed by these new patterns—a shrieking cry during the night's darkest hour, the sweetest softest breath, the slow fattening of limbs, my life a syncopated rhythm of fear and a deep abiding affection. And then my dresses, never taken back in, were growing tight again and I realized I would be repeating the experience.

I named Rosamund before she ever arrived: my promise to and ask of her. Her name means rose of the world. It is perhaps too much to ask of a child, but she faithfully followed through. Healthy and round. Somehow her appearance in our lives, instead of doubling my troubles, seemed to halve them. The two of them balanced me, tugged me in opposite directions so that I was stabilized in an upright position. Finally willing to turn toward, if not look at, the light.

WE SPENT A HANDFUL OF GOOD YEARS ON THAT LEASED ESTATE, MEMories I revisit often. The smell of the lavender bush that flowered beneath our bedroom window. The warmth of a bath prepared in a copper tub. Afternoons without responsibility. Rosie lining up seashells Henry brought home from a trip. Mathilde stepping on a broken bottle, and Henry cradling her head as he withdrew the shard. Afterward, I watched him lift her young foot and kiss it.

Because our happiness was not overwhelming—because it was subtle and constant and threaded through every day and every interaction—I did not know to covet it, to hold on to it, that it might suddenly be taken away.

I will just say it directly because it is easier this way: Henry—who was the bark to my tree, who held my head between his hands, whose presence was a happy ending—died. (The drip at the back of the throat, the soft tissue between your vertebrae, the plum-colored crescent from a fingernail dug into skin; grief is felt in so many more places than the heart.)

On a long, warm summer day, the kind of afternoon where the light feels endless—insects buzzing, flowers and trees backlit, a fuzziness around the edges of your vision, the sun burning with such steady reassurance you forget there is anything in the world to fear—Henry's eldest brother arrived with the news.

They had been traveling together. A trip involving trade negotiations for nutmeg. His death, illness from contaminated water—in a nameless inn, in a nameless place—was sudden.

I had the wherewithal, then, to think of my father and brother, and the letter I had gotten with the news of their deaths. How a letter could also be a gift. Because instead of clutching a scroll of parchment, of being able to fall to the floor, I had to offer my brother-in-law tea and refreshments. Had to send the servants scuttling for a tray. Had to avoid looking at the liquid hanging from the tip of his nose.

It was only after he left that I could fully collapse and, shutting the door to the daylight outside, wish for darkness. How could the sun still shine on such moments?

Henry did not die at home—a cause of deep, enduring grief. I wanted to ask him: Did you collect any more seashells? Did you suffer? Did you know how much we loved you?

Of course, he wasn't there to answer.

THERE IS NOTHING NEW TO SAY ABOUT GRIEF. IF YOU'VE GRIEVED, then you know sorrow, and if you have not, then I will warn you: There will forevermore be days where happiness is forsaken. But there is no grief like watching a young child mourn a parent, though the inverse would be an amplification beyond comprehension. Rosie was six and Mathilde was seven. They did not need a cameo to remember Henry. He was soft flesh and pumping blood; he was every manner of being alive, throughout every day of their life—until, quite suddenly, he wasn't. How do you take a six-year-old's face in your shaking hands and explain this?

"He is never coming back?" Rosamund asked. And I had to repeat—made myself repeat—the word: *never*.

After our initial shock, we were left to ourselves. Our home was managed—meals prepared, chamber pots emptied—by our household staff. The girls and I had to learn to accommodate sorrow: a new companion and bedfellow in our recently diminished family.

During those weeks, I allowed Rosie and Mathilde to sleep in my room. Neither of them wanted to be on the outside edge of the bed, and so they took turns in the middle, their matching, indistinguishable bodies swapping all throughout the night, slithering over and under one another like snakes. Fear and grief had turned us cold and scaly.

Mathilde would try to console me. She would hold my hand, and once whispered: "We are not alone as long as we are together." Rosamund, who was already prone to tears, and becoming more prone to outbursts, would wake herself crying. I had so little left to console them. But, when they finally fell asleep beside me, each slumbering breath became a gift: the reminder of a purpose.

BESIDES THE SOFT EXHALES OF MY SLEEPING CHILDREN, I ALSO HAD to listen to another noise during those long nights. The sound of thrashing—and screaming—from down the hall.

Before Henry died, he had acquired a young falcon with the intention of training it. When he did not return from his trip, and our household became absorbed by its new rhythms, the bird was neglected—given food and water and little else. The peregrine grew increasingly agitated, making sharp and shrill noises, and banging against the sides of its room. I began to call him Lucifer.

Late one night, when the noises were loud enough to cut through my fugue of self-pity, I slipped out of bed and went through the dark house to the room Henry had used for his mews. Imagine my surprise when I discovered Lucifer was female.

She was so angry. Furious. An eye like a serpent's. A coldness in her stare. Beak open. She hated me, hated the world and everything she knew of it. And why shouldn't she, when she'd spent all her time in a dark room with no fresh air. She was terrified.

Imprinting a falcon means you have to teach it to trust you, a process that is painful and uncomfortable because you knowingly have to cause a living creature fear. (Again and again you expose them to their own fear—fear of you—until it dissipates.) It took me four days. It was an eternity. When you experience time alongside a terrorized bird, each particle of dust or muffled sound is a threat. I could see from Lucy's tightly held feathers, the quick swivel of her head, that she was miserable.

Each time I tried to get close, she bated, an awful eruption of feathers, and then would end up upside down. I felt like a monster in her eyes. I wanted her to trust me so badly. I was exhausted. She was exhausted. But at some point past midnight on the first day, I got her to eat some raw meat off my fist.

Let me just say this: A hawk knows. I had spent years flying birds with Henry, and, by his side, had already trained two. The falcons understand everything you're thinking. And to train a hawk, you must keep your thoughts neutral. Blank. Wooing my mind again and again into a state of unconsciousness in that dark room was the most soothing thing I could do for myself. Mathilde, and Rosie, too, would come and sit with me. Mathilde brought me food. Rosie would lay her head in my lap. *Live, live, live, live, live*, the darkness told me. It was what we had needed all along during those early weeks of mourning: to disappear.

Lucy, slowly, learned to trust me. On the second day, she accepted some raw liver. On the third, she let me take her out for a walk. And on the fourth, she willingly hopped onto my glove. I stared at the tiny, downy feathers on the bridge of her nose. In that hop, there was life.

Hers, mine, all of ours. For it is only in being gone that you are able to determine you have something to come back to.

WE—THE BIRD, MY DAUGHTERS, AND I—CONTINUED TO RESIDE FOR a short time on the leased estate Henry's family paid for. There was, ultimately, a question of what to do with us: the burden of a daughter-in-law they had never wanted; the future of two fatherless grandchildren; the expense of keeping us well shod and well fed. By this time, the Tremaines' fortunes had begun to shift. They'd slowly lost favor at court, and with it the contracts and arrangements that had once over-filled their coffers.

About seven months after Henry died, Henry's father came to the house. He did not visit often, and I dutifully lined the girls up so their grandfather could inspect them. But he avoided their eyes and motioned for me to follow him into my own drawing room. I gave Mathilde a reassuring nod and squeezed Rosie's hand and sent them upstairs.

Errol had positioned himself in an upholstered chair in front of the fire, which was lit, though it burned low. I had an ominous feeling about the conversation he intended to have, so I took my time adding a log to the hearth.

He did not wait for me to settle into the opposite chair to begin speaking, and so I was still wiping the bark from my hands when he said: "I've arranged for the children to be married."

I stopped and stared at him, astonished. "To whom?"

He cleared his throat and looked into the fire. "As their guardian, it is my job to see them taken care of, and we cannot support you three forever."

I blinked. Were we nothing more than a drain on resources? Could he not manage to see his own flesh and blood in the granddaughters who looked so much like his son? Finally, I managed: "Henry has not been dead a year. They are seven and eight years old!" My voice was

ratcheting up, and I lowered it, suddenly nervous the girls would hear.
I repeated: "To whom?"

Still, he stared into the fire. "A pair of brothers."

"Brothers," I echoed, feeling weak.

"Your girls will be close to one another. They're not of marrying age
yet, but they will be soon enough."

Both had had birthdays since Henry passed. Both were still children. "They are seven and eight years old," I repeated, in a hiss. I could
feel my body tightening, the muscles that wrapped my ribs so tense I
began to ache.

Finally, Errol turned to me, looking not apologetic, but withdrawn.
Certain. "They will move soon—so they can get used to the new locale."

"New—" I sputtered. "You cannot—"

"They'll leave in the spring, when the ice has melted and the ship
can make its way. I've made all the arrangements."

"*They?*" I repeated.

Errol looked at me plainly, answering the question I hadn't been
able to put into words. "The girls' marriage settlements do not provide
for you."

"I am their *mother!*"

"Your father did not negotiate a jointure when you married—and
is not here to support you in your widowhood. Dower rights might
entitle you to land, but you well know the only land Henry had was the
land *I* leased to him. There is no one to provide for you if you go with
the girls—and they're quite lucky we were able to negotiate *any* marriage given the circumstances. I've provided the dowries, but they are
not enough to include a stray mother. You'll remain here." He looked
around. "Under my roof."

I was completely powerless, with little in my arsenal to contradict
such bleak facts. "Sir, please." I felt my eyes fill with tears and willed
them away, to no avail. "Could we not wait until they are a little older?"

"You should be grateful." Errol stood, signaling the conversation was over. However he felt, whatever he thought, the deal, to him, was as good as done. "I do not believe the brothers are keen to wait."

"Sir!" I cried out, and then clapped a hand over my mouth, both to quiet myself and in horror. My daughters would need to marry, but I couldn't stomach it at their age, couldn't stomach the thought of the distance. Rosie still made up songs that she sang under her breath. Mathilde slept with a wooden animal she'd carried around for years. I wanted to tell Errol about all these little facts, but he stared at the fire impassively. Unflinchingly. The flames had grown high, and I could feel their heat on my face.

It took but an instant: I resolved to remarry. It was the only way to protect them.

CHAPTER NINE

Rosamund's wails had been drowned out by the thick stone of the tower keep, but when I descended the stairs, they arose once more, increasing in volume with each passing step. It is difficult for a mother to feel immune to her child's tears, but after a certain volume, after a certain number of years, the innate response becomes, at the very least, muted.

I found Mathilde in the study, sitting in front of her ledgers.

"I wanted to check we had paid all the appropriate levies," she said, without looking up. When she did, her brow was furrowed with worry. "We have."

"I don't doubt it." I sat down across from her. The room was one of the many we had stripped of valuables. There were darkened squares on the walls where paintings used to hang. The shelves sat empty. But the account register on the table in front of my daughter was filled with meticulous notes. She explained: "I thought if I found an error, perhaps we could fix it."

I felt the weight of my secrets and looked down at the desk. "I doubt it would be that simple." The surface was covered in organized piles of Mathilde's things: half-written letters, neat stacks of old books, a writing quill, and a dried inkpot. Noticing a familiar volume beneath her register, I reached out and nudged the ledger aside. An open book, bound in green. I knew it well. "Mathilde," I said, in exasperation.

She stuck out her chin. "There is no prohibition on women hawking."

Down the hall, Rosie's crying reached a new intensity. As with all musical arrangements, crescendos must naturally, and eventually, find diminuendo. I waited a moment for this softening before responding. "Just as there is no approbation for a lady hunting. If you're looking for a pastime, I could suggest ten other things worthy of your attention." I picked up the volume—Henry's edition of *Practical Falconry*—and pulled it toward me, running my fingers along the spine. "Your father did not even use the book—it just sat on his shelf."

"*You* cared enough to keep it." Mathilde reached for the manual, but I moved it to my lap, and she widened her eyes in frustration. "He would have allowed me if he were alive! He taught you."

The small tome sat heavy on my knees, and I closed my eyes at the exhaustion of a repeated argument. "Please, Mathilde."

She scowled. "If I am not introduced this year, we will have to wait until the following season. I will be one-and-twenty. And even then, there is no guarantee of a happy outcome. I may never find someone you deem worthy of marriage, and there is not infinite time. You might be willing to leave everything to chance, but I am not. And it is *my* future we are discussing."

I pressed on my temples, willing away the stories of unwed women. The bodies in the streams. The bellies beaten black-and-blue. "Your best chance at a happy life is to prepare yourself for the ball—"

She tossed her head back in exasperation. "To which I am not invited!"

"And to comport yourself properly and continue to work on your accomplishments so that when you are—"

She placed both hands on the desk in front of her, and though she did not slam them down, the movement had all the dramatic impact she needed to silence me. "I need to be able to take care of myself!"

"You *do*. You boil the sheets and carry your own water. I must draw the line somewhere. You must keep up appearances. I do not want a future where you must rummage for woodcock and snipe in order to eat your supper!" I looked out the window, toward the apples, and then back at my daughter, hair falling around her face, her worn hands splayed on the desk. I reached out and took one of them between my own. She had large knuckles and thin fingers. I saw, despite the rawness around the nail beds and the thickness on her palms, beauty, and strength. (I saw, also, all her hands from all her years: Her newborn hands and her three-year-old hands. Her five-year-old hands holding a quill and her eleven-year-old hands peeling grapes.) Her fingers pulsed in mine, as fragile and full of life as a small bird.

"You know well," I told her, "that I have always done *whatever* was needed to take care of you."

After Errol's visit—and proclamation—I was determined to find a different way forward. I shed my mourning black and set about attending a litany of parties, balls, and dinners, saying yes to as many as I was offered, with the idea, or goal, of finding a suitable partner for marriage—for myself. My actions had nothing to do with grief, which still throbbed like an animal trapped under my skin. But if I could secure a second husband, our marriage settlement would present an opportunity to negotiate. I could find someone willing to take the role of guardian of my daughters, to cover their future dowries, and in turn, wrestle control from Errol and his looming intentions. I had no doubt he'd be willing to give us over easily.

But finding such a second husband wasn't without its challenges. Though I was elevated in status by my first marriage, I now had two daughters, no land, and a meager amount of coin. I was not as young as most women on the marriage market. I could only consider widowers, most of whom were so far beyond my own years, I felt like a child bride myself. Still, I said yes to each invitation: I had only a few months before the girls were meant to board a ship that waited for them like a curse I could not break.

One evening I went to a supper hosted by a wizened neighbor who, I believe, understood my situation. After I arrived, Tabitha pulled me aside. "I've seated you next to Lord Robert Bramley. He is visiting and titled and has every one of his teeth. A well-tended estate in the southern province, if you don't mind me being direct. He lost his wife five years ago, and also has a child, and, from what I hear, has been uninterested in taking a new wife. Yet every woman I know would throw themselves at his boots. Goodness." She glanced over at her husband, who was twisting his ear hair while listening to another guest. "I would, too, if I had half a chance."

It was an illustrious send-up for a man who, I soon discovered, spoke so softly it was as if he had swallowed his own sentences. Perhaps, I reasoned, that was why he gave the impression of being so sought after: People had to lean toward him to hear what he said.

Once we were seated and introduced, I turned to face him. "It seems we have been placed together because you are without a wife." He looked surprised, but I leaned in, adding a twinkle to my eye. "And I without a husband. You have a daughter, our host has told me, and I have two. I think that should give us sufficient material for discussion, and if we keep it up properly"—I put a hand on his arm—"we may avoid chiding from dear Tabitha yet."

He glanced over at our host, then back to me, and swallowed. "Two daughters," he repeated.

I looked at him carefully. He had a pale complexion, blond hair, pillowy, purplish lips, and the posture of a person unused to their own body. I dropped my arm and decided to take a different approach. "They are seven and eight. Insatiable ages, and yet I miss them the moment I step away."

"Mine is seven and a half." He withdrew a watch from his pocket and flipped it open. On the inside of the gold lid there was an engraving of a young girl, maybe three years old. "When she was younger, of course."

"She looks like a cherub," I exclaimed, though it was hard to tell what she looked like at all from the simple etching.

"Her mother had it made for me." He shut the face of the watch abruptly and, in the hurry to shove it back into his pocket, dropped the gold object onto the floor, where it rolled under my chair. He colored, embarrassed.

"Allow me," I assured him, bending over to retrieve the timepiece from under my skirts. "We cannot let our precious objects escape, if even for a moment." Upright once more, I handed it to him. The watch was heavy and likely worth as much as a horse. "Tabitha tells me you are from the south."

"Yes—near the palace. Just a quarter day's journey."

"Do you spend much time in the city?"

"Not much," he admitted, eyes distant.

"Do you not care for it?"

"I do. But I don't. In some ways, I find it all right. In others . . ." He trailed off, as if flummoxed by the question.

"So, you prefer the country, then." I nodded. "I love a good walk in the countryside."

Our small talk continued in such a vein until an attendant interrupted us, offering a choice between regular wine and sherry.

"The wine," Robert asked, "is it good?"

The attendant nodded. "A fine year, my lord."

"But you'd say the same of the sherry?"

"Both are excellent choices."

"Indeed," Robert said softly, but continued deliberating until the silence grew unnatural.

"Sir?" The attendant held out one of the bottles. "Shall I pour you the wine?"

"That should pair nicely." Robert nodded. "But perhaps—would you suggest the sherry instead?"

The attendant cleared his throat, perplexed. "I think you'll be pleased with either."

"The wine, then," Robert decided. "No—the sherry."

The man could not make a decision. I leaned forward and addressed the attendant. "Please bring another glass. Lord Bramley will have one pour of each."

Robert slumped into his seat, relieved, and nodded at me gratefully. Sweat beaded on his brow—from the warmth of the nearby fire, or the anxiety of choice. There would be no hawks or blackberries, no nestled cups, but I decided in that exact moment, we would be married. It wasn't only the money and the title and his docile nature: I would be able to shape him to do as I saw fit with all three.

I nodded toward the pocket in which he had secured his watch. "A daughter without a mother? That must be quite a heartache. Though no doubt your closeness makes up for a great deal."

"I try to make up for it." He smoothed the tablecloth with his hands, which looked soft in the way that came from lack of challenge. "I do."

"Naturally," I encouraged him. "I am sure you've had plenty of opportunities to remarry. But no one could replace her real mother." I felt a pang then, something far more genuine than all the other feelings I had had sitting next to him. The quick throb of loss that pulses until you push it away. Discreetly, I wiped my eye.

He nodded in agreement. "Or a father," he acknowledged, respectfully, averting his gaze.

"Do forgive me." I tried to smile. Sometimes the false self and the real one become so intertwined you do not know where one starts and the other ends. "Though I do not think anyone else here would understand as you do." I dabbed at my eyes again. "And if I may overstep, perhaps it is not a woman's touch your daughter needs, but rather a mother's."

He cleared his throat.

I nodded, confirming my meaning. He smiled back, uncertain. The rest of the evening was much the same: like pushing a rock down a hill on which it was already rolling. I directed. He received. All his timidity landed somewhere soft and unpleasant on the back of my tongue. But I thought of Rosie's songs and Mathilde's animals and knew I could make peace with a lifetime of the feeling for the sake of my girls.

In a few weeks' time, all was settled. There was no one to ask permission of—a detail that held satisfaction and heartache in such equal balance, I could not be convinced there was any way but forward.

I have wondered: Was it deceitful to orchestrate a marriage based on my needs? We are all designed to sate our desires—and what is hunger if not a drive to survive? Is deceit less insidious if it is with noble purpose? There is nothing more noble than taking care of children—even if they are your own.

HEARING A HICCUP BEHIND ME, I TWISTED IN MY CHAIR AND LOOKED back across the study. Rosamund stood in the doorway, tearstained and swollen.

"Mother," she said, and I extricated a hand from one daughter to offer it to the other. She sank down beside me and put her head onto my skirts. "What should we do?"

"Whatever do you mean, *do*?" Mathilde watched her. "We can hardly show up in front of the palace and juggle to catch their attention."

"I know that." Rosie lifted her head to narrow her eyes at her sister. "I don't know how to juggle."

Mathilde sighed and spoke before I could. "We wouldn't make it past the gatehouse."

"We could petition. Or at least ask." Rosie turned to me once more. "Mother," she pleaded.

"I don't see what you're hoping to accomplish," Mathilde said.

Rosie paused her tears and frowned. "I am not crying for my own amusement. It is not frivolous to be concerned with one's future."

"Are you concerned with your future, or about missing a party?"

"Well." She sniffled. "Why can't it be both? Many great futures are decided at parties."

"Just as many great parties derailed many futures," I said. But my girls' pleas and the unending talk of the near hereafter twisted in my gut. I looked around at the bookless bookshelves. How could I allow Elin, younger than Mathilde, to be introduced and not offer the same chance to my daughters, my own blood? I heard my father: *You use the tools you have.* I would do whatever it took to protect my family. I always had. In all the years, nothing had changed: Whatever shred of pride I had, the scraps I'd coveted, I would trade for them.

"I suppose," I said, "that I could pay Sigrid a visit."

The girls glanced at one another, and then back at me, a question on their faces.

There are boundaries you make for yourself that you still end up crossing. There are selves that your children do not know. I nodded, confirming. "Before she married the king, her name was Sigrid White." I sucked in much-needed air. "Sigrid Camelia White."

They realized, both at once, and gasped.

"You know—" Mathilde began.

Rosamund finished: "The queen?"

They looked at each other, and then back to me, aghast.

"Yes," I said. "Yes, I suppose I do." I looked down at my own red, raw hands. "I'll need gloves."

CHAPTER TEN

FOR SO MANY YEARS, I KNEW EVERY INCH OF MY CHILDREN'S BODies. The creases at their wrists. The crooked teeth pushing through inflamed gums. The folds of their groins and the pebble shapes of their toes. And that body familiarity goes in hand with such a deep sense of knowing—of voice, of habit, of every intention—that even years after their initial demands for privacy, that primordial knowledge still sat, a bedrock, informing our every interaction. (*You, you, you, my darling, you.*)

A mother gets to choose. My body, my mind, were not made available to Rosie and Mathilde for such scrutiny. And though proximity offered them undeniable knowledge, it couldn't be mistaken for a complete picture. In the sharing of every detail of Henry they had asked for, in the recounting of the many stories that were demanded, I still chose to omit.

My omission: Sigrid. All of her. The whole of her. Not just the wasps, or the birds, but the fact of her in my history. All the more egregious, for she—my onetime rival—had gone on to marry the man who became the king.

☙

WHEN HENRY ASKED FOR MY HAND, FOR A FEW BRIEF WEEKS, IT
seemed as if all the world had tilted in my favor: Life had indeed put
a check on Sigrid's expectations and surpassed my own. But, shortly
after my wedding, at the Tremaines' main manor hall, I received a letter:

Dearest Ethel—or shall I call you Mrs. Tremaine?

*You may soon call me HRH, for I do have news to share. I am back
home and have finished convalescing. My hand is much healed,
though I likely have my mishap to thank for my present circumstances. A trade most would take. I am to be married—to the king's
first son! We met at my dearest sister Mary's wedding to the king's
third cousin, as you may recall. (And she thought she was the one
orchestrating a triumph!) A lovely bit of happenstance, though you of
all people would understand sometimes luck is by design.*

*I owe you my thanks, for perhaps if it were not for you, I might
find myself spending the rest of my years married to a third-born
with a penchant for feathered fiends. You did me a great kindness
and I will look back on our summer of girlish closeness fondly. I would
say that when we should see one another next, we shall embrace as
friends. Alas, I do not expect to see you very soon, for it is now determined that we will live very different lives. The sun does not think
about the other stars, after all, for it is the sun.*

Your friend always,
Sigrid Camelia White

The news had felt improbable. I had only just bid Sigrid adieu a
few weeks before, feeling satisfied and victorious and regretting little.
But in one swoop, she had recast my victory. Thrown a shadow on my
triumph and sapped its pleasure. How had she done this, I wondered, in

horror and awe. How does one meet and marry a prince in such a short time? How do some people appear to find soft carpet beneath them, no matter where their feet fall?

Henry's family had been thrilled for what they understood the news to imply: friendship with the future queen. I knew better. For all the following years, the Tremaines—and I—were not invited to court. Errol's long-promised peerage failed to materialize. The family was not rewarded their annual royal charter on spices and lost their monopoly. There were sudden fines for breaking trade regulations that had never been enforced previously. Protective tariffs were withdrawn, exposing the family's wares to further competition. It took but a small handful of years: The Tremaines quickly grew further from social grace and power and, eventually, their money. And I grew a disdain for the crown's rule and developed a jealousy of its splendor.

The seasons ticked by, and news of Sigrid's life was unavoidable. She had her first child—a boy—the same year I had Mathilde and the kingdom rejoiced. After the death of his father, her husband became king and Sigrid was crowned and her face put onto coins. Her very likeness burned into metal and jangling in my pockets. Later, her daughter's name day fell around when Henry died, and I had to listen to pealing bells and walk past flapping celebratory banners as my own joy turned to ash in my mouth. As I watched my daughters grow, observing them learn to navigate the world, seeing how their futures became like pawns on the increasingly desperate Tremaines' chessboard, Sigrid's presence—her pervasiveness—only served to underscore my growing conviction: Those who played by the rules, who laughed sweet laughter and sang songs and weaponized the tools given to us—who turned the rules into a ladder, then a dagger—did best.

You could place a kind of blame. The Tremaines' ruin stemmed from Sigrid's acrimony over Henry's choice. A choice I had tried to force. The seeds I had sown with the venom of a thousand wasps.

And still—*still*—I was choking down the rotten remains of that harvest.

CHAPTER ELEVEN

HENEVER THE NEED AROSE, ALICE WOULD DRESS HERSELF in men's attire and oversee the chaise, drawn by Arno, our spindly horse. Alice sat, in cap and livery, waiting for me. "Goodness," she exclaimed when I finally emerged from the house. "What a charming sight!"

"You're one to talk," I scoffed, but we regarded one another with a shared smirk, and then I pulled my skirts up with one hand so I could climb into the carriage beside her. My dress—one of Rosamund's elaborate patterned concoctions, an affair so draped and pleated my head was like a decoration on top of a cake—had elbow-length sleeves with flared cuffs and a two-foot train. I arranged the fabric around our feet so it wouldn't dirty. "Shall we open the calash?"

Alice clicked and Arno lurched forward. "Might rain."

I looked up at the cloudless sky. "That's the spirit."

"Don't let them see those." She nodded at my feet.

"I know that!" I slid the old leather latchets behind my skirts. With the exception of my footwear, I had been cinched and tied into the shape of respectability. Over a linen shift, I wore bone stays, followed by a quilted silk petticoat, a bow-covered stomacher, and an open-faced robe. Engageantes and combs decorated my elbows and hair. Though I carried nothing but a fan and gloves, I could not have looked more prepared if I had been wearing a knight's brigandine.

"Just . . ." I waved my hand in the air. "Drive."

Alice looked forward, not quite hiding the roll of her eyes. The calash remained closed. And we were on our way, bumping along the country road until it could be called that no more.

EVENTUALLY, THE CITY AROSE BEFORE US, APPEARING FIRST AS A smoke-covered anomaly in the green country hills, then making itself known through the increase of hagglers and traders and children running amok as we reached its outskirts. We passed under an arched gate in the ancient outer walls and made our way through crowded streets. The air thickened with the smell of woodsmoke. As we approached the city center, people and livestock filled the mud-slick roads. When we could move no longer, Alice directed Arno to the side of the road, stopping behind an old man selling roasted nuts from a cart.

"You'll make better time on foot." She climbed down and held out a hand. "Watch the muck."

"An appropriate city motto." I held on to Alice as I lowered myself, wishing I could give her a shilling so she could buy some of the chestnuts. The cart's aroma might at least disguise some of the other smells: The open sewers and the sulfuric stench of a tannery and the blooming algae from the palace moat.

"Best of luck," she called.

There was no need for directions. Though the city's buildings had, over time, grown up and out in pieces, each new extremity jutting over the street to block the light and view, the castle was on yet higher ground, and I could see it perched on the rise of the hill. As I got closer, my surroundings hardened: both wood buildings and earthen streets turning to stone. Proximity to power desired permanence—and was not without its dangers. The sun occasionally caught on the castle's blue-gray turrets, causing brief, bright moments of blindness. I used a gloved hand to hold the fan above my eyes.

As I neared the outer walls, my path, lined with topiaries and stone benches, filled with people. Courtiers rushed past, tittering and clucking in groups of two and three. A bearded man played a stringed instrument beneath the shade of a maple tree. A youth, missing his leg, leaned against a marble plinth, attempting to adjust his bandages. A pregnant redhead sat on a bench, crying into a handkerchief. Castle servants hurried in currents around us all.

I crossed a small bridge over the green-watered moat. The guard house, a squat functional building, attached to the palace wall like a growth. Next to it, the massive gate lay shut. A smaller door, cut into the wood, was partially ajar, though flanked by a uniformed guard standing on duty. He watched me approach.

"Good day." I nodded.

He remained expressionless. "State your business."

His eyes were small and high on his forehead, giving the impression that there was not much space for thought inside. He had a cut on his chin from a poor job shaving. "I am Lady Tremaine," I told him. "I request an audience with the queen."

His expression barely changed. "Time with the queen isn't doled out based on request."

"Nevertheless, please pass the message that Lady Tremaine is here for an audience." I stared at the cut on his face for a moment too long and he raised a hand, unconsciously, toward his chin.

"Her Majesty isn't available." When he lowered his finger, there was a spot of dried blood on its tip, which he inspected.

"The man operating the gate doesn't determine who gets an audience," I scoffed.

He squinted at me, the scab forgotten. "Do you know how many people come here demanding to be let in?"

"My name is Lady Etheldreda Verity Isolde Tremaine." I enunciated each word with clarity. *Soft voice, controlled pace*, Agatha reminded me. "I am here to request an audience. Duty obliges you to relay my message."

Finally, the guard looked me over, taking a moment to examine my dress, pausing on the series of bows down the front of my stomacher. I did not look the same as the crowd—the people of missing limbs and falling tears—that lined the path to the gate.

"Lady Tremaine," he echoed.

I gave him a curt nod.

After a moment's hesitation, he shrugged. "I'll relay the message."

"As you're obliged to."

His small eyes narrowed. "A response may take a long while."

I set my jaw. "Then I shall wait."

LADY TREMAINE DID NOT EXIST. OR RATHER, SHE WAS NOT A REAL person. But, though it was not the world's name for me, it was my truest one: An accurate depiction of what I gave and took from each of my marriages. Tremaine was the name from my first, the marriage of my heart. My title came from my second.

After marrying Robert, arriving at Bramley Hall that first day was like unwrapping a gift I'd chosen for myself and then forgotten. Spring blossoms blanketed the trees, scenting the air and scattering their petals like aromatic snow. The ground was dry, and the house looked bright and clean, and larger than I had allowed myself to imagine. Though I held Robert's purple lips in no higher esteem than the day we had met, as he helped me and the girls down from the carriage, I could not help but think: If the future were a person, I would kiss them.

The staff was all lined up in front of the manor. Housemaids and kitchen maids and footmen. I insisted that Robert introduce me and my daughters to each one in turn. We went down the row—bobbing to the scullery maid and the groundskeeper and the coachman who had driven us over—until the end, when it became more obvious that it was *only* the staff who stood to greet us.

"Where is Elin?" Robert asked.

A tall, thin woman stepped forward. The housekeeper, a metal ring of keys attached to her belt. Alice. "In her room," she informed him, with an efficient nod.

"She should be out here, shouldn't she?" Robert asked out loud. I wasn't sure who he was asking. The staff remained quiet. He turned to me. "Should I fetch her?"

"Perhaps—" I began.

"Or should I send someone to get her?" He peered upstairs at the mullioned windows.

I glanced over at Rosie and Mathilde, who had jostled for days in a carriage to come to a new home where they knew no one. They stared back at me, open-eyed. "We might—"

"It is cold out. And if she comes here, then we will just end up inside anyhow," Robert mused. "But if—"

"We will all go inside now," I said, firmly. "And meet her where she is."

From down the row, the cook gave me an approving nod.

OF ALL THE STAFF THERE HAD BEEN NO NURSEMAID, WHICH EX-plained, amongst many other details that would come to light, both Elin's absence and why she was alone in her room.

"Elin," Robert called softly from the doorway. "Your papa is home. And I've brought you your new sisters."

She was playing with her dolls, turned away from us, sitting in front of empty plates laid out on a child-sized table. I could not see her face, but the conflict that must have been upon it reflected itself across her shoulders. I was not offended by her shyness. She was a motherless girl surrounded by baby dolls. And a new family *was* an unexpected arrival, even if her father had written ahead. I watched as she lifted an empty teacup to a doll's lips and poured air down its throat.

When the pouring was finished and still she did not turn, I took Rosie's and Mathilde's hands and brought them one step forward into Elin's nursery. All three of us looked around in astonishment. There was a peach chaise and peach walls and peach tapestries and peach curtains. The room was like being inside a cloud if a cloud was also filled with toys. The surfaces were covered in every manner of doll and animal. Exquisitely realistic dolls with porcelain faces and curled hair. Little-girl dolls in lace gowns and baby dolls in bundles and blankets and cradles. Unable to contain herself, Rosie shook off my hand and ran forward, stopping short in front of one doll that was discarded, face up, on a cupboard. Extending a hand, she touched it gently with the tip of her finger, turning back to me after, eyebrows raised in a belated request for permission.

Mathilde took another step forward, into the room. "Hello," she said, thinking carefully about her words, and straining to make a good impression. "I am Mathilde. It is lovely to make your acquaintance."

"You have *so* many wonderful things." Rosie spun to take in the room once more.

Still, Elin had not turned. "Elin," Robert called, again. "We have visitors. Come say hello to your papa."

Because it was a direct order, she stood, and, without looking at us, went toward her father. When she was near enough, she closed the distance between them with a quick run into his arms and buried her face into his chest. I firmed myself against a pulse of my own grief. *Henry!* I wanted to say his name aloud.

I had seen, when we walked through the great hall, a portrait of a woman I could only assume was Robert's first wife. The resemblance between the woman and the girl in front of me was striking: bodies so slender you had a sense of the bones beneath skin, hair so blond it was at risk of losing its color, and eyes so blue they managed to be both startled and startling at once. It was difficult to decide if they—both mother and daughter—were stunningly beautiful or strange and unfamiliar. Either way, it was difficult to stop looking at Elin.

When a proper amount of time had passed, I began to speak to my new stepdaughter. "Hello, Elin," I said, softly. "My name is Etheldreda. I have been very much looking forward to meeting you. As have my two little girls, Rosamund and Mathilde."

Still, she did not look at us, and instead began to sing a nameless tune into Robert's chest. He chuckled and looked over. "She's like this. Head in the clouds. She has the heart of an angel—you will see."

She fit his description. The girl was light personified. Pale skin, white eyelashes; her color had evaporated. She'd float away if she were not anchored by her father's arms.

"Elin, darling," Robert continued, "perhaps you might choose a toy to share with each of the girls."

Mathilde's hand, still clasped in my own, jumped. I heard, from Rosie, a quick intake of air. There had been no new toys or gifts the past year. Elin pushed back from her father's arms, and for the first time, turned to face us with those startling eyes. She opened her mouth. Her gaze flitted up to the ceiling, down to the floor, up once more, and then, in one smooth collapse, she fell, lifelessly, against her father.

I ran a few steps forward, dropping Mathilde's hand, as she spun around in surprise. Rosie cried out. But Robert, cradling Elin fondly, quickly explained: She had only fainted. A harmless ailment. It happened often, and at random.

As the initial days passed, I had a chance to observe for myself.

When Elin was gently scolded by the housekeeper for opening her nursery windows and letting the rain warp the sill—Elin fainted.

When Mathilde, tentatively, shyly, asked if they might play together—Elin fainted.

When she learned that I, Robert's new wife, would be taking her seat beside him at the dinner table—Elin fainted.

When Rosie found her unlatching the door to Lucy's mews, and walking away with the opening ajar—Elin fainted.

When she was questioned after Mathilde's wooden animal went missing and it was discovered in Elin's room—Elin fainted.

She was but a child, acting against change and grief in childish ways. But it did not take long for me to come to my own conclusion. We don't all draw our angels with the same hand.

THE DIFFERENCES BETWEEN MY NEW HUSBAND AND I QUICKLY MADE themselves known. Though I was out of black, my loss was still new and fresh. In contrast, Robert's first wife had passed years before. Now he spoiled his daughter, lavishing her with gifts and ribbons, and more of those discomfiting dolls. In return, Elin, his angel, his small fountain of girlish virtue, dined with the adults, had no friends her age, and was her father's primary talking companion. I believed in rules and had children who knew how to follow them. Robert could not deprive Elin of a thing, for she had already been deprived of a mother.

Jealous was not the right word for what I felt. Rather, Elin and her deceased mother were an unaccounted-for imbalance in my life, like I had calibrated the scales and then found extra weights on the table. Elin's mother had decorated Bramley Hall, and—though I tried to expunge her, the nice ghost—you could not enter a room without seeing all she touched. She was there in each silk and brocade, the elaborate carvings in the stairwell, and the crest that marked the lintels.

A few weeks after our arrival, I was wandering the hallways, familiarizing myself with my new home, when I came to a stop in front of my predecessor's bedchambers. I had already discovered, during previous meanderings, that the room had been left untouched. Half-full bottles of oil and perfumes sat on a polished vanity. Vases decorated the bedside tables. Heavy curtains muted the light from the oversized window and contrasted with a delicate lace canopy hung over the bed. Through the open archway to the dressing room, I could see the graceful specters of outdated dresses.

I had paused to marvel at these details—a pair of silk dressing slippers still awaited their mistress at the side of the bed—before realizing someone was in the room. Elin stood in front of a row of dolls she'd placed on a chaise that faced the window.

"Look, ladies," she instructed. The dolls were her pupils. "This is where my mother painted." She gestured toward an empty easel and stool across the room. "Papa says a woman is capable of never-ending accomplishments. She must think of herself not as a piece of art to be finished, but an ongoing project."

She went over to the mantel, where a small selection of volumes were wedged between bookends. "And here are her books. A lady must be learned and well read." Selecting a thin booklet, she opened it, paged through, and sounded out the words: "'Let every young woman aspire to high degrees of purity, excellence, and unsullied virtue. Since mothers are never mothers until they have become daughters—and mothers are the ones to go on to raise sons—let us presume that the education and instruction of daughters is the responsibility not just of the daughter herself, but society as a whole. Such a charge is . . . indubitably'"— she slowed, struggling with the word, before picking up her pace once more—"'paramount, as mothers, in their omnipotent influence, may sow the seeds of malevolence with as much fervor as they sow good. Hence, the inculcation of virtue becomes an endeavor of the utmost gravity in the education of all of the world's daughters.'"

Elin lowered the booklet, biting her lip. "I do not really remember Mother," she admitted to the dolls, shifting from the voice of authority to that of a small girl. "Only from the painting. But Papa said that she was a proper lady and that I will be like her if I am a good girl." She turned her face upward and addressed the lace canopy above the bed. "I will try to be a good girl always, Mama, and not to . . . sow malevolence."

She waited, as if expecting a response, and I could not bear it. Could not let her statement go unanswered. I stepped into the room, making enough noise to announce my presence, and Elin's chin snapped back down.

"Hello, Elin," I said softly. I looked around—at the soft light, at the porcelain figures on the chaise. "This was your mother's room, wasn't it."

She had gone cold and quiet, the book now shut in her hands. "Yes, Stepmother."

"It is hard to miss someone, isn't it?"

"Yes, Stepmother," she repeated, stonily.

"In missing someone, we keep a part of them alive within us, you know. I'm quite certain your mother would be very proud of you."

"Please excuse me." Taking the booklet with her, she made for the door. "I must go find my father."

She left me in the room, alone, her useless porcelain dolls—skin cold, eyes blank—staring back at me from the chaise.

Much of my efforts with Elin, for weeks after, went the same.

Robert, for his part, was careful and polite but vaguely disappointed by the initial weeks of our marriage. He had not married for feminine company; he did not often visit my rooms. He had not married for domestic support; he had a household that ran itself—with a housekeeper that kept a firm eye across every detail. He had, I believed, hoped to offer Elin another feminine figure to sit amongst all the other dolls in her room: a mother.

But everything I knew about motherhood came from ushering Rosamund and Mathilde through each step of their lives. I knew every orientation of their hopes and failures. We were a unit of three. (*Live, live, live*, I had told Mathilde, but it was them who gave my life meaning.) After my initial overtures with Elin were rejected—and rejected again—I did not know how to begin anew with a girl of nearly eight years. I knew nothing of Elin's hopes and dreams. She suffered by comparison to my feelings for my own girls. As I am sure I suffered by comparison to whatever she felt for her own birth mother. But most critically: She did not want my mothering. And I did not know how to be an unwanted mother. I did not know how to grow love from infertile ground. It was unnatural for both of us.

My girls adapted a bit better. Rosie, who had been tearful and petulant when she learned of the prospect of a new home and new family, fell into the rhythms of Bramley Hall—the formal meals, the lady's maids—with relish. And Mathilde, who had accepted my decision with a steely determination to support it, seemed to draw, at least in part, some reassurance from the tightly held articulations of our new schedule. Meals at set times. Each staff member with their own domain and role. And though Elin never embraced their offers of friendship, the situation was not without corporeal pleasures. We ate well. Each bath was drawn warm, and, that first winter, hot stones were placed between our sheets. It was easy to accept this new life with our bodies, however reluctant our hearts.

I missed Henry—*Henry!*—but I recognized there was no way to go but forward. So I tried with Robert. I tried to overlook his blood-sausage lips, and I tried to get used to his soft hands, and I tried, again and again, to be useful to his daughter. I tried, also, to help him move on from his own loss.

A HANDFUL OF MONTHS AFTER I ARRIVED AT BRAMLEY, I ASKED Robert to remove the portrait of his first wife from the hall. I understood— *Henry!*—the ties that bind one's heart, but if we were to live together, we did not need those blue eyes watching every time we crossed the room.

The piece was hung high on the wall, above the mantel. Robert did not want anyone else to touch the revered painting and went up the ladder himself. I watched from the doorway: his blond head bobbing in front of his wife's varnished face, hovering as if he meant to kiss her. Gently, slowly, he took each side of the frame in his long fingers, his soft hands, and unhooked the art from the wall.

The shift in balance caused the ladder to sway. A slight wobble. I saw, as if time slowed, Robert's look of alarm. He was within a foot of the mantel. He could have reached out and steadied himself, but he was holding the painting. He glanced down at the floor, and back at the mantel, and then down at the floor once more.

I tried to tell him to drop the painting. The fool. But time would not slow enough for me to get the words out, and all I managed was: "Robert!" It was a large room and I could not get there quickly enough. The ladder pitched. Robert fell, soundlessly, and struck his head on the base of the stone hearth. Still clutching the painting. Its frame now cracked. In his indecision, he had saved neither himself nor the portrait.

AFTER ROBERT'S FALL, HE SPENT TWO DAYS IN BED, FACE GRAY, UNTIL his death, which felt like the slow-motion snuffing of a candle. A practical part of me reasoned I already owned the mourning clothes. So, I was surprised by the grief, real grief, that rose when his eyes closed for the last time. Another father, gone. What would the girls think of the world? The picture we all beheld, finality, loss, blood, pain, was not inaccurate. But I did not think our hearts were meant to reckon with such perceptions so frequently.

I couldn't have realized that initial loss—*Robert!*—was only the beginning.

A few days after his death, Alice bid me into the study. The testator had come. Once inside, she brought out a folio and explained: She was named executor in Robert's will. That a housekeeper was sorting my dead husband's affairs felt no stranger to me than the fact of the dead husband itself. But my numbness soon gave way.

The testator—a phlegmatic man I had never seen before—told me what was obvious: that Robert had no male heirs. He continued to explain that the law was that the estate would go to me. (*His* becomes *hers*.) His own papers decreed all other money—which there was so much less of than I could have imagined—would go to Elin, to be marked in a trust and used only for her dowry.

"I don't understand." I pressed my fingertips to my temple. But I did understand, I just hoped it was not true. "None of the money is available for our use?"

Alice confirmed with a tight nod, eyes sympathetic.

"How will we run the estate? What will Elin live off of until she is able to make use of her dowry?" The questions continued in my head: To what extent was the situation intentional versus a task deferred? To whom could I turn now? "Can Elin sign over the money? Could she contribute—could it be used toward the expense of raising her?"

"The money is not technically hers," Alice explained.

The testator nodded. "Her dowry will go to her husband. She is your ward until that happens."

"There's something else," Alice interjected.

The testator cleared his throat. "Lord Bramley has not paid taxes on the estate—the hall—for some good years. There are more unpaid taxes owed than it is worth. So, if you were to sell it, the taxes would be due, leaving you with debt. The house and the debt are one and the same."

Alice said the number.

I did not blanch. By then, her serious face and somber tone had prepared me: I had been impoverished while Elin had been given a future. In one move, Robert had tied me to his house and to his daughter: my ruin, her gain. I exhaled, though it felt like there was no breath left in my chest. "I . . . see."

"Yes, m'lady." Alice slid a carefully folded handkerchief across the tabletop.

The title, I realized, meant so little. The house was an opulent weight that could only pull down. And I faced a graver issue: I had no means to take care of my girls.

❦

My long wait outside the palace guardhouse was made all the more uncomfortable by my doubts. I was not certain my plan to gain entry would work. After all, I suspected my daughters had been left out of the messenger's invitation intentionally. But I knew Sigrid would recognize the name I had given.

I walked up and down the walkway. Paused in the shade of a tree. Sat on a stone bench. I looked at all the people I had passed earlier. The lute player, likely hoping for employment, played his sad songs. The pregnant girl continued to cry. The youth perpetually wrapped and unwrapped his bandages. And the ladies-in-waiting—none alike yet all similar, continually replenishing themselves—waited by their very nature.

After an interminable amount of time, the guard, scab now picked fresh off his chin, approached me. "You can go in," he said. "Follow the page."

"You have something," I told him, tapping my own chin. "Right there."

I followed a bespectacled attendant along a cobblestone path, passing a series of silent, erect guards. When we entered the castle, we climbed a stone staircase and came to a long gallery, our footsteps echoing on the blue-and-white checkerboard floor.

The room was only half lit; every curtain on every east-facing window had been pulled shut. Walking at a pace that felt slower than natural, I passed gilt-framed painting after gilt-framed painting. The blank stares of nameless faces. A room of artificial eyes.

I came to a stop in front of an oversized family portrait. The slight tilt of the head and the half-pursed smile of the woman at its center was unmistakable. Sigrid still looked beautiful. But the lordliness in her expression was unnecessary. The fur-trimmed robes and jeweled crown might have done that work for her.

I had seen a likeness of our king plenty of times before—kind-eyed and sharp-boned—but the two children who stood at his side were new to me. The prince was as tall as his father, if not taller, for I did not think a royal portrait would depict any man standing above the king. He had the same warm brown eyes, with a crop of his mother's honey hair, as if an unseen hand had deigned to mix the best from each parent. By contrast, the girl who stood on the opposite side was her mother in miniature. Red lips and flaxen tresses. Blue eyes like looking into my own past: I could practically hear Sigrid beating her heels against the Tremaines' rock wall.

We kept walking. Lady Tremaine—had it worked? I had spent years wondering if Sigrid hated me, resented me, blamed me for her accident. But seeing the likeness of her family, each clad in velvet and fur, and then following the attendant through the palace rooms, passing fabric-covered walls, oil paintings, and statues, high-backed chairs and inlaid-tile ceilings, through blue rooms, pink rooms, velvet rooms— each its own acidic bite of opulence—gliding past a thoughtless wealth of wealth, every jewel tone rendered in a color brighter than nature, it occurred to me: She had no reason to think about me at all.

When, at long last, the guard slowed ahead of a closed door, I felt a sense of relief. Nervously, I began to fidget with my gloves. They were uncomfortable—hot in the summer and not warm enough in the winter. The whole kingdom wore them because the queen did.

Gloves, after all, were a clever way to cover a missing finger.

CHAPTER TWELVE

EXCEPT FOR AN ATTENDANT PULLING THE DRAPES SHUT OVER
the east-facing windows, Sigrid was alone. This surprised me, for
I had pictured her surrounded by musicians and courtesans and ladies-
in-waiting. She didn't rise when I came in and didn't acknowledge the
footman when he announced me. I curtsied, and then stood, waiting.

"Tremaine," she said, thoughtfully. "I thought it might be you."

"My thanks for receiving me." I stood still, and then, remembering,
added: "Your Majesty."

"Come closer," she commanded. I complied and walked toward her,
allowing her to inspect me.

"It has been some time," I offered, beginning what I hoped would
be a round of pleasantries.

"Sit." She nodded at the chair across from her, on the other side of
a small, round table. I arranged my dress and consented. Wordlessly,
Sigrid began to prepare tea, using a silver spoon to scoop the leaves
into the pot. We said nothing as it steeped for several long moments.
I watched as she added loaded spoonfuls of sugar, more than I could
stomach, to porcelain cups. When she had finished, she handed me

a saucer with a brimming cup of scalding liquid. "Have some," she instructed. "The leaves are all screened from the sun by silken shades."

I raised the cup to my mouth. I could feel the steam. It was too hot.

"Drink," she said, and I did, feeling the water burn my tongue. I couldn't taste anything through the heat except the sugar. Satisfied, Sigrid nodded. I returned the cup to its saucer, and we regarded one another.

She wore a low-necked peacock-blue dress adorned with dramatic folds of lace that created bells at her elbows and covered her chest in a transparent screen of feigned modesty. It was a shock to see the age on her face—like a mirror, it confirmed the passing of time. Unlike the painting, she was freckled and puckered. Her eyebrows had thinned and she wore two bright spots of rouge on her cheeks, reminding me of a doll. But her eyes were as shrewd as ever.

"What an unconventional introduction," she mused. "If I recall, Henry didn't have a title."

"No," I acknowledged. I looked down and stirred my tea—Agatha, who had come roaring back into my subconscious the moment I got to the palace, reminded me: *clockwise*—to cool it off, careful not to splash or clink. "The title is from my second husband, Lord Robert Bramley."

"I heard Henry died." Sigrid measured more sugar into her tea, stirred twice, and discarded the spoon with efficiency. "But you remarried? A step up, it appears?"

"My second husband also died."

"What a touch you have!" She had lost her habit of pairing smiles with her insults. Instead, the queen watched me coldly.

The room felt, suddenly, airless. The heat from the fire too warm. The drapes at the windows too thick. Helplessly, I complimented her— her appearance, her room, the finery of her porcelain. "It is," I added, at the end of my soliloquy, "so wonderful to catch up." I was incapacitated in the face of our many imbalances, our strange history: I could not right the kilter of our conversation.

"Indeed." She took a small sip of her tea.

"Time has been kind to you," I lied, and I could see her catch the lie, and then want to believe it. She looked satisfied by a few degrees, and I continued: "As little girls, you gave me beauty tips. I should have listened."

Idly, she examined her fingertips, which were covered by her gloves. "Do you live near here?"

"A two or three hours' journey south," I said, carefully. Her tone had suggested she knew exactly where I lived.

"Far cry from that pile of rocks you grew up on. And just look where you stand today!" She dropped her hand. "Do you remember how the wind used to whip and moan at night? And the food. Hardly anything grew out there! Waterfowl for every meal. I'm partial to sweet things. Red meat. Oh, I do enjoy a bit of reminiscing."

She turned away before I could respond and, to the air, said aloud: "We will take our refreshments."

The paneling in the wall sprang open and through a hidden door came three servants bearing trays of cakes and fruit towers. A silver bowl filled with so much whipped cream it looked in danger of slumping onto the table was placed between us. We said little, compiling our plates, until, unable to stand the silence, I asked: "How is your sister?"

Sigrid ladled a small mountain of cream onto her cakes. "Fat."

Under the table, I held on to my fourth finger, squeezing it, again and again. "She is married to the king's third cousin?"

"Yes."

"Lovely," I managed.

"I met Stellan," she said, referring to her husband, "at her wedding. He was a bore. Still is!" She laughed at her joke—laughter meant to include me, thus protect her from any judgment. "Hated dancing. And I was in no mood to dance. So we sat and I listened to his little stories—he loves to recount his childhood. What I would give to never hear another mention of his dead mumma again. He said that his mumma used to love the smell of huckleberry, and I said that I loved the smell of huckleberry. I couldn't have told you a thing about it. Now he's filled the gardens with the shrub."

"A romantic gesture."

"It's for his mother. He sits on the bench out there each morning and talks to her. When he's in town, of course. He's off doing his tour of the kingdom."

I watched her, trying to make sense of these intimacies. She was like a doll that lived inside of another bigger doll, that was inside yet another hollow doll. I was sure I was not yet looking at the smallest version.

"Tell me," she continued, "do you still go hawking? You used to be interested in hardly anything else. Or was that just . . ." She waved a hand. "For Henry's benefit?" She brandished his name like a knife—one meant to cut a sharp and sudden line into the past. She didn't pause to see how deep it had cut me. "I dislike birds. Hunting—and eating. Though my son enjoys a hunt. Are your daughters accomplished?"

I thought about the smell of rotting apples and walls stripped bare. "Mathilde is an ambitious reader. Rosamund is a marvel with her embroidery. Elin, my stepdaughter—" I considered. "Is a paragon of virtue."

"No instruments, then?" Sigrid helped herself to more whipped cream. "My daughter is an accomplished player. She applies herself diligently."

"And your son?"

"Who has time for instruments when you're to be king one day?"

Every minute of the conversation pained me. "He sounds dutiful."

"Duty." Sigrid shook her head. "I hate that word." She tapped her gloved fingers on the tablecloth, also ready, it seemed, to do away with our niceties. "Etheldreda." She picked up one of the colorful cakes. "What brings you to my doorstep?"

"Your invitation, of course," I said, with a game smile. "I wanted to thank you."

"Invitation?" she said, with a kind of surprise that was so false I assumed she wanted me to read the lie. She finished chewing and patted a napkin to her lips. "Oh, the ball. So you've heard, then, we have to find my son a wife."

"I wish him every happiness."

"Happiness!" She laughed at the idea. "It is hard enough to find him a suitable match, let alone a happy one."

"One might endeavor for both."

"The kingdom loves my son. The most popular prince in history, it is said, though one scholar claims popularity can be fickle to measure." She chortled before growing serious. "But I love my son more, which does make it a challenge to find someone, well, worthy. We couldn't settle for half rate. Of course, it's also a ball, and everyone loves a good ball."

"Actually"—I chose my words carefully—"the invitation only included my stepdaughter, Elin. But all the girls are of age. You see, they're not connected with the property. There likely isn't a record of them." In a gesture of intimacy, I put my hand to my chest, fingers splayed. "I would love you to meet them, after all these years."

"And you'd like them added to the invitation . . ." She trailed off.

"Yes." I nodded.

"Let me see if I have this rightly understood." Bored, she reached forward with a gloved hand and scooped some whipped cream onto her finger. She licked the cream off the fabric. Appalled, I had to stop myself from looking away. "Your daughters were not invited to my ball. And you'd like them to be?"

"Yes," I repeated, experiencing the humiliation exactly as she had intended.

For the first time that afternoon, I saw one of her brilliant smiles, starting slow and spreading across her face. One of her incisors had turned a different color, a fleshy gray, so that it stood out from the rest. Decay that no amount of raw egg or beer wash could have stopped. Then her lips snapped shut and she finished the last of the cream off her gloved finger and, without raising her voice or turning her head, called: "Send Otto in."

Sigrid sat back with a subtle look of satisfaction. As if my request—and admission—had been what she was after. Saying nothing, she helped herself to lemon cake, which she sliced with the edge of her fork and ferried, in slivered bites, to her lips. When she chewed, a few trembling wrinkles puckered around her mouth. Though I desperately wanted to say something, to put an end to the quiet in the room, to find the right combination of words to ameliorate my shame, I could think of nothing appropriate. My request had laid me bare.

After some time—the lemon cake long finished, Sigrid regarding me like a plate of unwanted crusts—the same paneled door swung inward once more. A tall man with black hair and dark eyes came through. I stared, wide-eyed. He was the stranger from the woods. When he saw me, his brow knit. He straightened, briefly, and paused, before continuing toward Sigrid.

"You," I said. Remembering myself, I placed my gloved hand over my lips.

The footman reentered behind him and announced me. "Lady Etheldreda Tremaine."

"Bramley," I added, this time. "Lady Etheldreda Tremaine Bramley."

Momentarily confused, he pushed forward with his introduction, gesturing at the stranger: "His Honor, Counselor Otto Abensur."

Gone were the man's peasant clothes and undecorated sword. Now he wore a fine tunic, trimmed in fur. And was a counselor. To the royal family.

He looked at me, expressionless, before ducking his head down in a quick nod of acknowledgment. I realized—with a lurch of my stomach—that he remembered me, would be able to connect the woman in the woods, the mud, back to me and, by extension, my daughters.

"You know one another?" The queen looked back and forth between us.

"We have, ah—passed at the village market. Once." I watched the stranger, to see if he would contradict me. My heart in my throat. He watched me back and remained silent.

"The market," she repeated, interested. "Say more."

"Aye, Your Majesty," he finally spoke. "Our paths crossed when I was out with the carriage issuing invitations."

His presence in the woods now made sense. Why had I not thought to connect the stranger to the carriage that had appeared moments after he had?

"Lady Tremaine," Otto said, emphasizing the title, as if confirming it to himself. "How can I be of service?"

"She wants her daughters to be invited to the ball," Sigrid said, sounding bored. She yawned, without bothering to cover the action. "Good of you to come," she added, directing the words at me.

I realized, belatedly, that our tête-à-tête was over. There were no goodbyes. And, as the footman escorted me out, I saw Otto Abensur lean over and whisper into the queen's ear.

My heart thrummed. Information was currency and the man owed me nothing.

As the footman walked me back through all of the rooms, their details—the dazzling chandeliers and inlaid tiles and painted frescoes—gave color and context to my thoughts. Sigrid had been right that our lives would take different paths. We passed mirrored overmantels and coats of arms and, by my count, six different servants attending to candles. And, while I did not doubt being queen came with its own set of burdens, I couldn't help but think, as we walked around a man polishing a row of decorative weapons, that burdens were easier to bear when you sat on feather pillows. We were moving through a room where everything—walls, furniture, and drapes—called to mind the exact shade of a mint leaf, when a voice called from behind: "Lady Tremaine."

I turned back. Otto, still expressionless, approached and addressed the footman. "I will see her ladyship out."

Without looking at me, he began to walk forward. I hurried to match his pace. Once or twice I thought to make conversation, but glancing over at him, and the oyster-sized muscle clenching his jaw, I thought better of it. In his fine clothes, he gave an entirely different impression than the man in the woods. He was quite tall, and had a severe, attractive face with a hard look about his eyes, as if he had been drawn in charcoal with too heavy a hand. We continued through the rooms, lavender and teal and one entirely of polished mahogany. At length, as we moved through a chamber filled with preserved and stuffed animals, he spoke: "You are far removed from the woods this afternoon."

I nodded, gut tightening. "You, too, have transitioned from the wild." I pictured him as he had been on that dark path in the forest—worn steel and fine boots—and frowned at how I had spoken to him. How he had spoken to me in return. "I did not place you as a member of the royal retinue."

He looked over at me for a moment, as if to say he would not have placed me, either—woman of the bird and the rabbit—as the lady of the nearby house. "I am dispatched to keep watch, but there's little to oversee in verbose invitations orated to ladies in fancy gowns."

A moment of silence, during which I could hear only the swishing of my own fanciful frock. "One should never underestimate a lady's ability for metamorphosis."

He did not respond, and, walking ahead, remained inscrutable. After a long while, he looked back and said: "Indeed."

I gestured around us at the animals—foxes and rabbits and, in the corner, a stuffed bear. "Though these rooms are not a far cry from the woods. It seems the spirit of the forest has followed us."

He turned to face forward once more. "The woods have their place and it's not within these walls."

Nettled, I quieted, and we fell back into silence as we entered and crossed the checkered gallery. Without breaking a single rule of propriety—he opened doors, pointed out a rolled carpet we would need to step over, and walked on the path side when we exited the castle—Otto managed to be disagreeable. As we got closer and closer to the castle wall, I was increasingly ready to bid him adieu.

At the gate within the gate, he offered me his hand to step through. I pretended not to see. We both looked down as I stepped over the threshold and saw, simultaneously, the worn leather of my shoe. Mismatched and out of place with the fine cloth of my gown. Otto cleared his throat.

I colored. Nothing, I thought to myself, escaped the man's attention. If I had failed in my errand, my pride could suffer it no longer. I could not get away from the residue of Sigrid's venom and her taciturn myrmidon quickly enough.

When I was on the other side of the gate, he called again: "Lady Tremaine."

I turned back, without taking trouble to hide my irritation. The counselor had to stoop to fit his head through the opening.

"The queen welcomes all your daughters at the ball."

I nodded, doing my best to keep my own countenance as expressionless as his. It was a victory, and I should have felt triumphant—but I had not expected success to taste so bitter.

CHAPTER THIRTEEN

I ASKED ALICE TO HURRY US HOME, AS QUICKLY AS ARNO COULD manage. We flew over the ruts and the bumps. "Were you successful?" she asked, raising her voice over the rattle of the chaise.

"In a way," I acknowledged.

The panels creaked and the chains shook and the horse's feet pounded on the stones beneath us. "What?" Alice shouted.

"In a way," I cried, raising my voice.

"Speak louder!"

"Never mind, then!" Unable to engage in conversation, I was left to peer into the trees and make sense of the day.

I had been humiliated. Of that, I was sure.

That had been the bargain I had come to drive. All self, all *me, me, me, I, I, I,* bent in supplication to my greater purpose.

And in that, I had been successful: The girls would go to the ball.

But I didn't feel relief. No sooner had I achieved what I'd wanted than I'd realized how much more there was to want: It was like summiting a hilltop to see, from a new vantage point at the top, an entire mountain range ahead. When I'd first heard the rumors, I wasn't afraid of not being invited to the royal ball; I was afraid of one existing. For if it existed, we must go. And if we went, we must succeed. And if we were successful, my daughters would be married and move away from me forever. My own desires contradicted each other. And Sigrid's many derisions had left me feeling sour.

But I had accomplished what I came for: The girls would go to the ball.

Everything would require management to a precise degree. We would need dresses, and not ones easily refashioned from those we owned. New gloves. Introduction cards. A refresher on deportment and etiquette for interacting with the royal family. And transportation—a carriage was a potent symbol of status. It would not do to arrive in a rented hackney.

I wished, pointlessly, and for the hundredth time these many years, that we might have been able to use some of Elin's dowry for Elin's share. It seemed only fair: Rosie and Mathilde would need the dresses and the frills and every appearance of being proper ladies, for they had nothing else to recommend them. Elin was the daughter of titled no-bility and came with an inheritance. And, I reminded myself, she hardly contributed to the work in the house. It was unfair indeed that all our hard-earned pennies—made from Rosie's embroidery and the fruits of all but Elin's labor—had to be equally shared when their circumstances were anything but equal. There were not yet any scrimpings from her ashes.

I slumped down in my seat, exhausted already.

"All's well, m'lady?" Alice called, frowning in concern.

Whether fortune awaited or disaster loomed, the wind would only take my words. So I said nothing at all.

When we neared our gate, Alice stuck an elbow into my side. I looked up to see: A man sat at the helm of a refitted hackney coach, half blocking the road in front of our iron arches. His carriage was piled high with all manner of goods and instruments. Different-sized tabors and citoles and shawms. Inside the carriage compartment, I could see a gourd-shaped hurdy-gurdy and a rebec swinging from hooks that had been screwed into the roof. This entire mountain of chaos was pulled by a sole horse, and it was a marvel it moved at all, for the animal's black bangs entirely blocked its view. Unlike the man himself, who was regarding me with amusement.

"My lady!" he called, grinning widely. He had a normal-sized body—softening out in the middle—but delicate, tiny hands, which he used to twist the end of a short, pointed beard. Above, a pair of brown eyes were marked by smile lines, which deepened as we approached. I could see his every tooth, including the space where one was missing in the back. The rest were bright and white against his sun-worn skin.

I climbed down from our chaise and frowned at the jongleur. "You cannot stop right here." Each year the itinerant minstrel came and each year I tried to send him away, with decreasing conviction. I directed Alice to maneuver around his cart and take our own horse up the drive. And, when she and Arno were safely past, I turned back to the man, hands on my hips. "Hello, Moussa."

He laughed. "You are all dressed up. Are you having a party?"

"I'm quite serious," I told him. "You're half blocking the road. You might be seen. I am not running an inn!"

"And I haven't asked you for your charity," the man said, still smiling.

I began to walk past him, and almost stumbled on an apple in the road. Bending down, I picked it up. "I do not doubt you are about to ask me for something!"

"My lady!" He mocked hurt, a hand on his breast. "I am going to offer you something. I have things you will want to hear. Magic things. Things you wouldn't believe—"

"I have no use for sweet songs today," I cut him short. "Or any songs. And more to the point: I have no food for you."

He nodded, unconvinced.

"Moussa, no food. None." I glanced down at the apple in my fingers and tried to move it out of sight.

The creases around his eyes deepened. "My wagon can fit many, many apples . . ."

"Benefitting you, it seems, more than me."

"Which you might be able to take to the market—and sell."

"In exchange for some price you have not yet named."

"A price that costs you nothing. A place to park my coach. A bit of cider you've already brewed. The market is in a few days," he sang.

We regarded one another. And I calculated, weighing, weighing: apples and balls and money.

He wiggled his fingers, conjuring unseen riches. "I can fit four times as many bushels as your own carriage."

"All right," I finally agreed. "Pull in, up behind the hedge, where they can't see you from the road."

Maneuvering Moussa's towering cart through the gate took a good quarter of an hour. To make the hard turn up through the arches, he painstakingly marched the horse—inopportunely named Lucky—one step forward and one foot back, again and again, until the load was appropriately oriented. Then, as if I hadn't been standing watching the whole time, hands on my hips and a scowl on my face, he dismounted and came over to me. We clasped hands.

"It is good to see you," he said.

"Poor Lucky." I shook my head. "Next year she may outright refuse."

"She has nothing to complain about."

I raised my eyebrows and looked at the burdened cart. A small tambourine fell from the top and landed on the ground.

"A sign!" Moussa clapped his hands. If the traveling singer was capable of anything, it was reinterpreting events in his favor. "We must drink."

"And I suppose you'd like me to supply the ale?" I went over to the horse and gave her a pat. "Hello, Lucky." I offered the apple, which she took in her teeth, her lips tickling my palm.

"She gets to see the whole world. The moorlands and the cliffs and the ocean. She is the—"

"Luckiest horse in the world," I finished for him. "I'll add her to the stable with Arno."

❧

I COULD HEAR ROSAMUND AND MATHILDE TALKING AS I ENTERED the hall. Rosamund, sitting in a deep-set chair by the window, was using the day's last light to sew a ribbon to a hat. She held it up to look at her work. "Perhaps I will wear it to market this week."

Mathilde, reclined on a chaise next to a low-burning candle, turned a page of her book and did not look up. "I would not."

The room offered evidence of their afternoon's labor. Mathilde's ledger lay open, the ink still drying across one of its pages. A spinning wheel had been brought out, and a fresh bobbin of thread sat on the table. A set of clean sheets lay folded on a bench. And a new pile of firewood had been carefully stacked next to the lit hearth, which filled the room with a weak warmth.

Rosamund frowned. "Well, I did not offer it to you; it is my hat!"

"Allow me to rephrase—you should not. It is an unbecoming hat."

"You dunderhead! You only wish you could have a new fontange." Rosie huffed, dropping the hat back into her lap. "And now I shall never make you one!"

Mathilde used a finger to hold her place in her book and leaned forward to address her sister. "It is I attempting to offer you wisdom. One might presume that you want to wear a new hat to draw attention and impress people and perhaps have an excuse to flirt. None of that can be accomplished in the ugliest, most regrettable hat in the kingdom."

"Neither of you are going to market this week." I stepped into the room. "So, you do not need to concern yourself with the hat any longer."

"Mama!" Rosamund sprang up and rushed to my side. "What happened?"

Mathilde followed and kissed my cheek.

"Hello, darlings." I kissed them each in turn.

"Tell us everything. Every single detail," Rosie demanded. "Do not leave out even the tiniest observation. Were the queen's slippers pigskin or silk? Does she reveal her petticoats or keep them covered?"

"In good time," I promised. "But first . . ." I turned to the curtains in front of the window seat, under which I could see the tips of two shoes peeking through. "Elin, would you please join us?"

The window dressings twitched, and, after a moment's hesitation, were pulled aside. Elin stepped forward, pressing, between her hands, her constant companion.

"You were in there this whole time?" Mathilde scowled.

Elin nodded, eyelashes fluttering like escaped pieces of down. "Far be it from me to disturb such sisterly revelry."

We all stared at her, and she, only slightly abashed, continued: "And I must thank you both. To listen to the silence between words is a wonderful opportunity to meditate on meaning."

"Yes." Mathilde's frown deepened. "And the space between curtains makes a good place for eavesdropping. What does your little book say about that?"

Elin blinked. "It counsels the importance of prudence." She began to sway on her feet, and I wondered if we would need smelling salts.

"And what," I asked, taking her elbow and leading her to a chair, "did you determine in your moments of cautious listening?"

"After consideration, I might now tell Rosie that I do not think her hat is ugly."

"See?" Rosie sniffed, glaring at Mathilde. But her elder sister only crossed her arms and raised a questioning eyebrow at Elin.

Elin, cowering under the force of Mathilde's glare, explained at last: "I was reading. I must have dozed off for I didn't hear you come in, and then it was too late to reveal myself. It does get awfully hot behind those curtains."

Satisfied, I turned back to the girls, but Elin continued: "Though, if I may—I beseech you to scorn your vanity. Appearance is but a fleeting shadow. The pursuit of inner beauty should be your greatest endeavor—"

"Elin." I stopped her. The girl, soberly dedicated to properness and correction, could not see her own contradictions—or how fine a line lay between preparation, which she esteemed, and pride, about which she lectured. "When a young woman does not have the opportunity to speak, it is, on occasion, only her appearance that she can use to recommend herself. While we're on the subject: How is your dress coming along for the ball?"

I had given her a length of fabric to begin working with. I was waiting until market day—and hoping to see some of her pennies—before purchasing the rest.

She hesitated. "I have been working diligently. Though—I am greatly troubled by a few trifling details. The bodice, and the arms." She paused a moment. "As well as the skirt."

"I see." I nodded. Elin had learned to stitch the perfect sampler, but had never been required to complete the finger-breaking work of piecing together an entire dress. More diminutive than her stepsisters, she had benefitted from hand-me-downs that only required minor improvements—bits of lace and bows. "And the coins you are to give me?"

"Wenthelen is helping me with the ashes."

"I see," I said again, feeling the beginnings of a curdling inside of me.

"For the dress, I thought, perchance, Rosamund may find the kindness in her heart to assist me." She turned to Rosie. "'Knowledge is a treasure: In the pursuit of it, do not hesitate to seek guidance.'"

"Rosamund will have no time to work on your dress. She will be working on her own." I glanced to the other two young women. "For we are all going to the ball."

Rosie shrieked, a high-pitched squeal of unbridled excitement. "Oh, Mother, I do not know what to say. It cannot be true. It must be. I thank you!"

Mathilde, looking pensive, sank back to her chaise. "We will have to get started on everything right away."

"Yes, we will," I agreed. I looked around at their upturned faces. "We'll start by picking some apples."

Elin, for once, was silent on the matter of virtue.

OVER THE YEARS, I HAD LEARNED MANY WAYS—SENDING WENTHELEN to market to sell apples chief amongst them—to save or make small amounts of money. Cutting barley and rye and oats into your wheat lowers the cost of bread. If firewood is scarce, meat can be boiled. Old scraps of linen can be collected into a rag bag and sold to a paper maker. Bones make good fertilizer. Textile guilds will pay good coin for home-spun white warp. Brickmakers will even purchase dust.

After Robert died, when our financial situation was made clear, I had all three of the girls stand with me when I gathered the staff in the entry hall. Here was our retinue: footmen and porters and grooms and cooks. Buttoned fronts and stiff, correct posture. I had only been introduced to them as their new lady months before. Now, readying to voice our collective turn of fate, I stood without Robert at my side.

"My late husband," I said, trying to hide my tremble, "has left this household in a sorry state. I have been made to understand many of you are owed wages. We do not have the funds to pay you."

An angry murmur rippled through the entry. A laundress's face contorted in rage. A gardener began to protest, and I felt the girls' fear beside me. I held up a hand. "In exchange for your discretion, I can outfit you handsomely with goods from this home. I will pay twice your owed wages in goods. They will all catch a fine price in town. You'll see me in Robert's office by order of your stations."

The anger dissipated, and so did the people. All the stiff backs slumped. The crowd began to collapse and flow down the stairs and out the door. So quickly our life was leaving us. How easily I had spread our ruin. "Anyone who has no place to go," I called out, "is welcome to stay here for however long is needed."

Alice helped me. She made suggestions about which pieces in the home—small paintings and candelabra and textiles—were worth what, and how they might be doled out. Rosie offered me her ribbons, which were not worth much. Mathilde went through the house gathering silver, and then sat at the table beside me, dutifully recording the depletion of our lives, the redistribution of each bound book and polished spoon, in her neat and even hand. The immediate problem—paying the staff—was solved, but I did not know how to do what came next: how to cook, how to clean, how, even, to wash my own hair.

After the day ended, I went to Elin. She sat on a swing hung from the oak behind the hall, listlessly pumping herself forward and back, wearing the hat and veil and gloves that protected her sensitive skin from the light.

"I am certain all of this has been disorienting beyond reason," I said. Wishing I had a chair to sink into, I stood in the grass, facing her. She watched me through the veil, in her unblinking way. She had just lost her sole remaining parent. She was eight years old.

"There's little I can say to make it better. I know that from my own experience. But I wanted you to know you are not without family." I took a breath. "Elin, I know I'm not your mother, but I'll do my best to be a mother to you."

She tilted her head, considering. After a moment, she said: "No, thank you." Her voice was sweet and her tone polite.

"But, Elin," I said, faltering. "It's only that . . ." I trailed off. I had no will left to argue with her, no desire to force her to me, after all my own losses. I had daughters who had now lost a father figure twice over. I had to spend another year in black. I had a faceless future that was only a mouth: open, gaping, and hungry.

"Stepmother? You need not concern yourself." She withdrew her mother's booklet from her pocket—it had appeared more frequently after Robert's death—and read aloud: "'The compass of virtue guides one through the seas of challenges. Even in the darkest of nights, if a young woman nurtures the seeds of virtue—gentleness, goodness, docility—within her heart, life will only reward her.'" She closed the book and raised her eyes to meet mine once more. "Don't you see? All will turn out fine."

"I do see," I said. And, looking back, I wish I had.

WITHIN A FEW DAYS, MOST OF THE STAFF HAD LEFT US. WENTHELEN and Alice stayed—they said they would not be able to find employment elsewhere at their age, but I also sensed attachment, to Elin, and to a manor they had come to know as home—as did a few others, though our numbers dropped each day. We had food, but our halls, once busy, echoed. I began to see, to understand, how much work had happened around me without my ever noticing. Curtains opened in the morning and then closed at night. Fires lit and grates emptied. Water for wash-basins replenished. Mud cleaned from my shoes. The motionlessness of the house felt not like solitude but like stagnation, reinforcing with each passing day just how much our lives had changed.

Dazed, and with my daughters in tow, I tried to pick up the pieces. I remember, clearly, Alice showing me how to scour a pot: the initial soak in hot water, followed by scrubbing with straw and potash. And Wenthelen, lecturing Rosie that all the drippings she was tapping into the dirt could have been saved and sold. That a kitchen fire had to be started before first light. That if you used black soap on cambric, it turned the cloth to gray. That apples stored in the hoardhouse could not be touched, or else they would mold. We all had to learn quickly.

Elin still self-governed with the expectations of the daughter of a lord. She had little ability to think for herself. She had, instead, her book. Her listless behavior was marked not by cunning, but by belief in virtue and its ability to protect—and save—you.

One morning, Elin did not come down to breakfast, and so, leaving

Rosie and Mathilde to string vegetables for drying, I went to check on her in the peach room. I found her under her bedsheets, though she had dressed and styled her hair.

"Are you unwell?" I asked.

"Not at all," she assured me. "It's only that . . ." She trailed a finger along the top of her quilt.

Something about her manner made me impatient. "Yes?"

"I used to have breakfast in my room."

I leaned over and picked up one of her dolls, which had tipped over, and set it right. "You are welcome to bring your tray in here."

"You see"—she nodded toward her book, which lay on the nightstand—"I believe, well, the book says, that habit and established routine are essential for a well-ordered life."

I turned away to survey the room filled with toys and dolls, so many of which she'd outgrown. They would gather dust in the coming months. I wondered what they might fetch if I were to sell them.

"Elin." I wanted to speak gently. I wanted to use a voice that acknowledged all that had happened to her, no matter what had happened to me. I do not know that I was successful. "The girls are downstairs now, stringing the onions and carrots that I asked you to string last week."

"They have not molded."

"And you've yet to help carry any of the wood inside."

She widened her eyes, a trace of genuine surprise in them. "You know I cannot easily go into the sun without burning."

"There is no one but us to pickle our fish or pinch the fleas from the sheets. Surely, you understand that circumstances have changed."

She sniffed but did not answer.

"And," I continued, "I hope it does you some good later, but there are a healthy number of years before you can touch your dowry. You must learn to take care of yourself." I looked down at my own dress, which was covered in a work apron. "We are all learning to take care of ourselves."

She pulled the covers higher, closer to her chin. "I will take care of myself by staying true to my course. Otherwise, there will be no one who wants me and my dowry."

"The course has altered," I replied, more sharply than I meant to. But I myself was learning to draw and carry my own water, to clean silverware, to scrub floors. That very morning, I had dirtied my arms up to the elbows securing a side of pork to be smoked in the chimney. Trying to soften the blow, I explained: "Every one of us will have to keep up appearances. But what happens here, behind the walls of our home, must change."

Her eyes fluttered. I wondered, briefly, if one could faint if they were already supine. I reminded myself: She had lost her mother, her father, her entire life. Even, in some sense, her home, which now belonged to me: the woman who was not her mother. And there was no malice in her reluctance. Not, even, an insistence on being coddled. Elin believed, truly, in the necessity of her own gentility. It was all she had left.

So, I allowed her to fall back into her pillows, to remain under the sheets, to let my statements go unanswered. I even went so far as to bring her some breakfast that day. Whatever empathy I had had for Elin made it hard, in those initial months, to enforce any kind of change. And soon our habits and patterns were established.

Rosie and Mathilde were quickly required to scrub their own dirty linens, to chop firewood, to make soap. They carded wool and darned stockings and kneaded dough into bread, all the while keeping up with their reading and writing and the outward appearance of being little ladies. They watched Elin—practicing her instruments, copying her verses, reading her book—from the corners of their eyes. Any wish for friendship was soon abandoned, then sneered at.

Elin was not always treated kindly by my daughters. My daughters, who, because of my insistence on their adjustment to our new circumstances, soon lost some of their youth and beauty. I could not fault them for lacking grace during the transition. Could not fault them for voicing some of the thoughts that were in my own head.

You can sniff at someone for being resentful, but I challenge you to take an icy bath in the depths of winter when, for all the years before, someone else has heated the water. Did you know that lye, when not handled properly, burns your hands? That thrice-used tea leaves could still be stored and sold for money? That it takes a near hour of continuous, relentless churning to make butter? That the act will give untested palms blisters, which will swell and tear and bleed? We did not, but we learned, quickly.

All of us but Elin.

MOUSSA FIRST APPEARED DURING THESE WEEKS. JONGLEURS TRAVEL around, looking for larger households to pay them to stay and entertain. He sang and played instruments, but—he made it explicitly clear—he did not juggle. The size of Bramley Hall made it seem that we would have work, but, I told him, standing on our massive doorstep, we had nothing for him. The truth of the statement must have shown on my face, for he believed me.

From his place a few steps below in the gravel, he observed: "You have met misfortune."

"My husband has passed." I didn't say more. We still had Bramley Hall and we still had our titles. No one knew what happened inside of our gates. Even with an itinerant, it was necessary to keep up appearances. "I assure you, there is nothing for you here."

"If you are hungry, I shall share my food, though there isn't much. And I can offer song. There is no better music than the sound of a cittern. Do not misunderstand me—I do not require payment. The city is so full of pipers, there is no room left for myself. I'll sleep in an outbuilding. And if you have a pint of ale to warm my belly, I would only be grateful."

I looked him over. The punishment for a vagabond was to burn a person through the gristle of their right ear with a hot iron the compass of an inch. The man needed somewhere to sleep. I didn't need his food—we still had plenty in our stores—but I wondered if a bit of his song might cheer up what remained of our household. I soon found myself showing the jongleur a place to make a bed and pouring him something to drink without fully realizing I had given him what he'd asked for in the first place.

❀

That night, Elin, Rosie, Mathilde, and I were serenaded as we ate in the great room. Moussa's songs covered wide territory. They were ranging, in scale and in subject, flipping from quick and merry to the slow notes of mourning. Fingers moved across strings and breath blew into hollows and came out fresh and woody, reborn as sound. When the notes became too sad, he made them happy. And when the music was happy for too long, it ended. After Moussa finished, he looked around at our applauding hands. As if registering, for the first time, the size, or lack thereof, of his audience, he asked: "Is it just the four of you?"

I didn't perceive any threat in the question, so I nodded. "For now."

He glanced over at Wenthelen and Alice, who had been listening to the music from the doorway. Their hands were clasped between them. "And them?"

"And them." I nodded.

"Such a small group. They don't dine with you?"

I glanced at the servants' faces, which remained blank. Their fingers, so carefully interwoven, remained entwined. "Staff does not traditionally dine with the household."

"We also have a bird," Rosie volunteered, hoping to increase our measly head count. "Lucy."

"A falcon," I corrected.

"A bird?" Moussa said, with delight. "Is it tamed?"

"It's trained," I corrected, once more.

"May I see it?"

"She's in the mews," Mathilde interjected. "Outside."

"Does she not come into the house?"

"One cannot bring a bird in the house," Elin replied in surprise.

"She's right," I acknowledged.

"My lady, if it is your home"—Moussa glanced back to the doorway, the carefully blank faces—"is it not yours to handle as you see fit?"

It had not, until that moment, occurred to me.

"Yes." I looked at him. I looked around. "Yes, I suppose you may be right." I turned to Wenthelen and Alice and bid them to our table.

CHAPTER FOURTEEN

A FTER I REGALED EVERYONE WITH THE STORY OF MY DAY—THE many stiff-backed guards, the queen's mountain of whipped cream—I took supper in the kitchen, hunched over a wooden bowl of soup, eyeing our cook as she moved around me.

"You must not help Elin with the ashes," I instructed Wenthelen, pausing to blow on a spoon of hot broth.

"What's the difference if you get your pennies?" Wenthelen scoffed. She stopped her bustling and settled into a wooden chair by the hearth, crossing her tired feet in front of her.

"Fairness."

She removed one of her boots and scratched her heel on the floor. "Nothing about this life is fair."

"You don't help the other girls."

"They don't need my help."

"Elin won't learn how to be on her own."

"Mayhap she won't need to!"

"I think that is the same gamble she's been willing to make." I finished the last of my stew and pushed the bowl away. "But listen to me—I forbid you from helping her anymore. It's a deal she and I made, and she must do her part."

"Forbid me?" Wenthelen crowed, tilting back in her chair with some delight.

"Yes." I nodded. "You are henceforth proscribed. Now, fetch me an extra bowl. I'll bring some supper to our guest."

I found Moussa in his camp, crouching by the light of a small fire. I handed him the stew and a small pitcher of cider and sat down on a roll of carpet he had laid on the ground.

"One for me," I commanded. I waited, watching him pour the cider into two wooden cups.

"I pour, you choose," he suggested, squinting as he ensured the drinks were even.

"Oh, come along. We have plenty more cider."

"That you keep under lock and key. You should be selling this cider." He held his cup aloft. "I think about it every time I have pond-water ale."

I crossed my arms. "A lady doesn't sell things."

"A lady doesn't sit with a minstrel on a roll of carpet."

"Hush, you old graybeard." Moussa had come through seasonally since that first year, and we had learned to barter what we could—a dry place to sleep for dance lessons, a warm meal for a night of song. But his circling of the territory had begun to slow down. "It is not just your carriage that creaks when it moves."

He grinned and then laughed.

"I'm quite serious, Moussa! You are getting older."

"So are you."

"I am not forty years. You are—"

"Young at heart."

"And gray at the chin and crown."

"And when you are gray, you will see it is nothing but a color."

"When I am gray, I will accept that my years of labor must come to an end."

He took a drink from his cider, unbothered by the thoughts I was voicing out loud. "May you be so lucky."

"Well, the alternative is the house collapses upon my head. Hopefully the girls will be long gone by then." I stuck my feet closer to the warmth of the fire. "Now, tell me of your travels."

He looked at me over the rim of his cup and then lowered it. "I played last week at a home that was to have a grand feast. All day they prepared. They were to serve mutton and pork and veal and teal and snipe and curlew. There were marzipan confections in the shapes of wild animals. They had, they said, slaughtered an ox, just for the occasion."

I interrupted. "Are you saying you are above the stew?"

He held up his hands to quiet me. "But my patroness, the wife of a rich gentleman, grew increasingly distraught as the day wore on, embarrassed by her daughter's behavior. You see, her daughter had picked up my bandora and was practicing playing upon it. Her mother thought it beggarly and kept insisting she play something more appropriate, like the virginals. I did not mind. She was quite adept. But it's been on my mind ever since. An accomplished young woman is meant to learn some instruments behind closed doors, yet is scorned for playing others. I, unaccomplished, by most estimations, am paid for playing any of them. Not well, I might add."

"Are you pointing out an inequity or complaining about having to share an instrument?"

"I am just telling you a story. And I am not done. My patroness grew so frustrated that she canceled the feast. The ox was already dead. The food was prepared." He shook his head. "So much food—the jellies alone—went to waste. I could have taken some with me. And there was no feast, and so no need of music. I did not get paid."

I shook my head at his story, less inclined to feel sorry for Moussa than for myself; I could not hear stories of other people's splendor without noting the lack of my own. "Well, you are not the only one who has encountered wasted opulence."

"Oh?" Moussa raised an eyebrow.

I told him how I had gone to see the queen, and his eyes grew round, and the pupils dilated, for there was nothing Moussa liked better than the tales of those better off.

"Tell me," he demanded. "Were there any musicians?"

I thought of the castle. Of all those empty and beautiful rooms. "Not that I saw or heard—I was too busy trying to memorize the details. The tassels on the curtains looked like they were woven from gold."

"Ah." He waved me away. "The royals have smelly jakes just like the rest of us."

"The palace has quills that bring water, right into its walls."

"Yes, and if an eel swims up into those pipes, they, too, have to wait until the fish decomposes for the supply to resume." Moussa winked at me. "I would have been good at being rich." He paused. "But I've settled for being good-looking." He twirled his little beard and smirked to himself.

I sighed. "There is always someone richer."

"And now you are rich with company. Mine." Moussa put an elbow on his knee and held his face in the cradle of his small hand. "At the ball—you are going to introduce all three daughters at once?"

"What do you know of introducing young women?"

"I play music in their halls! I see and hear every little thing. Lace sleeves, you must have them. Pompons all the rage. Are the little women ready for it all?"

"Ready enough. Except . . ."

He pursed his lips, the smile only in his eyes, as he waited for me to finish.

"You know the latest dances, do you not?"

"Give me another cup of that cider." He winked. "And you shall find out." He rubbed his hands together. "I can picture it. One of these young ladies in the castle. Mathilde's neck is stiff enough for a crown."

"I suppose," I said. With cider in my belly, thinking of all those rooms—their gold leaf and sparkling crystals, the statues, frozen in time—had unhinged something inside of me, an unruly, wild kind of desire. But here I was sitting on a carpet roll.

"You wouldn't want that for them?"

"I would," I admitted. I stared off toward the house, which was dark against the dark sky. I felt myself grasping. If I had golden tassels, I would have had to sell them long ago. What would happen to my girls? What could I do for them? I had not felt this kind of longing in a long while. My desires—insatiable, and yet, they had to be satiated, for I could not accept failure—were a prism that, in refracting and repeating my hunger back to me, only served to amplify my appetite.

I wondered: Was it possible?

"It is possible," Moussa reasoned, as if he could hear my thoughts, and I glanced up. "The prince, after all, *is* having a ball for a reason—to select a potential wife!"

"Your company is corruptive." I frowned at him. But what was to stop me from at least examining the possibility of the prince considering one of my girls? What was to mark them in any lower esteem than every other woman who would be at the ball? I did not meditate on the delta between my own crumbling walls and the many-windowed halls of the castle. I did not believe this line of thought was a kind of moral failure. It was not opulence I wanted for Rosie and Mathilde; it was permanence. Maybe this desire was a kind of strength. Maybe, more than just hoping and wishing for something to come true, you could create change by your own volition. For what use is a named desire if there is not also a decision to pursue it? What is there to do in the face of humiliation except to climb to stand and face it all head-on once more?

"So," Moussa interrupted my thoughts. "What do you think? Shall you endeavor to aim high?"

"As in a prince?" I looked back at the house again, where everyone was already in their beds. Opportunities came and they were small and unlikely and easy to overlook. You had to stick your fingers into them and pinch the edges and pull. You had to widen the aperture of possibility. "Yes," I agreed, finishing my own cider, and turning to face Moussa. "Yes."

"Good." He nodded, pleased. "We'll have our first dance lesson to-morrow."

"Very well. But Moussa," I said, standing to go back to the house. "What happened to the girl? The one from the feast?"

Moussa twisted his beard, lost in thought. "I don't know. But I left her my bandora."

CHAPTER FIFTEEN

✦

WE SPENT OUR DAYS IN THE ORCHARDS, PICKING APPLES. Rosamund stitched and stitched. I repeated the etiquette lessons that had been instilled since their earliest days. We picked more apples. Moussa gave dance lessons in the hall, walking through minuets, quadrilles, and cotillions. We reviewed posture and deportment: how to stand, how to walk, how to exist in a room. We picked more apples. We discussed titles and calling cards and accepting dances. We practiced the art of polite conversation. Still, we picked more apples. Moussa tapped out the beat of music on the floor of the hall. We sorted the apples. We resized our corsets, and panniers, and petticoats. Elin sewed a sleeve to the hem of her dress. We sat through rounds and rounds of fittings and alterations, pinching and pinning, and stitching, and hemming, until even Rosamund wanted to sew no more.

For a girl's royal introduction, her dress needed a train exactly three yards long, and she had to wear a feather on the back of her head high enough that it would be visible to Her Majesty when she entered the room. Despite the season, necks and shoulders were to remain bare.

The girls had little experience with such outfits. Country dances and small dinner parties were trifling by comparison. Channeling Agatha to the best of my ability, I explained to them, step-by-step, what they must expect:

"Leave your wraps in the carriage. Do not bring them into the ball. As you enter, walk with your train folded carefully over your left arm." I stood in the middle of their small sewing circle and demonstrated with an imaginary dress. "You will await your summons in an antechamber and then, when called, make your way to Her Majesty. Let down your train, which will be spread out immediately by an attending lady- or lord-in-waiting. Before you enter the room, hand the card bearing your name to the attendant, who will announce you."

"What will you wear?" Rosamund asked.

"Neither feathers nor a train."

"Will you dance?"

I laughed at the question. "Now, when you see the queen, you must curtsy until you are very nearly on the floor." I demonstrated this as well, bowing to Mathilde, who sat up, happy to play the part of the queen. I took her hand in my own and kissed the back of it, close to her knuckles. "Kiss the queen's hand. Just so."

I turned now to Elin. "*You* are a lord's daughter, so she may instead kiss your forehead. You will need to watch her carefully and follow Her Majesty's lead."

Addressing all of them once more, I continued: "Rise, and then do not forget to curtsy again. Do not talk unless she asks you a direct question. Back out of the room. Do not turn your back to her, or any other royal person in the room. Only then"—I twirled my wrist, indicating an imaginary party ahead of me—"do you enter the ball."

"If our necklines are bare, then we must have lace trimming," Rosamund announced.

"And we do not yet have hair feathers," Elin worried.

"I have used all my fabric for the train," Mathilde said, "and have none left for a matching petticoat."

I looked at the concern on their faces and did my best not to mirror it. I had already sat down and charted the expenses. Even with a wagon-load of apples going to market, there would not be enough to cover what was needed. When I had tallied my columns, the numbers gave me a kick in the gut. I had already cut so many corners, I was holding a circle. I did not know where else to trim.

"Mama," Mathilde continued, "I know we have not the resources, but I do believe we need these items."

"Elin," I snapped. "I still have not seen those pennies from the ashes. You'll pay me after market tomorrow and you'll get what you need." I turned to Rosie and Mathilde. "And you, too. Keep picking the apples, as many as you can."

If it took ten wagonloads of fruit and the ashes of a thousand fires, I was resolved: Our household would not show so much as a hairline crack in our facade.

✿

THE NEXT DAY, MOUSSA EMPTIED HIS COACH OF ITS WARES. AS ALICE and Wenthelen loaded the carriage with bushels of apples, I carried Lucy to the outside mews.

"You're going to have to stay here for a little while," I told her. "We have to be proper ladies now and I can't have you in the house muting all over the place."

She didn't so much as blink at me.

"I will find time to take you hunting soon," I promised. We had skipped our hunt that morning—and a few others—in service to our preparations for the ball. "But I did prepare you a bath. See?" We neared her block, which sat on a circle of gravel. I had set out a basin of water.

She stepped freely into it, taking time to first gnaw at her talons and then, more extravagantly, use her wings and tail to throw water on her back. When she was finished, she began to preen, sliding her beak through each feather and letting out small noises of content.

"It's just for a little while," I said.

She ignored me and continued her preening. I waited, looking around at the back of the house, out at the trees, and up at the sky, as if a falcon deserved its privacy.

I had brought along my mother's cameo, and, as Lucy roused, I took the necklace from my pocket. The depiction, carved from shell, was strung on a strand of seed pearls. My mother had had a patrician nose and tapered jaw. I held her countenance against my lips—readying myself—before sliding it back into my pocket.

I left Lucy, fastened to the iron ring on her block, to weather in the yard. She did not look at me as I walked away, but instead had her eyes trained somewhere in the distance—toward the forest, the trees, the smaller birds, and the insects. It reminded me of staring out the window during my lessons with Agatha. "I'll take you out for a hunt soon," I promised.

THE MARKET WAS HELD ONCE A WEEK ON THE ROADS THAT BRANCHED from our village's central square. The fruit and vegetable sellers grouped together—vendors yelling over one another, women weaving through the crowds with baskets of soft persimmons and strings of onion—and the grains, oats, barley, and rye were sold on the other end. Down one narrow lane, shoppers perused crockery and baskets. On the outskirts, where there was more room, farmers held chickens and pigs and goats in makeshift pens and at the ends of fraying ropes, bartering with slaughtermen. As a titled lady, I didn't operate the apple stall or go near it, so when we neared the village, I bid Wenthelen and Moussa adieu and ventured off on my own. Passing criers delivering news and a woman selling fly-covered meat pies, I skirted tables of textiles and weaver's goods. The pawnshop was situated behind the market stalls between an apothecary and a tailor. I pulled my hat down around my face before stepping inside.

"Lady Bramley!" The pawnbroker rubbed his hands together in delight as I came through the door, its bell tinkling above me. Leonard, a portly man with the sad eyebrows of a hunting dog, always made an effort to counteract his role as a trader of others' sorrows with abundant solicitations and cheer.

"I'm sure you're happy to see me," I said. He had benefitted greatly over the years from the steady cycle of goods—furniture and picture frames and candelabras—that had streamed in from Bramley Hall. Leonard was one of the few people who would have been able to guess the extent of our lack of means; the stripped-bare walls and the empty mantels.

He spread his hands out on the wood counter in front of him. "We have a marvelous samovar—and look, the matching cups, a complete set."

"Mm-hmm." I pretended to browse. The room was filled with cabinets and shelves, upon which sat all kinds of objects. Silverware and fine porcelain and musical instruments. Books, old and new, and coins and garments in various states of repair. In the back, there was a harpsichord.

"A set of three fans—imported lace—came in yesterday."

I bent over the jewelry display case. Both Leonard and I did not acknowledge the string of jet beads that had once graced my neck and now sat, dust-covered, behind the glass.

"Thank you." I did not want to see the lace fans.

"And silk ribbon, perhaps for Miss Rosamund?" He held up a spool.

"Lovely," I mused, attempting to be dismissive. We both knew I would not be purchasing any ribbon, but I was appreciative of his tact. "While I am here," I said, attempting to make it feel like an afterthought, "I have this old piece—I never touch it. What would it fetch?"

With care, I retrieved the necklace from my pocket pouch. I had to turn away while Leonard inspected it through his loupe, listening to the small noises he made in the back of his throat, then the scratch of the quill on his ledger.

I reminded myself: I would be able to get the cameo back. I needed the money to cover the day's purchases—fabric and trimmings for all three young women—but I'd soon have the apple profits and Elin's rag-and-bone money in hand. I hoped to return for the piece as soon as the next day.

"The pearls have some minor imperfections," he said, while I pretended to look at a case of eyeglasses. "And the cameo exhibits good craftsmanship and has no wear. But the portraits go for much less—it would be better if it were a mythological figure or landscape. Who is the woman? Could we say she is a mythological figure?"

To me, I thought. "No," I said, out loud.

"Did you know her?"

"No," I repeated, because that was truthful in its own way.

He named his price, which was less than I had hoped for, and I accepted without argument. "It likely won't sell for a while," he said, handing me my coins.

"Thank you." I stole one last glance at my mother's profile—for the sake of my daughters, I reminded myself—and then turned my eyes to the portly pawnbroker. "Keep it at the back of the case, will you?"

"Of course, my lady." He cleared his throat. "Of course."

I WAS A FEW STEPS OUT OF THE SHOP WHEN I HEARD SOMEONE CALL my name: "Lady Bramley!" At the sound of the nasal voice, I felt a quick surge of alarm.

Lavinia Enright had the unique distinction of being both the wife of the district's largest landholder and its most grating personality. She and her husband were often at court. I had, somehow, cultivated a friendship—by exterior measures, a great success. By interior, a greater sacrifice. But this day, I had specific need of her. "Lady Enright!" I cried, thinking ahead already to what I would ask. Or rather, suggest. "What a pleasurable surprise!"

"Well, you know me." She bustled forth, mound of curly hair swaying as she sidestepped two customers emerging from the apothecary. "I try to avoid the market days, the hoi polloi, but what with all the recent turn of events—" She paused to raise her eyebrows up and down a few times, and then, sotto voce, whispered, "The royal ball," and glanced surreptitiously over her shoulder, as if the common people would overhear and show up en masse. "We needed a few odds and ends. The timeline! They've given us no time to prepare!" She held up a hand as if I had started to speak, which I hadn't, and turned to face her two daughters, twins who waited behind her in matching dresses and bonnets.

"Girls, say hello to Lady Bramley."

The twins curtsied in unison. "Good day, Lady Bramley."

"Hello, Bethesda," I said, not quite making eye contact with one. "And Bethia," I added, vaguely, to the other. I could never tell them apart. The matching names did not help. One of them, Bethesda, was easily perturbed by fast-moving objects. I had once seen her driven to tears by a falling pine cone. But, unless there were a rapid movement to aid me, I was at a loss. "You're both looking . . ." I searched for a word. "Fresh." The girls had no chins. An unfortunate aesthetic trait they had inherited from their mother. The Enright family had ten thousand acres, two carriages, tenant farmers to work their land, rental income, and social influence. There were four children, including a male heir, Finnian, who was now a page to the prince. The Enright progeny didn't need chins. (And besides, what Lavinia and her brood lacked in a jawline, her husband more than made up for. He had, by my latest count, three.)

"How fortuitous to run into you," I exclaimed. It was for women like Lavinia that I had to maintain our facade. Finnian, even at seventeen, was technically a potential match for my daughters. "Rosamund and Mathilde and I were only just saying how much we missed you all."

Lavinia nodded confidently. "There is nothing as reassuring as female friendship."

"Certainly," I agreed. "The ball will be a marvelous time for them to see one another. I am in town myself looking for their feathers and some extra cloth." I hoped this would explain my exit from the pawnbroker's, but we stood in front of a whole row of shops: shoemakers, glovers, tinsmiths, and drapers. I could have come from any one of them.

Lavinia was distracted by the knowledge of our attendance. "I had the girls' dresses made in the city ages ago—always be ready for a ball, that's what my mother used to say. Summer and winter gowns at the ready. One must be prepared."

I paused, overwhelmed simultaneously by Lavinia and the noxious fumes coming off a nearby dung heap. She used the opportunity to take hold of my arm. "Come, let's walk," she insisted. "If you don't have something made, the silk merchant will be the place to look." She began to lead me along the road, past a long line of timber-framed houses. "Girls, come, come!" The twins fell in line behind us, and we proceeded as a quartet.

Lavinia continued, pulling us to one side to avoid a particularly messy-looking patch of mud: "It is a merry circumstance indeed, all our girls coming out at the same ball. Mine are a bit young, I know, but this is a season not to be missed." Again, she fell into an exaggerated whisper. "The prince," she said, and pursed her lips with pleasure, imagining, I was sure, a match for one of her daughters. Glancing back to look at them, I couldn't help but feel, despite their sallow faces, a little stir of competition.

"I have heard some conjecture that he is looking to marry," I acknowledged. Through a gap in the timbered houses, I could see laystalls in the rear yards that had been filled with animal entrails, feces, and rotting vegetables. It explained the smell.

Lavinia cut in: "He is marvelously talented. A wonderful conversationalist. Extremely handsome. He cuts a dashing figure, to be sure."

"You are lucky to be so acquainted!"

"My Finnie tells me all. And he has told me this is not just any ball; it's a chance for the prince to choose." She told me this as if I had not shared the same information a moment before. "Of course, I heard he had an engagement to a princess from one kingdom over"—she lowered her voice again—"and it fell through. Anyhow, my girls have known His Royal Highness for years; they've been to many of the same places and even occasionally at the same time! I wouldn't be so presumptuous as to say there's a good chance one of them could be spending more time at the palace, but I bet they'll get a dance in at the least."

A glance backward indicated the twins had little opinion—or perhaps say—in the matter. I offered an encouraging smile before turning back to their mother. "Your Finnian is surely a fixture at court by now." Young Finnie probably weighed one hundred pounds. I doubted he was a fixture anywhere. "You must miss him."

"Where else would I have him? I see him plenty. He's back now, this very moment sitting drinking ale with the other men, right here in town. He's here to scout one of the hunting expeditions. You know we have the perfect marshes on our land for waterfowl? Finnie has naturally suggested the property as well situated for a hunt. His father minds not in the least. Not in the least! In fact, Finnie has proved invaluable because of his knowledge. They've put together a party and are going after grouse and bustard—"

It was easy to let Lavinia talk. You only had to make small noises now and then and she kept going. We had almost managed to go the length of the street, which ended at the silk merchant's shop, and I hadn't needed—or been given an opportunity—to ask a question. When Lavinia had nearly exhausted herself, finally pausing to take a breath, I found an opening. "Are you staying in town for the ball?" I interjected.

"In an inn?" She wrinkled her nose.

"It's just not proper. For the girls." I shook my head in agreement. "But it's *such* a long carriage ride for them. So boring. They'll be like wilted flowers when they arrive."

Lavinia furrowed her brow. "They'll have to perk up."

I leaned toward her. "After all that time in a hot carriage? With such a low roof and little air?"

Lavinia trembled at the thought.

"If only," I thought out loud, "there were a way to keep them fresh. Some way to keep them entertained—"

"I know!" she cried. "We'll bring them together. They'll keep one another amused."

Though I was delighted, I protested: "Certainly that's out of your way! And far too generous!" I didn't mean a word of it. The Enrights had a massive carriage with equipage pretty enough to make up for two hours in a confined space with Lavinia.

"Nonsense," she disagreed. "We have the extra seats; you'll come with us. We'll drop you off again at the end of the evening."

We had reached the silk merchant's and came to a stop. I shook my head before going inside. "Well." I sighed. "You've given me no choice but to accept."

AFTER SECURING THE CLOTH FOR THE GIRLS, I HAD ONE LAST TASK. The village had three drinking houses, and instinct alone sent me looking for Finnian in the least respectable of them. The dim lighting and thick air did little to disguise seats missing their upholstery and the lingering smell of unwashed bodies. Weathered faces and dull eyes stared into duller tankards of beer. Near the sole window, an old crone could barely keep herself on her stool. In my silk jacket, I was as noticeable as a dahlia growing in a barren field. I was relieved when I spied young Finnie in a corner.

He was pink in the face, alone, though there were enough empty tankards around him to suggest he had once had company. Had I looked under the table, I was certain his feet would be dangling a few inches above the floor.

"Finnian," I said sternly, waving some of the pipe smoke out of the way, though the gesture did little good.

He tried to focus on my face. "Yes?"

"You must tell me when you will be hunting with the royal entourage."

He narrowed his little-boy eyes and hiccupped.

"Come on, then."

"What do you care for hunting?" He hiccupped once more. "You're a woman." He slumped a little at the observation.

I rubbed my hands together, impatient. Down the row of tables, a man with a scarred face and mismatched shoes fixed me with a stare. "I commend your powers of analysis."

"What are you doing in an alehouse?"

"There are other women here." I glanced around. There were no other reputable women there. "Your mother couldn't help but sing your praises in the market just now. And I thought: I bet Finnian could assist me. She said you knew every little thing about fowl this time of year. I am planning a party and I want the perfect bird on the table. I thought perhaps you could get one for me during your next hunt. When is your next hunt?"

He watched me. "It's true. I know everything there is to know about teal. And mallards."

"A verified expert, I hear." I waited a moment, then repeated: "When is the hunt?"

He held up a finger. "Take mallards. The female quacks are softer. More subdued. Males have a distinct and louder quack."

I nodded. "That does not come as a surprise—"

"And they follow their mother from birth."

"Yes, and then we eat them. Your knowledge must be prized at court."

He bobbed his head enthusiastically, and I interrupted, before he could tell me more about the ducks. "Will you tell me where you will hunt this evening?"

"I can't," he protested. "For we are not hunting until tomorrow."

"Shame." I tutted. "For the party is tonight."

But I smiled to myself as I turned away, for I had gotten the information I needed.

CHAPTER SIXTEEN

A SCHEME WAS FORMING IN MY MIND—A DESIGN STEADILY UN-
folding. It required, of all things, items that had belonged to
Elin's mother.

Remnants of Bramley's history were tucked away in its forgotten
attic, an area of refuse I had combed through countless times searching
for sellable treasures. My footsteps were noisy in the dim expanse, each
creak of the floorboards echoing off the aging and broken relics: an old-
fashioned spinning wheel, a fractured stool, a looking glass with a crack
down the center. My own battered trunk—carted from my childhood
home to the Tremaines' manor to Bramley—collected dust in a corner.
As I passed, I ran a finger along its lid, looping a quick *hello* into the
grime on its surface.

After Robert died, when there was no one left to dust the perfumes
and oils in his first wife's quarters, when the only hands that might have
fluffed the pillows and swept the floors were my own, I decided it was
time to put her personal belongings away. I undertook the careful folding of her garments into cedarwood chests and the stacking of her half-
finished paintings, ferrying the remainders of the unknown woman

into the recesses and hollows above our head. All her belongings still sat, neatly stacked, covered in cobwebs, under the eaves of our home.

I pulled out a few of the woman's half-finished canvases, inspecting the artwork in the weak light. Blank circles of stiff cloth stood out against dark backgrounds. A primary hobby of Elin's mother had been, it appeared, painting bowls of fruit. Apples.

"Naturally," I said out loud, and tried to blow some of the dust from the canvas. I could not escape the hard fruit.

We had sold almost all the bushels Moussa had carted into market—and it had been just enough to cover the day's purchases. Cloth for the dresses, three yards of lace, new feathers, and wages to Alice and Moussa that were so small they were solely symbolic. The earnings had not covered Wenthelen's requested essentials—no meat, nor any cheese—let alone the recovery of my cameo.

I selected two small paintings. The incomplete canvases needed a good dusting but would suit my purposes. Tucking one under each arm, I picked my way back across the wide floorboards, and descended back downstairs.

Her mother's apples were as good a reminder as any—I needed to talk to Elin.

I FOUND HER PLAYING A GAME OF PATIENCE BY THE WINDOW OF THE drawing room, the cards spread out on a small table. "Stepmother!" She stood when she saw me.

"I have brought you the fabric you needed for your train and petticoat." I watched her carefully. "And I do think it will be a good match for the gown." I laid a parcel upon the table. "Go ahead, open it."

She worked on the string, and, when it had loosened, took care unfolding the paper. I continued: "I think the color will set off your hair. We'll dye your feathers to agree. Of course, if it is not a good color match with the other pieces you've started, there is a trunk of your mother's old items in the attic, and perhaps we can find something in there."

I waited.

"Thank you," she said, at length.

"Is that all?"

She stared at me. "The color is pretty."

I looked down at the maroon fabric, which had cost me my cameo—at least in part. "Do you mean to say you have not gone to the rag-and-bone man and collected the money?"

She glanced away. "I have every intention of repaying you."

Holding my breath, I unfolded the cloth I had bought for her, covering the cards on the table. "I secured this as a kindness for you, at great personal sacrifice. I expect to be repaid."

"Certainly," she said, nodding. "Trust is a fragile bloom that must be nurtured in the soil of steadfast commitment. I give you my word that once I am married and have my dowry, I will repay you."

"You are not even engaged." I thought of my mother's countenance, trapped beneath the pawnbroker's glass, and fought an urge to slap her. "And you are sitting here playing cards."

"I have indeed made you a promise, and follow-through is the heartbeat of integrity!" Elin clasped her hands, genuine in her regret. "But as the daughter of a lord, ought I not concern myself with higher matters? Soot clings so dreadfully and does not come off without that horrid-smelling soap, and the water is frigid this time of year . . ." She gestured at the table where the cards lay under the cloth. "I am practicing for future gatherings."

"Elin." I was unable to keep the poison from my tone. "You are lucky I have not asked you to scour the countryside for the dog droppings the tanyards would buy. You *will* go round and collect the ashes from every hearth. You *will* take them to town and bring them to the rag shop. You *will* collect the earnings and bring them straight back to me." I gathered the red cloth in my hands and twisted it, fighting the desire to bloody Elin's pristine knuckles the way Agatha had once bloodied mine. "I do not care how you manage it."

Her eyes grew. "You would not ask Rosamund or Mathilde to do these things."

"Because they have earned their keep in one hundred other ways." My voice pinched and my jaw clenched with a seething anger. "You will do as I say, and you will do it promptly and without hesitation."

I didn't bother to wait for her reply. My anger stayed with me as I left the drawing room and went down the hall to Rosie's room and then after to Mathilde's, giving both the same message: "Ready yourself for a picnic in the morning," I said. "Wear your best flattering day dress and do your hair."

"Why?" asked Mathilde.

"A mother may command as she likes," I rebutted.

"And a daughter may comment when her mother does something out of the ordinary," Mathilde observed. "We have hardly any days left to finish our dresses for the ball that *you* have deemed so important."

I turned on my heel. "Then *you* shall work in the nights."

CHAPTER SEVENTEEN

THE FOLLOWING DAY WAS BLUSTERING AND CRISP. THE SKY HAD turned a clean, bright kind of blue, and the light felt long and sharp, as if intending to bestow upon each leaf and blade its very own shadow. My daughters and I were sandwiched into the bench of the chaise, along with a stack of quilts, a rolled carpet, two easels, paints, the half-finished canvases, and a basket of biscuits, tarts, fruit, and three loaves of bread.

"It is not entirely fair that Elin must repay you, when you used the apple money from apples we all picked." Rosie had twisted herself into a small degree of concern for her stepsister and sat, eyeing Mathilde and I, with a look of mild reproach.

"She picked one apple for every five I got down. Every ten!" Mathilde, sitting on my other side, was distracted by retying the ribbons of her hat.

"Rosie." I bent toward her, adding some slack to the reins in my hands. "We have been selling your embroidery bits for years to buy what we can. Both of you have worked and worked." I shook my head. "It's so much more than apples. I am done compensating for her indolence."

Mathilde finished her bow and leaned forward to look at Rosie, across the bench. "Why do you suddenly care?"

Her question was ignored. "Why are we going out today of all days? We need to work on our dresses."

"Today is more than a picnic." I peered into the bushes at the side of the road, looking for the right spot to pull over.

"It's because she complimented your hat, isn't it," Mathilde said, more to herself than her sister.

Rosie ignored her and bent forward to nudge the cloth off the top of the food basket. "How do you mean it's more than a picnic? There is nothing but bread and fruit!"

"Any half-wit would know she isn't talking about the *food*, Rosamund." Mathilde sighed. "She has a plan."

"If I am a half-wit, then you are a crotcheteer—"

"Better a grouch than a popinjay."

"If you two would pause your debate for one moment . . ." I held the reins aloft. "We are nearly there."

We were close to the Enrights'. Another half a mile and we would see the fence for their enclosure. I clicked at Arno and directed him to pull over to the side of the road.

"*Here?*" the girls asked, in unison. There was not much around us but a field of high grasses, and a ditch that edged the thoroughfare.

"Here," I confirmed.

My daughters unrolled the carpet and arranged our picnic while I unhitched Arno and led him to the shade of a small sapling.

"Make it look perfect," I called, watching them orchestrate the food. "Put the biscuits into a pyramid on that silver platter. When you've finished, set the paintings upon the easels and spread some fresh paint on the pallet and mix it around. You must make it *look* like you are painting."

Mathilde gave me a questioning glance, but did as I requested, holding the brushes away from herself so as not to dirty her dress.

When it was all arranged as I had directed, I had them sit. "Mathilde, go next to your sister. No, not there, the other side. Now, turn your body to face me."

"You poked me!" Rosie scowled at Mathilde.

"One cannot help sharp elbows."

"But they can mind where they've stuck them!"

"You make a beautiful scene," I called. Their little fingers, their pretty lips; they looked like a painting themselves, except a painting couldn't have captured the field rippling in the breeze and their dresses rising and falling on the same drafts of air. Nor would it have caught their bickering. "As long as you are not talking."

I went back over to the chaise, stopping at its rear. I could hear birdsong and closed my eyes to listen. A wren's rapid trill and a skylark's elongated call as it hovered above. So rarely did I get to see these small birds—those that quieted when Lucy was nearby. Wishing for luck, I opened my eyes, and placed my palms against the back of the small carriage. Using all my weight, I leaned forward to shove it into the ditch.

"Mama?" Rosamund cried, alarmed.

I pushed harder.

"Mama!" Rosamund repeated. Both girls' mouths were open in small O's of surprise.

With a final heave, I managed to get the chaise to lurch ahead. The gig rolled forward into the ditch, flipping on its side.

Mathilde turned to her sister. "She's lost her senses."

Both started to stand.

"Sit back down," I called. "Don't move, I've only just positioned you." I looked down at the cart and frowned. I had not anticipated its flipping. One of the wheels had also broken. "God's bones," I whispered to myself.

"Positioned us for what?" Mathilde demanded.

"You'll see shortly."

I was operating on a series of assumptions. I knew from Finnie that the prince was hunting that day. And that the party would be looking for fowl on the Enright property. The retinue would have to be large—large enough that the group couldn't stay at most halls and would have come from the direction of the city—and they would need to take the main road for their many wagons and carriages. The best time for hunting was late afternoon. I hoped they would pass us, and slow to offer assistance. I had positioned the girls close enough to the road that their faces might be remembered by a passing prince. The wind in their hair. Sun-kissed cheeks and a paintbrush held aloft: a tableau of feminine grace and artfulness.

But, for a long while, nobody came. The sun dropped lower in the sky. The girls' silence turned to complaints. Biscuits were pilfered and eaten. And, when, finally, there were hoofbeats, the dust revealed only a farmer and his wagon.

He tipped his hat and slowed, looking at the carriage. "You need help," he yelled, as he got closer.

"No," I called back. "No, thank you!"

He began to pull on his reins.

I shook my head at him. "No, sir, do not stop!"

"You need help!" he repeated, more plaintively.

"I do not," I called. "Be going. Move along."

Confused, he scratched his head.

"Shoo!" I shouted. Glancing over my shoulder, I could see my daughters' looks of consternation.

The farmer shrugged, unbothered. But watching his cart trundle away, I felt less confident. I didn't believe in fate or luck; rather that you had to take a situation in your weathered hands and wrestle it into whatever shape you required. But what if those instincts only served me a broken chaise in a ditch? We couldn't afford a wheelwright. And I couldn't do without a chaise. Dejected, I went back over to the picnic to eat another biscuit, further ruining the shape of the pyramid.

"When your father and I traveled after our wedding, the staff would set up a lunch like this every day," I remembered aloud. "There were tables and chairs and even silver."

"Yes," Rosamund said. "And insects would get trapped in the canopy of the tent."

"And the women were not supposed to talk," Mathilde added. "And you had to sit in silence and listen to the men."

I realized it was a repeated story—and perhaps not as sweet as my current recollection.

"Forget tables and chairs," Mathilde said. "A picnic would be more enjoyable if you could eat all the food." She stared longingly at a bowl of pears.

I was about to permit her one when the birds and insects went quiet. I lifted my head. A moment later, we felt the vibration in the ground, then saw the dust in the road, and, after a brief pause, a train of coaches. This was no farmer's cart.

I leaned forward and, as gently as I could manage, slapped Mathilde across the face.

"What—" she cried, raising a hand to her inflamed jaw.

Before she could turn, I slapped her other cheek.

"Stop!" Rosie cried, confused.

"For color," I explained. I handed Rosie my handkerchief. "And wipe yours. You have too much rouge."

They stared at me.

"Do not move off the carpet," I called over my shoulder and hurried toward the road.

Standing alone at the edge of the byway, I watched as the carriages drew near. One at the middle, marked by the royal coat of arms, was larger and grander than all the rest. I was overwhelmed with quick relief—I had been right—which soon gave way to focus: It was imperative that the caravan stop, if only briefly.

A glance over my shoulder confirmed the girls were still in place: framed by pretty grasses, their yellow dresses as eye-catching in the browning field as if they had been glowing lanterns. I stepped out into the road as the caravan's first riders neared. Armed guards and men on horseback.

I opened my mouth to call out but found I could summon no words. I recognized the first man, not only for the richness of his dress, but for the same yellow hair I'd seen in his portrait. The foremost rider was not an attendant or huntsman, but the prince himself.

I shut my mouth and sank into a curtsy, murmuring "Your Royal Highness" into the dirt.

I HAD HOPED THAT I COULD PLEAD FOR HELP FROM A GUARD OR hunter, and that, in the brief delay, the prince would see my daughters through the window of his carriage. That he might notice them, and later remember them. That, seeing their faces amongst the many, many women at the ball, there would be a sense of recognition. I had thought the attendants would quickly pull the chaise from the ditch. I had not accounted for the flipping, or the broken wheel. I had not prepared myself to converse with Prince Simeon directly. As I rose from my curtsy, Agatha had no advice for me, but I felt her presence in my breath and in the staccato of my heartbeat.

"You are in distress," the prince observed, face marked by the faintest trace of a smile.

I rose and peered up at him. He had brought his horse to a stop and was staring at the overturned chaise with interest.

"A small mishap," I explained. "We came to enjoy a picnic." I gestured back toward Rosie and Mathilde, who were looking on with wonder. "The horse spooked. He is, thankfully, fine, as are we, but I am afraid our carriage is not."

Behind Prince Simeon, his caravan was coming to a noisy halt, horses stamping at the ground and men talking, calling ahead. He turned and declared to those milling closest: "We must help these women!"

The prince began to dismount, leaning into one of the stirrups and

throwing his other leg over the top of the horse with ease. Two attendants rushed forward as he landed on the ground and he waved them
away, saying, instead, to me: "Their entire role is to help me on and off
a horse. And people wonder why the royal coffers run low. Now." He
rubbed his hands together. "Let's see about that carriage."

He strode over toward the ditch and, in one quick motion, hopped
down and landed in the muck at the bottom. He circled the chaise,
muddying himself in the process. "I see the predicament. We won't be
able to just push it out."

"I—we are much beholden." I was at a loss for words.

"Do not thank me yet." He smiled up at me from the bottom of the
ditch. "The chaise is still stuck in the mud."

"Regardless, we owe you our gratitude for your willingness to
help—" I paused, hearing hoofbeats approach behind me. Otto, the
royal counselor and the stranger from the woods, was making his way
from the back of the caravan. He rode a muscular steed with a shiny
black coat that had been brushed and cleaned well. My spirits plum-
meted.

"Lady Tremaine," he said, barely touching his brow. I curtsied.
"What is the problem?" Otto addressed the question to Simeon.

"You know one another?" The prince was rolling up his sleeves.
"How disgustingly small our kingdom is."

"Allow me to present Lady Etheldreda Tremaine . . . Bramley," Otto
replied, stiffly, as if the words were sour in his mouth. He surveyed the
cart and then glanced over at Arno, who was ignorantly switching his
tail in the grasses yards away. "The horse did this?"

I lowered my gaze. "I am afraid the wheel has cracked."

Otto stared down into the ditch from the back of his steed. "Why
is the wagon perpendicular to the road?"

Something in his tone made me forget my timidity and restored
my voice. "It is strange indeed." I held his eyes, lifting my chin slightly.
"I was setting up the picnic and did not see what spooked the horse."

"And yet the horse is untouched." Otto looked at the cart and back at me with the prowling, feral energy of a watchdog. Despite his nose, which looked to have been broken more than once, he might have been handsome—except he held a constant look of distaste.

"Come, Otto," Prince Simeon called. "And get down here and help me push it out."

"You have a crowd of thirty waiting to hunt." Otto turned to face the prince. "It will be quicker to pull it out with the ox."

"You'd give my opportunity to be chivalrous to a bull?" Simeon raised his hands—a mock gesture of defeat.

"Wouldn't want you injuring yourself again." Otto turned his horse around. "I'll get the men."

Simeon scrambled up and out of the ditch, and held out his arm to show me his injury: nothing but some cuts and a bruise. Lips pulled sideways in amusement, he explained: "Otto will use even the smallest hunting accident to keep me from having any fun. No enjoyable activity is worth doing without a little bit of risk. Not that Otto would agree. All he does is try to reduce risk. And here I am, unable to help a maiden in distress."

I was no maiden. Under the force of those clear eyes, I blushed as if I were.

With a quick gesture, Simeon rolled down his sleeves and buttoned them once more. He had an ease in his own skin—and a tall frame with broad shoulders—that reminded me, a little, of Henry. I tossed my head in the direction of Rosie and Mathilde, waiting on the carpet behind us. "Might I introduce you to my daughters?"

He met my eyes with a broad smile that was impossible not to mirror. "Certainly."

⚜

THE GIRLS WERE NERVOUS, ROSIE REACHING SELF-CONSCIOUSLY TO twirl a lock of her hair, and Mathilde measuring her words so carefully she had pursed her lips in concentration. But Simeon turned to me after our introductions and said: "Lady Bramley, your daughters are as charming as this setting." I surmised he meant the undulating grasses that surrounded us and not the massive ox that was twenty feet away, being led toward the ditch.

But he soon put us at ease, listening as Rosie and Mathilde answered questions about our home, the apple paintings, and the provenance of the biscuits, which were quickly offered to him. My daughters' nervousness turned into a flirtatious kind of alertness when the prince settled himself onto our carpet.

The picnic had been prepared as a prop—a diversion to be observed through a carriage window from afar. I couldn't help but see the bruises on the fruit and the crumbs on the carpet, but Simeon appeared to notice neither, taking an oversized bite of a biscuit and then returning the rest to the plate in front of him. "Forgive me for trespassing on your lunch. I would dine outdoors more—the point of a picnic is to experience the peacefulness of nature. But I can't go anywhere without people in tow, which defeats the purpose." He leaned back, sinking his weight into his palms, which pressed into the carpet behind him, and eyed the men of his caravan. He huffed—a private acknowledgment of a thought I couldn't read on his face. A desire for freedom? Autonomy? It occurred to me, not for the first time, that privilege was its own kind of burden. He sighed, nodded to his men, and added: "Even now, the few feet of separation makes them nervous."

I laughed. "As if three ladies in the grass could cause you harm."

He joined my laughter and turned to Rosamund. "That was an exceptional biscuit."

"The best in the kingdom." She offered him another with a sweet smile.

"Though I would be scared to say otherwise to our cook," Mathilde mused.

"She is formidable," Rosie agreed, gazing at the prince through her eyelashes and fingering some of the ribbons at her neckline.

He leaned closer to her. "The world is afraid of kings and armies, but there is nothing scarier than the wrath of a woman." Simeon's hair, which was naturally wavy, had been brushed and lay back, but as he leaned closer to Rosie, a lock fell across his forehead and into his eyes. He flicked it away, mindlessly, and when he looked up, he caught my eye. Or rather, caught me looking at him.

I hadn't expected to like him. He was a prince, but he was also flesh and blood, and, if I had wanted to, I could have reached out and pinched him. "We are lucky you happened to be here," I said. "And we had a chance to meet before we attend your name day celebration."

He looked pleased. "You are coming?"

Over Simeon's shoulder, I could see the men working to right the chaise. Otto was nearly out of sight, for he had gone down into the ditch himself. I hoped he would be down there a long while.

Simeon tilted his head, observing us. "It is I that am the lucky one— for I never would have gotten a taste of the kingdom's best biscuits otherwise."

"A fair trade, I hope, for keeping you from your hunt." Rosie's face was soft and open.

With a quick gesture, Simeon affectionately fingered a lock of her hair. "You ladies have so many options when it comes to being accomplished. Apple paintings! And all the things you do with a needle and thread. Books. Poetry. Language. Art." He gave an appreciative nod to the two easels and dropped his hand. Rosie reached up to touch her curls where his fingers had lingered, listening. "I have but cards and hunts. We go out nearly every week and I do not even like hunting."

"Then why go?" Mathilde interjected.

He nodded at the men of the caravan. "They like it. And they are my friends." Seeing that the counselor was striding toward us, he added, "Even Otto." He called out so Otto could hear him: "Have we succeeded?"

Otto waited until he had reached the edge of the carpet to respond. He stood stiffly and clasped his hands behind his back. "The chaise is righted, but you won't be able to drive it away. Needs a wheelwright."

"Alas," I exclaimed, though that outcome was more than obvious:

The chaise stood upright in the road and one of the wheels was missing a piece.

"We'll escort you home," Simeon reassured us.

"You're lucky no one was hurt." Otto towered over us. He glanced at the easels. "You were painting?"

"The girls love to paint." I widened my eyes at Mathilde.

"Oh, indeed," she added, quickly.

Rosie, a moment later, hand still tangled in her own lock of hair, managed: "The meadows are so inspiring."

"And yet, I cannot help but notice you are not painting them." Otto looked over the canvases on the easels, both of which were filled with apples. He leaned forward with an extended fingertip, as if to test the paint's wetness.

"Nature is inspiring to one's senses," I called, my tone a reprimand, "no matter the focus of the piece. Is it not?"

Otto straightened and turned to Simeon. "We'll lose daylight."

"Good gods." Simeon sighed, pushing himself up off the carpet. "The carriage will take them." He turned to me, conspiratorially. "I'm afraid we seem to have upset dear Otto's plans, but then Otto is invariably upset by almost everything I do. If I were to do as he suggested, every one of my days would be boring. I'm afraid you'll have to settle for a ride in my carriage. And I will see you all at the ball."

I matched his tone. "There is nothing boring about a ride in a prince's carriage—even if he is not inside of it."

Otto grunted and turned on his heel.

MAKING PROMISES OF HAVING OUR CHAISE RETURNED TO US—ARNO was led by an attendant who was to follow—Simeon himself handed us up into his carriage, which was every bit as opulent inside as its exterior. He paused for a moment at the open door, offering his well-wishes, which we accepted and returned with our thanks, and then a moment later the door was closed and we lurched forward. I stopped

Rosie and Mathilde from speaking by raising a finger to my lips. We clutched one another's hands and squeezed—grasping, grasping, at our wonderful turn of fortune. There was a world of riches and splendor, inaccessible to most, that shone so brightly. But we had just touched it—Rosie was still twisting that same lock of hair—and could see the sheen on our fingertips.

CHAPTER EIGHTEEN

W E REPEATED OUR STORY BREATHLESSLY TO WENTHELEN
and Alice and, I am sure, individually picked it apart and
wove it again as we lay in our beds that night, each with our own details
to hold and examine. How the sun caught on a golden carriage. How
a lock of hair shone when twisted around a finger. How the air itself
shifted and melted, reducing the entire world down to the size of one
carpet.

During our picnic, as I watched the prince alternate between teasing each of my daughters, I had asked myself what either—or any
woman—had to intrigue a man in his position. Beauty was a given, but
even the most splendid trifles can lose their allure when countless trifles are on offer. My girls had no money, but a prince needed none. An
accomplished woman—one well read and properly trained and polite
and virtuous—was appealing in words but perhaps not in flesh. But
I had seen—had felt—a flash of interest in his eyes. The way he had
fingered Rosie's hair.

Perhaps it was only the removal of life at court. The placement of
two women in pretty dresses in an empty field. It had also occurred to

me, as Simeon moved his attention from Rosamund to Mathilde and back again, that it might have been the very contrast, the tension of two, the attention of two, that had worked in their favor.

Either way, my instincts were right. Two days after the picnic, a gift arrived.

ALL OF US WERE IN THE HALL: IN ONE CORNER, ROSIE PINNED Mathilde's hem. At the table, Wenthelen tied little bundles of herbs with a ball of twine beside Alice, who was repairing a basket. Even Elin, who had made herself scarce since we'd had words, was nearby, kneeling at the hearth and using a scoop to fill her ash box.

"The other thing," Rosie said, apropos of nothing, "is that he handed us into the carriage. He did not have to do so. He might have had one of his footmen do it, but he chose to help us himself."

"He didn't gift you his carriage; he just held your hand as you climbed into it." Mathilde frowned down at the top of Rosie's head.

"I think he seemed lonely." Rosie ignored her sister. "A kind of sadness about his eyes. But it detracted from his looks not a little."

"Maybe it's that he doesn't know who to trust," Mathilde mumbled.

"Yes!" Rosie agreed. "Exactly."

Mathilde turned so Rosie could get to the next section of the hem. "What with everyone fawning over him everywhere he goes."

"He knew he could trust *us* because there was no artifice," Rosie protested. "He stumbled upon us in a field!"

"No artifice," snorted Alice, without looking up.

Wenthelen paused her bundling and squeezed Alice's knee. "Let them enjoy it."

"The *girls* had no artifice." I paused the stitching in my lap and narrowed my eyes at Alice.

She returned the expression, placing one of her hands on top of Wenthelen's. "You gained a prince but lost a chaise. What now?"

"A trade anyone in their right mind would make." I stabbed my needle into the cloth in front of me.

"And what will that right-minded lady do next Thursday, when there is no chaise to take to market?"

Over at the hearth, Elin let out a sneeze, sending a cloud of dust into the air. Mathilde stepped backward, into Rosie, to protect her dress. "Watch yourself!" she exclaimed, as Rosie let out a yelp of pain.

"I cannot help it!" Elin cried.

"If you did not make such little scoops," Wenthelen suggested, "you might finish sooner. Just as I showed you."

"Wenthelen—" I warned.

Elin released another sneeze and, after a small ash cloud resettled across her skirts, looked down at herself in dismay.

"Bear your head high," I called. It was satisfying to see her like this, after so many years. To watch her working. "For they'll wash off fine. Just don't touch any nice cloth until then."

"I need to work on my dress," Elin protested, eyeing the pinned flounces on her stepsisters.

"You've had plenty of time for that." I tutted.

"Simeon said he does not like to hunt. I wonder if he is an animal lover," Rosie said, now through a mouthful of pins.

No one responded, for we all heard at the same time the noise of a carriage outside.

"Who is that?" Mathilde asked.

"Not another royal messenger," Wenthelen worried.

Elin stood in alarm. She had her hair tied under a rag and soot on her face.

"Is it—" Rosie stood, hope cresting on her face and lighting her from within.

"No," I said firmly, tossing my mending into the basket. I went to the window. "It's our chaise." Otto was in the driver's seat, his own horse hitched and pulling him forward.

I turned to Elin as I made toward the door. "Go upstairs to your room—you'll be mistaken for a chambermaid looking like that."

"I cannot be seen as such." Elin stood straight, consoling herself. "Internal charm always translates to external grace."

"Regardless of internal charm, I advise that you peer into a looking glass," Mathilde said. "For you are covered in cinders."

Downstairs, Otto was dismounting.

I insisted: "Elin, for God's sake, and for your own sake, go upstairs. Before you're seen."

I ignored Alice's and Wenthelen's looks of admonishment.

"Very well," Elin said, meekly, adding more soot to her face as she wiped the bridge of her nose with the back of her hand.

OTTO WAS WAITING IN THE GRAVEL, STANDING NEXT TO THE CHAISE. When I came out the door, he frowned down the drive. "You have a peddler camping at your gate."

"A jongleur," I corrected, reproaching myself for not thinking ahead and entreating Moussa to move. The bird in the woods, the broken cart, a peddler's camp—every circumstance of our interaction seemed designed to lower me in Otto's esteem. Not that he mattered. I only cared about those he influenced. But, for my daughters' sakes, I would once more try to curry his favor. "We owe you our thanks for returning the carriage."

I realized, belatedly, that if the carriage had been driven, then the wheel had also been fixed. "And mending it," I added.

"Couldn't have brought it back to you if it wasn't mended." Otto's expression didn't change. His presence was a mystery—any attendant could have returned the chaise. But that question soon answered itself. Without looking at me, he turned and marched back toward our carriage. "Prince Simeon wanted to send a gift."

"A gift," I repeated.

Otto reached the back compartment of the gig, which, I now saw, had a cloth-covered rectangle and a horse saddle inside. He shifted the saddle to retrieve the rectangle and pulled off the cloth. It was a painting. Of apples.

"For your daughters," Otto explained.

"Apples," I said.

He coughed. "Prince Simeon said it is because they like pictures of them."

His discomfort provoked within me a deep sense of satisfaction. As did the fact of the gift—regardless of what the canvas portrayed. "They will be honored."

Otto thrust the painting, which was surprisingly heavy, into my arms and began to unhitch his horse from the chaise. "I need to return before it grows dark."

I stood aside, uncertain what to do with myself or the unwieldy artwork. "Prince Simeon was quite thoughtful to send a gift when it is he that saved us. I do not know what got into Arno. Our horse."

Otto nodded. "Simeon possesses an undeniable skill for charm."

"Skill implies practiced effort," I mused. "I would say his charm is more constitutional."

Otto only tilted his head in response and then went to the back of the chaise to retrieve his saddle. He concentrated on putting it on the horse, while I, arms growing weak from holding the heavy painting, attempted to sustain our foundering discourse.

"You know your way around this area well," I observed.

"Yes," he agreed.

I waited half a minute. Then: "Have you been in the kingdom a long time?"

"Yes."

"You are not from here."

"No."

It was clear he did not wish to have a conversation. After many long moments—him fastening the girth and adjusting the stirrups— I exclaimed: "You have a penchant for silence."

Otto straightened, ran a hand through his hair, and fixed me with his dark eyes. "You, it is clear, do not."

I glanced at him, sharply. His hand dropped to rub his mouth. Half shutting his eyes, he said: "I apologize. That was impolite. I am preoccupied today."

"I thank you for the painting," I told him, voice tight. "And I'll trust you to see yourself down the drive."

I was finally willing to concede: I would not win over Otto Abensur.

✹

ROSIE AND MATHILDE CAME TO MY CHAMBERS THAT NIGHT. They climbed up into the bed beside me and settled, one at each of my sides.

"Mama," Rosie whispered. "We finally finished our dresses."

"With almost no time to spare." Mathilde sank back into the pillows next to me.

The ball was the day after the next. I held a hand in the air, the candle causing a flickering, oversized shadow on the canopy above us. "You have done the impossible. A gown in a week, and all the other work as well. Not to mention, charming an actual prince."

"He is just polite, not charmed," Rosie said. She waited hopefully, and both Mathilde and I laughed and contradicted her.

"I saw his eyes lingering on you," Mathilde cried. "Polite eyes do not linger."

"Who would not be charmed by your sweet, happy disposition?" I asked. "And any argument should be put to rest with one glance at that painting."

Rosie pawed at the blankets. "What could he mean by it?"

"That he is thinking of you. That he wanted to do something for you," I ticked off the list. "That he is a prince and can send grand gifts on a whim."

She nuzzled into my shoulder. "Do you think he might ever love me?"

I considered. "Your father and I were an unlikely match. He wasn't a prince. Or anything close to it." I laughed to myself. "But it wasn't expected." I took each of their hands and laid them in a little stack upon my lap and pretended to climb them with my fingers. "You must learn the rules and then climb them like a ladder."

"We have a surprise for you!" Rosamund cried, pushing herself up off the mattress.

"Go on," Mathilde told her, and then we both watched as Rosie rushed from the room and returned a minute later, her arms full of layers of taffeta.

"You are going to a royal ball, too. And you need something to wear, even if you won't have feathers in your hair." She spread the dress out across the bed, on top of me.

"Rosamund did most of it; she is so quick." Mathilde watched my face.

"But Mathilde did all the seams along the hem, and the petticoat."

"Yes, and," Mathilde continued, taking a hesitant breath, "we know you pawned your cameo."

I wiped my cheek with the back of my hand, careful not to wet the material in front of me.

"I was going into your jewelry because I wanted to match your wrap to the color of the shell," Rosamund explained.

Mathilde continued: "We feel you should take the frame off the prince's painting and you can use that to get your necklace back."

I could not think of the words to express exactly what I felt, so I gathered each of them in my arms and kissed their shining, twin braids. One after the other.

CHAPTER NINETEEN

THE MORNING OF THE BALL, I YANKED MY CURTAINS OPEN AT first light, allowing myself a moment to appreciate the blushing daybreak. The sun rose with all the shyness of a new bride. But, like the muffins Wenthelen served us for breakfast, this initial calm crumbled quickly.

Mathilde, whistling past as Elin carried a bucket of hot water upstairs, sneered: "It'll be cold at the rate you're going." Rosamund, unable to find her flowered hair ornaments, accused Mathilde of borrowing and losing them. Elin, advising Rosie that virtue was the source of happiness, not hair ornaments, earned herself an icy look of scorn.

In the end, all three of them took turns washing in the same tub. I sent them to their chambers to begin dressing and left to take my own bath, alone, in my room.

Half submerged, I looked at my naked torso. Bony knees that rose from the bathwater like islands. Once, long ago, I had been attended to. Hair washed. Oils rubbed into my skin. Herbs scattered in the tub. Now my body bore the marks of living. Skin that had gone milky. A belly that had stretched for children. Hands—wrapped, now, around shivering shoulders—that had labored. I was an aging lady of the house, pruning in tepid bathwater, because there was no one to heat it for her.

I was older than my own mother had ever been. And yet, I did not feel old. I recognized the face that I could see in the looking glass. I knew the beating heart in my chest. I felt vaguely astonished to have children who were adults themselves. I squared myself, squeezing my shoulders. So many years had ticked past—through drudgery, necessity, injury—as if leading to this moment. To the evening's ball. To what I hoped would be a turning point.

I had reason to be hopeful. The gift the prince had sent was proof. Simeon appeared to be favoring my daughters. The painting now sat in Rosie's chambers. Propped against the window, a dark square backlit by sun. She was likely whispering to it as she readied. Making eyes at the frameless canvas.

As my girls had bid me, the day before, I'd removed the thick gold frame and taken it into the village. The gilded molding had sat on the seat of the chaise beside me, covered in a sheet, blind to the scenery—muddy farms and untrimmed hedges—along the lane.

As I drove, I reassured myself. It had only been a few short days since I had pawned the cameo. The pawnbroker himself had thought it unlikely anyone would be interested in a depiction of a strange woman. My mother was no mythological figure.

But, from the moment the bell rang above my head and the pawnbroker looked up, I knew his news would not be good.

"Lady Bramley!" Leonard rushed from behind the counter to take the sheet-clad object from my hands. "What is this? What have you brought? Allow me to help you."

The shop looked the same as ever: boxes of flatware and shelves of pottery. A sword missing the jewels in its hilt. "It's a picture frame. Genuine gold leaf, you'll see. Here, put it on the counter."

As he began to pull aside the sheet, I looked him in the eye. "Do you still have it?"

"Lady Bramley—" he began.

"You said you would keep it set aside. And that no one would be interested in it."

"Lady Bramley—" he tried again.

"And it is ever so important to me, so I hope that it is right where I left it." I was delaying, I knew.

"I am sorry."

I nodded and looked away. "Who took it?"

He wrung his hands, apologetically. "You know I cannot share."

"Who has the picture of my mother?" I demanded, then quickly put a hand over my mouth. I had not intended to reveal the depth of my desperation. I saw, in the pawnbroker's eyes, pity.

I made myself turn away. My anger was misdirected. It was not Leonard who had cost me the necklace. It was a stepdaughter who hadn't followed through on what was promised.

And now, rising from the lukewarm bath, I found I had no kindness left for Elin.

I could see my dress waiting for me, hanging from a picture rail. The garment was as delicate as a flower, held together by neat and even stitches, gathered in at the waist and then expanding, the skirt falling and barely grazing the floor.

When it was lowered over my head, Wenthelen fastening the buttons down my back, I could see in the looking glass that the layers of fabric and all the careful handiwork had done their job.

"Not half bad," Wenthelen observed.

I nodded, smoothing my hands over the lemon-colored taffeta, and caught Wenthelen's eyes in the reflection. "Pull in those laces until I cannot breathe."

ROSIE AND MATHILDE CAME DOWN FIRST. "YOU LOOK WONDERFUL," I told them, and meant it. My hands, as they always did when I felt surges of affection, sought out their faces, and my children shied away from me as I patted and fixed their hair, fingers fluttering around their necks. Then we stood in the front hall, waiting.

"I am so impatient. I wish we could leave this instant." Rosamund sighed.

Mathilde worried the lace on her sleeves. "We shall be late."

"We are expected to be." Lavinia and I had agreed, via letter, that we would arrive at half past the start time, as was the custom. But, because the journey to the palace would take a good while, the sun was still high in the sky. The ball felt close at hand and yet there were hours to get through before we'd set foot inside the castle.

"And Elin has not come down," Rosie said.

"I am here," she called, and we all turned.

She stood at the top of the stairs, lit by a beam of light that reached through the glass above the door. The deep wine color of the dress set off her pink cheeks. Elin held her folded train with an elegantly extended arm. Her figure, normally thin and straight, benefitted from the undulations of her dress.

My girls and I walked toward the base of the stairs, faces upturned. Elin began to descend. With each passing step, the pretty image she had presented fell apart, slowly, and then all at once. Elin had, I saw, not finished her hem, and the rough edge of the cloth dragged on the floor. Her eyes looked red, as if from crying.

"Why," Rosamund said, with genuine surprise, "that is my hair ornament!"

"I can see your undergarments," Mathilde said, in dismay. Sure enough, her smock was coming through a seam at her waist.

"Elin," I reprimanded. Her sleeves were different lengths. "You were not able to finish your dress."

"No." She shook her head. She came to the bottom step and stopped in front of us. "And it ripped when I was putting it on."

"It wouldn't last for one dance!" Mathilde reached out and plucked at the open waist panel, which began to tear away.

"Oh!" Elin cried.

"You could have asked me," Rosamund said.

"I did!" Elin protested.

"You should have made it clear what, what . . ." Rosie searched for the right words. "What the situation was!"

"Surely you don't intend to wear it," I said.

Elin looked down at the dress. "You insisted I do the ashes first."

"We did not know help was needed"—I fingered the panel of the dress Mathilde had removed with little effort—"quite so badly."

"Might she borrow something?" Rosamund wondered.

"She cannot wear a dress that does not meet the requirements—the train, the neckline," I reminded. The uneven clatter of horse feet outside indicated Lavinia's carriage had arrived. "And we do not have enough time."

Elin's eyes glossed over, wet with tears. "I have nothing to wear."

"Well, you cannot wear that," Mathilde observed. She turned to me, plaintively. "She will be laughed out of the room. We will be laughed out of the room."

"She's right," I said. Then, more softly: "You cannot wear that to the ball. And we cannot keep the Enrights waiting."

Elin's tears spilled over.

I did not feel so sorry for her. Elin might have worked on her dress from the very beginning. She might have used the days we were at the picnic, at the market, in the fields picking apples. She might have told us sooner. At long last, she would see the consequences of her own ineptitude. But even this was only half true: All was not lost for Elin. To her, this was just one ball. A singular disappointing night. She, a pretty-faced daughter of a gentleman, also had an inheritance. Her life offered choices whereas my girls' lives were confined to a solitary opportunity. And I would not allow her to jeopardize their chances.

Her unfinished hems trembled as she swept back up the stairs. Rosie and Mathilde turned to me, questioning. Perhaps they had the same doubts. Perhaps I could have helped Elin more. Perhaps I should have spent more time looking for a solution. Perhaps I had smudged the line between self-preservation and cruelty.

But the Enrights were knocking at the door, and I could not overlook the fact that my stepdaughter had cost me my most prized possession.

IN THE ENRIGHTS' CARRIAGE, THERE WAS MUCH EMBRACING AND kissing of cheeks and exclaiming over one another's dresses. Lavinia had, ludicrously—for a man can only marry one woman—dressed the twins as she usually did: matching outfits.

She sat in between her daughters in the forward-facing seats, so I squeezed into the opposite side with Rosie and Mathilde, grateful that circumstances had kept Elin at home. There was hardly room. Our knees all met in the middle.

"Bethesda," I greeted one of the twins.

"Bethia," she corrected me.

"Bethia," I amended, nodding.

The other leaned forward. "Bethesda."

"Bethesda," I repeated.

"Girls," Lavinia said. "I need more air. You must move to give me a window." They stood and crouched and reshuffled, a frenzy of oversized hoopskirts and petticoats. When they had resettled, I realized I hadn't managed to track which twin sat where.

There was a two-hour carriage ride to sort it out.

AS WE APPROACHED THE CASTLE, AT LONG LAST, AN AFTERNOON OF waiting came to an end and all accelerated. The sky had gone dark. The path to the palace's walls was lit by a series of torches, and the large gate, surrounded by white-coated guards, stood open. Ahead of us, and behind us, there was carriage after carriage, like a strand of pearls.

We left our wraps in the carriage and, bare-shouldered, were handed down by royal footmen and ushered inside. The entry hall was filled with flowers and lit by hundreds of candles, moving pricks of light that danced in the chandeliers and sconces and on the many tables.

Gloved men and women gathered in groups, jostling for their moment of presentation. We lost Lavinia and her children in the crowd. Young women eyed one another, holding their trains over their arms, before they were ushered in small groups into the royal antechamber.

We moved closer to the double doors at the end of the chamber, awaiting our turn. My daughters were breathless and overwhelmed. Rosamund bloomed, spinning as she looked at the painted ceiling above. I gently pulled on her arm to still her. Mathilde had gone grim—her way of showing she understood how serious this all was. All over, mothers were muttering last-minute instructions into daughters' ears.

In the antechamber, an attendant helped each girl lower her train and smooth it behind her. We could partially see ahead, into the throne room, and watched as each was presented. Some simpered and smiled. Some held small bouquets or sprays of flowers. Some were so nervous they could barely speak.

"Where is the prince?" Rosamund whispered. "I do not see him."

"He must have stepped out." I fought dismay, for I did not see him, either. "Hush now."

Nervously, I pulled the girls aside, pretending we needed more time with their trains, waving other women ahead of us. Finally, when we could delay no longer, Rosie and Mathilde handed their cards to the herald at the door and we walked through, into the throne room.

SIGRID STOOD ON A RAISED PLATFORM WEARING THE LARGEST PAN-nier I had ever seen. Her hips extended by feet on each side. A jewel the size of an egg hung from a necklace. We moved forward, into the stronger light, as the herald announced us.

"Miss Rosamund Tremaine and Miss Mathilde Tremaine of Bram-ley Hall," the herald announced. "Chaperoned by Lady Etheldreda Bramley." The three of us sank into curtsies.

Sigrid watched with interest. "Why, they look just like you, Ethel-dreda. Who would have thought there could be three of you."

Behind us, I felt the room tighten with attention: The queen was talking.

"Indeed, Your Majesty." I stood back up. "Though I see their father as well." All the ghosts of Agatha's little wounds were making themselves known to me. A throbbing in my knuckles. The feel of fingers grasping my upper arm.

"So, Henry's daughters have made it to my ball after all." Sigrid's expression was unreadable, but my attention went to Rosie and Mathilde, whose necks had gone taut. I could not see their faces, but I watched the discomfort in their shoulders. They had not expected mention of their father—had not expected to be singled out by the queen.

"We are honored," I replied without smiling.

Sigrid laughed. "I am sure of it. Where is the third? The . . . half daughter? Stepdaughter?"

"Ill," I said, too quickly. I wanted to ask where Simeon was but couldn't bring myself to reveal my interests. Instead, I added: "I hope we will have the honor of greeting the princess as well?"

"Ill," Sigrid replied, mimicking the same intonation of my own invocation of the word.

All three of us, Rosie, Mathilde, and I, made the quick implied noises of sympathy the occasion demanded, but we were saved from formulating any real response when a side door opened—a disguised panel springing forth from the wall—and the prince entered. He strode to his mother's side, turned, and saw us.

"Hello," he said, in a tone of both surprise and familiarity—one that threw the room into quick relief. Agatha released her tight grip on my arm. The girls, wrapped and cosseted in all their finery, goose bumps on their shoulders, loosened. How the inflection of one word could promise the world! So much was riding on a moment—a bat of an eye, a gesture with a wrist. All of us curtsied, murmuring quietly.

Sigrid covered a look of momentary consternation—she had not known we knew her son—gratifying my hurt pride. But the small satisfaction was somewhat nullified when the queen put a hand on the prince's arm. It was an intimate gesture, the worrying, rubbing grasp of a mother—the unconscious bid to secure your child to you, to confirm them, to feel them. What devotion could be communicated in such small friction. It was my first moment of viewing them side by side, and understanding, more instinctively and less rationally, the extent of their connection. They looked so alike. That yellow hair. The same curved pull at their lips. A question started to form in my mind, an uneasy prickle, but the prince shrugged his mother away and sauntered two steps toward us before I had a moment to examine my feelings. "Splendid of you to come," he said, stopping in front of Rosie.

She looked back to me, as if for confirmation, face aglow. "Your Highness," she replied, turning.

He gestured toward the ballroom doors. "I just have to finish all this"—a wave of a hand in the air, insouciant and suggestive of plenary and oppressive duty—"and then we will dance."

We, he had said. A promise. A delightful, fat little promise that offered the possibility of an entire kingdom. I couldn't meet Sigrid's eyes, for I did not want to see anything on her face that denied it.

The attendant had ushered in another girl behind us, and we took our cue to step forward. Rosie and Mathilde kneeled. Sigrid held out two gloved hands and they kissed her knuckles. I was distracted from the discomfort of this—my daughters, kneeling, before Sigrid— because I noticed her glove did not have an empty finger. It must have been stuffed with cotton. A small vanity reminiscent of a lace ribbon tied to a blood-spotted bandage.

It was all over quickly. We were soon backing from the room, making way for the next round of girls in feathers, pushed along like jewels on a strand, the great moment behind us.

My daughters' eyes widened as they took in the ballroom. Skirts made from every manner of silk and brocade swirled and swayed across the dance floor. Sumptuous drapes partially shrouded an entire wall of enormous windows. Oversized mirrors reflected countless chandeliers and sprays of flowers. Silver and crystal-laden banquettes supported towers of exotic sugared fruits and spherical pastries. Wealth had been measured and displayed in every manner of sugar and glass.

"The music!" Rosamund clapped her hands. Her curled hair sat in a luxurious pile on her head, escaping tendrils prettily framing her beaming face. She looked with delight at the orchestra playing at the other end of the room.

"There is so much food." Mathilde surveyed the banquettes. "Without there being much to actually eat." Along the edges of the dance floor, tables were covered in cascading bowls of punch and molded blancmange and goblets of mulled wine. Tureens of white soup—punch made from veal broth, cream, and ground almonds—steamed beside jellies and sweetmeats and platters of small biscuits and light wafers.

"Do not eat the prawns," I told them, eyeing the towers of shrimp. "If you must use the facilities, make sure you are accompanied at all times. And do not drink too much punch. You must not dance with unknown men. But do not refuse a dance if you are asked. Try not to be a wallflower. Avoid dark-colored liquids for the sake of your dresses. And I know it is your first ball, but *try* not to look gobsmacked, Rosie. And try to show some felicity, Mathilde."

"But I am gobsmacked," Rosie whispered, the light of a hundred chandeliers reflecting in her eyes.

"And it is hard to feel felicitous when you have persistently emphasized the great import of this evening," Mathilde accused me.

"Then pretend. Obviously." I widened my eyes back at them. "You must be presentable."

"Yes, Mama," Rosie said.

Mathilde put a pretty smile on her face. "Had I been aware that being presentable entailed diminishing one's sentiments to the point of insignificance . . . perchance I would have refrained from harboring any at all."

"Oh, hush," I snapped, for Lavinia had spotted us and was making her way over, daughters in tow. "And do not dance with just anyone, for your evening will get full and you won't be able to accept a dance with the prince."

"You have told us both to dance and not to dance, to avoid men and to accept them." Mathilde counted these instructions off on her fingers.

Rosie interrupted her, tugging on my sleeve plaintively, like a small girl. "Do you really think the prince will dance with me?"

"I think you have reason enough to hope for a dance—with him and any other eligible man."

We waited as Lavinia closed the final few yards between us. "Well, that was quite an ordeal," she exclaimed, fanning herself. "So many young women waiting in the antechamber! Girls, sure, but how about us mothers? Nowhere to sit and not a chair in sight. My knees were just screaming."

Bouncing on her toes, she continued: "But it went well. It went well. Did it not go well, Beth?" She tossed a glance over her shoulder at the twins. "I hope your girls fared as well as mine. The prince was not in the receiving room, but I do think the queen noticed them. Or at least noticed the pompons they wear in their hair, for I had the queen's own coiffeur fashion them." She turned to survey the room. "Good heavens, what a scene. No expense spared; you can see for yourself."

Addressing her daughters, she began to gesticulate toward the dancing. "Girls, girls. Beth. Take a turn around the room so that people might admire your figures."

The twins glanced at one another, alarmed.

"Go on, go on. Beth, go!" Lavinia began a shooing motion with her fan, the feathers quivering.

Rosamund stepped forward, offering her arm to one of them. "Come with me. I'll join you." Bethia—Bethesda?—looked up at her gratefully.

Mathilde looked at the other twin, resigned. "Come along, then."

The first twin—Bethesda, I had decided—leaned toward Rosie, nodding down at her dress. "Such delicate needlework. You must share your seamstress."

"Why, thank you! I made—" Rosie caught my look and stopped herself short. "I am ever so appreciative." She glanced back and forth between the twins. "Yours—both of yours—are ... the height of refinement."

Lavinia nodded, satisfied. But, a moment later, watching her daughters' pompons disappear into the crowd, she leaned in to my side and whispered: "If you call them both Beth, you never need tell them apart."

☙

THE DANCING CONTINUED AS THE NUMBER OF PEOPLE IN THE BALL-room swelled. So many young women. So many best dresses and herb-filled baths and rouged cheeks and cinched waists and dance lessons. A while later, when the prince had finished receiving, I could feel the hope in the room crescendo, every person waiting to see what would happen. The room did not hush, or quiet, when he appeared, but rather increased in its intense energy, the music picking up speed, the awareness of every person finely tuned to his royal presence. And so it was under the watchful eyes of an entire ball of people that the prince strode over to one of the banquettes and began to eat goose liver tart.

Sigrid went over to the dais and sat, the chairs around her quickly filling with courtiers and attendants and Otto Abensur, who had discarded his longsword for formalwear. They watched from the platform as the prince danced his first dance with a curly-haired girl I did not know.

"A cousin." Lavinia sniffed. "And not one to worry about."

For all my girls' gawking, I myself had never seen a ball like this. The dances in my hometown were held in the tavern hall and accompanied by a fiddler. It was not just the marriage-eligible on their feet, but young women and old, stomping their latchets and hooking arms to folk dances our parents' parents had danced as well. And, in later years with Henry, and then Robert, I had seen plenty of fancy gatherings—dozens of dishes at each course of a meal, peacock served alongside an

entire pig, women in velvet and fringe—but none that held a candle
to a royal ball, none that could compete with floor-to-ceiling opulence,
all-encompassing riches, and enough polished silver to sink a warship.

I took a glass of claret from the tray of a passing attendant, trying to
find my daughters in the room. Those dancing in the middle, performing
a slower processional, blocked my view. But then the music came to an
end and the dance floor emptied for a break. In the clearing, I was able
to see Rosie and Mathilde, both holding porcelain cups of punch, standing in a small circle of women that also included the twins. I couldn't
hear them, but I could see that Mathilde was talking and Rosie was
laughing, and they looked comfortable, and it felt, in watching their ease
from thirty feet away, that all we had sacrificed, all the stitches, and the
apples, and the performing, just might have been worth it. I'd wanted
this for them, and here they were, looking resplendent and fitting into
the room like a continuation of its sumptuous ornamentation.

I was so caught up in experiencing their pleasure from afar that I
did not notice the prince approach Rosie until he was in front of her.
From his every gesture—an offer of his right hand, extending across
the space between them—it was apparent that he had asked Rosie to
dance. This was confirmed when she placed her hand in his and he
led her onto the dance floor. I couldn't see her face. I wondered if it
mirrored mine.

Beside me, Lavinia clutched my upper arm. "My God," she breathed.
"The prince, Etheldreda, the *prince* has asked your Rosamund to dance."

"I can see that," I said, implacably. But inside, I was frothing over,
glowing, uncontained.

"Your younger daughter, at that."

I quickly glanced at Mathilde, who was now holding her sister's
saucer in addition to her own. But she did not appear upset.

"Rosamund is not wearing pompons." Lavinia sounded concerned.
"I wonder, do you think Prince Simeon prefers a more natural look?"
She glanced over at her twins, whose oversized headdresses stood out
from the crowd at the edge of the dance floor.

"I am sure the prince feels there is a time and place for pompons," I assured her. I wanted to extract myself so I could watch all that happened. I wanted to see every little twitch of Simeon's face, each intimation. I wanted to stand by and study—

Otto stepped in front of me. "Lady Tremaine."

Beside me, Lavinia looked confused. "Bramley," I corrected, eyeing her.

He did not look at Lavinia. "I must apologize again for my behavior the other day—"

"Not necessary," I interrupted, for he was blocking my view of the prince, and the dance was about to start.

"It is," he said. "Necessary." He paused. "May I have the next dance?"

"Oh!" Lavinia said, voicing the same surprise I felt. I was glad I had not yet introduced her.

"Dance?" I echoed.

He extended his hand, and I looked down at it, and then back up at him. The music had already begun. I could not leave the man with his hand extended in front of a room of people. Still stiff from the initial surprise of his question, I put my hand into his, glove nestled against glove, and let him lead me to the edge of the dance floor.

Across the room, Mathilde still stood with two cups. I caught her eye, and she looked back at me, astonished to see me amongst those preparing to dance. I tried to show with a lift of my shoulders that it could not be helped. The music began: a sarabande. The slow tempo of the solemn dance was suitable for Otto and I, but not what I would have chosen for Rosie. I concentrated on remembering the steps.

As if doing the same, Otto did not speak for a good amount of time. Finally, he said: "I am afraid I not only lack practice in charm, but also in dancing."

Over his shoulder, I could see Rosie and Simeon moving down the row of people, each of them with long arms extended in the shape of the neck of a swan. Sigrid watched it all from a raised dais at the center of the room, face unreadable. Heartened, I arched my eyebrows at Otto.

"I often think that dancing is nothing but a series of steps to learn. Memorization. But then I remember someone had to create those steps in the first place. That very first dance, I would wager, is real dancing." My good spirits—Rosie, dancing with the prince!—and perhaps the claret had loosened my tongue. I found I was, momentarily at least, willing to overlook my dislike of Otto.

He shook his head. "If I were to design a new dance at this moment, no one in the room would consider dancing with me again."

I laughed, in spite of myself. "Tell me," I said, pausing for a moment when we moved apart. When the steps brought us back together, I continued. "Dancing aside, do you enjoy a ball?"

"I am here in official capacity."

I was amused by his seriousness. "Are you dancing with me in official capacity?"

"No." I thought I felt his hand tighten slightly on mine but could not be sure. "I am dancing with you as a guest."

I tilted my head, looking at him more closely. Otto as a dancing partner was an entirely different proposition than Otto as a royal bloodhound. His leather boots had been replaced with fine ones shined to a high polish. And despite his severe face, somewhat marred by a perpetual scowl, he cut a smart figure in formalwear. With the exception of Moussa's instruction during the girls' dance lessons, it had been some time since I had been in such proximity to a man. Our hands were gloved, but each touch had a certain kind of power, a muffled memory of a kind of dancing that had little to do with choreography.

I said: "That is unfortunate."

He stiffened, taken aback.

"For to be two things at once—both a guest and an official—means you are never fully either. May I make a suggestion?" I did not wait for him to reply. "You should alternate and enjoy each more fully."

He did not respond immediately. On the other side of the dancers, I saw Rosie executing her steps with ease, smiling at something Prince

Simeon said into her ear. Sigrid had disappeared from the dais. All around the edges of the dance floor eyes followed the prince and ignored me and I was glad of it.

After a time, Otto said: "You may be correct, but I fear if I were only a guest and not an official, I would have no reason to be at the ball in the first place."

"You dance but do not like to. Is it," I wondered aloud, "that you do not approve of a ball?" I remembered how, the day he had escorted me from Sigrid's chambers, he had scoffed at the delivery of invitations to women in fanciful dresses. Now he was surrounded by hundreds of them.

His face held a trace of a scowl. "My approval is irrelevant."

"I disagree," I said with false solemnity. "One's approval is something they should hold in the highest of esteem; it's a personal treasure! Mine, for example, is like a favorite pet. I tend to it and offer it to others only in very specific circumstances."

I almost got him to smile.

"I am not a young girl of marriageable age," he explained to me.

"Do not sell yourself short."

"And I do not think it is the best way to choose a wife."

Involuntarily, I looked over at Prince Simeon and Rosie.

"The determinants of success in a marriage have little to do with receiving lines and dancing and"—he glanced around the room—"white soup."

"Do you really think this has no use?" I was surprised. "A kingdom has, at its center, a king, as Prince Simeon will become. And every tureen and candle and cream puff in this room is doing a part in ensuring he feels like a jewel at the center of it all."

"And who does not want a jewel?" Otto murmured, more to himself than to me. The dance was coming to an end, and we slowed, turning to face one another.

"But we agree on one thing," I told him, when the music stopped. "White soup is disgusting."

Otto returned me to the same spot he had taken me from, bowed, and walked away. I was a little breathless—from the dancing and from the conversation—and took a glass of sparkling wine from a banquette. Our conversation was not a dialogue I had expected to have, nor with a person I ever would have expected to have it. But it was a distraction from the most important matter at hand. I needed to find Rosamund and hear her retelling of every moment on the dance floor, every sentence uttered by the prince.

Lavinia located me first. "Well," she said, muttering, until she had sidled right up to my ear, which she whispered loudly into. "Who shall you dance with next? The prince?" She chortled.

"I think that was quite enough dancing for me," I admitted. I scanned the room, looking, still, for Rosie.

"I have surveyed the powers that be—the little birds—and the man you danced with is held in high esteem. How did you manage it? He is even feared. And his jaw is handsome. Handsome indeed."

I did not need to put quite the same stock in jaws as Lavinia. "He is a curmudgeon that does not recommend himself and does not like dancing."

"Plenty of eligible men here for you, too, you know. Quite! Indeed." She nodded to herself. "Widowers, for one. Take Sir Pike down there."

I eyed the ailing man leaning on a cane at the end of the room. "Sir Pike is two hundred years old."

"Brevity may be the point, dear Etheldreda," Lavinia admonished.

"I have been married twice." I took a swig from my coupe. *Tiny sips*, Agatha reminded me. "I am done childbearing, and the estate has expensive upkeep." It was the closest I could acknowledge to the truth of my situation. I had spotted my daughters—again happily engaged in a group of young people—and wanted to get away from Lavinia's needling. I held up my empty glass. "Too much wine, I believe. Excuse me, I am going to get some air."

WHEN I WAS OUT OF HER SIGHT, I STEPPED INTO ONE OF THE RE-cessed windows in the room, concealing myself behind the cascading drapes. I did not want to be asked to dance again. I did not want to be pestered by Lavinia. I wanted to watch my daughters in their happiness and to hope for the best and to believe, truly, that there was a way out of the squalor we lived in, that our circumstances would change, that this wouldn't become the one ball we had once attended that we talked about until we were ragged and gray. There was so much wealth in the room—of beauty, of feeling—surely there was enough for us, too?

I cracked the window, enjoying the cool air on my neck. I felt a little lightheaded. As I watched Rosie dance, the hope in my breast had become so alive that it was painful—more of a needful kind of want than I had ever experienced. The pain of two dead husbands and a crumbling house and a life constructed on a thousand lies. Oh, to see her well. To see her secure.

I took another sip of wine, observing the movements and tides of the room from a crack behind the curtain. There was a break in the dancing. The guests milled, gossiping and squealing with each renewed acquaintance. Rosie and Mathilde appeared to be holding court with a gaggle of fashionable young people. Rosie was pointing to the stays of her dress, likely explaining its construction. A young man nearby vomited into a potted plant. A woman's earring fell into her punch glass and had to be fished out.

My happiness also felt like a kind of sadness: the letdown of realizing a rehearsal was actually a final performance. We had done it. We had ended up here. My daughter, a few moments before, had been in the arms of a prince. But all her gains would be my loss. I did not want to give her up. I thought about Rosie's sweet smile. I thought about Otto's shiny shoes. And it was no sooner than I thought of them that I noticed them on the ground, in front of me. On the other side of the drapes.

"All is as expected," Otto said. Not to me. Alarmed, I took a step back, completely concealing myself.

"He is behaving himself, at least." A woman's voice.

"Aye, Your Majesty."

I realized, with no small horror, that he was talking to the queen. And neither had any idea I was standing in the recess behind them.

"There are plenty of pretty girls here to choose from," Sigrid said.

"Yes," Otto agreed.

"Otto," Sigrid said, with great familiarity and teasing. "Your role is not to agree with everything I say."

"I'll disagree when I disagree."

"Make sure he dances with more girls."

"As you said, there are plenty of pretty faces."

"He needs more than a pretty face."

"Yes." Otto's voice became more serious. "He needs someone who is a suitable match . . . in every sensibility."

"I saw that he knows the Tremaine girl." Sigrid paused and I could feel my heart pick up. "Yes. Her." I could not see but I imagined they were gesticulating around the room. I imagined Rosie, unaware she had caught the queen's attention. "They danced."

"They are acquainted," Otto acknowledged. I realized the queen knew nothing of the picnic and broken cart and delivery of the oil painting—and Otto had not used the opportunity to tell her.

"I knew their mother. Let me just say that apples do not fall far."

I leaned forward.

"Neither of the Tremaine daughters is a suitable match," Otto said, severely. "We should do all we can to discourage the acquaintance."

I put a hand over my mouth.

Not a suitable match! The effrontery—

"You are probably right." Sigrid sounded bored. "I'll put an end to any interest."

If there had been luck left in the evening, they would have moved on, but the music picked up again and the conversation continued, and I was trapped there, unable to hear full sentences, and unable to move, burning at what I'd heard and fearful I'd be discovered.

The nerve of the man. I felt furious, then insulted, my heart hammering—and then remembered my own run-in with Otto in the woods. I had been stupid to think an evening of beautiful dresses could erase the impression of a muddied woman. Had it been my own rule-breaking that led me here? Had my own actions cursed the possibility of everything I ever wanted? The noise and warmth of the room tilted on me. I turned, quietly, and pushed my head through the open window, gulping in the cold night air.

I had, from above, a fine view of all the palace's grounds. The neatly trimmed topiaries, the many fountains. The outer wall that curved like a snake in motion, containing so much manicured splendor. I had been foolish to think such loveliness was within my reach, that my pinching and prodding might amount to anything at all. How many times would I have to relearn? Dreams by their definition were impermanent.

I saw moonlight reflecting in shallow pools, and, down along the east side of the castle, a wall that contained a trellised garden and a number of roses—bare and trimmed in the season. The stone wall attached to the palace itself, with no gates or gaps or arches. A peculiarity, for it meant the garden inside was entirely inaccessible. I thought of all the curtains that had been pulled shut, darkening any chance of a view, on all the east-facing windows. Even inside a palace, there were realms and rings and hierarchies. Secrets that had been bricked over.

Beneath my window, the line of carriages had dwindled. But another one, a familiar shape, was heading up the path. I watched it, disbelieving, for it was decorated in gold and pulled by two white steeds. When it was close enough, my suspicions were confirmed: It was the same shape as Moussa's carriage. And Moussa was driving it.

"It can't be," I breathed, forgetting myself. "She wouldn't dare."

The carriage, a few days before, had carried apples. That night, it carried Elin. She emerged, not in her wine-colored scraps, but in a dress of the palest blue. I thought of Henry. I thought of the smell of mint and two cups nestled. I thought I might throw up.

It was my wedding dress.

CHAPTER TWENTY

I THINK OF MY WEDDING DAY IN A FEW BROAD STROKES: ME, CAREful not to dirty the hem of that organza dress of the palest blue. Henry, hair clean and clear-eyed. Saying goodbye to my father and brother and house, a palm held flat on the wall of my childhood bedchamber. And then that blue dress falling to its puddle on the floor, only to be put into my trunk and accompany us on our six-day journey. Later, it was moved to our leased estate. And then it came with me to Robert's.

It had stayed tucked into the travel chest. I had not seen the blue organza in some time. I could not look at those buttons without thinking of the hands that had undone them. And so, I had kept it bundled in the paper, safely stowed for a day when seeing it on one of Henry's daughters—*our* daughters—might restore some of the same happiness I'd felt the only time I had worn it.

Grief has an uncanny ability to unexpectedly overwhelm. To pull memory—the feel of that organza, the warmth of a man's fingers on skin—to the forefront. As I stood in the alcove, trapped behind the curtain, grief wrapped its gray hands around my heart and squeezed, the feeling rising from my breast and into my throat. How could a person live with such pain without the knowledge that it would dissipate? Anger helped. I wanted nothing more than to run from the alcove and confront Elin in the antechamber. But I was still trapped by Otto and Sigrid, who stood in front of the drapes.

Their presence turned my small alcove into a prison—albeit one with a view of the room I was itching to make my way across. I could see, perfectly clearly through the crack in the curtains, when Elin appeared in the double doors of the ballroom.

She stood alone, silhouetted by the massive doors, her pale shoulders warmed by the candlelight. She had somehow altered the wedding dress. She was so much shorter than I. Inches were missing from the bottom, though the train lay intact, dragging behind her. The sleeves were gone, her arms bare to the tops of the long gloves. Her appearance was timed to the end of the dance, and as the guests streamed off the dance floor, the herald's announcement of her entrance rang across the room.

Hundreds of faces turned to look at her. The beautiful latecomer. The strange guest.

She peered back at the room, at all the people, up at the chandeliers, over at the banquettes, and then, wide-eyed, to the sky. Unblinking eyes taking in hundreds of candles. Thousands of flowers. And countless eyes looking back at her.

"Don't do it," I whispered.

"Who is *that*?" Sigrid wondered aloud, in front of the curtain.

"Don't you dare," I breathed.

But Elin did. She fell, a dead faint, straight to the ground.

THE HUBBUB AND CONVERSATION THAT RIPPLED THROUGH THE ROOM was enough to dislodge Otto and Sigrid. They moved forward with the swell of the crowd, and I was able to step out from my hiding place, joining the surge of people. I weaved through the onlookers, trying to see what was happening ahead, and looking for Rosie and Mathilde.

The crowd parted. Prince Simeon was striding across the room, with purpose. Something inside of my chest hitched, and then tightened when I saw him reach his destination and look, with interest, down at the collapsed woman.

Lavinia appeared at my side. "My wonder," she observed. "That is your Elin."

"It is." I craned my head to see.

"She dusted off nicely."

"She did." I wanted, suddenly, to sit down.

"She is lying on the floor."

"She is."

"Will she be all right?"

"She will."

"That blue makes her eyes look like pure sapphires! And now the prince is helping her."

I felt unable to have a proper conversation. I didn't want to look anymore. I wanted to rip the dress off Elin's body, and anger left un-quelled for too many moments begins to feel like poison in your system.

Simeon was helping Elin stand, a hand on her waist. The room watched as he offered her a sip of punch. She blushed and accepted. The music started once more. The crowd pretended to disperse. The prince took Elin's hand and led her to the center of the ballroom.

THREE DANCES LATER—EACH OF WHICH SIMEON HAD SPENT WITH Elin pressed to his side—Rosie and Mathilde found me in the side room.

"Where did she get the dress?" Mathilde wondered, bewildered. Rosie sank into the chair next to me.

I shook my head. "She must have gone up to the attic and into my trunk."

Rosie's voice broke. "How did she even get here?"

"I haven't a clue." I was perplexed myself. Where had Moussa gotten the white horses? What had transformed the carriage?

"It is just a dance—right, Mama?" Rosie asked.

"Just a few dances." I shook off my stupor and sat up. "And you." I turned to clutch her hand. "Tell me about *your* dance. What did Prince Simeon say?"

"We hardly talked! We were dancing." She started to say more, but her voice had taken on the crimped sound of someone trying not to cry. She stopped herself.

"Rosie," Mathilde said, softly. "There are plenty of other eligible men in the room. If you are in here, they won't be able to see you."

I nodded at Mathilde, agreeing, though the prospect felt cumbersome, and the hour was late.

"Yes, but . . ." Rosie looked down at her lap. "The one I want to dance with isn't interested anymore."

"You don't know that," Mathilde protested.

Her sister gathered her skirt in her hands. "Should I have worn blue?"

Rosie's wet eyes and dashed hopes pained me, enough that I could set aside my own disappointments. I took one of her hands. "Oh, darling. He was always going to dance with other women. That doesn't diminish his interest in you. He could hardly dance with one person for the entire night. And he picked you first. After his cousin, that is."

"There's not a girl here in a prettier dress than you," Mathilde offered.

But it only caused Rosie's tears to spill over. "I could not bear it if he chooses her."

"He will not," I said, but I had a suspicion that making the promise would undermine all my others.

When we came back into the ballroom, Elin and Simeon were still partnered on the dance floor. The mirrors reflected them back and forth, so that, from our vantage point, we were surrounded by infinite Elins and princes—a glass ball that extended to eternity. The dissonance of watching my hopes fulfilled, but with the wrong daughter, was like listening to a song I knew played in the wrong key.

By morning it was the talk of the kingdom: The prince had danced with Elin, and only Elin, for the rest of the night.

CHAPTER TWENTY-ONE

ARLY IN THE MORNING, I WENT TO LUCY. SHE WAS STILL ASLEEP on her perch—shoulders dropped, eyes closed, wings crossed over her back, one foot invisibly tucked up inside of her feathers. Such peace. Utter stillness. The light just breaking, the interior of the mews dark. If I found my falcon spectacular in the midst of a hunt—the thrill of a fast-paced stoop, fledged body hurtling through air—in slumber, she was breathtaking. A statue's stillness belying predatory might. I wanted to reach out and touch her, to run two fingers along her feathered breast, but some inner hawk's sense alerted her to my presence, and she was up, head high, staring at me with flinty eyes.

"Morning," I said, mildly.

She blinked at me.

"I see you've not made your castings." I gestured down at the ground, which was empty save for the chalky excrement beneath her perch. "And you know very well I cannot take you out to hunt until you do."

Lucy fluffed the downy feathers of her neck.

"We'll keep up your carriage, then, and go for a short walk." I nodded, as if she'd suggested the idea. Using one hand to untie the falconer's knot that kept her on the perch, I extended the other—gloved—and she hopped on, mantling her wings for a moment before settling on the gauntlet. Properly secured, she clenched her formidable talons tightly on the leather.

Back outside in the gloam, we went along the edge of the orchard. Lucy's face turned to a sky that threatened rain. We walked until I could see Moussa's coach dimly lit in the trees ahead of us. I slowed and stopped and looked over at my bird. She looked back at me and, steadily, turned her head sideways, then completely upside down, so her beak was to the sky.

"Lucy!" I said, in delight. She had not played in such a way since she was young. Without taking my eyes off her, I reached out and plucked a dead leaf from the nearest tree. She righted herself and took it in her beak in one swift movement, crunching on the foliage, and then, after a few noisy munches, tossed it into the air. The pieces fell around my feet in a tiny cascade.

Enthralled, I plucked a second leaf and watched as Lucy repeated the game. The crunching, then the scattering of the pieces.

"You are just what I needed," I told her. Less enthusiastically, I reverted my gaze back to the jongleur's camp. "Now, let us hasten to conclude this whole affair."

When we got a bit closer, I saw that Moussa's coach had been turned into a poor facsimile of a wealthy man's carriage. He had used gold paint to make the wooden frame look gilded. And the curtains and drapes I had seen from a distance were just sheets of canvas that had been tacked inside of the windows. Moussa was wiping paint from the door of the carriage, removing a poorly drawn coat of arms.

"It is amazing," I said, when I was close enough, keeping Lucy near my body, "what can be passed off as opulent in the absence of informed comparison."

"And with darkness as an aid. I added apples," he told me, gesturing to the heraldic symbols in front of him. "For the apples, of course. And a bird for Lucy." He nodded to the falcon. "Morning, Luce."

"No one has apples in their family crest." I frowned. "And Elin already has a crest. It's on the lintels."

"This is *your* family crest," he explained.

"Moussa." I exhaled. "How could you?"

After we'd gotten back the night before, I'd waited until I heard his carriage return. He'd driven Elin all the way up the drive to the front door, and she had exited and slipped inside. I didn't leave my room to welcome or confront her, but it was only after they were home that I allowed myself to sleep.

Moussa dropped his rag and stood, slowly, a hand on his back.

"Do not give me that routine now," I scolded. "You should have discussed it with me!"

"It was just a bit of theater," he protested, straightening. "You'd already left. You said she was allowed to attend. I merely attended to her attending."

"You ferried her without a chaperone—without my knowledge. Without a modicum of sense!" Ever attuned to my emotions, Lucy tightened her talons on the glove. "And how? Was it a plan all along?"

He twisted his beard. "We improvised! She altered her dress with pins, and I worked on the carriage."

"And where did the horses come from?"

Moussa gestured over at Lucky, who was munching clover under an apple tree. "And Arno, too. I used wig powder and wheat starch. Enough until they shone in the moonlight."

I felt the beginning of a throbbing in my temples. "Do not mistake a bit of cider and a place to sleep as an invitation to involve yourself in such ways."

"She'd perfected her minuet just so." He dropped his eyes and gestured at his carriage. "Do not worry. I am leaving this day."

"Yes," I told him, already turning to take Lucy back to the mews. "Best not to linger."

A short while later, when I heard—then saw—the royal carriage through the window, I allowed myself the briefest moment of hope. One cannot help but wonder if a congealed romantic interest may change their mind. Perhaps, I reasoned, Simeon had come for Rosamund after all. Perhaps he had worried over her sudden departure. Perhaps absence does impact the heart, or at least draw its spotlight. But when the prince emerged from the open mouth of his coach, his first words were: "You did not tell me there was another sister!"

I had come outside alone to receive him, hastily untying my apron and storing it behind a tapestry, doing my best to smooth my hair and cover a housedress with a more elegant mantle I placed over my shoulders. I had no idea of the state of the rooms inside, though I could say with certainty none was fit to entertain a prince.

"We cannot keep track of ourselves," I said, from the depths of my curtsy. When I rose, I saw that Simeon was still in his clothing from the ball. He couldn't have slept, I realized, if he was arriving at our home so early.

"Lady Elin lives here." He eyed the house behind me.

"Welcome to Bramley Hall," I confirmed, and watched, in surprise, as Otto climbed through the door behind him, like a spider I couldn't rid myself of. He nodded at me without meeting my eyes and my breakfast soured in my stomach. *Not suitable.* Of course he had come. Of course he stood at Prince Simeon's side. Of course the loyal bloodhound was the only one wearing a smart set of clean clothes.

I realized the prince was waiting for me to speak.

"Elin is inside and, I apologize, but still abed," I explained. "She has not finished her toilette."

"I'll wait for her," the prince said, gesturing vaguely toward the house.

"Wait?" I repeated. Otto watched me, expressionless.

"Yes. I will wait until she has finished her toilette," he explained, gently, as though talking to a child. And indeed, I did feel a bit stupefied.

"We are honored by your visit . . . Your Royal Highness." I was delaying the inevitable.

Simeon kicked a pebble with the toe of his boot. "Perhaps you will let her know?"

Otto cleared his throat.

"Of course." I nodded. "I'll let her know at once."

Inside, Wenthelen and Alice were huddled in the entryway, trying to watch through the crack of the door.

"Shoo," I told them.

"He asked to see Elin," Wenthelen whispered, delighted. She turned from the door and stayed close at my heels. "Our Elin!"

"What happened at that ball?" Alice demanded, stepping in front of me. They had not yet heard us recount the whole story—but they had been kept up half the night by Rosie's incessant weeping.

"I do not believe for one minute that you didn't help Elin ready last night." I glared at both of them, looking up at Alice and then down at Wenthelen. "So you know very well that Elin managed to come after all."

"Of course we helped her. What else would we do!" Wenthelen tutted at me and went back to the door.

Alice frowned. "The girl deserves the same chances as her sisters."

"She has more chances—" I began.

But Wenthelen, nose back in the crack, cried out: "Oh, he is handsome as ever. A face as sweet as a lamb. What does he want with Elin?"

"What does a man ever want with a girl?" Alice retorted.

I stepped around her.

"Shush," I whispered, heading up the stairs. "I will have plenty of words for you both later. Do not wake Rosie or Mathilde. If they rise, tell them to stay in their rooms. And ready some coffee. More than one of us will soon need it."

When I was out of sight, I picked up my pace, hurrying quickly through the house, down the hall, and toward the tower keep.

Not suitable. I heard Otto's words in my mind again. Did they apply, only, to my Tremaine girls? Was Elin exempt from the same contempt? I wished I might have been able to nurse this wound in peace. To have better protected Rosie and Mathilde from judgment. To have never seen those blue buttons fastened around Elin's torso.

Once again, I had to duck my head to get into her room.

"Get dressed," I told her, for she was still under her quilts. "The royal carriage is here. For you."

She sat up, her colorless hair tumbling down around her shoulders. "The prince?"

"The prince," I confirmed. "And you're still abed."

She pulled the covers back hastily. "I was embracing the stillness of the morning for clarity of mind." Going to a basin of water, she began to wash with a cloth. She made a face at the temperature, and then kept going.

I walked to her dressing area and saw the sky-colored wedding dress, hanging from a peg. I touched its hem. "Though it should hardly surprise you after last night." Turning, I glared at her.

She turned, and hurriedly began to undress, pulling off her sleeping gown. The interest of a prince had stripped her of her modesty. Her skin looked nearly blue. Her nipples pebbled. So thin I could see the articulation of each rib and knob of her spine as her hands searched out the sleeves of her smock.

"You are upset that I came?" Her face emerged through the neck of the undergarment.

I handed her a pair of stockings. "You wore my dress."

She sat to pull them on, the white silk climbing her calves like a snake shedding its skin in reverse. "It was in the trunk in the attic—"

"It was my wedding dress," I hissed.

"No." She paused, one leg extended in front of her, toes pointed. "You wore green." The stocking went up and over her knee. "I remember."

I picked up her basquine. "Hurry," I told her. She stepped in, and I began to work on the laces on the back. "Not my wedding to your father." I pulled the laces and then pulled them tighter. Elin exhaled a mouth of air. "My first wedding. To the girls' father." With a final vicious tug, I fastened the knot.

"I did not know," she protested, stepping into her petticoat. "Ignorance persists where ignorance dwells. You had said there was a trunk of my mother's things in the attic. And then I found yours gathering dust and did not think you would mind so much. The dress had a train and bare shoulders. It was out of necessity. How else would I have gone to the ball?" She went to the deep-set window. "How else would I have met the prince?" She turned back to me. "Let us set our sights on loftier ideals. Would you really deny me my happiness over a dress?"

I grabbed her kirtle in a fist and thrust it toward her. "I have never denied you a single thing."

She took the bundle from me. "Except going to the ball."

"Which you went to." I picked up what remained of my blue dress from the peg it hung on, gathering its folds into my arms.

"And you did little to support me—me, who has lacked a family since I was eight years old! When all I want is to make a new family, my own family, once I am married."

I held the dress against my chest, taken aback. "You have repeatedly been offered a family—this family!"

She shook her head. "It does not work that way. Families are not offered or negotiated. A woman—" She reached for her book, which sat on the end of her bed.

I spoke before she could begin quoting at me. "Of course families are negotiated. We are all in negotiation. A marriage begins with negotiation and continues to be one. And that is if fortune smiles upon you! If you are not viewed as chattel, or property. Do you really think it will be so simple? You will go to one ball, and your world of sorrow will be resolved in a single stroke?"

Her eyes darted to the foot of the bed. "A good wife is a man's best wealth."

"You stupid girl." I shook my head. "For even if that is true and there is a prince downstairs, you are not yet anyone's wife and you still live here with us." I went to the door, unable to stomach any more from her. I did not look over my shoulder as I told Elin: "Be downstairs in three minutes and no later."

I STOPPED IN MY OWN ROOM TO LAY THE DRESS ON MY BED, TAKING care with the fabric and folds. The organza had not lost its color, though it had gained the brittle, stuffy smell of years in storage. I could not check for the stains since the sleeves were missing. Rubbing the cloth between my fingers, I wished I could unstitch so much of what had happened. I thought of Otto's shiny shoes, stomping beside mine on the dance floor. Of Mathilde's gray eyes, searching my own for reassurance and answers. Of the yellow dress my daughters had made me. Of the blue one, that had been entwined with it all. Mostly, I thought of my poor Rosie, who might rise at any minute to see a prince's carriage in the drive, only to have her renewed hopes dashed, once more, like a bad dream that insisted on recurring.

Outside, Wenthelen had offered hot coffee. Otto waited empty-handed and the footmen stood frozen like statues, but Simeon had sprawled onto the front steps, holding a steaming cup, boots thrust forward into the gravel. I had never invited him indoors, but my sole-cism appeared to have gone unnoticed, for he was content, picking at a bit of lichen on the stonework. Nearby, Otto peered about the property with predatory focus.

"Elin will be right down," I informed them. "And if you'd like to wait inside, I—" I was about to make apologies, but Otto interrupted me.

"We'll stay outside," he insisted. "And won't put you out long."

Not suitable. I nodded, curtly. To Simeon, I said: "The ball appeared a great success."

"We ran out of punch," he confirmed. "Did you try the hot chocolate? It was imported. The chocolate, that is. We heated it ourselves."

I was saved from answering, for Elin appeared behind me in the doorway. Simeon scrambled to his feet, leaving his porcelain cup on a stone plinth.

"Prince Simeon," she breathed, dropping into a curtsy. In the few minutes since I had left her, she had fastened her hair and added color to her cheeks. When she rose, she added: "This is quite a surprise."

The prince returned her obeisance with a short bow. "A happy one."

She donned a sweet smile. "If our existence is a play, the unscripted scenes add depth and spontaneity. I'll savor this unexpected visit for a long time to come."

"Quite!" Simeon turned to Otto, a look of mirth on his face, and then back to Elin. "Shall we take a stroll? You can give me a tour of the . . ." He nodded off into the orchard. "Trees."

I did not believe that the prince cared for the trees a whit. But the overcrowded grove might offer a bit more privacy than a drawing room with two chaperones. Otto and I followed a few lengths behind them as Elin and Simeon took the path along the side of the house, toward the apple trees. Ahead of us, Elin's uncovered hair looked bright and clean against the many gnarled trunks and wet grass and a sky that threatened unpleasant weather.

We walked in uncomfortable silence. I wished we could hurry. I was eager to finish this strange stroll, for the day was cold and I did not like journeys that had unclear endings. But, ahead, Elin was picking her way with dainty steps, taking advantage of the prince's proffered hand at every shift in the uneven terrain.

After a moment, Otto cleared his throat and nodded ahead to Lucy's mews. "That's where you keep the bird?"

I nodded. "She's weathered over there on that block." I pointed to the stump and circle of gravel.

He looked up at the sky and back over at the small structure as if making conversation pained him. "Why not just hunt here? The property is big enough and you have the open skies."

I stiffened at the reminder of our encounter in the woods. "There's nothing left to hunt here." Lucy had been trawling our grounds since we'd first arrived.

Otto narrowed his eyes at the laurel hedge—the same one I had hurried through the first day I had met him—in the direction of the little path that led to the stream. "A goshawk would be better for the woods. No need for all that land. It would hunt from your arm."

I glanced over, annoyed that he was explaining hawks to me—but more annoyed by the suggestion of a gos. Goshawks were not birds kept by the gentry. "What do you know of falcons?"

"Not very much," he acknowledged. "I used to know an austringer. To ride with him."

I did not want to discuss hawks or falconry with Otto. Not after he'd seen me covered in mud, holding a dead rabbit. Not after he'd deemed the very activity unsuitable. So I didn't respond until the quiet became uncomfortable, and only then to change the subject.

"It is a long journey from the palace." I turned to face the many apple trees.

"Aye." Otto's voice was gruff. "The prince was determined."

"To see Elin?"

"To see Elin." He nodded.

"You must not have slept."

"We slept in the carriage." He shook his head. "We shall not disturb your peace for much longer."

I wanted to be rid of Otto, but his desire to be rid of me, too, was irritating. I could not help myself. I narrowed my eyes and held his. "No," I said. "The prince need not spend any further time at the home of women who are *not suitable*."

Otto's eyebrows rose, surprised, I think, at first by my tone, but a subtle realization soon crossed his face. He stopped walking and I paused beside him. I felt the briefest pleasure—the certainty of a final tug after tying the loops of a knot. But as it cinched, I wondered if I had not gone too far.

He nodded. "The prince has . . . infatuations." He was carefully choosing his words in a way that focused my attention. "They do not last long. They are fleeting and . . . best left alone."

I sucked in some of the cold air. I was not clear if he was talking about whatever had been intimated with Rosie, or what was happening ahead of us in the apple orchard.

"Just as he has been left alone with Elin in the woods?" I nodded ahead. During our brief exchange, Simeon and Elin had continued into the orchard, out of sight.

Otto's head rose, sharply. He looked alarmed, and then, with a start, stalked off in their direction.

"They cannot have gotten far," I called, resigned.

"They should not be unchaperoned," Otto called back. He sped up his pace and I struggled to follow. We hurried, leaving the path and picking our steps over apples that had turned and layers of wet leaves, Otto rushing ahead, and then doubling back to hold branches out of my way.

"This is silly," I told him.

"They should not be unchaperoned," Otto repeated. I scowled at his back.

I saw a flash of fabric through the trees ahead.

"There," I said. "Elin," I called, peering through the trees. "Elin?"

She and Simeon, framed by the knobbed trunks, the near-naked branches stretching up to scratch the overcast sky, came into sight. They saw us and waved. The hands between them were clasped. Elin's cheeks were flushed and there was a leaf in her hair.

The prince held up her hand, as if presenting a prize. He spoke to Otto. "Isn't she the most modest, marvelous little flower? Just as I told you."

"Your Highness—" Otto started.

"So untouched," the prince said, moving the hand in his own to his lips.

Elin flushed. "Stepmother," she called, her cheeks pinking further, her eyes bright. "We are engaged."

"It's true," Simeon said, dropping her hand so he could cup her chin. "We are to be married."

Instinctively, Otto and I stared, not at them, but at each other.

It was only through his expression that I truly believed I had heard correctly. His face reflected the same astonishment and revulsion as my own.

CHAPTER TWENTY-TWO

"MARRY—"
     "Her?"

The girls stared at me, mouths agape. Rosamund turned away, rubbing at her eyes, and then just as quickly spun back to ask: "They are truly engaged? An actual wedding?"

They stood in their dressing gowns in Rosie's bedroom. After the prince's departure—after much hand squeezing and promises and reassurances between him and Elin—I had quietly pulled Mathilde from her own chambers and bid her to follow me.

I do not know who decided that bad news was best delivered in person. Watching Rosie try to compose herself, I thought perhaps it would have been kinder to give it to her in a letter. There is a kind of mortification—hurt and upset with no small amount of shame—that wishes for privacy, that needs a few moments alone to curdle into something more manageable. Instinctively, both Mathilde and I turned away, trying to give Rosie a moment of solitude, if only by gesture. So many times in my daughter's life I had watched her shed tears and dismissed them. I wanted to collect them, just then—those salty drops—and assure her of their validity.

Rosie went to the window, looking out over the trees in the direction of the palace. "That means she will be queen."

"Queen!" Mathilde cried in realization. Her countenance shifted from a mask of concern to one of anger. "That conniving, silver-tongued, insufferable, superior fountain of false virtue!"

Rosie did not turn from the window. "I wonder what he sees in her."

"*Sees* in her?" Mathilde snorted. "She is practically translucent."

Nothing united my eldest to her sister like a shared foe.

But Rosie turned, wiping at her cheeks with the back of her hand, and shook her head at Mathilde. "I cannot fault Elin. She didn't know the extent of my hopes. And who would turn down such attention?"

Mathilde protested: "You need not defend that honey-mouthed, hollow-hearted—"

"Ladies." I held up my hands, palms facing out, and then lowered them slowly. "Watch your tongues." I glanced at the door. "Or at least speak softly. We've suffered a blow, but we must not lose our heads."

I brought my fingertips to my temples and dropped my voice to a whisper. "And while I am as surprised by this development as you are, we cannot lose sight of the situation. Your sister—" I paused, already feeling discredited by my own falseness. "Stepsister," I conceded, "is going to be a part of the royal family."

Going to Rosamund, I tried to pull her to me, to comfort her, to impart every ounce of feeling and regret and love that was hammering in my temple and pounding in my throat.

She pushed me away.

"How can I call her sister now?" Mathilde attempted and failed to match my whisper. "When she is to be queen one day? And there is little sisterly feeling between us?"

"Mama," Rosie interjected. "Her whole world has changed. But what will that mean for us?"

"That is precisely my point." I held out my hands. Neither of the girls took one.

Through the window, I could see the weak sun had all but disappeared from the sky, which had turned to a dark, threatening gray. A steady rain had begun. Down below, Lucy would need to be exercised. Water required fetching. Firewood demanded gathering. Beds called to be made. Returning to the ongoing activities of our daily lives— churning and cleaning and mending—felt improbable in the face of all that had happened. How many other guests of the ball had had to rise that morning and remove a film of frost from their washbasin? How many of them had to wash the chicken dung off the eggs that went into their morning omelets? Still, I stood, hands extended. Neither daughter was willing to return the gesture.

A knock on the door, and we all stopped breathing. But when it opened, it was only Alice who stuck her head through the crack. "There's been a royal summons."

I looked around. "Elin isn't in here."

She frowned. "You, my lady. The queen wants to see you. Immediately, it says."

I looked at her, my own mouth now agape. My hands fell to my sides.

"You can't go on that drive in this weather," Mathilde protested. "It isn't safe!"

"Please, Mama, stay here." Rosie reached for me, finally willing to take one of my hands.

I looked back and forth between them. "I can't not go. It's a royal summons!"

"I'll ready the coach." Alice's voice was sober.

I didn't meet my daughters' eyes as I rushed to get ready. There was no time to marvel at how quickly shifting allegiances laid all else bare.

✺

ON THE DRIVE TO THE PALACE, I SAW THE WEATHER HAD TURNED toward winter. Many of the trees we passed branched upward with a nearly naked grasp. The fallen leaves had revealed oversized crow's nests from seasons past and these sodden bundles loomed above us, empty cradles waiting to be used and repurposed once more. The steady, drizzling rain came, not just down from the sky but misting inward; it covered cheeks and kissed tender necks and curled a halo of little hairs at our temples. Alice and I had bundled ourselves, but our outer layers had gone damp and it was hard to tell how much of the jolting, shaking movements of our bodies was from shivering or the jostle of the chaise itself. The miserable wetness, the grayness of the day, felt fitting—my feelings and the world around me alloyed as one.

"M'lady." Alice interrupted my thoughts with a nudge of her shoulder. I ignored her and tightened my soggy cloak around my neck. I was wretched with disappointment. My darling Rosie. I had made a home of hope and wishes and asked her to live inside—only to watch the walls crumble. I had ticked through every evidence of her anguish—the hitched breath, the rending of her skirts in her hands, the wet pillowcase in the morning, the grayness of her skin as she stood by the window—remonstrating myself for each one in turn. The only subject that had succeeded in distracting me from my expostulation was my own humiliation. I had been summoned to Sigrid's side like a criminal. I wondered what new mortifications I would be subjected to. What ways I would be told the girls were unsuitable. What slights I would have to swallow under the guise of Sigrid's smile. What news I would have to bring back to Elin, who had already begun stitching her trousseau, smiling placidly at some private vision of the future.

"M'lady," Alice said more forcefully, chin jerking forward. "Look ahead."

I peered through the precipitation. An envoy made its way through the mist. Black-booted guards and plumed horses and an oversized carriage. Pennoncels dampened by weather. It could only mean one thing.

Alice said it first: "The queen has come to you."

We stared at one another with worried eyes. Neither able to produce an explanation for this odd turn of events—this urgency—that didn't foreshadow some kind of misfortune.

AN OUTRIDER ESCORTED ME THROUGH THE TEAMS OF HORSES AND guards. Men and animals alike stamped and snorted and braced themselves against the cold. I was led to a large carriage marked by heraldic symbols painted onto its leather—the real version of what Moussa's artifice had attempted to emulate. Feathers burgeoned from the roof's corners, though the plumage had become bent and bedraggled in the rain. The windows were glass, but the interior curtains were drawn, so I did not see Sigrid until a footman helped me climb inside.

She started talking even before I could settle to face her. "Traditionally," she said, speaking as I clambered over her feet, "this conversation would happen between two men. But my husband is traveling, and you no longer have one. So, the details about how to proceed are left to be worked out between the two of us."

"Your Majesty," I said, settling into the bench facing her. The carriage was overwhelmingly warm, and the windows, though covered, had fogged.

"Mind the coals." She nodded toward a cylindrical brass container on the floor that had been filled with burning embers. I shifted my feet away. Sigrid, sitting under a pile of fur blankets, did not stir. "I feel keen to assure you, Etheldreda, when it comes to my children, I do not muck about."

I took a breath. "And I can assure you, Your Majesty, I am as surprised by this development as yourself."

I had no view of the men I had passed outside, and little light crept in. But I could see Sigrid's face well enough. She flicked her eyes away, toward the covered window. It reminded me of her long-ago habit of staring off into the horizon, despite obstructions in her view.

She ran a gloved hand along her furs, against the nap. "Someone sits at my door when I sleep. Someone else wakes me in the morning. Do you know I am never alone? Except in this carriage. When no one is looking, I can put my feet up on that bench where you sit. Except now you are sitting on it." She leaned forward. Her furs slipped down off her torso, and she made no move to retrieve them. "I will admit I was surprised that fortune is so intent on keeping our paths intertwined. But I should not have been. You have always managed to badger about until you get your way."

"My way." I realized Sigrid viewed Elin's engagement as a triumph on my part. The heat from the coals. The smoke in the air. The smell of burning. I felt thickheaded and encumbered by my layers, which, in the heat, had begun to give off the fetid barnyard smell of wet wool.

Seeing—and misunderstanding—my dismay, Sigrid laughed, but it was a gentle chiding, not the self-satisfied chuckle I would have expected. "No doubt you've recognized all the ways the wedding will benefit all your daughters. One doesn't need to marry a prince to gain from his majesty."

"The wedding," I repeated. I was doing a poor job of keeping up. It was like playing a game where your opponent knew every card in your hand.

"Oh," she said, and sat back. "I presumed you had no objections. Your eagerness being on full display." Her lip twitched, as if in contact with her own poison. "But fate has a sense of irony. Who am I to argue with the tides that guide our children? I have made it clear to Simeon that there is no reason to delay the union. We've determined they should be married in three weeks' time."

I managed to say "That is quite soon" through my surprise.

"Yes, but enough time for you and I to put our scratching aside, I think, and at long last embrace as old friends. A union like this would make us practically sisters." Sigrid's fingers crept along the edge of the blanket and then she reached forward and took hold of my hand— a gesture of female complicity. We sat there for a moment, my glove in hers, and she squeezed my fingers. She could not have shocked me more. I resisted the urge to pull away.

I tried to steady myself in the miasmic air by peering at the carriage canopy, which had been painted like the night sky. The constellations reminded me of Sigrid's long-ago letter: *The sun does not think about the other stars*, she had said, *for it is the sun.* But what are stars if not suns themselves? Lowering my chin, I looked straight ahead at Sigrid—her yellow hair now faded, her cheeks beginning to sag—and said: "It would make us mothers-in-law."

"What are two mothers if not sisters of some sort?" She dropped my hand. "I can assure you of the king's support in the matter. Elin's father was titled. You all live on a gentleman's estate. You're in good enough standing. So there you have it. My son has set his heart. We will host a reception, and you will all be the better off for it."

We stared at one another. Sun or star, there are moments when you must tuck in your tail. If I could overlook all the thorns—the unfairness of Elin's dowry going to royal coffers, the acrimony of my own embarrassment, the plain fact of Rosie's hurt—a simple truth remained: A royal marriage in the family would improve my own daughters' futures. However *unsuitable* they might be, the proximity to court would be life-changing.

"I have no objections," I said, after a long moment.

"Do not worry, Ethel. They will live happily ever after." Sigrid held my eyes. "I will make sure of it."

BACK OUTSIDE, I FELT GRATEFUL FOR THE COLD, WET AIR. ALICE AND I waited until every member of the royal retinue was well out of sight before I recounted all that had happened.

"He really, truly means to marry Elin? And the queen supports it?" The reins in Alice's hands went as slack as her jaw.

"It appears that way." I nodded. I myself was still adjusting to the idea.

"It's odd, innit? The urgency?"

"Plenty of weddings have been planned in less time." I looked out at the wet landscape. We moved at a slow pace, for the rain had turned the road to muck. "I wish they had gotten to know one another more formally, but they're already engaged."

"A royal ball is the epitome of formality."

"Aye."

"But I don't mean the wedding date, m'lady. Why would the queen ride out and meet you in a muddy field?"

The ground around us was more brown than green. "Even royalty cannot stop the rain from making mud out of dirt."

Alice only clucked at Arno, who did not need clucking at. Her way of disagreeing with me.

"I do not think we should pick at it," I told her. "This wedding has the capacity to change everything. Not just right now, but forever." My daughters lived in a society where women were taught to hold their tongues and say little—where we were measured by our ability to disappear. Currying favor in this context was like being challenged to speak without a voice. If Sigrid was allowing the marriage, then I would likewise need to put aside my own humiliations—*unsuitable, your eagerness*—and embrace an undeniable truth. My girls still had no dowries. They had little means to advance themselves. But, now, they could have something else: kinship with a future queen.

"Then you shall continue your ruse." Alice sighed.

"It's not a ruse." I bristled. "It's a performance. And artifice is a language as common in the courts as it is in the hamlets. The only difference is it is called *orchestration* if you have money and *deception* when you don't."

"And if your performance is found out?"

I clenched an unseen fist beneath my cloak. "It won't be."

"Right now all the girls are guilty of is poor circumstances. What if your charade unravels? You'd leave them worse off than they started." Alice gave up her clucking and shook her head at me directly. "The house is going to fill up with every manner of visitor and guest, not to mention the royals themselves. You're going to have to feed and entertain them, with little help and no money. Forgive me for saying so, but you are treading a precarious path."

"Then we must be sure of our footing." I nodded, staring off, lost in thought. Alice was right, in her own stiff way. "The house must be ready to receive, always. We'll need to open more rooms, have more food. We'll need more people to help us."

"No, no," Alice reprimanded me. "That is not what I meant."

I pointed ahead. "Drop me off at the village and I'll walk the rest of the way home. Go to the walls outside the palace. There are people in need of work there. See who will come and who will work in exchange for room and board."

"No one will want to work without pay."

"People are hungry. Find someone hungry enough."

Alice's gray eyes went grayer.

"Come on, Alice," I implored her. "Success seldom comes without a bit of risk. The nearer you draw, the more hazardous the journey."

She turned toward me, her mouth pressed into her signature grim line. "The problem with risk," she countered, "is it can also lead to ruin."

I looked ahead. The rain had stopped, as if reacting to my sheer will. "I have faced ruin." I held my head high. "If she comes again, it will only be an opportunity to meet an old friend and then send her on her way once more."

CHAPTER TWENTY-THREE

W HEN ALL THE LANDOWNERS HAD PLANTED HAWTHORN hedges, the primary intention—making use of the bramble's thick growth and thorns and impenetrability—was to keep people out. But, as I hurried along the muddy lanes between the village and Bramley, I could not help but appreciate how the vegetation also offered seclusion. Sludge covered my shoes and water ruined my hems. On such a day, when any puddle could hide a pothole that might break a horse's ankle, no one else was traveling. I was completely alone—the haw-covered branches providing a thorny echo chamber for my every thought.

I had initially been disappointed at the prospect of Simeon and my stepdaughter—the sight of Elin and the prince on the dance floor as slippery and loathsome as a slug of milk gone sour. Naturally, I had championed my own daughters for the position. And, naturally, I had been thrilled when Simeon had shown interest in Rosamund.

But our family knew how to endure. Rosie's tears would dry. And my personal feelings were of little matter. No matter to Sigrid's superior smile, either. No matter to Otto's condescension. No matter to Simeon's choice. And, because it was necessary, no matter to Rosie's tears. We would make an advantage out of this wedding, and, if I had my way, we would polish and burnish and finagle until even the slightest advantage turned to a golden opportunity.

By the time I arrived at Bramley, my feet were soaked through, but I was in high spirits. As the house came into view, I pictured it fixed up and overflowing with guests. Light glowing in each of the mullioned windows. The library filled with books once more. Feet pattering up and down the back stairs. Smoke at each one of the chimneys. Companions for Lucy—a bird in every chamber of the mews. Each improvement so fractional from what was in front of me, it was impossible not to believe in the possibility of fruition.

The front door swung in and Wenthelen hurried out, hesitating for a moment at the mud, and then rushing forward once more. "Thank goodness you're back!"

"I am fine," I assured her.

"M'lady—" She caught sight of my hems and clicked her tongue at them. "Oh, you're a sight."

"The engagement is confirmed," I continued, as she came to my side. "I've sent Alice into the city for more help."

"I've been waiting—you see—after—" She abruptly turned and tried to keep pace as I marched toward the entrance. She was flustered and breathless.

I tried to slow so that she might keep up with me. "I do hope Alice finds someone. You'll have to ready rooms. We must give them good rooms at least, and food, which we will have to sort out."

"M'lady," Wenthelen repeated, panting. She came to a stop. "You see—well—that is the problem."

I paused and turned back to her. "We'll thin the soups and slice the roasts into thinner pieces. Whatever we must do, we shall."

"Not the soups. The *rooms*. M'lady, you see, the rain this morning was—at long last—too much."

I sighed and marched forward once more. "No one will go upstairs to see the leak."

"But," Wenthelen called. "But!"

I slowed and turned. "But?"

She exhaled, her great chest heaving. "Well, you might as well see for yourself."

THE ROOF HAD CAVED IN. THERE WAS NO LONGER JUST A LEAK: A large support beam had softened and splintered into two and the rooftop it held up had, in its entirety, fallen into the upper floor of the west wing. Wenthelen showed me: oversized splinters and rotten planks and scattered wood shakes. A pile of rubble composed of decades of dust and dirt.

Initially speechless, I had wandered through the debris, the weakened floorboards creaking beneath my feet. The rooms were not ones we used, but the damage was withering. A film of plaster dust was in the air, and covered, more thickly, the evidence of the breakage: beams fractured as though broken bones, crown molding jutting out in pieces. A bent chandelier sprouted from the pile, as though—as it were—the world had turned upside down. Standing close to the refuse, I could see straight up into the gray sky above.

Bramley Hall was not endless. On my first afternoon, so many years before, Robert had completed an efficient tour: the great hall, the gallery, the bedrooms in the east, the old tower. The upper floors of the west wing were where his first wife had kept her chambers, alongside Elin's peach nursery. Both had long ago been emptied. But, that first day, he had clicked through each chamber, softly explaining the details that Henry would have put last. Robert murmured about dour paintings in a room that had a view of the treetops. He fingered some decorative ornamentation and ignored the amount of light the windows let through. He was wan and eager to see me pleased. But I had been pleased—with the views and the windows, yes, but more so with the thick-framed paintings, the heaviness of the ornamentation, the weight of the years of prestige that coated the halls. I craved, by then, more than views and light. I wanted solidity. And Robert, with this home, had provided me the security I'd sought. The walls were built from brick and stone. I didn't love Bramley; I clung to it, the way a beggar grabbed for a tossed coin. And I clung to it still, all these years later.

With all its debt and depreciation, its sags and unbecoming bulges, Bramley might have spelled my destruction. But Bramley, too, was the grand stage I so badly needed: It assured, it bolstered, it asserted—with all the force of a mighty building, all the visual pageantry it could muster—the right of its occupants to want more and to want better. What was a performance without a stage? Staring at the rubble, I felt as though I had been holding the roof myself for all the years since Robert's death. As though, in its falling, my own body had failed. With an anguished crack of my wrists, I had allowed the sky to fall upon us.

❦

"WELL, AT LEAST NO ONE WAS HURT," ELIN SAID AT SUPPER THAT evening.

Prior to the afternoon's catastrophe, Wenthelen had prepared a celebration feast for her engagement. Cheese pie and blanched almonds and persimmons instead of our usual pottage and stew. Despite our shock—Rosie had not emerged from her room that day—and the dust that covered the halls, I had insisted we all sit together to eat.

"Obviously," Mathilde responded from her seat at the table. A quick look from me and she added: "And for that we must be grateful."

"She's right," Wenthelen said. "Someone could have been hurt."

"But they weren't," I contested. "We don't use the upper side of the wing, for the very reason of all the leaks. The rooms were uninhabitable, therefore uninhabited when the eaves collapsed." I looked up at the ceiling of the great hall, which was covered in a painted motif of apples on trees. We sat directly beneath the pile of rubble, and, if you looked closely, you could see a stain was growing above the dining table.

"But—" Mathilde protested.

"You are right," I spoke over her, tearing another piece of cheat bread from the loaf on the table. "We must be grateful."

Rosie—who had sat through most of the meal with silent forbearance—stared down at her plate. For all my blustering, I was inclined to join her. No one had been hurt, but, from the rear of the house, anyone standing on the lawn might see: There was a yawning mouth, a gaping hole, through which you could observe a mess of rubble and dust. It was so much more than the blemish of overgrown hedges and graying whitewash: The hole was a festering sore, the weeping kind of wound that, if not properly tended to, would become fatal.

I was glad Alice was not there, for the moment, at least, to say *I told you so*. But Mathilde, hungrily finishing her tart, seemed more than happy to assume the role. "This could jeopardize everything," she announced to the table.

"I do not understand why a hole in the roof jeopardizes anything!" cried Elin. "Accidents happen. People are not punished for them." She nodded to herself—not defending me, I realized, but rather, asserting the stability of her own future.

"The hole is from years of neglect, and it cannot just be hidden," Mathilde said. "We have no means to fix it."

"The prince is not marrying Elin for her house." I glanced at Rosie, who still had not looked up from her plate.

"No, but we live in it. What happens after the wedding? The hole will not be fixed on its own and we cannot afford to fix it. And that is if it isn't seen before!"

"You cannot see the hole from the front drive. You cannot see the hole from right here." I knocked on the tabletop. I had carefully traced the route: You could ride or walk all the way up the drive and get through the front door without seeing the destruction. All one had to do was keep guests from going to the west wing, or anywhere near the back of the house. "We will need to keep it out of sight. Until the wedding. We'll have to discourage any visitors."

"No." Elin cleared her throat and then dabbed at her lips with a napkin. "No, we must prepare for that eventuality. Simeon told me he is coming for dinner the day after tomorrow."

I stared at her, feeling, suddenly, less hungry. "You are telling us this now?"

"Now is when I am seeing you."

I turned to Wenthelen. "We will need meat."

Wenthelen frowned. "Perhaps woodcock?"

"And something sweet. A marmalade? We must prepare."

"Breast of veal in white broth," Wenthelen mused. "Or mutton with salt-and-vinegar sauce."

"How," Mathilde interjected, "would we get veal or mutton?"

Wenthelen continued: "A sucket for something sweet. Is that too sweet?"

"I could try to hunt some bustard or pheasant," I suggested. "Gods, Lucy does need to get out."

"He is not coming for the meal," Elin exclaimed. Then, suddenly, viciously, she blushed, a redness that crept from her neck and touched her chin but went no farther. "He said he wants to see me."

"Nevertheless, he is coming for *a* meal," Wenthelen retorted, brow furrowed. "Therefore, a meal must be cooked and the rooms must be cleaned and your mother must figure out how to disguise the fact that half the house has caved in."

"Stepmother," Elin corrected.

Mathilde leaned forward with an expression I could not quite read. "Elin—the prince has picked you, but what are your thoughts on the prince?"

Elin, who sat in the middle, turned from facing Wenthelen and I, back down toward Mathilde. "Whatever do you mean?"

"You are happy?"

"He chose me!" Elin replied, half in protest, half in delight with the affirmation. "Of course I am happy!"

Mathilde pursed her lips, glancing quickly at Rosie, who kept her eyes down. "But what do you feel about him?"

"Why—I love him, of course!" Elin splayed a hand on her chest, as if her heart were proof. She glanced down at her own fingers. "He said he will get me a ring. There was not enough time."

"But you've only just met him. You love him? You would go to the ends of the earth for him?"

"I would." Elin nodded.

"You would die for him?"

"Die?" Elin repeated.

"Mathilde," I warned.

She kept going, undeterred. "Would you contradict all—no, let's not say all, how about just one of the little maxims you live by? Will you discard your booklet once you are queen?"

"Mathilde!" I called down to her end of the table. "That is enough!"

"You are hateful and envious," Elin said, empty hand now hidden in her lap. She turned to me. "And this home has been in my family for generations. It only took one for it to fall into ruin."

"Your father left me this house and nothing to take care of it with," I protested. "It is like caring for a plant with no sun, no water!"

Mathilde pointed at Elin. "You are a self-righteous little prick." She dropped her extended hand to the table, took a whole persimmon, and bit from its side. Still chewing, she continued. "Or a pricklet, if you prefer it. You always have been. I just hope you are not also a fool."

"And you—" Elin's eyes watered. "You have the manners of a boar."

Rosie stood, pushing back her chair with a loud scrape, and dropped her napkin upon her untouched plate of food. "I wish you would all just stop. Just stop."

"Rosie." I reached toward her. But she had already turned on her heel and, with a few great strides, left the room.

I looked around at all the faces that remained at the table. "So, we are in agreement, then? We will do all we can to keep anyone from seeing the damage on the roof?"

"What happens when the other half falls in?" Mathilde scoffed.

I ignored her and turned to Elin.

"Yes," she agreed. "Yes—we must."

"Well," Wenthelen said to herself, sawing into a slice of tart with the edge of her knife. "I think I will make the sucket after all."

WHEN I WENT UP TO MY BEDCHAMBERS THAT NIGHT, I FOUND, FOLDED in a pile on the foot of my mattress, a neat bundle. I undid it. Twin slips of blue taffeta, the fabric sliding and slipping onto itself. Two long sleeves—those that had been severed from my wedding dress. A stain near the wrist. Long-ago tears that had been as happy as they'd been sad. The duality was a fitting mirror—I could not tell if the blue scraps were Elin's peace offering or her admonition.

After refolding them carefully, I went back down the hall to Rosie's bedchamber, wondering if she required company. Upon entering, I saw that she already sat with Mathilde.

The room had been cleaned. The various puffs of silk and embroidered kirtles folded and stored away. The crumbs cleared. Rosie perched at the end of a bench, hunched over a lavender bodice, sewing needle in hand. Behind her, Mathilde plaited her hair.

"That's your old piece." I recognized the long waist and embroidered flowers on the purple cloth.

Rosie pulled a nearby candle closer to her but did not look up. "Elin will need something nice to wear if the prince is indeed coming to lunch, and it's easily refitted to her size."

I nodded, pleased that my daughter was feeling a little better. "It is smart of you to recognize the advantage offered by the situation."

Rosie paused her stitching. "It is not for you, and it is not for us. It is for her."

Mathilde finished the braid and extended a hand for a ribbon, which Rosie supplied. After deftly securing the end of the plait, she placed a palm on each of her sister's shoulders and leaned forward. "You are not bound to help the pricklet."

Rosie looked up at Mathilde. "Nor do I gain an advantage in hating her." Grabbing ahold of her own braid, she pulled it over her shoulder to inspect it. "She is our kin. Some version of kin, at least. You should be helping her, too. Even if she can be a . . ."

"Pricklet. I am more inclined to help you, my true sister."

"Well, then you shall help me help her," Rosie retorted. "And she is right anyway. You do have the manners of a boar."

Instead of arguing, Mathilde let out a disdainful snort, mimicking the sound of a wild pig.

"You should not," Rosie cried, half horrified.

Mathilde did it again and a sudden eruption of laughter seized the both of them, all tension dissolving into shared amusement. But Rosie's laughter quickly transformed into a series of hiccups, and fresh tears adorned her cheeks once more.

"Oh, Rosie." I took a step toward her.

She swiftly rose, gesturing for both Mathilde and me to depart. "I am"—she got a faraway look—"quite tired."

I QUICKLY FOUND MYSELF BACK ALONE IN MY OWN CHAMBERS, SITTING next to the delicate wedding sleeves. The frayed edges, the beautiful cloth—they were as fitting an emblem as any of all my joy and sorrow. Falling asleep, I wondered if their very presence was a potent symbol, or if the two slips of fabric were just remnants from a distant, better-forgotten past.

CHAPTER TWENTY-FOUR

❧✿❧

"**I** AM CROSS WITH YOU," LAVINIA SAID, BEFORE SHE HAD EVEN stepped from her coach. Like a dog bred to sniff out weakness, she had arrived the next day—interrupting our flurry of preparations—flushed a deeper shade of scarlet than usual. "To find out from gossip and cackle and idle chatter"—she landed in the gravel and steadied herself—"that my dearest, closest, most cherished friend has a child to be wedded to the prince?" She pushed past me, into the entry hall, which was filled with candlesticks waiting to be polished.

Finnian emerged from the carriage mouth behind her, but I did not have time to greet him. Lavinia was already inside, opening the door to a state room we did not use. It was the wrong space to entertain in—we had kept the drawing room and hall to much higher standards—but it was better than if Lavinia had marched around to the back of the house. Happy to allow her to settle far from the view of the roofline, I followed. In the briefest of moments she had been alone in the room, my *dearest friend* had already established herself into one of the chaises.

"The position I was put in," she continued, "where I could neither confirm nor deny to others, when all it would have taken was a letter." She paused, finally, and looked around. "Did you redecorate?"

"We are in the middle of finding new things," I explained at a brisk clip.

"Finnie! Finnian!" She craned her head toward the open door. "We are in here!"

Her son appeared at the doorway. His hair had been zealously combed and his ears had the pinkness of a recent washing. "Don't dawdle!" his mother called. "In! In, in, *in*! We can't keep Etheldreda all day, she is clearly preparing for company." She swiveled her head and held me with a steady gaze.

I took hold of a brass bell on a dust-covered table, and rang it, hoping someone would hear and come to my assistance. I nodded. "We are indeed—"

"And my children asked me this morning if they would be included in these events, and I assured them, naturally, that there was no question of it! Not with a friendship such as ours." She turned a shrewd eye back to the room. "My dear, where are your paintings?"

"They are being restored," I lied.

She clicked her tongue. Finnian, taking a seat beside her, said nothing. I rang the brass bell again, more forcefully.

"It is difficult to find responsive help, isn't it?" Lavinia sighed.

I stood. "If you'll excuse me, I'll go find someone to assist with some refreshments."

She breathed out wearily. "Excused."

THE KITCHEN WAS BUSY WITH PREPARATIONS FOR THE PRINCE'S VISIT. Mathilde sat in a flour-covered apron, punching dough alongside Alice, who had returned late the night before. Wenthelen was in her usual place, overseeing the bubbling dishes on the hearth and in the ovens. And at the table, a woman sat, her legs stuck straight out on the floor in front of her. She held a polishing cloth, but there was no silver or brass laid out.

"Who are you?" I asked, in surprise.

"This is Morwen," Alice informed me.

"Morwen." I nodded as she stood. Turning back to Alice, I asked, "Just one?"

"Just one," she confirmed.

"Botheration." I released a tired breath. "Did no one hear my bell?"

"Who has time to pay any mind to a bell?" Wenthelen wielded an iron poker to push a pot closer to the embers of the fire.

"The Enrights are here, and—"

"Morwen," Alice interrupted, "this is the lady of the house."

"We're roasting our guts in here preparing for tomorrow's luncheon." Wenthelen wiped her brow on her upper arm.

Morwen, broad-shouldered and clean-haired, watched us, but avoided my eyes. From her bewildered glances between Wenthelen and myself, I deduced she had yet to make sense of our unusual dynamic. I looked her over. She was the same age as I, or close to it. Had she been younger, I would have benefitted from the authority of age. Older, and I would have the advantage of youth.

"I cannot wait on the guests," I protested.

"*I* can help you and let all the food burn to black bits or *you* can figure it out," Wenthelen told me, matter-of-fact.

I turned to Morwen, worried her mouth might fall open. "You are capable of serving."

"No, my lady." She crossed her arms defensively. "I am a lady's maid."

"She won't even polish," Alice interjected.

"I do not know how," Morwen protested.

"You hold a cloth and polish," Alice scoffed.

"I am a lady's maid," Morwen repeated, turning to me plaintively. There was no argument in her features, but rather a bovine kind of obstinance—a lack of understanding. I felt, suddenly, more gentle, the way one wants to hush and assure an animal through its discomfort.

I exhaled and turned to Mathilde. "Mathilde, go upstairs and entertain Lavinia, please."

My daughter paused her kneading. The dough sat in front of her in a shaggy mound. She held up her dirty, sticky hands. "Must I?"

"You must." I handed her a rag to wipe herself. "I will be up presently."

She stood, gave the dough a final, decisive punch, and removed her flour-covered apron. I turned back to Morwen. She waited, fidgeting, hands picking nervously at her waist.

"Morwen," I started. "We do not run a traditional household here at Bramley. We are ladies, but we don't require lady's maids. However, I do require help."

"I do not know how to be a scullery maid." Morwen gestured toward the polishing cloth. She spoke with a hint of learned, appropriate deference. She did not have to add: *And it is beneath my station.*

"You agreed to come for no pay." I looked her over, wondering what had brought her here, to our hearth. She was clean, but her shoes were worn, and she wore a smock made of lockram instead of cambric or holland. She held my gaze for a long moment, a bit of boldness that might indicate she had been in a household of strong standing, been valued, even, and comfortable. But at the last minute she dropped her gaze and directed it toward the planks of the floor, unwilling to reveal to me her secrets. "Only in exchange for a place to stay," I finished. "I deduce you do not have many other options."

After a moment of hesitation, she nodded in confirmation, as if it were difficult to acknowledge even to herself.

"We're grateful for your help and, as I said, your help is needed. But you'll need to step beyond the bounds of your role. I need you to wait on our guests. You've seen it done plenty of times. Just bring up a tray and go about it properly."

"A tray of what?" she asked.

"Wenthelen will show you," I said, and stepped from the kitchen before I could be punished by our cook's response.

✿

In the state room, Mathilde was sitting across from Lavinia and Finnian, barely disguising a frown.

"Oh, good, you've returned," Lavinia said. "Finnian has brought a nosegay and a love letter he would like to give to your daughter."

Taken aback, I managed only a quick glance at him. He nodded in agreement, and, I saw, was holding a small bouquet of posies. He patted his breast pocket.

"I—ah—which one?" I managed, not daring to look at Mathilde.

"Well, that's what we must discuss. Which do you think is better?"

I could not stop myself from coughing.

Lavinia went on. "Rosie may be better suited to him in stature and inclination, but I understand if you'd want to see your eldest married first—it would be a terrible blow to Mathilde otherwise."

The door swung inward and behind it, Morwen pushed through with an oversized tea service. We didn't have new tea leaves and I was quite sure the biscuits were two days old, but Wenthelen had seen that the appropriate silver had been used—polished, already, in preparation for Simeon's visit.

"On the table there," I told Morwen.

"And," Lavinia continued, "I was not sure if Rosie's affections were still fixed on Prince Simeon. No boy wants to follow in someone else's wake."

I noticed, from behind, that Morwen had straightened and was listening. Certainly, our household was confusing—motley and now, it was revealed to her, adjacent to royalty.

"They had a dance," I acknowledged. "That is hardly something to hold against her."

Lavinia's countenance shifted from hawklike to delighted. "A dance with one sister and an engagement with another."

"The prince danced with many." Refusing to meet Mathilde's eye, I watched Morwen hurry to finish, nervous on her behalf. One of the teacups clattered in her hand.

Lavinia chortled. "If I didn't know better, I would say your family has worked out some kind of magic charm." She turned to her son. "Finnian, what do you think of the matter?"

"I—" he began, reaching with both his hands to tuck his hair behind each ear.

She nodded. "Yes, I agree. It should be Mathilde."

Mathilde half stood, abruptly, and catching herself, sat back down.

"Mathilde," I repeated. I looked at Finnian, the heir to the largest estate in the county. He was not bad-looking, he just had not yet grown into his face. I reasoned that he might be suitable indeed in a few years' time—what with his inheritance and his parents' oversized property. And it would place one of my daughters just down the road. "We are flattered," I said, decisively. Mathilde was practical. Unlike Rosie, she wasn't interested in an affair of the heart. Already, I could see how Elin's engagement might turn our fortunes. It was easy to forget about the roof upstairs. About Rosie's cracked heart. About the prospect of Lavinia as a mother-in-law.

Mathilde opened her mouth to protest, and I held up my hand, silencing her as effectively as I could.

Lavinia cleared her throat. "Etheldreda, please come with me. I have something in my carriage I need to show you."

"Very well," I agreed. Still unwilling to risk eye contact with Mathilde, who stood, fully this time, hands pressed to her stomach as if it pained her.

"Please," she said, "I would love to see the carriage as well."

"No, no," Lavinia called. "You mustn't."

"Mama—" Mathilde turned to me, her fingers digging in further at her waist.

"We'll be back presently," I assured her.

"Please," she said again, but when I began to follow Lavinia to the door, her hands shifted from her belly to her hips and she glared at me.

When we were through the doorway, Lavinia turned back to me and revealed, in a fake whisper: "I did not really have something to show you."

I kept my eyes ahead, ignoring my daughter behind me. "I assumed."

"But," Lavinia continued, "young love must have space and air to bloom."

And money, I thought. I did not judge myself—for it is true and I did not say it aloud.

✿

I DO NOT KNOW EXACTLY WHAT TRANSPIRED IN THE STATE ROOM after Lavinia and I exited, but when the Enrights' carriage departed a short while later, Mathilde did not wait until it was out of sight to turn to me. "Surely, you are jesting," she hissed.

"Be practical," I insisted, hand still raised in a farewell gesture. I lowered it. "Why else did you go to the ball if not to encourage visits such as this? We have a window of opportunity. Think of your future."

"That is exactly what I am thinking of!" she cried.

"Then we are aligned." The carriage now safely out of sight, I turned and headed along the path toward the side of the house.

"This is preposterous," she called after me, and then picked up her skirts to follow. "Mama, he is seventeen years old. His chin is covered in spots. We have nothing in common!"

"He has not even proposed," I told her, over my shoulder. "Do not discourage affection until you understand your options."

"He spoke only of mallard ducks."

"You do not have to accept. But it would do you well to consider it."

"Ducks!"

We rounded the corner of Bramley and came to the rear yard, the hole in the roof visible above us. "We will obtain more proposals and choose which is best. Mathilde, do not make that face at me. This is a good thing. Elin's engagement bodes well. You have to see the possibilities of every situation, to see the possibilities in your life," I urged her, stopping at the path that led to the mews. "To believe in what you are able to become!"

She shook her head at me and then gestured up toward the roofline above us. "Mama, the line between possibility and fantasy is proving to be exceedingly fine."

I looked up at the hole, which had not improved itself overnight.

"We only have to get to the wedding," I assured her.

Mathilde paired no words with her look of disgust and, exasperated beyond measure, turned on her heel.

THE AFTERNOON WAS BUSY WITH EVERY MANNER OF PREPARATION. Sweeping the floors and beating the carpets. Placing new candles in all the rooms. Hanging pomanders to ward off the smell of smoke and rot. Everyone helped. Mathilde finished the bread and cleared the prior day's storm debris from the drive. Rosie assisted Wenthelen with the roast and sweetmeats. Alice gathered firewood and set the table, with Morwen's assistance, laying out our best—and our only remaining— silver and crystal and porcelain. Even Elin helped, folding lace-trimmed napkins into a ruffled pile.

I took Lucy out in the afternoon to hunt. She killed two pheasants. A good catch, but we had had a miserable go of it: Gone was the playful bird from the day before. She was hungry and jumpy and agitated, less satisfied with her bounty than she should have been. I was eager to get her back to her mews, and, after I handed the birds to the kitchens, I secured Lucy and excused myself to the cellar house.

The distinct, yeasty smell of fermentation always invokes memories of my father: the rough cloth of his apron, the crumbs that would catch in his beard. Our cellar, a damp and dark outbuilding filled with cider barrels, smelled more of fruit and of rot than the bready aroma of ale in my father's clothes and hair. But the dank room still called him to me—an edge of comfort in an otherwise cold space.

Near the door, next to a pile of rusted garden tools—a long-handled axe and a crusty shovel—a row of open vessels housed cider in various stages of fermentation. I lifted the cloth from one barrel and saw the sediment had settled well enough. There was little active bubbling; the drink was ready to be poured. I was readying a funnel over an empty barrel when I heard a noise behind me.

Morwen stood in the gloomy light. "Oh!" she said, as if it were I who had surprised her.

"Come and help me." I shifted so she could hold the other side of the barrel, which grew heavier in my arms.

After the briefest hesitation, she took hold of the vessel. "They said I'd find you here."

Together, we tipped the contents into the barrel. The liquid glugged slowly.

"You make the cider?" Her chest heaved from the effort.

"We'll serve it tomorrow." I waited and then lifted the fermentation vat at the last moment—to keep the sediment from pouring. Then we both straightened, righting the cask once more. "One of those." I nodded toward the racked barrels on the other side of the room. "I just needed to transfer this one when it was ready." I leaned down to secure the bung in the side of the barrel and added: "We all make it."

She nodded, more to herself, as if confirming something. "Ma'am," she said, "I thank you for taking me in. I cannot stay."

I was surprised. "You are giving notice?"

"I will take leave in the morning."

"Whatever do you mean?" Despite Morwen's earlier reluctance, she had proved capable for the rest of the afternoon. Polishing, yes, but she'd also wiped the tables with wax and cleared some of the white dust that had drifted from the upper west wing. "You cannot leave!" I stopped and corrected myself. "You may leave, but I do not want you to."

"I've already packed my things." She avoided my eyes.

"I am sorry our household is not more traditional." I sank to perch on one of the nearby sealed barrels and watched her, standing uncomfortably on the dirt floors. I could not help but feel, as I had when I'd met her, that she was hiding something. "Morwen," I asked her, crossing my arms, "what is your story?"

"My story, ma'am?" she repeated, alarmed.

"Where do you come from?"

"My prior employer—"

"I mean where are *you* from. Do you have a family? Anyone to return to?"

She hesitated. "No, ma'am." She shook her head. "I had eight siblings but my mother made it clear when I left that there was no room for me to return. And that was years ago yet."

I settled fully onto the barrel and surveyed the room. "Growing up," I told her, "we had a cook and one maid, and then, when I was older, my father hired me a tutor. Agatha."

"Ma'am." Morwen eyed me.

"You see, there were no women in the house. I had no sisters. My mother was not alive. And so this tutor was brought in to show me all that was involved. To make up for what I supposed my father thought of as years of missed instruction. Agatha was so intimately involved in my life. More than lessons. She meted out my punishments. She hit my hands with such force. I remember, still, watching the blood snake into the wash water after. Like little forked tongues."

Morwen made a small sound of objection, but I continued: "I do not mean to say she was cruel. Rather, that she was so wholly involved in the administration of joy and pain throughout my day. She's a part of my life, still, in that her many lessons are carved into my memory. Indelibly. Inescapably!" I laughed to myself. "My father thought she was the best thing for me. She was well paid and highly valued. And despite how I hated those lessons, despite that pink wash water, she proved to be immeasurably valuable to me over the years. Yet—"

Here, I paused and hopped down from my place on the barrel. "Yet, she lived in a little room at the top of the house. She took her meals there or in the kitchens and did not eat with us. I realized, later, that she was such a part of my life, and I knew—still know—nothing about her."

I shook my head, shaking away, too, the small amount of shame I had conjured. "It was she that taught me about lady's maids, though I did not have one. The great art of what you do, and all it entails."

Morwen watched me, waiting.

"I gather," I continued, "from your position that you must know a bit about security and trust. A lady's maid is involved so intimately in her lady's life. I may not need help with the same sorts of things, here—the letter writing and management of my chambers and assistance with my toilette—but I do need the same things you've been trained to provide. Someone to trust. Security. And I can offer those things in turn, to the best of my ability."

When Morwen was certain I was finished—she waited for a good pause, a light flush crawling up her neck—she ducked her head. "Your daughter is marrying Prince Simeon." She sucked in air. "I am a lady's maid as you said. I am not trained or capable of waiting on him. I am not a parlor maid. And I must," she said, her voice wavering, "give you my leave."

Her nervousness made me suspicious—as did her intimate knowledge of the hierarchies of royal staff. But the waver was a small opening. "You need not stay with our household long," I agreed. "I do not know if it will serve you. But I beseech you: Please stay for a little while longer."

Morwen looked up, warily.

"A matter of weeks," I assured her. "It will make all the difference for us and give you time to determine what you'd like to do next. I will not ask you to do too many tasks outside of the role you prefer. You will not wait on anyone at the luncheon."

"I will not"—she spoke so quietly I had to take a step toward her—"wait on the prince?"

"Wenthelen will need some help in the kitchens," I agreed. "And you do not have to tell me your story, but I think you will find, after a few weeks, all the trust you need."

She hesitated. A brief gesture, as if wanting to reach toward me. Then, she stilled. "A few weeks, then," she asserted, without much confidence.

So it seemed all in life was narrowing toward the date of the wedding. Three weeks—three weeks to see it through or see our futures undone entirely.

CHAPTER TWENTY-FIVE

THE HOUSE TICKED LIKE A CLOCK, WAITING. TABLE SET AND FOOD prepared. A line of loaves down the center of the table. Pewter bowls of fruit decorating the mantels. Curtains drawn and candles lit. I walked through the rooms checking all. Fussing with cushions. Pinching bits of lint from the upholstered places it clung. Fretting, because the accumulation of these details—wiped dust, polished mahogany—did little to hide how Bramley had gone shabby around the edges. I hoped the high ceilings and ornate friezes, the oversized fireplaces, and the columned great hall—the solid leftovers of Bramley's wealth—made up for it. A vestigial disguise.

When we heard the clamor of arrival—grinding gravel and the hollow thunking of hooves, reliable as a door knocker—I rushed down to the kitchens to gather the staff. Wenthelen, Alice, and Morwen were busy with last-minute preparations.

"They are here," I told them. "Get outside for the receiving line." I removed my apron and put it on one of the pegs by the back door. "No one—no one—is to be allowed into the back."

Alice retied her apron strings, but Wenthelen remained inert. She nodded to a copper pan in the hearth—the sucket. "Syrup'll burn if left on by itself."

"I'll watch it," Morwen offered.

"It needs to reduce." Wenthelen peered into the pan, then nodded at the candied rinds. Fruit and root preserved in syrup of sugar. "A proper sucket should go for twelve days."

I used my hands to smooth my hair, to check my dress. A fingertip on each button to ensure it was in place. "Everyone upstairs. The syrup can sit for a moment."

"Do you not care about the sucket, then?" Wenthelen sniffed.

Morwen frowned at me. "You said I would not wait on anyone."

I blinked at her. "And you will not."

"I will stay here," she announced.

"Morwen," I exclaimed. "We are all—"

"No," she said sharply. She bent over the syrup. Something in the set of her shoulders stopped me from arguing. Stubbornness, yes, but also fear.

"Come along, then." Alice brushed past me on her way to the stairs.

WHEN SIMEON EMERGED FROM HIS CARRIAGE, WAVING AWAY THE footman and helping himself down with the handrail, he observed the lot of us women with a subtle grin. "If I had realized how few men were in your household, I would have brought more."

He was surrounded by them. Two more footmen, riding up front, and a page holding on to the back of his coach. Men-at-arms on horse-back, the horses themselves plumed and armored. An echo of Sigrid's own retinue. Otto—the prince's shadow—had come, too, riding atop his black-coated horse.

All of us women were lined up and waiting. The girls had arranged themselves: Mathilde and Rosie, looking so alike, and so much taller, on one side of Elin in the purple bodice that turned her eyes so blue the sky felt gray in comparison.

The prince went to Mathilde first, at the end of the row, and kissed her hand. She nodded impassively. Rosie was next. I did not envy her position. Did not envy the discomfort, the inherent awkwardness, of having been passed over. But Simeon lingered a little longer in front of her. She, who had spent extra time readying, looked becoming. Even then, committed as I was to the march we were all participating in—forward! To the wedding!—I'll admit it brought me pleasure. A little salt to sprinkle. Whatever charms she had mustered worked their small magic, for Simeon held her eyes and did not drop her hand too quickly.

He stepped over to Elin. "My darling," he murmured. Instead of kissing one hand, as he had done with her stepsisters, he took both of Elin's in his own and leaned forward, planting a kiss on each of her cheeks, which flushed upon contact. Spellbound, she peered back up at him.

When he tore his eyes from hers, he stepped ahead, to me, the last in line. He took my hand, too, in his own, and raised it to his lips. "You could not have arranged for a more perfect day for a visit." He held my hand and my eyes with his own but used a free arm to gesture at the skies above.

"The gods and the clouds both complied," I agreed. Under his gaze, I found I wanted to elicit his good graces. "Welcome to Bramley Hall."

I heard a throat clear and looked up to see Otto had come forward. He did not greet me, and instead asked: "Where shall the men rest their horses?"

"Take that path"—I jutted my chin toward the outhouses—"to the stables. Do not stray off the walkway. We are reseeding the grounds. Alice will show you the way." She had been instructed to keep a close eye on the men—and not to let any wander to the rear of the house.

"I'll join you for your dinner," Otto said, as if the invitation were his to issue.

"We need not sit right away," Simeon protested, tilting his face up toward the light. "Perhaps Elin and I will take another stroll in the orchard."

All of us eyed the path that wound along the side of the house, toward the trees, and right past the view of the hole in the roof. Rosie looked down. Mathilde kept her eyes resolutely forward. Elin blushed. No one dared contradict a prince.

"I'm afraid the rains have made the fields impenetrable," I said.

"A modicum of slush has never stopped me." Simeon's hand reached for Elin.

"I think—" She stepped toward him and looked back at me, be-seechingly. "I think—" Simeon took ahold of her arm and began to walk her along with him, toward the side of the house.

Rosie nudged Mathilde to help, and she called out: "Elin, you must not catch cold!"

"Yes," Rosie agreed. "We have such a warm fire inside."

Elin looked at Simeon. Her blue eyes suddenly less blue. "I am a little . . ." Her voice was so quiet I could barely hear her. "Cold," she finished.

"I will keep you warm." Simeon pulled her arm with a small amount of force. Instinctively, Elin stepped backward, and the tension between the two caused a rip in her dress, an inch of her undergarments poking through the sleeve. Embarrassed, she whipped her hand up to cover the rend.

Instinctively, I reached a hand toward Elin, who was inspecting the tear with dismay. Beside me, Otto tensed.

"Alack," Simeon exclaimed, shaking his head, though I perceived no real regret in the set of his brow.

"Your dress." Mathilde took a step between them. Rosie hurried to her side. Their bodies a small wall of protection.

"I am clumsy." Simeon looked around, ever the prince once more, hands held up in apology. "Elin is cold. We'll go inside."

IN THE GREAT HALL, WE RINSED OUR HANDS IN THE BASIN AND TOOK our seats, Simeon at the head of the table. He unfolded his napkin and looked over the tableau—two days of work manifested in a series of dishes. "I am glad you haven't done anything extravagant on my account."

"A light meal," I assured him.

"There is nothing worse than a feast where the food does not stop coming. I was hosted recently, and they brought out lamprey pottage and salmon in mustard sauce and venison in sauce of ale and some concoction of green leaves and bustard and I ate to my heart's content and only then realized it was the intended first course. It is refreshing to eat as you eat." He reached forward and began to serve himself some carved pheasant. "To dine as you dine in your everyday lives."

"You do not need to worry," I said. "The food you see is the food we eat." Memories of oat cakes and watered-down stews contradicted the words in my mouth.

"I do not have a sweet tooth." Simeon turned to Elin. "I prefer smoked herring to pickled. Venison is my favorite meat. I cannot stand lamprey. I do not want to see lamprey, ever. There is something wrong with their round, teeth-filled sucking faces." He cocked his head at her reassuringly. "You will learn all this in time. My preferences. And we will ensure our cooks learn yours."

"No lamprey," Elin repeated, nodding, diligent.

Simeon continued as the rest of us served ourselves. "People always try to impress with the most exotic things—stork, bittern, that sort of thing. Porpoise. Seal."

"Seal!" Elin's brow furrowed.

"Yes, and what they do not understand is there is nothing as appealing or as humble as a good loaf of bread." He nodded toward the row down the center of the table. "A simple roast. I do not need to eat curlew to feel appeased. Food is about satiation, after all. Gratification, yes, but hunger, that is what food is for. So I thank you kindly for the bread."

On Simeon's other side, Otto withdrew a knife from his own pocket and used it to saw off a hunk of the loaf that was in front of him.

"Do not be worried," Simeon told Elin, helping himself to the salt-and-pepper box, "by all my prattling. I like to hear myself talk. And if you want an elaborate wedding feast, we will serve swans for all I care."

Otto put his knife back into his pocket and chewed the bread. Silent.

"Well," I carefully interjected, "we have plenty of bread. As much as you want, and more for your guards."

"They are terrorizing your kitchens, no doubt." Simeon offered an inscrutable smile, and the rest of us—the women—chirruped.

"I wanted to ask, if you will permit me a question," Mathilde said, and waited for him to nod. "Do you need guards? Riding through the countryside?"

Elin leaned forward. "Are you not safe?"

"Of course I am safe." Simeon waved off her worry. "But it cannot be helped. The guards—and Otto here—are like a cage that moves forward on wheels. And backward. Where I go, they go."

Rosie shook her head, sympathetically, a physical echo of the tutting noises Elin was making.

Mathilde eyed him, interested. "And what kinds of threats rattle the bars of your cage?"

Simeon laughed. "None! That's my point precisely!"

"You do not need them," Rosie asserted.

"One day I will shake them off. Slip away." He wiggled his eyebrows at Otto, who ignored him.

Elin sat back. "They would not allow you to be unprotected."

"I will find the seams and leak—or lash"—he slashed at the air, playacting with an invisible sword—"my way out."

Otto cleared his throat. Glancing at him, his seriousness struck me as an effort to counterbalance Simeon, as if by holding words back, he'd make up for some instability in the room. By comparison, Simeon's talking felt, suddenly, childish.

I changed the subject. "Bread or swans, we all look forward to the wedding. And to meeting the king. I am sure you are eager to introduce him to his future daughter-in-law."

Simeon stifled a yawn. "My father is touring the kingdom. He won't be back until the wedding itself."

"Oh." I sat back, in surprise. "I hope there will be no ill will for having the ceremony so soon." It was odd—very odd—that the king would not meet his son's bride until the matrimonial feast. That there wouldn't be a series of royal banquets and festivities leading up to the grand ceremony. Each an opportunity for our ruler to bestow his blessing.

Simeon did not share my concerns. "You have to have will to have ill will." He chuckled. Otto, more forcefully, cleared his throat, but Simeon continued: "It's my mother who oversees it all. Iron fist, soft glove, that kind of thing." He held up a tight hand and then rapped it on the table, loudly, to make his point. Some white dust sifted and fell from the beams above us onto the platters of bread. "*He* has no stomach, and *she* has only appetite."

Otto glanced up, eyes following the path of the falling dust, then tracing vines and apples on the ceiling. If you looked closely enough, the edges of the stain were obvious. Not just marked, but wet, dark. Something in Otto's prowling eyes and Simeon's insouciant dismissal of his father was not sitting well. It was more than my own deception—what that stain belied—that made the room go off-kilter.

"You are the heir," I said to Simeon, "and Elin will mother the future heirs. Surely, the king would want to see her . . . before . . . to show the kingdom the union has his benison . . ." I ended up losing courage. But the conclusion of my thoughts wasn't necessary to voice. Otto had lowered his eyes and was watching Simeon with focused attention.

The prince took a measured breath, making a visible show of his patience. I thought of the stiffness I had seen in Morwen's shoulders. I felt, inexplicably, fear. But Simeon soon smiled, a generous smile, all traces of his forbearance gone. He turned to Elin. "Your stepmother is sweet. She wants to see you get the honors, the fanfare, you deserve." He reached out and placed his hand over hers on the tablecloth, his long fingers arched, his hand calling to mind an oversized spider. He directed his gaze back to me. "The king is making his way back. It is only that Elin and I cannot stand to wait. We are ever so impatient. Young love. You must have known it. I think, in fact, I recall my mother knows a bit about both of your long-ago, ill-fated engagements. Each were only a few weeks, were they not? My condolences, by the way. Twice over. But you understand the heart has a sense of urgency. Even just yesterday, I was itching to ride out here, to set eyes on my pretty flower." His hand flattened on Elin's. "Isn't that right, darling?"

"Yes," she assured. Yes—the conditioning of her book. Yes—the dreams of a girl. What else but yes?

Simeon's smile, which had remained in place, relaxed. He stretched his neck, chin extended toward the sky, revealing its whiter underparts, skin untouched by sun, the cords around his throat taut. His head snapped forward once more. "And rest assured, Elin will get all the fanfare she wants. A lifetime of it."

"Indeed," I said. My own version of *yes*. Decades of being habituated to accord. For I had said the word, smoothed all things forward in our perpetual march, despite having realized what was bothering me. Since he had first mentioned it, I had been turning over Simeon's elaborate metaphor of a cage. Walls were designed to keep danger out. A cage was built to keep a threat contained.

I felt a prickle of concern—a sense of something going off course. I stood, needing, suddenly, to leave the room. To breathe air that wasn't shared. "I will go see about something sweet." I looked at Elin, her pink cheeks. "To eat," I added. "Something sweet to eat."

SUCKET WAS MOST OFTEN CONSUMED WITH A DOUBLE-ENDED UTEN-sil. On one side, there was a two-pronged fork, a devil's spear, which was used to stab and ferry candied fruits to waiting mouths. On the other, there was a flat spoon, used for scooping and slurping the leftover syrup. The liquid was all sugar. Boiled and reduced and boiled once more. More sugar added. More reduction. It was decadence—a concentration of the most expensive ingredient. And Simeon had said he didn't care for sweets.

Balancing a tray of forks and the sucket, the fruits bobbing in their cloying syrup, I pushed back into the hall. The prince was alone with the girls. All my daughters were turned toward him, like flowers to the sun. He was still eating.

"Put it just there." He nodded to the space in front of him.

Looking down at the candied fruit—citrus rinds in curls and spirals—I wondered if Simeon himself was a sucket. Flesh and skin boiled in its own syrup.

"Your Highness." I placed the tray where he had directed and began to pass out the forks around the table. Otto's seat sat empty. "Will the counselor not be joining?"

Simeon picked up a sucket fork and held its prongs to the light. "Probably seeing to the horses."

But, above us, the ceiling creaked, and some more dust sifted. Mathilde's gaze lurched skyward at the sound of footsteps from above. Rosie, who had been twirling a lock of her hair, went dead still. Elin, not realizing, reached for her own fork.

I had seen Otto glance upward. Had seen him watch the dust filter through the cracks. I looked up now at the mural. The many apples. The faded red. I felt a little nauseous.

"I forgot . . ." I didn't finish the sentence. I made for the door.

I COULDN'T BRING MYSELF TO HURRY. THE ACT WOULD CONFIRM MY fears were valid. And so I went to the entry hall and up our grand staircase slowly. The steps creaked and moaned under my feet. And, when I turned at the top of the stairs to go to the west-facing wing, my legs moved as if weighted by lead. Dread had personified into slow motion. But all my delaying had little power to stave off the inevitable: When I got to the double doors that concealed our rubble, they lay open.

Like a long-boiled sucket, disappointment, reduced down into one puckered image: Otto, posture stiff, hands behind his back, in front of the pile of rubble. He turned to me, frowning. "Were you trying to keep this concealed?"

I was indignant. "You cannot just go prowling—"

"It is dangerous."

"This is my home, and you've not been invited—"

He ignored me and stared into the rubble pensively. "The debris is heavy and could fall through on the heads of everyone who sits downstairs."

I gathered myself. "I assure you, the matter is well in hand."

He turned back to look at me. "Your roof has fallen in."

"And will be repaired."

"I am going to tell the prince to leave. You should advise your family to do the same."

He turned and made for the double doors, and with him, I worried he was taking our entire future.

"They are to be married in a matter of days," I called, and he slowed. "They barely know one another. Would you truly deny them a chance to spend a little time together?"

Otto's jaw ticked. He didn't respond and continued toward the doors.

"Stop!" I called, and he did.

He turned back to me. "This is grossly irresponsible."

His words burned and then my own tumbled forth: "You have done everything in your power to prevent my happiness. To prevent a union between one of my daughters and Prince Simeon. At every turn, you have been a blockade."

"My lady," he said, grimly.

"Do you deny it?" I cried.

"I do not deny it."

Not suitable. I was unable to speak for a moment.

"You are right that I did not want your daughters to match with the prince. And you are right that I did what I could to prevent it."

To hear it stated, to see him tell me with such little emotion, forced the air from my chest. "What right have you to interfere?"

"It's not a matter of right. It's a matter of duty."

Insulted, aggravated, I had to ask: "And what in your duty insists my daughters are not a suitable match?"

"Etheldreda." He looked me over. "You mistake me. It was not the prince I was trying to protect. It was your daughters. And in that I have failed. You have my apologies." He bowed, stiffly.

"I always seem to have your apologies yet I am left the one insulted."

He looked pained. "I must remove everyone from the dining hall." He half turned again, then stopped, and pulled from his pocket something so familiar I thought my heart might stop. There, in his gloved hand, was my mother's cameo. "I knew you would want it back."

I could hardly move. "I don't understand."

He thrust it forward, so I would take it.

"How did you know it was there?"

"It is my job."

"Were you following me?"

"It is my job," he said, again.

"To have me followed?" I could not make heads or tails of our conversation.

"To ensure the well-being of the kingdom. And its constituents." He still held out the cameo. The carving was undamaged, but my mother's profile appeared emptier to me. Unchanged, yet somehow, a bit hollow. For what silhouette could contain a woman's multitudes? I snatched the necklace from Otto's hands.

"Will you tell?" I whispered.

He shook his head, disappointed with me. "You ask the wrong questions."

I knew, deep down, that he was trying to tell me something. But I was distracted—by the rubble, by the departing prince, and by the surprising weight of a new fact: Otto's dissatisfaction with me weighed as heavily as any message he could have imparted.

CHAPTER TWENTY-SIX

~⚘~

THERE ARE FAR-FETCHED STORIES OF HEADLESS MEN THAT WAN-der, bodies that keep walking without skulls. But I've killed enough chickens to know: Sometimes a torso just keeps going. The last pumps of the heart. The legs moving. The final stumble before the collapse. The rest of the afternoon had the energy of that kind of fall—everything moving forward, but with no more grace than a terminal lurch. A staggering pitter-patter of footwork toward some inevitable end.

I didn't know what excuses Otto made to Simeon. By the time I made it back to the great hall, everyone was already standing, heading toward the doors. A series of quick goodbyes and reassurances from the prince to Elin. *Darling*, he called her. And he was off, back in his carriage, all the guards gathered, the men on their horses, Simeon safe, once more, in his cage.

Inside, I did not allow anyone else to clear the table. I did it myself, glancing, when I was able, at the mural, the stain, on the ceiling above. If Otto was right, if all those apples could not bear the weight of the rubble, then I had put everyone in danger. I pushed away the thought.

Hurried to empty the room of dirtied dishes. The bones of two pheasants. The remaining loaves of bread. What was left of the sucket was covered in a thin film of white dust.

Otto had been following me. I turned this over in my mind. Thought, with shame, of all the things he might have seen, had most certainly seen: Me, in the mud, with the rabbit. Pawning my last jewel. Straining to catch the love of a prince in an empty field.

But it had worked. For the unintended daughter—foolish Elin, ungrateful Elin, a girl dimmed by the axioms she thought protected her. But it had worked nevertheless. So why would Otto—in all his efforts to separate our family from the prince—ever have the gumption, the gall, to claim he had been trying to help me?

Not suitable, he had said.

I had felt the abuse of the words like a brand on my own skin.

You ask the wrong questions, he had said.

I could not help but wonder—clearing the last of the loaves, whipping the diamond-patterned linen from the table, shutting the doors to the great hall behind me—not suitable for what?

MORWEN WAS THE ONLY OTHER PERSON IN THE HOUSEHOLD ATTUNED to the last stumbling steps I was certain we were all taking. I found her in her bedchamber, packing a satchel. Seeing me at the door, she strode over to a window shade and pulled it shut, as if securing the place for her absence. "You cannot change my mind this time." She gave the tie a proper tug.

I took a step into the room. There was little furniture left except for the bed, which sat like a moored ship in the middle of the floor. The walls had once been a deep blue, but large swaths had since been bleached by the sun. "Morwen, you must tell me what you know about Prince Simeon."

"I am a lady's maid—" she began.

"By God's bones, I know." I held up a hand. "And you were not trained to be a parlor maid, or scullery maid. But that doesn't explain everything." I walked across to an uncovered window. A dead beetle lay on the sill. "I am not insisting that you stay, I am asking—what do you know about the prince?"

She tensed and turned away, not wanting to look at me.

I thought of training hawks, how you must make yourself nothing in the room. How trust comes slowly, by degrees. I was silent, for a while, and then picked up the beetle and carried it to the fireplace, which was empty and offered no warmth. "You said you had siblings." I kept my voice soft. "Surely some of them are sisters."

"What makes you think I know something of the prince?" Fear, again, in the set of her wide shoulders. Her nervousness felt discordant with her capable body, like she was wearing clothes stitched for someone else.

"A lady's maid with experience in a good household should have no trouble finding work. She certainly wouldn't need to come here, for no pay." Still, I spoke softly. Willing myself into nothing. If I could have muffled my heartbeat, I would have. I had only a short amount of time to get her to trust me. "I sense you have a story."

"Most do." She didn't elaborate.

"Most would trade their front teeth for a chance to see a prince. Not hide in the kitchens."

"He's not worth a donkey's tooth," she spat.

"I am only asking for information," I said, though she had just given me some. "It need not change anything. So that I might better prepare them. My daughters. Elin. Wouldn't you want the same for your sisters? Morwen, please tell me—what do you know of the prince? Have you waited on him? Did he visit your last household?"

She snorted.

"That's a yes, then?"

Morwen sank her face into the heel of her hand and took a deep breath. Glanced at the open door to the room.

"Come, come into the dressing room, then," I assured her, leading the way. An ornate tub sat empty above wide-planked floors. Little light came through the solitary window. "No candles," I told Morwen, as she followed me in. "But more privacy. Come in, no one can hear us in here."

She stepped in, after me, but remained silent.

"Go on," I told her, gently.

But she remained silent, stubborn—or unwilling.

I reached out and grabbed ahold of her arm. Squeezed harder than I should have. Dug my fingernails into her soft flesh. "Please, Morwen."

She looked down at her arm. "You're hurting me."

I dug in a little tighter. "They are my daughters."

Morwen held my eyes for a moment. I released her arm, and, as I did, she exhaled. "I used to work in the palace," she explained.

I nodded, though my pulse began to thrum. Some part of me thinking, *Here we are*.

"I was Princess Hemma's lady's maid," Morwen continued.

"Simeon's sister." I nodded. "What of Simeon?" I didn't want to say anything to deter her from speaking.

"What of him?" Morwen's face went dark.

"Please," I told her.

She nodded. "His nature is common knowledge."

"At court?"

She chose her words carefully. "He is charming, yes, but . . . something else, too. He has an ability to make you feel complicit in his desires, in the moment, but after leaves one wondering what happened."

"What happened, then?"

"People know to avoid him," she tried to explain.

"Does he harm women?" I asked, too quickly. My fingernails digging into my own flesh now.

She stiffened. "Ma'am, you misunderstand me. Princes are princes. Power is power. People are not concerned with how he treats the women."

I lost whatever gentleness I was holding on to. "Then what is it that you are telling me?" I demanded. "What is it that I need to know?"

"I am trying to say that his engagement—they could not arrange a marriage for him. They could not find a noble man or cousin willing to marry off his daughter. The ball—that is why they invited all the country women."

"To find him a wife."

"To find him a wife." She nodded. "And quickly."

Three weeks, I thought to myself. I drew in a breath, trying to connect the pieces. To understand the thread. "But why? Because he is a brute? You are saying he is a brute?"

"Haven't you wondered, ma'am, why you haven't seen the princess? Not at the ball, not ever?"

I hadn't. I had never wondered. She was only a girl in a painting. Abstract and meaningless to me. But I thought, then, of all the closed curtains at the palace. Of the walled garden. Of her absence at the ball. A woman could be kept so quiet it was hard to notice when she disappeared.

I watched Morwen, waiting, but she did not answer her own question. I reached for her arm, again, intending, this time, not to use my fingernails, but to reassure. Morwen pulled away and whispered, "She's pregnant," as if the fact itself was my fault.

I blinked at her.

"Kept under lock and key," she continued. "They dismissed her entire staff, but I knew. She told me. And Simeon must marry quickly, for they—he and his mother—plan to pass the baby off as his own."

A noise came from the door, which swung in. We both started.

But it was only Mathilde, who stood, a look of shock on her face. We turned to her. Me, dismayed. Morwen, afraid. We were caught together in those last, stumbling footsteps.

Mathilde looked back and forth between us and the headless body fell with a final, echoing thump.

CHAPTER TWENTY-SEVEN

WHEN I WAS A GIRL, A BUTTERFLY FLEW THROUGH A CRACKED window, into my room. It knocked back against the parchment, trying to find a way out. Into sunshine. Into air. Chalky wings palpitating. I reached for it, wanting to help. Tried to grab it, cup it in my hands, so I could deliver the thing back to freedom. But my gesture, my very touch, brought injury. The butterfly fell to the floor, wing torn.

Why, after however many years and bloody ends, however many animals gutted and disemboweled by Lucy, however many chickens plucked for supper, did I think of a butterfly? I had tried to help, and I'd hurt. I'd gotten myself caught in the surprise of the mismatch of intention and outcome. The unfairness: a rend, a mangled wing, by my own hand.

I did not sleep well. Or at all. It is difficult to mark the moment you cross over from your own wild thoughts to those of unconsciousness. But I thought of butterflies and white dust falling on golden loaves. I thought of Elin and Rosie and Mathilde. Of Morwen. Of what had happened already and what was still to come. I thought of deceit.

I reasoned: What I had learned was deception, but it was not quite injustice. For an unmarried girl—a princess no less—being with child was an unrecoverable blow. A woman had only her reputability. Her wifely ideals, her chastity, her projection of following all rules, her performance, meant survival. A swelled belly counteracted all of that. Do not forget the pregnant maidservant whose torso was beaten black-and-blue. Do not forget those swollen bodies in the stream. Some might have preferred a knife in the gut.

So perhaps there was another way to look at what Simeon and Sigrid were doing. Deception, yes, but also a kind of familial chivalry. The protection of a beloved sister and daughter. Would I do it any different? I thought yes. I thought no. I could not get my thoughts to settle.

I ROSE AS I USUALLY DID, BEFORE FIRST LIGHT. FEET SEARCHING FOR slippers. The same sprint to the dressing area. Hoary frost, thicker now, clinging to the windows. Lucy no longer inside.

In the gloom of the hallway, Mathilde was waiting for me in the open cavity of her doorway. She held a candle. Her sable hair streamed around her shoulders. Her face marmoreal in the firelight. Her eyes dark. I got closer and saw another figure, just behind her. The white of a nightgown. The glint of a wet eye. Rosie was in Mathilde's room, and I could tell, from her expression—the accusation, the need, the laid-bare question—that Mathilde had told her what she had overheard. And somewhere above, Elin slept soundly.

They came toward me like ghosts behind that raised candle. Mouths open, teeth chattering, breathing out the need to know, the need for reassurance, the demand of the promise that all would be well. Each face the mirror of the other. Determined. Certain I could fix the problem.

I wondered if all my life I had misled them. Placated. Made promises. Held their limbs and fretted over every accident of the body and heart—the stubbed toe, the scraped knee, the slipped knife that nicked the finger. All our goodbyes made easy by vows to return. My mothering had always been an offer of certainty. Of protection.

"You are going to the city?" Rosie asked, voice but a whisper.

"Yes," I confirmed. Still offering that false reassurance. For I did not understand the problem. I could not feel the terrain of its surface, I could not foresee its size. It was like hugging a boulder: my body pressed against rock, my arms reaching, hopelessly unable to meet on the other side. Heavy and immovable. And the girls, peering at me with their oversized low-light pupils, little pools of black, looking at me like I could turn granite to dust.

"You will see about this news," Mathilde confirmed.

"Yes," I said again.

"And you will mend things?" Rosie, whispering again.

"Yes." And to give strength to the lie, I said it twice: "Yes."

As I saddled Arno, I wondered: What was mending things? I was still unclear about what had broken. Postponement, or even revocation, of the wedding was impossible. We had come too far. We had a hole in the roof the size of a small cottage. But accepting the deceit of the situation left a bitter taste in my mouth, as cold and metallic as a knife on the tongue. I could not shake the thought of Sigrid, leaning toward me from her pile of furs, revealing her pointed little gray tooth.

I did not know what to tell Elin. Did Simeon care for her? Or was it only weakness that had attracted him—the instinct of a moth drawn to the needed flame of her vulnerability? A fragile flower who had collapsed from the overwhelming opulence of a dance floor. A delicate, obedient girl who wanted to please.

But Elin would still become a princess, and later, a queen. And my girls, no matter how their view of the world might have to reshape and form again, would be set up with more advantageous matches, would rub better-adorned shoulders, than I ever might have wished for. Once again, my thoughts looped back around to the protection the queen and prince—mother and son—were offering the princess. An unending cycle of thoughts in my head, ruminations that contradicted themselves, weaving and melding into a tapestry ugly enough to make me feel mad.

I rode Arno hard the entire way to the city. The horse lost his stamina by the time we arrived. Leaving him at a run-down stable far from the palace walls, I had to finish my journey on foot. Hood up. Past men sleeping on the edges of the street. Past a child missing an eye. Past a beggar, who tried to clutch at my riding skirts. As if all the world were the same boulder I was trying to wrap my arms around.

The guardhouse knew me this time. Or knew my proclamation: I was the mother of the woman betrothed to the prince. Queen Sigrid was expecting me, I said, and I was let in, without delay. Power, proximity to it, felt greasy. Doors sprung open. Guards stood at attention. I walked up to the palace, and right into its mouth.

I WAS LED THROUGH THE LONG GALLERY WITH THE CHECKERED floors and oversized paintings. This time, I read the portrait of the royal family differently: Saw intensity in Simeon's posture. Weakness in the arched back of the king. I could not read Hemma at all—her pouty pink lips, her yellow hair, were inscrutable. Before I could weave any of this into a semblance of understanding all I had learned, we were continuing into the series of sherbet rooms that followed. Each as sugared and frilled as the next. All the curtains pulled shut on the east-facing windows.

I kept my eyes on the walls. Looked for cracks in the silk wallpapers and gaps in the tapestries. Motes of dust and places where the air came through. I thought of Otto, bustling out of the panel in the wall. Simeon, stepping into the throne room from a door that had sprung from nowhere. I knew the rooms, now, for what they were, what they had always been: varicolored jewel boxes of deception, paper palaces, constructed to conceal as much as they showed off.

I counted the chambers as we passed. When we had gone far enough, I stopped, and turned back to the footman escorting me. "I require a moment for personal matters."

He paused, a stockinged foot thrust forward. "My lady?"

"A long journey without rest, and personal matters beckon." I gestured to my torso. Embarrassed, he pulled his foot back and stood up straight.

"Of course, just through these doors." He gestured ahead. "If you'll allow me—"

"Personal matters," I repeated, holding up a hand.

He nodded. "There is a privy three rooms forward. Would you like me to call a lady's maid?"

I hid my smile—Morwen had already given me all the assistance I needed. "That isn't necessary."

I glanced back only once to ensure the footman did not follow.

The walls of the privy room were covered in a mural of a hunting scene. It depicted only men, leaning forward from horseback in billowing robes. On one wall, a dead boar lay on its side, a spear stuck into its gut, blood pooling. The artist had used only one shade of paint for the blood. Death, they must have reasoned, being simple. I searched the mural, looking for flaws, a variation in the pattern. And there, in the back, I saw it, blended in, but noticeable if you knew to look: an outline of a door.

Morwen had explained that the inside of the palace was made up of a series of servants' hallways, used by staff and royalty alike. Windowless corridors that ran alongside the rooms like veins that kept the palace supplied. The hidden panel swung inward easily.

The passageway was dark. Walls of rough, raw wood—in complete opposition to the pomp of the rooms it sat next to. There was little to see by, except for rectangles of light that came from doorways ahead and behind. I began to move down the hallway, just as Morwen had instructed. Some of the rectangles—the doorways—had voices on the other side. More often, they were silent. I picked up my pace; I could not be caught.

Morwen had said to follow the passageway all the way to its end, and take a set of stairs to the right. I was nearly to the stairs, I could make them out ahead, when I heard voices and a door swung inward, ahead of me. I sucked in air. I had no time to check. I reached for the nearest rectangle of light without any idea of what awaited me on the other side.

The room was empty.

I was not sure what I was after. Why was I taking such risks? Proof, perhaps. Something about the look in Rosie's and Mathilde's eyes. *Information*, I had told Morwen. But what does one do with information? Wield it? Trade it? I only knew I felt urged forward.

I looked around the bedchamber I stood in. A white sheet covered what appeared to be a desk and chair. The bed had a coverlet, but no pillows, and beneath the cover the mattress was bare. On the other side of the secret doorway, I could hear the voices—two chambermaids, it seemed—get closer.

Here, too, the shades were drawn on the east-facing windows. I pulled them aside to reveal a view of the enclosed garden I had seen from the ball. In daylight, I could see its outer wall was new. No vines grew upon its surface, and the stones had the flinty look of a recent quarrying. As I had noticed before, the wall was unbroken by gates or breaks or arches. Inside, there were roses. A series of fountains. A copse of trees. No people. The whole thing—well manicured, thoughtfully looked after—was empty. Inaccessible.

When the voices from the passageway had passed, I listened at the secret door for a moment longer, and, hearing nothing, pushed back into the inner hallway. I found the stairs at the end of the hall. Went down them, and through an archway, past a pile of mops and hazel brooms. From there I reversed directions and counted doors—rectangles of light—and came to a stop in front of the seventh.

The entry was locked from the exterior with an iron dead bolt. *I* could open it—what lay beyond was what could not get out. But there were no ghouls or beasts or demons in this cage: If Morwen was right, inside, I'd find a pregnant woman.

With a scraping noise, the bolt loosened. I pushed through, intent on reaching Hemma.

❧

I UNDERSTOOD RIGHT AWAY.

Elin's malleable delicacy—her fainting, her weakness, her years of conditioning by the sweet maxims of her well-worn book—was appealing, certainly. The nature of a girl who could be cajoled to participate in a lifelong ruse. But she had been picked for her looks.

Hemma's hair was as colorless as Elin's. Icy, near-white tresses. She had the same pinkness around her eyes. Skin so pale it looked translucent. Even if the girl's dress hadn't belied an obvious swelling at her belly, I would have seen the truth of Morwen's tale in an instant: The women looked too similar for the story to have been made up. The princess's baby would look like Elin's without raising any suspicion.

"It all makes more sense now," I said, to myself, more than to Hemma, who was staring at me, the stranger who had burst into her room, with alarm. She had sprung to her feet when I came through, and held, still, the sampler she had been working on, the needle now brandished like a weapon.

"Who are you?" she demanded. Clutching the hoop in her other hand.

A part of me wanted to laugh. At the absurdity and intelligence of it. On Rosie's behalf. After all my orchestrations—the market, the picnic, the damn broken chaise. Both of my birth daughters had sun-kissed skin and dark, abundant hair. Hair that flowed black. There was no amount of performance, no beauty, that could have passed this inevitable test. Otto had been right: For this task, they were wholly, undeniably *not suitable*.

Something had loosened inside of me, some tightness I had been holding on to. The world unspooling. "I am Etheldreda." I took a step toward her. "The stepmother of your future sister-in-law."

My announcement did not relax Hemma. The hand that held the needle flipped and rested protectively in front of her belly, as if the splayed fingers might disguise its swelled form. "You should not be here."

"I already know about your . . ." I eyed her torso. "Condition."

"Who sent you?" she demanded.

"It is clever," I said, ignoring the question, "how much you look alike. You and Elin. Your painting, the one in the gallery, looks otherwise."

Hemma's eyelashes quivered and her hand fell. "I was painted to look like my mother."

"She had you painted other than you are?"

Hemma's coloring was the same as Elin's, but she had had years of being conditioned as a princess. She fixed me with an even stare and narrowed her eyes. "She said I look depleted in the original. Bats and fleas, my brother used to say, drain all my blood when I sleep. Now, tell me—what are you doing in my rooms?"

From the size of her abdomen, I guessed she was a little less than halfway along. But she had small hands. A round face. The girl was just a child.

"Is your plan to deliver in secret? Keep the baby squirreled away and try to pass it off as Elin's nine months after the wedding?"

"*My* plan?"

"I suppose people won't really be able to tell the difference in size after a few months," I mused aloud. *Such a big baby*, people would exclaim. *The blood of a king*, I could imagine Simeon saying. A hand on Elin's arm squeezing too hard. I shook off the image. The princess was being kept in a locked room. The beautiful tapestries on the wall and the feather bed in the corner were no different than when Sigrid had tried to put a lace bow on the bandage that had covered her missing finger. "Morwen is worried for you," I told her.

Hemma let out a small huff of air. "What do you know of Morwen?"

I didn't say anything and waited.

"Where is she?" she asked, more plaintively. She set her needle back down on the tabletop, making a show of the gesture.

"She's tried to see you. She's been turned away."

The princess glanced at the door I had come through. "If Morwen sent you, then you are certainly not supposed to be here."

I thought she was going to tell me to leave, to point at the door—but instead she stepped toward me and grabbed my wrist. Her fingers so thin. Delicate. "Someone might come at any minute. Please, I need to hear of Morwen. Let's go to the gardens."

She beckoned me through a set of doors that led outside and pulled me along a trellised walkway. Explaining over her shoulder that we had to stay under the arbor. Her mother's chambers looked over the enclosed yard. We must not be seen. "She had the garden built with no entrances except to and from my own rooms," Hemma went on, "so that I could go outside, and no one would stumble upon me. But my mother worries, still, that someone will see from above."

The girl was given an outdoor pen like a common animal. But it explained the rows of closed curtains. I looked up to all the mullioned windows—closed eyes—in the palace walls.

Hemma followed my glance. "My mother cannot see me with anyone other than her maidservants."

"Surely you have a lady-in-waiting or an attendant?"

"There are two servants that attend me, the only ones in and out, and they are my mother's. Everyone else was sent away." Hemma shook her head. "That is why Morwen was dismissed. They could not have anyone partaking in the secret." She let out a bitter laugh. "I had already told her."

I felt a wave of dismay. "You are not allowed outside of your rooms?" How lonely it would be for a young girl to be given only a needle and thread to pass all the hours it took to grow a life inside of her.

Hemma gestured to herself. "How could I go anywhere? Now, please, give me news of Morwen. She attended to me since I was eleven."

"And you are now?"

"Sixteen."

"Morwen is safe," I assured her, trying to keep the alarm from my face. "But unable to find employment. She was turned out with no references."

We'd come to the end of the trellis. Sparing a worried glance toward the windows, Hemma led me farther, to the copse of trees. "No one can see us here," she told me. "And I shall be Morwen's reference."

"Write one, and I will give it to her." I thought of the lock on the door. "Are you confined here against your will, or by choice?"

"I cannot go out and about like this." She gestured at herself again, as if imploring me to see: She could not go out and about in her own body.

"So, you are hidden—you will stay hidden—until the babe comes, and then return to the life of a princess."

"There is no life for an unwed princess with child." Her lips puckered, as if she were swallowing something sour. "My life has always been these rooms and these walls."

I looked at the trees around us. Their trunks still weak with youth. I was trying to make sense of it, of being here in this walled garden, in the construction of the garden itself, when Hemma might have just been sent away to a summer home. "Why are they not just giving it away, your child? Why will they pass it off as Elin's child? Why keep it in the royal family?"

"It is royal." She stared at me.

"But—it will appear to be the firstborn child, the heir to the kingdom."

"Yes, exactly." Hemma watched me closely and looked, for the first time, unnerved. She shook her head. "Elin is your daughter? You are here for her?"

"Stepdaughter." I nodded, feeling, again, the sensation of trying to wrap my arms around a boulder.

"And you say we are alike?" Hemma glanced worriedly at the palace windows. "Have you not wondered why Simeon would agree to take a wife so abruptly? Why a future king would stoop to such levels?"

"Stoop?" I repeated, offended. "He must care about you, greatly, to go to such lengths. Or your mother does, and he is doing as she wishes. But I cannot make sense of—"

"Stop," she demanded, frustrated by my words.

I agreed with my silence and Hemma held my eyes, trying to say so much with her own.

"Who got you pregnant?" I asked, stupidly, because I knew a second before she said it. I was sorry to make her say it aloud, but it was too late.

"My brother." She didn't look away.

"Simeon?" I was still stunned by the confirmation.

"King of the beasts," she confirmed. Her whole body tense.

"You two are—"

"No," she whispered.

"You did not want—" I couldn't bring myself to finish the sentence.

"No, I did not," she confirmed, with less vehemence, her shoulders falling.

"He preyed on you?" I asked, appalled. I could not help but think of my girls. Mathilde's scar. The twin braids. The freckle on a calf. How easily all the world's children become your own.

She shook her head and whispered, as if frightened: "Not just me. Not only me. *Also* me."

The wall around the garden felt, suddenly, monstrous and suffocating. Not only a snake—a constrictor. "You are his sister." I did not want to believe her. I did not want to accept her story. But—I thought back to the wound I had seen on Simeon's arm, the day of our picnic. His apologetic smile. His haste to dismiss it. The sleeve pulled down. The lesion had had a distinctive pattern. Semilunar and curved: It followed the crescent shape of human teeth.

Hemma was quiet. "Woman first, sister second." Then she looked up and held my eyes. "She deserves to know."

CHAPTER TWENTY-EIGHT

>πー**ꟼ**ー✕

T HERE WAS NOT TIME TO EXAMINE HEMMA'S STORY. TO GET EV-
ery detail. To compose the questions that were swirling, half
formed, around my mind. But did the *how* or the *when* or even the
why really matter in the face of the *what*? No amount of information
changed the *what*. And I could barely stand to make the princess—
drained by bats, her brother had said—recount it all. I did not blame
Hemma for her haste to dispel me from her chambers. She wrote a
servant's commendation for Morwen on a short scroll of parchment,
and I was sent back out into the service passageway. I locked her door
behind me, leaving Hemma in her gilded cage.

As I felt my way forward in the darkness, my thoughts were jumbled
and indirect. The harm of one child always calls to mind the possibility
of the harm of your own.

As a mother, you must accept that death and its partners—pain and
anguish—are coming for your children. Fear is the steady little hiccup
that drives you, wakes you in the night, stealing sleep and forcing extra
kisses at each goodbye. You hope, beyond all measure, that when death
or anguish come for your children, it will be peaceful, late in life, and

long after you are gone. What a contradiction: to have to accept that your entire role—giving life—was impossible, short-lived, fleeting. But it was not unjust.

Cruelty was different than fatality. Cruelty was not a necessary condition. And no matter which way I turned it—rushing through that dark passageway, losing count of the doors—cruelty was not something a person ever should, or could, make peace with.

I felt reckless. I was lost. I did not wait to listen at the lit rectangle of the next door I saw, but pushed forth into the nearest room. Acid-turquoise walls and drapes. Gold mirrors. I had no idea where I was.

I should have waited. I should have gathered my thoughts. Lessened the heat of my emotions. But I was a mother, and I could not help it. I found a footman at one of the doors and approached him. He looked up at me in surprise, and I told him, lacking no confidence, feeling, in that moment, entirely certain: "I am here to see the queen. I've gotten lost looking for the water closet. Take me to her at once."

I was led back outside, across a different part of the gardens—low boxwood mazes, conical evergreens—to a hothouse filled with orange trees. Inner warmth fogged the windows, but as soon as I stepped inside, I could see: Sigrid was having breakfast with three ladies-in-waiting, each at one side of the table.

The room was overfilled and a bit steamy, like a fantasy that Sigrid had concocted out of magic and will. Citrus bent leaf-covered branches. The clouded windows blocked the view of the winter-barren gardens and the festooned guards. The outside world no longer existed.

The queen eyed me with surprise. I felt the weight of all I had learned. The pregnancy. The molestation. I was speaking to the boy's mother. And she was the queen. If ever there were forces to ensure you chose your words carefully, these were them. But I summoned all my will, all my fury, all my horror, and announced: "I have come to annul the engagement."

The ladies-in-waiting quieted, turning to me, glancing back to Sigrid, their attention as jumpy as little morning birds. Sigrid watched me over the rim of her coffee cup. Then she set it in its saucer, decisively. "Oh, what a dirge you have come to sing!" She reached forward and selected a pastry from the top tier of a platter of sweets. The ladies around her relaxed.

I looked at the group of them, sitting in their tabbies and blonds, surrounded by fans and feathered muffs and tiny crystal glasses of fruit juice, sniggering at their queen's bidding. The whole group of them—Sigrid and her pastries included—disgusted me. All these years, I had thought Sigrid sat beside the sun as it shone on the rest of us, but, really, she had only climbed up into air. Into nothing.

"I know about the babe," I said.

The queen looked at me for a long moment, measuring, I think, what I was capable of. Around her, the ladies-in-waiting had again begun to make faces, using their fans to cover smirks without any intention of covering them at all. The fans dropped abruptly when the queen said: "Leave us."

I waited as the ladies stood—floating puffs of violet and pink—and filed from the room, ignoring their resentful looks as they passed.

"You've interrupted my breakfast." Sigrid speared a tiny sausage link with her fork.

"It's your own daughter." I spoke quietly, watching as the sausage was ferried to Sigrid's plate. Her face did not change. "Your son," I added, and thought I saw the slightest hint of a flinch.

Sigrid steeled herself, her face settling into a mask. She sawed the sausage in two. "As if there is no precedent for royal bastards. We are born to breed, are we not? That's what us women are for. That's why we're married off and so carefully managed. And then after we breed, we protect. To do any differently would be to live in contradiction with your own makeup."

I tried to hold her eye, but she was still sawing her sausage. "Not if you are protecting a monster."

She nodded. "Perhaps I am a monster, then. Perhaps so are you. Perhaps we are monsters raising more monsters. It doesn't change the outcome. A monster, after all, needs a mother, too. This is what we do for our children, Ethel. What we do for ourselves. If you think you and I are any different, I suggest you take a long, hard gander in the looking glass."

"Having a monster is different than enabling one!"

She dropped her fork with a clatter. "Have you ever loved a single thing more than your own child?" She began tugging on her glove, pulling finger by finger. "Have you ever felt what you feel about those little apples of yours, for a man, or a bird?" The glove loosened and she pulled it off, revealing her hand beneath. The stump of a finger. She wagged those that remained at me. "I would cut off the rest of them myself for Simeon—for Hemma, too. And now I've found a solution that suits everyone. Hemma is protected. Simeon's firstborn will stay in the family, where it belongs. The bloodline isn't even polluted. And your Elin ends up a princess, no less, with no pain, no effort. A guaranteed child! If only we all had such odds. And even you—and your other black-headed girls—will benefit by association. So I am not sure what you are hoping to accomplish, coming here."

I didn't know what I was hoping to accomplish, either. I wanted to make arguments for what was right and what was just, but rightness and justice had little to do with the kind of power Sigrid wielded. "Elin is a young girl looking for love and fairy tales. She will not do well with the arrangement," I said, voice low. "They will not do well together. You solve your immediate problems and set up a lifetime of trial, for everyone."

Sigrid laughed. "What is doing well? Elin will have jewels and gowns and acolytes."

"She will be a puppet!"

The queen shook her head as if I were being foolish. "All wives are puppets until they learn to master the strings."

"There are other solutions. You need not wall Hemma in—"

Sigrid's eyes flared. "Do not talk to me of Hemma." She took a breath. Sipped from a glass of ruby-colored juice. The red marked her lips when she set it back down. "Your protest is boring me. Why all the fuss? Elin is not even your real daughter."

"She is someone's daughter."

"All women are someone's daughter," Sigrid replied with irritation. "If you think any of yours will find peace or security without my blessing, you are sorely mistaken."

My stomach twisted. I believed the threat. I believed in her willingness to enforce it. Sigrid continued, eating her sausage, the stub of missing finger at the center of her fist. "If you want a future for your daughters, for all of them, this wedding will proceed."

"We have nothing to offer," I protested. Desperation squeezing the words from my mouth. "We are poorer than we look. No better than peasants."

Sigrid watched me.

"We are," I continued, racking my mind for the right words, "not . . . suitable."

One of her smiles. The shiftiest, most vicious of her dancing bears. "Don't embarrass yourself."

"I speak the truth."

"I already know all about your pitiable circumstances. All the more reason for you to embrace the wedding." With a definitive gesture, Sigrid finished her juice. The crystal glass was set back onto the table and she wiped her lips with a square of lace. "You know our secrets now, so do not think you'll escape our grasp. The wedding will happen. Elin will be a princess. We will fix the sad state of your financial affairs. They will *all* live happily ever after. You can use your imagination for what will befall you if you choose the alternative."

I started to make a noise, but she held up a finger. "I'll put it to you as I would to a lackwit: You do not have a choice."

❧

Back outside amongst the leafless trees and under the bleak sky, a footman hurried me forward, toward the gate.

"Sir," I called ahead to him. I pulled out the little scroll of parchment Hemma had given me, with the royal seal. I held it up when he looked back. "The queen gave me this—to deliver to Sir Otto Abensur."

"I am to escort you to the back gate," he protested.

I waved the scroll, showing the seal. "And the queen said to deliver this first."

He eyed me. Eyed the emblem stamped into the wax.

"Go on," I said.

We changed course.

Otto sat behind a desk, fingers tented over a series of maps and scrolls. He looked up to see me and the footman and then frowned, confused, before standing.

"I have just gone to see the queen, and she gave me a message for you." I held up the scroll.

Otto glanced at the footman and then back at me. "You talked to the queen?"

"Yes." I nodded and eyed the footman at my side. "This is to be opened in private, she said."

"Wait outside," Otto told the footman, who nodded and stepped out, shutting the door behind him.

I lowered the parchment, putting it back into my pocket. "It is not from her. I—I wanted to come to . . ." I looked around the room. It was not fitting for a bloodhound, but rather filled with books and framed maps. Bookshelves rose to meet the ceiling. I wasn't sure why I had come—I was torn between thanking him for his attempts at protection and accusing him of complicity, of failing to protect us.

Before I spoke, he took one step toward me. "Did you actually talk to the queen?"

"I know about the pregnancy."

His jaw ticked. "Aye."

"And I know Simeon is the father."

Otto shook his head, slowly at first, and then as if ridding himself of the thought. His face darkened, and then, in one even movement, he violently swept all the items on the desk—ink and quill and the maps and scrolls, rolled and unrolled, a short pile of books—to the floor. An inkpot, unopened, rolled across the room. He straightened, running a hand through his hair.

"You did not know?" My voice was quiet.

He shook his head. "You told the queen? What you know?"

I nodded.

"That was a mistake." He didn't wait for an answer and strode over to the door, yanking it open. I thought he was going to see me out, but instead, he called for the footman, and instructed him to find the whereabouts of the prince, as quickly as he could. "Run," he finished.

That Otto had believed me, did not question me, was a testament either to his trust in my word or his own impression of Simeon. Perhaps both. When the footman had departed, he turned back to me. "You need to get home."

"You did not know?" I asked, again, needing confirmation.

"Not of . . ." He didn't finish the sentence, his face tightening at the thought. "I knew of the child," he admitted.

I shook my head. "I cannot . . . I do not know what to do." I trusted him. The necklace, perhaps. The *not suitable*, maybe. All my expectations, my understanding of who people were, had been turned over.

"Etheldreda." He put an arm on each of mine, held me firmly, urgently. "Simeon is . . . there is a foulness. And Sigrid will have warned him. You need to get back to your house, as quickly as you can. Immediately."

"Oh" was all I managed to say. For Otto was pushing me out the door.

CHAPTER TWENTY-NINE

I MADE MY WAY BACK TO THE STABLES ON FOOT, PUSHING THROUGH crowded streets, sidestepping peddlers hawking baskets of eggs and pouches of tobacco. I avoided the heavy feet of men's horses and livestock. Arno was not saddled, and was in no hurry to be, resisting the bit and snorting at me. Once on the road, we moved slowly, the poor horse already exhausted from the morning ride.

Despite Otto's urgency, I did not mind the delay. Whatever waited for me at home was not something to relish. Rosie's and Mathilde's upturned faces. Elin, confused or still unaware. I did not know what information to share with the three of them, did not know how to share what I had learned, nor if sharing was the right thing to do in the first place.

But even this kind of hand-wringing felt false. Sigrid had put forth all in clear terms: No matter how I struggled, no matter which way I turned, the situation was fixed. We were mothers, both of us, and whether a parent of predator or prey, I understood the instinct. (Felt, even, the briefest flash of pity for her, balancing motherhood of both predator and prey, hunter and hunted.) I still wanted to protect my own. And in this case, it had been expressed to me that the best means of protection was to do nothing. Let your horse stop to eat clover. Let yourself sink into the saddle. Let your daughters—*live, live, live!*—stay afloat.

Still, doing nothing did little to abate my revulsion. All my dedication to—my rapturous optimism about—climbing the ladder had diminished. If these were the tools I had, I was better off without them. A part of me was still saying *but. But—. But—.* Even to myself, even in my own mind: I could not finish the sentence.

Rosie and Mathilde were waiting for me at the bottom of the drive. I clicked and urged Arno to hurry, to no avail, and when I was close enough, before I had a chance to dismount, the girls began to inform me of what had happened. They spoke quickly, talking over one another, but it did not take long to parse out their message: Simeon had come to the house, already, and left with Elin.

I had been half expecting it, but Rosie was shaking her head, disbelieving. "She knows better than to put her honor on the line." My daughter was shocked. But I had always understood Elin's virtue was just a stepping stone, a pathway to get what she was after.

"He said he wishes to have a private wedding," Mathilde explained, frown deepening. "But he came alone, dressed in common clothes."

"The only need for such subterfuge is if he does not intend to marry her!" Rosie cried.

"We did not know if we should tell her about—" Mathilde didn't finish the sentence. The baby. Princess Hemma. Her outdated bit of half information. "We tried to talk to her, to talk her out of it, but she would not hear anything, would not be convinced otherwise—"

"If he does not marry her, she will have disgraced herself, going off with him." Rosie clambered forward. "And that pollution will smudge the whole family! And without a dowry, without family reputation, we will become untouchable."

I handed her the reins so I could dismount from Arno and then took them back in hand, pulling the tired horse so he could finish the last part of our journey up the driveway unburdened. "He will marry her," I assured them.

My daughters were concerned with Elin's reputability. But I knew more than they could ever understand: Sigrid needed Elin. She had sent Simeon to ensure they would be married. An elopement—or at least a forced change of atmosphere—would keep my stepdaughter away from those who might put a stop to the union. All was clear; even if we *attempted* to interfere, Elin would remain within the golden cage of the castle walls and royal influence. It would only be us who were cast out.

Rosie wrinkled her nose. "What of the—the news?"

Her sister, more forcefully, demanded: "What did you learn?"

"Morwen's gossip cannot be true," Rosie insisted. "Surely you found out otherwise."

I could not bring myself to look either of them in the eye. If they were to know all I had found out—how much worse things had turned out to be. How depraved the prince was. And I had urged them to Simeon's side! The shame of this—the blindness of it—disgusted me. I gave another sharp tug on the reins in my hand, picking up my pace as Arno trailed behind. "It is true," I said, without looking back at their faces.

I heard Rosie make a little noise, an effort at speaking. "Perhaps," she said, at a loss for words, "perhaps . . . we are not giving his character enough credit. Perhaps the prince is doing it for his sister, and he will broach the subject with Elin and they will figure out this situation together."

My sweet Rosie. I had tried to come to a similar conclusion myself.

Mathilde was flintier. "Elin deserves to know before marrying him."

An unvoiced accusation. "Then you might have told her before they left," I retorted.

"But you had not returned to verify the information!" Mathilde cried.

I listened to our shoes crunch in the gravel for long moments. Glancing back, I saw the girls exchange a look I could not decipher, some secret language of sisters designed to exclude me. Something in the look, something in Mathilde's tone—some small finger of blame that laid the situation at my feet when I had only ever tried to help them—filled me with frustration. "How could you let her go with him!" I cried.

"We are not her chaperones." Mathilde's voice was cool.

I knew my anger was misdirected, but the choler in my chest felt unbearable. "But you could have used your heads."

"He is her fiancé," Mathilde said quietly. "You have tried at every opportunity to put us before him, and your schemes worked. If we had gone to her and jeopardized it all and been incorrect in our accusations, you would have been furious."

"We were but following your suit," Rosie agreed. "And you did everything to fan the flame of love in my breast and the moment he chose her, you swung right over, as if it were the most natural thing in the world. The rest of us do not just . . . pivot quite so easily!"

I stared at them, wondering if part of Rosie's anguish over the past few days had also been directed at me. I had spent so much time perfecting the little dollhouse of our existence, that I had forgotten about the dolls living in its rooms. There was hurt on Rosie's face, but also a different kind of feeling—one that was adjacent, or tied, to disappointment. A child believes everything you say, everything you tell them, and there is a precise moment, you feel it exactingly, a little tap in your gut, when the belief snaps.

For her part, Mathilde looked furious. Perhaps after what we had both learned the day before, she had supposed I could take such information and turn it into a weapon with which to defend ourselves. Perhaps, after learning of Elin's departure, she had expected me to cry out about dishonor, to leap back on the horse shouting that we had not a moment to lose. But I was familiar with loss. I knew the contours of its prowling, animal body. And I believed that perhaps if I were inert, lay down, did nothing, it might only sniff and pass. I had spent too many years building the dollhouse to give up on it now.

I stalked forward, hurrying up the drive, and, when I reached the top, looped Arno's reins through the hitching post and gave the knot a hard tug. As my children came up behind me, I turned to them. "Enough, girls. Go inside."

Mathilde put her hands on her hips. "You need to go get Elin."

Rosie, halfway between the two of us, looked back and forth, and then, decisively, went to her sister's side. "Yes, Mama. You cannot just let him take her! Not if the news about the *baby*"—even alone in our driveway, even when it was just us, she whispered the word—"is true."

I sighed, impatiently. "Get her from where? They could be anywhere, in any direction. The only thing to do is go inside and wait."

They scowled at me, in unison, without needing to consult each other. "You cannot let him marry her," Mathilde said, compelling me, as best she could, with her eyes. I wished that I had more power. I was glad they didn't know the full truth of the situation, for then they would also see how little I could do about it.

I shook my head. "If I interfere, then your futures are imperiled."

But Mathilde wouldn't accept my response. Raising her voice, she called: "Are you worried about Elin, or worried about reputation?"

"Of course I am worried about Elin!" I exclaimed. "But she will be a queen. If I worry about reputation, it is for you."

Mathilde glared back at me. "You've never asked us what we want."

"It is not a matter of want!" I threw my hands up. "I was trying to find you security. And I am still trying, if you'd allow me. It is the only good that might arise from this entire circumstance if you would just allow it. Come," I begged both of them. "Let's warm up inside and we will figure out what to do."

Rosie made a move to step forward, but Mathilde stuck out an arm to stop her. "Security?" She laughed. Beside her, Rosie's eyes were round as teacups. "At what expense!"

"I am trying to protect you," I bellowed.

"You of all people should know there is nothing"—Mathilde gritted her teeth, each word ground out and carefully measured—"protective about marriage!" She inhaled. Slowed down. "All your talk of our futures, Mama, but what about what is in front of you? Look around! The roof has fallen in. You've confined us to a prison of performance. You choose a false kind of safety for us again and again. And then take freedom for yourself!"

"I am not free!" I cried. "I have worked every waking hour of every day for you."

"You go out into the woods with Lucy and cover yourself in dirt. You have the freedom to decide what you do with your days, even if it is just gathering firewood. You oversee your own life, and we do not."

"Lucy." I raised a hand to my throat. For after my sleepless night and my rush to the palace, I had forgotten to feed her that morning. I spun away, leaving my daughters huffing behind me on the front steps, needing to pacify, and return to, a hungry falcon—a monster of my own making.

LUCY WAS NOT THE BIRD I KNEW. HUNGRY BEYOND REASON, SHE HAD become a dark-eyed murderer—a creature hell-bent on killing and killing alone. Her talons held my fingers so rigidly I could feel her beating heart—her anger, her hostility—through her feet. She stared at me, hackles raised, feral, waiting for me to untie her jesses.

The bird had always represented some wilder part of me—the part that wanted to get out, to break free. Perhaps the part that felt more ruthless, more brutal, than I was supposed to be. A part that I had neglected in recent weeks, a part I had tried to tamp down. And as a result, Lucy was nervous and high-strung, head swiveling at each movement of the trees, each passing insect.

"I am sorry, Lucy," I told her, though I also felt sorry for myself. My daughters were furious with me for not pursuing Elin, for not righting some wrong that I had no capability of making decent. But if I went after my stepdaughter, if I tried to put a stop to the wedding, I would curse my own flesh and blood.

I began to untie Lucy from the gauntlet. The feathers on her chest rose and her toes went tight on the leather. She bent down, swift, and pecked my arm: the spot of skin showing above the glove and below my sleeve. I covered the wound—ripped, white flesh and the beginnings of blood—glaring at her in surprise. But I'd dropped her jesses, and she was free, suddenly, uninterested in the gash or my face. Pushing off the glove. Wings flapping. Except she did not go to her block, or toward the great oak, or to circle above. She was moving farther downwind, floating, then gliding, flying away from me.

No one tells you how to mother. It is presumed to be buried within you, a deep, primordial instinct that awakens in your body—in your breast—when the time is right. We mothers are expected to have that instinct. Our intuition. Our supernatural understanding of our children's habits and bodies and rhythms. You learn to trust your knowledge. I thought I could trust my knowledge of Lucy. I thought I knew each intimation of her head and chest, the feel of her flying weight, the subtle strength of her muscles.

But time affects our reading of that rhythm. Like a clock, we lose our accuracy as years pass. Fallibility squeezes in. I knew before Lucy left my sight. I knew after those initial flaps. Something hitched inside of me, a small voice saying that the cadence was off. I had read it all wrong. I had lost my way.

I was running, but I could not keep up with my bird. I looked around, wildly. She was not at the horizon. She was not in the trees. She was not anywhere. It was as if she'd found a tear in the sky and slipped through.

I moved madly through the foliage, whistling, calling for her. The branches and leaves whipped against me. Each lash felt like a reminder: Lucy, lost. Elin, fled on the wings of a broken prince. Rosie, crestfallen. Mathilde, enraged. All of them, gone to me at once, in their own ways. If I needed a sign, a moment of reckoning, I had found it.

Pursue Lucy, and I could not pursue Elin. Pursue Elin, and I was damning every hope and dream, potentially even the lives, of my most cherished girls. Hissing and spitting and hating me, but I cherished them still.

All of them.

Lucy, who I had let down.

Mathilde, who had only ever pushed me, in her own tireless way, to be better.

Rosie, who, until that day, had still looked at me with the clear eyes of a small girl.

And Elin. The pinnacle, perhaps, of my broken clock. How I had resented her over the years. How I resented her, still. I'd always thought: How different things might have been if she had accepted me from the beginning. If she'd taken me as a flesh-and-blood mother instead of reaching to the cold pages of her book. But when you accept a child as your own, you aren't just accepting them, you also must create a new self to love them with. I hadn't been willing to change my rules and expectations for how she should be. It was me who could have changed, and I hadn't.

I paused, panting, when I could run no longer. Lucy still nowhere. The sky empty.

What would I do if it were Rosie whom Simeon had selected? How would that have changed my calculus? I imagined her fine freckles. I thought of the crescent shape of human teeth. I was certain, that if the roles had been swapped, I wouldn't still be pondering.

The hypocrisy set me off in the opposite direction.

I reversed, stumbling back through the trees; the same branches and brush that had grabbed for me before now poked and prodded me forward. Back through the dark leaves, over the mulch of the forest floor. Back across the lawn, feet catching in the divots and gullies of the grass. And, when I was close enough, I called as loud as I could for Alice to meet me in the front.

Arno was still tied up and I had not changed from my riding

clothes. I began to work on undoing the knot on the hitching post. Alice appeared, concerned.

"I'm going after Elin," I called. "And I'll need some food. Grab what you can manage from the kitchens."

Alice shook her head at me. "Arno's ridden too much today already."

"We'll take our chances. Please, hurry, Alice!"

She left and returned with some hard rolls. I loaded as many as I could into my skirt, talking to her all the while. "Lucy is out. She flew away from me."

"In the tree?"

I shook my head, unable to speak, my voice catching in my throat. Alice frowned, understanding. A trained bird can escape to the wild and do fine. But a bird with jesses was bound, one day, to get them caught or tangled in a bush or tree, to spend the last of their days caught, starved, or even upside down.

"Please," I asked her, "make a lure, and go looking for her. See if you can get her down." I felt a wave of desperation. "Do whatever it takes."

Looking up, I saw that Rosie and Mathilde had come to an upstairs window. We locked eyes. It was a long moment, a pane of watery glass between us. They stood, shoulder to shoulder, watching me, their mother. I was about to ride off into the afternoon, alone, with no direction, no plan, just an aimless, desperate desire to right the wrongs of the world and myself.

Alice took Arno's reins from me and held them.

"Perhaps I'll find them before nightfall," I said, ruefully. I repositioned my habit, grasped the pommel, and used the stirrup to lift myself onto the horse.

Alice handed me the reins once more. "Perhaps. And perhaps you might check the village inns or find a room there yourself."

Clicking, I gave Arno a little kick in his side. He took a step forward, then stopped once more. I tried again, and he did not respond at all.

"He's too tired," Alice called.

"Please, Arno," I begged.

He would not budge. I cried out in frustration, patting the horse's neck, and muttering encouragements. "I cannot give up now. Not now!" I cried.

But then Arno lifted his head and stepped forward. Not at my urging, but because there was another horse coming up the drive. A black one, with a shiny coat, twice the size of poor Arno. On its back sat Otto.

I dismounted and started walking down the drive.

"Where are you going?" Alice called.

"The same as before," I called back.

Otto continued toward me, following the path through the apple trees. When we were close enough, I demanded: "Pull me up on your horse."

He slowed, and offered his hand. "What of your things?"

"We do not have time."

He had a large saddle. I climbed up to sit on the leather behind him, legs hanging off one side. I was aware that my daughters, from their upstairs window, were probably watching. Aware that Alice stood just up the drive, holding Arno's reins. Aware that, without a handrail or straps, I would need to put my hands on Otto himself.

He urged his horse in a semicircle, facing now back toward the iron gates. He clicked and we moved forward. I reached for him, his body, and held on. Rescuers and saviors, or, I feared, fools.

CHAPTER THIRTY

WE FOUND NO EASY LUCK. NOBODY IN THE VILLAGE HAD SEEN anyone who fit our description of Simeon and Elin, and I worried that we were headed in the wrong direction entirely. But, in the late afternoon, at a lonely water mill set back from the road, Otto pulled over to talk to the miller and emerged triumphant.

I waited outside, with the horse, staring at the placid millpond. It was already late in the day. We had stopped at every small town and hovel we passed and received only half assurances: One farmer had seen a man who fit our description but was alone. Another had noticed a well-appointed coach, but not the travelers. I was surprised the strangers talked to us at all, but Otto had a coin purse. And coins could be compelling.

Coins or no, it didn't feel as though we had fortune on our side. I knew I'd been reckless. For running off with Otto—alone, on his horse, the sun soon setting. For marching into the viper's nest of Sigrid's castle, accusing her of all I knew. Reckless, yes, which left me wretched: Whether I found Elin or not, I was on an excursion I did not know how to come back from.

The millpond—a small stream dammed with wooden planks—was torpid, covered in dead leaves and a darkened reflection of the blank sky above. I wanted to pull the planks from the water, to see movement. Instead, I threw a small pebble, which the pond accepted with no more than a sucking plonk, extending a few ripples in return.

"They saw them," Otto called, emerging from the mill house. "Or the daughter did. From an upstairs window. A coach with two horses. Of fine make, she said. Except—it is why she remembered—she said there were scrapes along the side, as if made by a knife."

"They were attacked?" I asked in alarm.

"He probably tried to scratch the insignias off so they wouldn't be recognized." Otto hoisted himself up onto the horse, offered his hand, and pulled me up behind him.

"Then we are on the right course."

"Aye," he agreed. And we started moving forward once more, leaving the motionless water, the somnolent water mill behind us.

"I fear that even if we find them, we will be too late. They'll be married already. Or worse."

"If the prince intends to follow through on his plan, then he will need to ensure she is not with child for at least nine months." Otto looked forward so I couldn't see his face. The thought was reassuring—though no guarantee.

We had not spoken much over the course of the afternoon, which had given me plenty of time to study the back of Otto's head. His dark hair, threaded with strands of silver, was still thick and grew in a small whorl at the nape of his neck, which itself was tanned from the sun. Broad shoulders, and, I could feel from my hands on his sides, no lack of brawn, though he had the softness that also came from eating and aging well.

He was Sigrid's advisor. Simeon's. I wondered in what ways that might aid me, and in what ways he was putting himself at risk. We were both making bargains, but I did not know for what or with whom.

"Why are you helping me?" I asked, abruptly.

He glanced, briefly, back over his shoulder, and I saw the bridge of his cheekbone, a glint of his eye. "I was always helping you. Or trying to."

I sank into the saddle, considering his words. Re-forming my memories—perhaps Otto was not ill-natured so much as protective. Perhaps he was not aloof, but steadfast. "Does the queen know?"

"That I was trying to help, or that I am here?"

"Both."

He murmured some instructions to his horse—an animal that moved with twice Arno's speed—and then was silent. After a moment, he said only, "Nay."

"But—"

"But?"

"Why?"

He was silent again and I thought, after a long while, that he would say nothing. I could see only that small whorl of hair and the cords of his neck. But then, when I'd almost forgotten my question, staring off into the oak and ash trees lost in my own circling thoughts, he started talking.

"Before I came to this kingdom, I had a son." His voice lowered. "He died when he was one. As did his mother."

Except for the movement of the horse beneath me, I went completely still.

Otto continued, "He would have been the same age as Simeon. I didn't know him well. I was a soldier then, and mostly away from home."

"The pestilence?" I asked, quietly, thinking the timing was the same year as my own father's death, when illness had swept its black hands across every kingdom, overstepping the boundaries as if they did not exist.

"I was a cartographer—a surveyor—for the army. Where I come from, the land, the people, are marked by strife and struggle. For power. Contested borders. Factions vying for influence, control. I was always sent to the edges of the conflict, to mark and remake maps as land changed hands. And it changed hands often." His voice was marked by bitterness. "When I was away, those same wars came to my village. My wife and son were both killed. I do not even know by which faction. Or how. Or who buried them. But I came home to two mounds. It was a kingdom of sides. And I soon lost sight of which one I was on. Could no longer understand which one was right. So I left."

"And came here." I didn't have the right words. I worried that perhaps in acknowledging the calamitous part of what he had shared, I might discourage him from sharing further. But it also might have been the careful decision of a coward.

"My skills were in high demand. Your king—the king—hired me. And, over time, my advisory extended from maps to other matters."

"Watching Simeon?"

"Leaders that try to impose their beliefs on those around them are dangerous. I came to your land because your royals have little ambition beyond their tiny world, and that keeps people safe. If you keep those that steer the ships and direct the armies calm, there is less blood. Fewer mounds. And so I've made that my purpose—made the kingdom my responsibility. When it comes to Simeon . . ." He released his pommel and ran a hand through his hair. Glanced back at me. "I did not know. Or I did not understand the extent of it. I did what I thought I could. It wasn't enough. So I am trying to do more."

"I am sorry," I said, when he was finished.

"For what?"

"Your wife. And child." I had to push the thought of those two mounds away.

"They are at peace," he said, after a long moment.

I envied his certainty.

WHEN WE LOST THE LIGHT, WE STOPPED TO SLEEP AT A MONASTERY. As we knocked on the massive gate, Otto turned to me: "It will be easier if we say you are my wife."

"I will not," I replied, mildly offended.

"Then say nothing and let them assume."

I complied. The abbot gave us a little thatched hut to sleep in, with earthen floors, along with a jug of warm beer and two small loaves of cold cheat bread. When Otto and I were left alone, we sat on two overturned crates, holding our individual loaves and sharing the jug.

"I am sorry for the room," Otto said. "I thought we might get to an inn before nightfall. I will sleep outside."

"You'll freeze," I protested. Whatever damage was done with us sharing a room had been done already, and I did not believe he would touch me. "Do you think they're nearby?"

He knew who I meant. "They've got two horses and will be faster. They have a head start. But near enough." Otto watched as I tore off a hunk of my bread and chewed it. "Which is it? Are you the mud-covered huntress from the woods or the lady of Bramley?"

"Both. Neither. I'm a brewer's daughter. And this is a sorry excuse for beer," I told him, holding up the jug that held a murky liquid that had gone sour. "They fermented it too long."

He shook his head at some unspoken thought. "Do your daughters really know how to paint?"

I took a swig of the beer from the jug and did not meet his eyes, remembering how, at our picnic, he had reached for the canvases as if to test the wetness of their pigment. "Any accomplished young woman takes up an art." It wasn't an outright lie.

He smiled at me. "You mothers preen your daughters like race-horses."

"Better a racehorse than a dog's dinner." I looked away. "We're all just looking for some stability."

"There's nothing stable about life at court." He shook his head. "What about all the options in between? Cart horse? Plow horse? Respectable pony?"

"Because the world is so plentiful with options?" I scoffed. "What are Elin's options? What are Hemma's?" I did not say: What are mine?

Thinking of the princess reminded me of why I was sitting in a strange hut in the first place and soured me against Otto. I glared at him. "Would you really just thrust her child on someone so unsuspecting? Even if you did not know it was Simeon's?"

Otto's expression clouded, his face tightening. "Hemma is an innocent girl, even if, as I errantly thought, she'd made a mistake. There are worse outcomes for a baby. It was not my plan, and I did not like it, but it seemed to me—with the information I had—an all right outcome. Provided the mother was accepting. So many women would happily raise another's child."

"But not the noble ones. So the ball was arranged. And all the second pickings were invited."

"Aye—not the royal cousins. Or the great families. They care too much about bloodlines."

"Second pickings," I reiterated. "Tell me. Did Sigrid intentionally exclude my daughters from the ball?"

"Initially, yes." Otto spoke plainly. "Them and plenty others that suited her, or offended her somewhere along the way, or that she didn't like the look of."

"It's illogical. She was trying to saddle someone with her erratic, dangerous son. Who better than an enemy, or someone she dislikes?"

"But they'd still gain. Though I suppose that's the reasoning she looped around to, in the end." His jaw tightened. "I tried to discourage her."

"From the plan overall or from choosing my daughters?"

"A bit of both. Bits and parts. I am an advisor, not a puppet master. I push and prod, here and there, gently sometimes. Forcefully others. I cajole before I push."

"A bit"—I passed him the jug of beer—"like a mother with her racehorse."

"A bit," he conceded.

For sleep, we'd each been provided a sack, which we stuffed with hay from the floor. When Otto's was full, he took it to the opposite side of the hut. Lying on my own scratching, ill-shaped bag of dried grass, I marveled: My life had been hard in many ways, but I had never not slept in a bed. I had never lain in a room with a man who was not my husband. But curled up on that sack, instead of appreciating Otto's attempt to add some propriety to our context, as if sleeping on the other side of the dirt floor made a difference, I found myself wishing we might have settled a little bit closer—and not just for the warmth. Acutely aware of his nearby body, I found that I was glad, for just one night, not to be performing, or thinking of reputability. Despite the dirt and despite the sack, I slept well and with a sense of certainty that finally, at long last, I was doing the right thing.

I just hoped that I could get to Elin in time, for her well-being would not be measured by my intentions.

WE COVERED GOOD GROUND THE NEXT MORNING, CONFIRMING AN-other sighting of a man with an enclosed carriage and scrape marks on the side. But by afternoon our pursuit was slowed by rain. The roads were soon nothing but mud. And though the sun, somewhere behind the clouds, was not yet gone from the sky, we had to stop at an inn to wait out the water and dry off.

The inn was nothing more than a private home that had turned its hall into an alehouse. A crude establishment—wooden sign flapping in its iron bracket, smoke from a central open fireplace filling the room and filtering toward a hole in the ceiling—that had become overcrowded with people and travelers trying to avoid the weather. Fiddlers played in the corner, hats set out for coins. Otto carried two chairs to a small opening near the round stone hearth. We'd no sooner sat down than the alewife came over.

By then, I was bedraggled from traveling and a night spent on the floor, and the woman eyed me carefully. Deciding, it seemed, that I deserved little attention, she leaned toward Otto and offered a knowing smile. "Aren't you a sorry sight." She reached out and flicked his wet shoulder with a fingernail.

"Good eve," he replied evenly. "We're looking for a man, blond hair, fine dress, with a woman more blond than he. Have they come through this establishment?"

The woman leaned closer. "What do you fancy tonight?"

"Two ales," I interjected, eyeing the woman as she had eyed me. She was short and wide, though not stout, her body giving the impression of having been, at some point, flattened. I tried to flatten her further with my stare.

"That all?" she said to Otto, as if it had been he who ordered. She reached her hand toward his face, waiting.

"That's all," he said, gruffly, no small amount of derision in his voice. The hand hovered, then fell.

"Otto, she will not give us any answers unless you give her some coin." I sighed, after she had turned away, heading to the buttery to fetch our drinks. I looked at him, his face still stony. "Must you be so disagreeable? She might have told us what she'd seen."

"I am only disagreeable when I disagree."

In spite of myself, I laughed. I looked around at the room. Many patrons were red with drink, others well on their way. In the corner, one of the fiddlers played while the other clapped along. A couple nearby shared a pipe. "I think the ale will be better here than the beer last night."

And I was right: When the alewife brought two cups over, they tasted fine.

"Are you staying here?" she asked, curtly. "We have only one room left."

Otto reached into his pocket and placed two coins—enough for our drinks and then some—onto the small table we sat next to. Then he stacked three more on top. "The lady will take the room."

"The lady," the alewife repeated. She used an extended finger to slide each coin off the edge of the table into the cup of her waiting hand. "Haven't seen the people you asked about. You'll take the first door upstairs on the right." She straightened and winked at Otto. "Hope you and the lady enjoy the room."

When she'd left, Otto turned to me, lips pursed. "This is what happens when you won't say you are my wife."

"She did not even ask," I protested. "And I've been a wife. It invites a whole other set of problems."

He nodded.

"And thank you for the ale, and the room—I will repay you. When I can."

"All right," he said, but I had the feeling he was only agreeing to avoid argument. We fell into one of our now-familiar silences, each drinking our ale and staring into the forked tongues of the fire. With the passing minutes, some of the wetness lifted from our clothes. And I felt increasingly comforted by the sounds and smells of the tavern. The sweet scent of spirits. The sticky feel of spilled beer. Something was cooking, and it smelled like home—not my home, but a home, somewhere that people kept warm and ate meals together. Unmarried women did not get to spend time in ale halls. This strange journey with Otto, this rest stop, was a brief opportunity to slip in unnoticed. Even if the barmaid thought I was an immoral strumpet.

"I would like to better understand you," Otto said, suddenly.

I glanced over at him. The Otto sitting by the fire, boots on the floor, sprawled in his chair, was a different person than the formal and serious man I had observed at court. I smirked. "You mean outside of what you've learned from spying on me."

"Yes." He nodded, equably. "Outside of that."

"Well, you go first."

"I told you my story."

"No—tell me what you learned from spying on me." Embarrassed at what he might have seen, I twisted away to survey the room. Across from me, a man drained his tankard and belched. I shook my head. "I have not been in a tavern for some time."

"Besides market day when you talked to Finnian Enright?"

I turned back to Otto and raised an eyebrow. "Well, that is as good a starting place as any. What else have you learned?"

He tilted his head, considering. He was still relaxed in his chair, unperturbed by my questions. "You have a lot of apples."

"Anyone who has been within a mile of Bramley could tell you that."

"You can dance a sarabande better than I."

"I should hope so."

"Neither of your daughters can paint—"

I burst out laughing, and then covered my face. "Do not embarrass me!"

"You can man a bird better than any expert falconer I've seen."

I took a sip of ale to cover my falling smile—a stomach-turning flash of worry for Lucy. Otto pressed on, straightening in his chair and leaning toward me, voice growing more serious. "You were left in a tough spot by your dead husband. You have no money or means, but present as if you do. You're resourceful. You're stronger than you appear. You pretend to be one thing when underneath it, you are something else entirely."

I was silent a moment. When Otto had made his list, I had felt shame, but also something else—tiny and alive, a little flame that flickered when it was named.

"You've had loss," Otto continued. "Have you had happiness?"

I looked at the fire. Thought about my words before I shared. "My experience of happiness is that it comes in two forms: a potent dose so extreme that you are overwhelmed with fear it will disappear, or a subtle kind that envelops you with such stealth you're hardly aware of its presence. Both kinds are defined by their inverse. Extreme happiness is measured and held against its potential absence. Contentedness is only recognized once it's gone. Do they count?"

"Aye." He nodded.

"Have you completed your report?"

"Your roof has fallen in," he added, with a wan smile.

"When you first saw me, you thought I was a mud-spattered poacher."

"No." He shook his head and held my eyes. "That is not what I thought at all."

We didn't speak for a long moment. He reached out and put his hand on mine, firmly, on the arm of my chair. We were not wearing gloves and the feel of his strong fingers—skin on skin—felt so unusual, so warm, so reassuring, I did not know if I should lean in or recoil. My body was sore from a day of hard riding, and whether from the horse, or something else entirely, I felt an ache between my legs.

I moved my hand, abruptly, reaching for the ale again, wanting to dispel whatever had come over me. I was in a strange village in a strange inn with a man who was, essentially, still a stranger. The stranger from the woods. What of Elin? What of Lucy? How could I sit in a tavern and enjoy my ale? I could see through the small windows that the sun still had not set. "Should we continue on?" I asked. "Let's finish our ale and keep going. They are getting farther away."

Otto, still relaxed, still calm, sat back in his chair once more. "The horse can't continue in this weather. And he needs his rest, or he will be no use to us at all. Console yourself, though, for if we cannot move forward, neither can Simeon."

"I do not understand how he has gotten so far undetected."

He sighed and stared into the fire. "A prince without a retinue is just a man with bad manners."

OTTO SAW ME TO MY ROOM. THE SHEETS WERE DIRTY AND COLD, BUT it had a wash table and closestool, and I was happy to have a chance to freshen myself. After I'd washed, I lay under a pile of blankets and quilts, looking around at the wainscoted walls and a tin plate of dried flowers that trembled in the draft like shriveled insects. A far cry from the dirt floor of a hut, and yet I found I could not sleep.

There was too much to hold, to turn over, in my mind. If the first day away had felt like a breathless, slow-moving adventure, the reality of what was happening had finally caught up with me. I hoped beyond all reason that Alice had found Lucy. I worried I would be too late in finding Elin, but also worried about what would happen if I did find her. What would Sigrid do if the engagement was broken? What was I to do when no outcome was one I could stomach?

I was certain I would never fall asleep. The thoughts were overpowering. Except then, suddenly, I was roused by a knocking at the door, and I realized I had been dreaming. I pulled my dressing gown on hastily. The knocking didn't stop. "Who is it?" I called.

"Me." Otto's gruff voice.

I cracked the door. "It is the middle of the night."

"The sun rises in an hour. And I found them. Or I think I did."

I opened the door wider. "Where?"

"The innkeeper on the night shift pointed them in the direction of another inn, a few towns over."

I sucked in the cold air. "They stopped here, while we slept? How is that possible?"

"We don't know it was him for sure, but aye, it seems as if we passed them somewhere along the journey. They won't be far." He gestured back to the room behind me. "We must hurry."

I looked down and saw the stub of a candle and a horse blanket on the floor by my door.

"You slept here?" I asked.

"There are no locks on your door." He shrugged. "Be quick. I'm going to ready the horse."

WHEN I GOT TO THE SMALL STABLE, OTTO WAS FINISHING WITH THE saddle. "Good lot he does," he said, cocking his head toward the sleeping stable hand. I watched Otto, familiar already with the sight of the back of his head. He was capable and calm with the horse, taking care with its comfort. He moved easily, though he was likely stiff from sleeping on the floor outside my room. He checked the cinch and turned back to me, speaking over his shoulder. "I owe you an apology. I shouldn't have told you to say you're my wife." He turned to face me. "Or—"

I didn't think about it. It wasn't a decision. I leaned forward and put my lips on his. His head was angled, and it was not a perfect match. I found my mouth half pressed against his cheek. Rough warmth. My breath caught in my throat when I realized what I had done. I took a step back, glancing, worriedly, at the sleeping stable boy in the corner.

Otto looked at me, quizzically—the faintest breath of a smile—and then turned back to the horse, running a hand along its neck.

"Better get on with it," he said.

THE EMBARRASSMENT COATED ME—A ROILING IN MY STOMACH AND a lump in my throat. I had always made such a fuss about appearances and honor. And here I was, with the royal advisor, who was helping me on a rescue mission, kissing him. I was supposed to be a distraught mother. I was supposed to be crying fat tears and beating my breasts. Overturning every stone. Working tirelessly. Sacrificing endlessly. Thinking only of my children. All I did was supposed to be for them. *Live, live, live,* the very same as my heartbeat. And yet, I was no different than the woman the alewife had supposed me to be.

We were moving quickly on the horse and did not speak. I couldn't help but feel, sitting behind Otto, avoiding looking at the whorl of hair on the back of his neck, jostled against his back again and again by the pounding feet of his stallion, a shift in his posture. He was stiffer, more formal, reverting to some version of the Otto I'd met before. The stranger in the woods. The shared saddle suddenly too intimate.

After two hours of hard riding, when the sun was fully low in the sky, Otto pulled the animal off the road and directed it toward a small stream. Wordlessly, we climbed down. I went first, stood by a small tree, listening to the dribble of the brook. The horse took long drinks of water. The sun lit up the little copse around us, beginning to warm the dew-covered leaves and the cold earth. I shivered.

Otto took his time managing the horse, checking its hooves and then the fit of the saddle. He withdrew two apples from the saddlebag and handed one to me. We still didn't speak. I didn't know what to say.

Unable to meet his eyes, I polished the fruit on my skirt. Polished and rubbed its skin, though I had no appetite. I heard him crunch on his apple.

A sound of a boot in the brush. I looked up and he was right in front of me. My breath hitched. He reached a hand out, tentatively, and put it on my waist. Then, he pulled me to him. Closer, closer until our bodies were nearly touching. With the palm of his hand on the small of my back, he pressed me to him and kissed me. Slowly. Steadily. His mouth, his hands, warm in the cold morning. He tasted of apple.

After a long moment, he stepped back. A little twinkle in his eye. He took another bite of his apple.

"Well," I said, flustered. I smoothed my skirt down with one hand. Held my apple helplessly in the other. My heart beating madly. I was warm. It had been a long time since I had kissed anyone like that.

He still had not said anything. He raised his eyebrows.

"Yes," I said, nodding. "Yes."

He nodded.

I wasn't sure what he had asked me. But, in that moment, I felt certain of my answer.

It might have just been: Maybe apples aren't so bad after all?

CHAPTER THIRTY-ONE

FTER OUR PAUSE—DEW-COVERED GRASS, BABBLE OF THE BROOK, apple-flavored kiss—we had another short ride. Back on the horse, I was glad Otto couldn't see my face. Was it a failing that, as I rode forward to find my stepdaughter, my thoughts were on myself? I had some ease, and some embarrassment still, around what had happened. There were whole swaths of my life I had written off, unknowingly sentencing them to the past. Now I thought of my own future. And marveled how one kiss—one inane, stupid grappling—could cause a woman to open up her entire self, her entire hereafter, for examination.

Which is not to say I had no nerves about what lay ahead. I oscillated between rejoicing in an imagined success—coming home, with Elin, triumphant—and the simultaneous certainty that we were pursuing a dead end.

But, of all these ruminations, of all my wild thoughts, danger did not cross my mind. Blood was not something I considered.

Elin and Simeon's inn was bigger and noisier than the one we'd come from. Sitting at the edge of a small village, the building had a central courtyard, which was filled with coaches and clamor. When we entered, an ostler came over to take our bags. Seeing we had none, he directed us toward the innkeeper, who sat behind his desk in a cave-like entry hall.

Otto described what we were after, and though I thought I saw some flicker of recognition on the man's dour face, he shook his head. "Don't know 'em," he told us. "Now, either let a room or make way for folks who will." He added a *please* the way one slaps on a bonnet when headed outdoors.

Otto reached into his shirt and withdrew the coin pouch. He held it out. "Don't know them?" he repeated.

"Don't know 'em," the innkeeper affirmed but extended an upturned hand.

Otto put one coin in his fingers.

"Still don't know 'em," the innkeeper said.

"Good god." I stepped forward and grabbed the ledger on the desk.

"Hey!" the man cried in surprise. But we were divided by his wide table. I ran my fingers down the column, scanning the day's entries, and flipped one page back. A man and woman had checked in late the night before.

"Terrible penmanship," I reproved. To Otto, I said, "Upper north corner," and set the ledger back on the desk.

"You can't do that," the innkeeper growled.

Otto shrugged in apology and put another coin on the table.

"Two floors up on the left side." The man sighed, dejectedly collecting the second coin.

WE KNOCKED ON THE DOOR AND WAITED. THE CEILINGS WERE LOW, and Otto's head nearly touched one of the wooden beams that crossed the hall. After a few moments, when no one had answered, I knocked again.

"Simeon," Otto called, loud enough to be heard on the other side.

"Open the door." When we were met with silence, he knocked, more forcefully. After a long moment, he stepped back. "Perhaps they are here no longer."

Our journey up until that point had been hypothetical. Everything a long shot. And felt a long shot still. But we stood in front of the door we had sought, and I would not just turn around. I would not give up. Not when I was sacrificing so much, to come this far. Not when I had not followed Lucy. If they were inside, I would get through.

"Elin," I called, banging more loudly. "Elin, it is Ethel. Open up."

Another door down the hall yanked inward, and a man stuck out his head to see what the commotion was about. "Pipe down," he called, scraggly eyebrows knit into a scowl.

"You pipe down," I retorted.

"You—" He eyed Otto, standing beside me. His sword in its scabbard. The man slammed his door.

I turned back to banging on the wood in front of me. "Elin—"

The door opened. She stood on the other side of the frame, fully dressed. "Hello, Stepmother," she said, evenly. As if it were the most natural thing in the world for her to be barricaded in a room at an inn a two-day ride from home.

Still, I felt immediate relief, seeing her in front of me, in one piece, with no marks on her skin—a picture, at least, of bodily health. I tried to see around her, inside the room, but could make out only the end of a made bed and an oversized chest. "Did you marry?" I demanded.

"Where is Simeon?" Otto nudged beside me.

Elin pulled the door open an inch farther, and then stopped herself. She was surprised to see Otto with me, the confusion plain on her face. "Hello, Otto," she said, politely. "How do you do?"

The girl had run away from home, defied every rule of proper behavior, and was still acting as though we were dropping by for tea unannounced. "Did you *marry*?" I repeated.

"No—" she began, and my relief surged. She pursed her lips.

"Simeon is not here. He will be back soon. He ran out of coin and is off to get more." She paused, hesitant. "He said not to let anyone in."

I worried, from the way the door wavered in her hands, that she might push it shut in our faces. "He meant strangers," I said, quickly. "You're traveling, after all. It's wise advice. But I am family." The invocation of the word felt false, but I pushed forward. "Otto is Simeon's closest advisor." I took a step toward her, willing her to let us in. "We've come to take you home. Surely, you must see something wrong with this situation. Why would a prince run away with you? With no guards and no retinue?"

She fidgeted with the trim on her kirtle, and I saw her cuticles had been gnawed ragged. "To marry me!"

"And yet"—I lowered my voice—"you are staying with a man alone in an inn, and you are not married. What would your book of virtues have to say on the subject?"

"He means to marry me. And it is a woman's duty—a wife's duty—to do as her husband wishes." She swallowed and began to sway on her feet. "You do not think he means to marry me?"

"Please listen to us." I lowered my voice. "Otto is Simeon's own man. This situation is not right. Surely you can see that. Surely all your dreams of being swept off your feet did not look like a flea-infested room at an inn."

"I did not see any fleas," Elin protested. But she bit her lip and took a step back. I pushed through the doorway. Inside, I saw the room was simply appointed, with a table and chairs, the oversized four-poster bed, and a wash basin. A mirror leaned on the mantel above the small fireplace, and I could see in its reflection that Simeon was not present.

Elin sagged against one of the four posts of the bed. I looked around for smelling salts, but she steadied herself and turned to me. "You have not heard what he has said to me. The kindnesses. The words of . . . my nature!"

I reached for her. "Compliments are not kindnesses."

"He means to marry you," Otto said, coming into the room behind me. "And that is the problem."

Elin's face clouded further.

"Just come with us and hear what we have to say."

"He will wonder where I am." She shook her head. "A woman's duty lies in obedience to her husband's will."

"He is not yet your husband. And you may not wish him to be after you've listened. But it will be your choice. If you hear what we have to say and wish to be reunited, then consider us powerless to stop you," I promised. She looked uncertain, so I decided to put it in terms Elin would understand: "Knowledge is all we offer. And knowledge is the lantern that illuminates the path to wisdom."

She considered my words. "I suppose," she admitted, "if you love a bird, you should set it free and see if it will fly back to you."

I did not know if she was the bird or Simeon, but I did not bother to ask, for she reluctantly gathered her things and followed us back down the hallway.

OTTO SPOKE TO ME IN A HUSHED WHISPER AS WE WENT DOWN THE stairs. "We won't all fit on the horse. I'll go let a carriage. You should stay here, tucked away. Simeon is somewhere nearby and it will be much better if he doesn't see you."

Before he departed, he paid the innkeeper a few more coins to allow Elin and I to sit in the buttery. No one would think to find us there, tucked in amongst the barrels of wine and ale and beer, he said. But I could see Otto looking at the window. At the door. The habit of a soldier. Or perhaps the mind of a mapmaker. Charting our exits. The alertness, that careful awareness, reminded me that I, too, had reason to be afraid.

Elin and I settled on two barrels, for there was nowhere else to sit.

"This is unnecessary," she told me but, with a mind primed already to obedience, said nothing further.

Outside, through the one small, high window, I could hear that the courtyard was busy. Coaches leaving. Men throwing about trunks and strapping them aboard. Doors opening and shutting. When it felt that we had settled, lulled by the noise, I turned to Elin. "We've made a mistake," I told her. I tried to think of the right words to make her understand.

"I know you must be upset that I went off." She put her hands in her lap. "But he is to be my husband. I must listen to him. I know it is a flexible application of my moral duties, but I do believe it is for the greater good."

I leaned toward her, thinking of all the ways one can be harmed without visible evidence. "Has he . . ." The words were uncomfortable in my mouth. "Did he take your maidenhead?"

She blushed, a deep crimson, and shook her head. "We kissed." She said it as if this, too, were shameful. "He wanted to marry straightaway, but I insisted we at least do it properly, on the coast, as he had promised when he first came to collect me. He has been remarkably patient with me. In a hurry, yes, but patient all the same."

"He has not hurt you, then?"

She sat up straight, in surprise. "He has been nothing but kind! He has shown me no aggression."

I shook my head, to myself. "Why would he, when you are sweet and lovely and go along with every little thing he says? But what of later, when you have a want or need of your own, something that he does not want or need, or worse, contradicts his wants or needs. What would happen then?"

She frowned at me. "I do not understand why you would say such things. Happiness is not a thing to be scratched at."

I took one of her fragile little hands in my own, a gesture that felt awkward, even as I was making it. I had never done anything like this with her before. But I felt the need to offer some kind of comfort, however weak, however middling, as I recounted to her what I had learned. I told her without withholding the details, working chronologically,

from Otto's first suggestion to Hemma's shocking disclosure: the subterfuge and planned secret. The incest. Simeon's true nature. All the
while, I kept one eye on the blank frame of that small window, worried
Simeon's face might appear at any time. I wished Otto would hurry.

While I spoke, Elin's expression had remained unchanged, as if she
were filtering the information to herself slowly, receiving only a fraction
of the words. When I was finished, she stayed silent and tilted her head,
thinking. "Mayhap someone like him will change?"

Beneath my frustration, I felt a stir of recognition. Had I not attempted a similar bargain in my own mind? Hope for an imaginary
future allows you to overlook the horror of the present. Maybe, Simeon
would reform. Maybe, he would tame his most base inclinations. Or,
more realistically, maybe, Elin could learn to live with them. Maybe she
could still be a princess, still get, at the end of each day, to call herself
a woman in love.

"No," I said, as simply and clearly as I could. "Not with you. Not for
you. Not like this."

"But," she asked, "what am I supposed to do?"

"Come home with us and we will figure it out." It was a false kind
of reassurance—I had no more idea how we would move forward, ex-
tricate ourselves from this mess of a situation, than she did. But I did
know I needed to get Elin away from Simeon, and time was of the
essence.

I realized that the noise from the courtyard had gone quiet. It was
a hawklike instinct, my body aware a moment before my mind. Something in me coiled.

"Darling," Simeon said, appearing in the doorway. He spoke directly to Elin. "There you are."

"Simeon!" She stood from the barrel.

"Your Highness," I managed. My voice was not steady.

He ignored me. "I had to sell my fur to get us some more money,"
he told Elin. "It feels good to shed excess, doesn't it? A small sacrifice
for our life together."

"Simeon—" Elin said, again.

"I think it best if you go upstairs," he told her.

"Stay here," I instructed.

But she took a step toward him. Caught, I think, between the promise of his world and the deception that underlay it.

At last, Simeon directed the force of his attention in my direction. "You've sniffed us out, my lady," he said to me, a half smile on his face. I thought about calling out for the innkeeper, but he was likely the one who had sold us out in the first place. How else would the prince have known to find us in the buttery?

"It's hard to travel unnoticed in a royal coach."

"Eh, eh, eh." He wagged his finger at me. "Don't say that word." He lowered his voice to a mock whisper. "We might be found out."

He turned back to Elin. "Darling"—he leaned in to the sobriquet, twisting it around—"go back upstairs."

She took another step toward him. "My stepmother has come. I—I must go home with her."

"Home? What of our plans?"

"Only for now," Elin was quick to assure him. "I am to be—I am—your helpmeet, but my stepmother, she is right, we must do it properly."

"I don't understand," he said, plaintively.

"I am sorry," she said, with genuine regret. "It is only for now."

Simeon's eyes filled with wet tears. I was alarmed—where had he bid them from?

"Please," he begged Elin. "I don't understand. What is happening? Darling—please." His voice broke on the last word.

"I—I—" She twisted her skirts in her hands. "I cannot," she said finally. "Not now. I'm sorry, Simeon, but we must talk first. We must—"

He slapped her, across the face, with the back of his hand, something inhuman in his expression.

She stood back, shocked, for a moment. Her cheek turned, somehow, whiter. Then, a drop of red on her nose, down to her lips. A little rivulet. A few spots on the chest of her dress. Her eyes wide. I do not think she believed me, or understood all I had told her, until she felt the force of that slap.

"Yes, yes—your stepmother said things." Simeon watched us without any effort to control the muscles of his face. "Your life must be so simple," he said to me, after a moment. All the warmth, all the expressive feeling, the full range of human emotion, looked to be extinguished from his eyes like a light snuffed out. "To pursue me the way you did. You thought: I'll knock on the door and leave with her. And that would be the end of it."

"It could be." I tried to step between him and Elin. I looked at the doorway, which his body was blocking. Where was Otto?

"I am shocked you are here, actually. Your greedy little heart. All you've risked. All you've given up." He mused. "I never would have expected it! I was lazy, because why would you pursue us? You had every reason not to."

"I found out what you've done. What you are," I told him. Looked to Elin, who was silent.

He considered me. "I felt for you when my mother told me that you knew my secrets. Because you'd been reaching. Wanting to be one of us. Grasping. Always extending those hands, reaching, reaching, reaching. And so you caught something. Me! But I'm not what you thought at all. And what to do now?"

Thinking of my daughters, of Elin, of a kingdom of girls, I couldn't stop myself. "You are a beast," I told him.

"I am a king." Simeon exhaled. "And I'll let you in on another secret." He leaned forward—I could feel the thrust of his breath in the still air of the room. "Beast and king are the same. There is no one there to stop us."

But I did not want to stop him. I only wanted to exit the room. "Let us pass," I insisted, wishing there was more strength in the request.

He continued as if I hadn't spoken: "You know—I remember watching you," he told me. "All of you. Sitting on a pathetic little carpet in the middle of an empty field. Playthings arranged for my liking. And I felt sorry for you. Then, I saw her. Elin. Like a ghost at the ball. What a sense of humor fate has!"

Elin released a noise close to a whimper and he turned to her. "Your confusion is endearing, really. So shocked and offended. When you were using me, too. Happy to feast on me, really. As if I were a roast pig made of dreams, waiting for you, belly-up. All your hopes on a silver platter."

She started trembling then, again. I reached toward her with a steadying hand. I could not have her fainting on me. Despite the blood on her face, on her dress, I said: "He won't hurt you."

He laughed. "Of course I won't. Do you know we have a whole team of servants who are rat catchers? It's all they do. Trap them. Poison them. Dispose of their bloated bodies. You are just vermin that scrabbled its way into the castle. We should have chewed you up and spat you out. But we gave you a chance."

"Why?" I asked—stupidly. But I wanted to procure more time.

He sneered at me. "Because I live in a castle. And you live in a crumbling pile of rocks. Oh, yes, I know about that, too. Otto told me. Your upper floor a heap of rubble. It doesn't matter, in the end. You'll go back home and live in ruin, and I'll still be a prince. None of it matters."

"Then let them go," Otto said, stepping through the door.

Simeon looked back at Otto in surprise. Calculating. Wondering if Otto knew all that I knew. "You work for me," he sneered.

"I work for the kingdom."

"I am the kingdom."

Otto took another step into the room. "You don't take an unmarried girl, no matter the circumstances. Her mother has every right to collect her."

Something in Simeon's demeanor changed. He became playful. Light on his feet. "Now, Otto! Do not stop me from having a little fun."

Otto looked over at Elin, who was still trembling, and back to Simeon. "No one is having fun." He extended a hand to us women. "Come."

"You would defy me?" Simeon asked, eyes narrowing.

"I am protecting you. From your own inclinations." Otto took ahold of Elin's hand and helped her across the floor to the doorway. I followed behind, without looking away from the prince.

Simeon addressed me as I passed him. "This"—he gestured around himself at the buttery, the inn above us—"will be the stitch that unravels you. Mark my words, you are undone now. Ruin happens slowly. But you already have the stench of rot."

"We're done here." Otto undid the frog on his scabbard—a version of a threat—and waved us forward. I took Elin by the arm and tugged her through the doorway.

Simeon shook his head. "Rescued by a man with a sword."

"Sometimes," I said, quietly enough I was not sure I was heard, "it really can be that simple."

ON THE LONG CARRIAGE RIDE HOME, ELIN REQUIRED ONLY A PHYSI-cal kind of comfort. Her hands, which I again clasped in my own, were soft, smooth, and occasionally wet from wiping her tears. I found that even in this act of solace, I had a little bit of resentment. That some of the calluses on my palms might have been borne by her instead. That we might have shared more burdens.

As she nosed my shoulder, I thought about all she had lost. A kingdom. A life. A story. An exit, away from me and my daughters. She had no idea what I'd given up for her. Sigrid's threats were not idle. And yet—what do children do except take without knowledge of the sacrifice behind the giving? As I held her, proffering pats on the knee and reassuring squeezes of hands and shoulders, I was self-conscious in my offer of comfort. I had none of the bodily ease I enjoyed with Rosie and Mathilde.

When my girls were small, I would hold them similarly. So minutely aware of their skin, their pulse, the soft openings and closings of their lips. I would look over them—their nails, their hair, the thin skin stretched over the bones of their wrists, the rapid rise and fall of a sobbing or sleeping chest—and think, also, of the body that had created them. My own. I had made them. They were made of me. Sitting there, holding Elin, it occurred to me that all my empathy, my pain, had been for them, but also for myself. Perhaps mothers were no different. The *you, you, you, my darling, you*s were just another way of saying *me, me, me, I, I, I.*

I let go of Elin's hand and wrapped an arm around her shoulder. Tried to reassure her, saying inane things that came to my head. I was creating a whole new person to be with her. A new self to love her with. Each gesture, each intimacy had to be learned and earned.

She looked up at me. "I used to think, if I am good, if I am nice, then the world will be good and nice in return."

"So it should be," I said, looking down at the white-blond hairs on her head. The wet eyelashes. I resented her for all she had taken from me, and found I was still willing to give her so much more.

"But it isn't."

"No, it is not."

And we both stared out the window, thinking of the gap between *should be* and *is* and the morally vague expanse that you learn to make a home within.

CHAPTER THIRTY-TWO

EVERYONE RUSHED FROM THE HOUSE AS WE PULLED UP THE drive: Wenthelen holding up her skirts, and Rosie and Mathilde, connected by a pair of linked elbows. Alice brought up the rear. As if they had been waiting by the window, watching.

"Days you've kept us on our toes," Wenthelen scolded. She looked enormously pleased.

"What has happened? Where did you find them?" Mathilde demanded.

I embraced the girls first, one in each arm, pulling them against my body. "I am so happy to see you," I said into their hair. Kissing the tops of their dark heads.

Their upturned faces swiveled, and we all watched as Elin climbed down from the carriage behind me. There was a moment of hesitation—a half beat of breath—as everyone took her in, blood-spotted dress, lank hair, and then they rushed forward to surround her, too.

"You look older," Rosie breathed.

"It's been a handful of days," Elin protested.

"You've had an adventure," Wenthelen told her.

Alice, wordlessly, stepped forward and gave her an efficient, abrupt hug.

Elin fingered her dress self-consciously, but accepted their welcome, returned the smiles.

"You are all right, then?" Mathilde asked, and Elin nodded.

"Lucy?" I turned to Alice. She gave a quick shake of her head. I squeezed my eyes shut. I had expected it, but the confirmation still gutted me. I could not think of Lucy out there, alone. Trapped in a bush by her leathers. To have loved a thing for so long and then to be the reason for its downfall.

Opening my eyes, I tried to take solace in the tableau in front of me. My motley family, crying their relieved tears. Framed by Bramley, my fallen-down castle. We were missing a roof. But I was home. And I was certain that we were beating toward some kind of resolution.

Otto left quickly, telling me: "I am going to try to get back before Simeon. Try to talk some sense into Sigrid."

"She is not a little scrap that goes in whatever direction the wind blows." I frowned in the direction of the palace and then turned back to look at Otto. He had been so helpful to me—at a disadvantage, a danger, even, to his own self.

Reading something on my face, he promised: "I'll be careful."

I didn't know that I would need to be, too.

INSIDE, ALICE RECOUNTED THE PAST FOUR DAYS OF HUNTING FOR Lucy: She'd gone around and through as many trees as she could in the area, waving a lure with fresh meat. She'd asked the neighboring farmers to keep an eye out. She'd walked eight miles downwind from our house, and walked more fields, every day. She had spotted Lucy once—or a bird she thought was Lucy—but the hawk had been too far away to know for sure.

"Take some hope," Alice reassured me, with a light pat on my arm. Her version of an embrace. "She will not be far. Trained hawks don't wander."

"But they lose their training quickly," I muttered, sinking my head into my hands.

The adventure—the fear, the uncertainty, the final triumph—of the past few days had staved off a deep upset. I had held on to a hope, even, that Lucy would be safely secure when I returned. How many times had she gone up a tree only to return to us once more? But something deep inside of me knew that this time was different, that I had not kept up her carriage, her training, in a consistent enough way to guarantee her return to me. And every hour she had spent alone that week made her recovery less likely. After four days, seeing her again was nearly an impossibility. She had had a taste of the wild and would have lost her trust of man.

A part of me could not blame her. But I could not shake the thought of her getting trapped by her jesses.

ELIN AND I ATE TOGETHER—ROSIE INSISTING ON BRUSHING THE dirt from our clothing and Wenthelen shoving more and more food in front of us—and then collapsed in the drawing room. I felt settled, for the moment at least. Listening to the contented bickering of my daughters. Watching the firelight dance on all their faces. The world held at bay.

Elin, still, looked a little shell-shocked. Bits of red rimmed her eyes, though I had seen her shed no further tears since we returned home. It was Rosie who finally addressed it.

"You will move on soon," she assured her. "Because imagine the alternative."

"That is the problem," Elin protested. "I am imagining it! Poor Hemma." She turned to me. "What will become of her?"

But I wasn't ready to give my concern to Hemma. I still had not yet determined what would become of us. Sigrid—and Simeon—had promised ruin. But we were already ruined. I had been trying to scrabble our way out of ruin for years. The benefit was that I had no further to fall. I was left only with the same set of problems I had faced in the first place—though now with the added problem of the hole in the roof. And potential banishment from all of society.

"Hemma will be fine," I reassured her. But what I really meant was that Hemma would be as fine as someone with wealth and power could be. That life was filled with unkindness and so you had to meter out your sympathy. I was rationing mine, saving it for the people under my spotty roof. There was only so much rescuing one woman could undertake.

The evening brought a strange storm. Lashing wind and sheets of water did not discourage the moonlight from shining through the windows and covering the room. Long after everyone went to bed, I stayed by the fire, staring at the embers and letting my thoughts twirl through those dark places. Listening to rain pelt the windows.

I had wanted so much for my daughters, for so long. Had worked so hard and had pushed them harder. I had told Otto, just a few days before, that contentedness was only recognized once it was gone. Was that this very situation? Had I been striving for years, wanting, aching for more, more, more, unable to recognize the value of what was in front of me?

I was startled by a noise outside, which at first I took as part of the storm. But, as it grew louder, the noise of horse hooves on wet gravel drew me to my feet. I thought Otto had returned and went to the window. But it was not Otto.

I do not know why it hadn't occurred to us that he would come. Hubris, perhaps, or some stupid idea of victory's finality. The coach was mud-spattered. Curtains flapped through open windows. The sides had been hideously hacked apart—splinters of wood and peels of leather. The horses had uneven gaits and I knew if I were closer, I would hear their labored breathing, see blood in their saliva. And there, at the helm, drenched by rain, was a lone man. The driver.

"Simeon," I said, out loud. As if the name itself were a curse.

Our door was locked when we went out, not when we stayed in. And I did not think I could move quickly enough to bar him.

CHAPTER THIRTY-THREE

I RAN THROUGH THE ROOMS AND DOWN THE STEPS, STUMBLING, FOR I did not carry a candle. But my haste made no difference: By the time I reached the entryway, the front door had banged open, and Simeon stood in the frame, silhouetted by the rough weather and night behind him.

He looked wild. His hair mussed. He was in the same clothes as two days before. There was a high redness to his cheeks and a slackness at his jaw. I hoped he was drunk, for it might offer me an advantage.

"The door boasts a serviceable knocker," I told him, from the bottom stair.

He stepped forward, into the entry hall, streaming rivulets of water onto the floor. "You called me a beast. No man would name me so to my very face. But after you left . . . after you left, I thought: What self-respecting beast lets its lunch get away?" He was enjoying his own anger. "What kind tolerates disrespect without consequence?"

So he was here to eat me. Whatever that might mean. I came down off the steps, thinking to put myself between him and the rest of the house. I wondered if I might be able to placate him with deference.

"Your Highness—you're dripping wet. Allow me to remedy this, if it pleases you, and we'll talk."

But he had no interest in feigned civility. "Where are your daughters?" He pushed past me, with unwavering strength. I did not have the gumption to reach out and grab ahold of him, but I looked around, for a candelabra or anything else I might use if needed. He put a hand on the banister and turned back to me. "I am going to pluck their wings."

"Your argument is with me." I kept my voice calm, but a rapid pounding filled my chest.

"You're the chess master," he agreed. "But I am going to smash every piece on the board." He continued up the stairs, feet leaving wet marks.

The prince intended harm, but I had no way of knowing how much, how badly. I wondered if his arrival had stirred the girls, the sleeping women. I desperately needed help, but I did not want anyone to appear and put themselves in his way. I would have to expel or contain him on my own. I tried to think of Sigrid. Of her love for him. Of her ability to see the best, to want someone to be more than they were. "Prince Simeon," I called—hoping to placate, to stall. I did not know how to overpower him. "Think of your honor. Think of theirs!"

But he only laughed and kept going up the stairs.

I began to hurry up after him. "Your mother would not want this."

The invocation made him pause. "It is the mark of a mother that you think that would bother me at all." He turned toward the steps once more and kept going.

"How many people have you harmed?" I called.

He cocked his head. Tossed a glance over his shoulder. Curled his lips in something resembling a smile. "Stop trying to delay."

I was just behind him now. He could have shoved me backward, sent me tumbling down the steps, with a light push.

"Please," I begged. He turned—a blinding crack—and I received one of the backhanded slaps I'd seen him give Elin. A blue pain lit into the bone of my jaw. I gritted my teeth. Did not cry out.

"The harder you make it, the harder it is," he said, taking on Elin's affectations, as if spouting one of her maxims.

"Please—" I started to say again but thought better of it. I ducked my head. "I will show you the way."

Keeping my head down, I stepped aside, up, and around him, so I was ahead on the stairs. We were soon at the top. But, instead of turning toward the girls' bedchambers and the steps to Elin's keep, I went the other direction, toward the west wing.

My designs would not protect anyone for long, but I did not know what else to do. Maybe the girls had heard and would have time to hide or escape. Maybe I would find a way to subdue him. Knowing what was ahead, what he was capable of, I could not live with myself if I led him to the beating heart of my home.

The hall was dark and I could hear him breathing behind me, the squelch of his shoes, as we made our way forward. I kept one hand along the wall, to steady myself. Reaching, with some silly hope that my fingers would land upon a weapon. A long-forgotten sword leaning behind a tapestry. A family battle-axe that I'd never noticed. But my fingers remained empty and we made it to the double doors without incident. I pushed them open ahead of me.

In the moment it took for our eyes to adjust, I had only my senses. The air was moist. The rain must have come through the hole in the roof. The temperature was much lower. The wing of the house was incredibly still, silent. And then the pile of rubble, wet with rain, appeared in the gloom before us.

Simeon turned to me, understanding at once that I had not led him to Rosamund, to Elin, to Mathilde. I had expected fury—malevolence—but on his face, instead, was a kind of delight. "Still playing chess." He shook his head at me. "You've already lost." He reached out, and in one swift motion, had me by the neck, against the wall. "I told you. The harder you make this, the—"

He didn't finish the sentence. I had kneed him between the legs. He let go, groaning, and I ran. But he grabbed ahold of my skirts. I twisted away, hoping they'd rip, but he had them by two hands now. I scrabbled forward. With a yanking motion, he leveled me to the ground. I fell, landing on my shoulder with a cry.

He stood over me as I tried to push backward with the heels of my hands. Then, with a decisive movement, he was on top of me, straddling my hips.

The moonlight streaming through the hole in the roof lit him in an eerie gray. He looked beautiful. I could see the stubble of his jaw, the hollows of his temple. Like a sculptor's idea of a marble god. Like a sculpture, too, he had blank eyes—the emptiness had returned, and they had all the life of a pond of stagnant water.

He reached forward, placing both his hands on my neck. Squeezed. I could not breathe. I clawed at his fingers. Scratched my feet at the floor. Beat his back. But his grip remained firm. Viselike. Certain. No will or strength I could muster could undo that grip.

Beginning to feel faint, I wondered if this was how it would end. Something inside of me was starting to slow down. I tried to find leverage, to place one foot flat on the floor and thrust him off, but his weight was fully on top of me. A little bit of blackness at the edge of my vision.

I thought of Henry. Of gorse leaves. Of Lucy's baby feathers. The taste of apple in another man's mouth. A freckle on a calf. Twin braids. How do you make sense of your own life? What are the things that really matter, in the end? Did the girls know—*know*—how much I loved them? And would it be enough to sustain them once I was gone? A wish formed, in some emptying part of my mind: If only I had kept a list, a compendium, of all the things the girls should know. All that mattered. Instructions about how to live, how to survive. To share every part of myself, all the little pieces that made a person, to give them away, so that they might make use of them. My mistakes, my choices, my learnings could be the food of their lives.

My vision was going. Blackness, like a fog, creeping, fading. But I could still see Simeon, his face above mine. His unseeing eyes. What would he do when he was done with me? It was the thought of that—a continued prowl down the hall, the opening of the girls' doors, the stagnant pond water—that cleared my sight for one last moment. I stopped scrabbling at his fingers around my neck and instead reached up and dragged my nails down his cheeks.

He screamed. I'd drawn blood. Bright stripes of it. He let go of my neck to touch his face. His weight was still firmly on top of me, but the release of my windpipe gave me the briefest moment to draw a much-needed breath.

It was my only idea. Not premeditated, just there—the grasping of a dying woman. I licked my lips. Tried to whistle. Tried again, and this time the shrill notes came out. Three in a row. Low-high-low. I did it twice.

Simeon was looking at his palms now, at the blood. The sky behind him black. The moonlight made the blood look black, too. It dripped to his jaw.

"You little bitch," he said, voice cold, and reached forward to grab my neck once more. This time, I was certain, with the intent to kill me as quickly as possible.

I saw a figure above. Small and dark and darting. If it were my last image, I would have gladly welcomed it. The shadow took form and Lucy flew in through the hole in the roof. He had not seen her, still had his hands around my neck, but seeing me watching something turned his face upward. I willed her to listen, to follow her nature.

She could smell the blood. See it in the dark with her hawk eyes. She was fast. On his face in an instant. Scrabbling with her deadly claws. A talon in an eyeball. More blood. He began screaming, released me, and I shoved him, scrambling backward, putting distance between us.

My Lucy. She was safe. She had come. She was saving me. I felt a surge of love, watching her with ribbons of flesh in her claws.

Simeon, still screaming, reached up and grabbed her body—a talon stuck in his cheek, pulling it outward—and threw her, as hard as he could, against the near wall. A burst of plumage, a scrabbling, and her body fell to the floor. A wing bent, feebly twitching. Contorted. A quivering. Then, stillness.

"Lucy," I cried. But my voice did not work. It came out only as air.

Simeon turned back toward me, toward the noise I had made. I could not tell how much he could see. He was covered in his own blood. One of his eyeballs was distended. The muscle of his cheek showed through a rip in his skin. A monster on the outside that matched whatever was within.

"I will slay you, you pathetic, smelly cunt."

"My cunt made me a mother," I rasped.

I was still on the floor. Pushing backward. And he put his boot—sodden, rough—on my throat and stepped down. "I will end you and everyone in this foul, beggarly house. The worst kind of ruin. For each of your daughters. I will take you without mercy and—"

A loud crack. He collapsed. A straight fall to the floor. I could not see, could not make sense of it for a moment, until my vision cleared, and I saw Elin standing over him, a wooden post—a part of the damaged roof—in her hands.

"In resolving challenges one must look to the compass of justice," she said, staring down at Simeon. She turned to me, breath shallow. "I heard screaming."

Slowly, painfully, I pulled myself to sitting. Looked over at him. I do not think Simeon heard her or understood what had happened. I was reasonably sure—a spreading pool of blood, inert limbs, still lips—that he was dead.

Elin peered down at his body, eyes glistening. "He was not a gentleman."

My throat, which pulsed, felt crushed, like a stalk of wheat that had been bent and mangled. "No," I rasped. "No, he was not."

I put my arms out and did my best to soften Elin's fall. She had fainted.

CHAPTER THIRTY-FOUR

I HAD NEVER LIFTED SIMEON IN LIFE, BUT IN DEATH, THE BULK OF him must have doubled—blood congealed to lead, skin shedding life and gaining solidity as it stiffened.

Elin and I managed him between us, down the dark hall. I had his feet and she his hands, and we lurched along. "Take care with the blood," I told her. "Mind the carpet."

"I'll wrap his head in a cloth." Her voice wavered. "Not like he can see."

I waited while she fetched a rag—a fitting shroud. My fear was gone. My throat still hurt. "And you are untouchable," I whispered, to the body.

When Elin returned, she had composed herself. "I found a suitable piece." She bent to wrap the cloth around his head, taking care. Gentle hands. "Green suits him."

When we finally managed to get Simeon downstairs, she said to me: "All things find their proper resolution. See? Already the rain has stopped." She was right, though I attributed the shift more to our fickle climate than any kind of cosmic approval. Simeon's limbs, after all, were still dragging on the floor.

I put on a cloak and bid Elin to do the same. She waited with the body while I retrieved the one-wheeled wooden cart we used for the apple harvest. The plan had developed between us without words: I knew what to do, and Elin would follow. I might have marveled at her elasticity—the girl who would not dirty herself, the same young lady who insisted on an everlasting ballad of moral rectitude—except I, too, was moving forward with a kind of numbness. I felt no need to defend myself, even to the most vociferous inner critique.

When I stepped outside, I was stopped by the sight of the carriage. The horses stood, stamping, snorting clouds of breath into the air. I went over and laid a hand on the corded neck of the animal that was closer, willing it to be calm. It blinked, watching me with an oversized eye. Nervous. I stepped forward, without thinking, and laid my cheek on its neck.

Hugging the creature was the closest I could come, in that moment, to grieving Lucy, whose feathered body still lay on the cold floor upstairs. I wanted to feel the animal's warmth, even if it were afraid of me. I wanted to soak in a bit of its life, and to offer, or feel, something akin to love.

The moment was soon over. The horse nickered, unhappy to be a stand-in. Or just unhappy, for it had not been cared for or ridden well. Working slowly, making what reassuring noises I was capable of—for my voice was raspy and my throat ached—I undid the fastenings on its harness, and removed the bridle. When he was free, he walked a few steps forward. I did the same for his mate.

I could have kept them, used them. Sold them. But they were Simeon's horses and I needed to put a wide distance between them—however brown their eyes, however appealing the notion of their recuperation—and myself. Aiming to scare them away, I threw pebbles. Waved my arms. Frightened them until they moved at a steady trot down the drive.

All was dark in the cellar house. The hulking shape of the barrels indistinguishable from the dark air itself. I found the tools by touch. With the long-handled axe in one hand and the shovel in the other, I felt immediately better. My stomach surer. I placed them into the wheelbarrow, and went back to the house, willing my feet and hands to ignore the cold.

Elin and I loaded Simeon into the cart with difficulty. He did not fit well. His arms and legs flapped over the sides. The handles of the tools stuck up around him, like spikes he had been impaled upon. His covered head lolled back like a drunk man.

At the first row of trees, we paused. "Leave him here. We must take care of the carriage first," I told Elin. I walked over to the empty, horse-less coach. Raised the axe. Sank the blade into its side.

"Stepmother," Elin called, from her spot behind me. I brushed my hair back from my face and turned. She was pointing to the front door, which now stood open, Alice in the frame. Her gray hair was loose, and she looked grimmer than usual.

She looked at the carriage, the axe. I doubted she could see the cart in the darkness, but she was peering past me, into the trees.

"How can I help?" she asked.

"There is blood upstairs," I told her. "Scrub it."

"And us?" Rosie and Mathilde, holding candles, appeared just behind her.

"Put cloaks on and light a fire. A large one."

"Use the covered wood, ladies," Wenthelen instructed, coming alongside them. "It's dry."

We all looked at one another. At the empty royal coach. The hacked-apart sides. Everything still wet from the rain. And then, wordlessly, they all moved away from me. Alice, to the kitchens to select a bucket and coarse brush. Wenthelen and Mathilde to gather more wood. Elin and Rosie to fetch more cloaks. And I turned back to the job ahead of me, axe in hand.

They had asked no questions. Whether blind loyalty or trust, I was grateful for it. If I had needed them, the words to explain couldn't have done the situation justice.

The carriage was meticulously constructed from beautifully carved wood, with leather stretched over its top and sides. The windows were glass. The wheels marked by decorative carved spokes. I raised the axe again and again against the side of the coach. Hacking apart what remained of the heraldic symbols. Ripping velvet curtains from their frames. Smashing wooden wheels.

Each time I raised the long-handled tool, I felt grateful for the buckets of water I'd carried. The bundles of wood. The bushels of apples. The body of a hawk I'd lifted, again and again, arm extended, muscles taut.

Once the pieces of the coach were small enough, the women brought them, one by one, carrying the larger parts between them, to the fire they had built. Hot flames welcomed wheels and wood. Leather blackened. Carvings smoldered. Iron brackets glowed red. When the last of the dismantled carriage had been placed into the embers, we all stood around. Sparks flew up into the air. My girls' faces were lit by the blaze. Their twin braids gleamed in the yellow light.

Elin reached into the folds of her dressing gown and pulled out her little booklet. Alice caught my eye. Both of us concerned, momentarily, that we were about to be quoted at.

But Elin surprised us all and tossed the thing into the fire.

"I will not be saved by a book," she announced.

We said nothing, and instead stood for a moment, watching the cinders devour all those nice words of virtue.

ELIN AND I LEFT EVERYONE AT THE FIRE AND PUSHED THE CART across the property. Over the potholed, soaked grass. Past the rows of gnarled trees. I looked back, once. At all of them, circling the oversized flames. Working together in their ignoble pursuit.

We scraped ourselves going through the hole in the laurel. Shoved the cart. Emerged with leaves in our hair. But from there, there were no obstructions along the familiar path. Across the road, down the embankment. Past the many skinny-trunked trees. Along the winding dirt walkway. The dense growth even denser at night.

At the stream, we abandoned the cart and reverted to carrying Simeon by ankles and wrists. There was no avoiding the water. We went in, shin deep. The body got drenched. Elin dropped his feet. His torso floated between us. When we finally made it over, we lowered the prince into the soft mud, panting.

"There you are," I told him. "Royal land."

His head cloth had come off in the stream and I looked at his disfigured face. "I suppose we're both monsters now." The thought did not bother me. I was done pretending. I was happy to gobble people up. To eat them whole.

To Elin, I said: "We need to bury him."

I went back across the stream to get the shovel from the cart. We took turns, though I did the greater part of the labor. My body was ready for it, still running on some kind of inhuman fuel. Though it was a shallow grave, and the ground was softened by rain, the digging took hours. By the time we shoved him in, the sky had begun to lighten above us. A deep indigo that washed to gray. Just enough daylight to watch Simeon disappear beneath shovels and fistfuls of dirt.

Remorse still had not come. I thought of his hands on my neck. Of Lucy's feathered body, twitching on the ground. Of blood spurting from Elin's nose. Of a bite mark from unknown teeth. Of Hemma. I dropped another fistful of dirt on his ugly face and when we had finished, we flattened the ground with the soles of our boots. Covered the fresh dirt with old leaves.

We looked at one another a moment. We were sweating and our hems were blackened with mud. Dirt encrusted our nails. Elin's nose had begun to bleed again. "I have a blister," she told me, extending her hand to show me. And there it sat, in the meat of her palm. Round, white, perfect.

"It will heal."

She withdrew her hand. Inspected the bleb. "I do not mind."

We made our way back across the stream, wetting our hems anew.

"Should we have said some words for him?" Elin wondered.

"When they figure out he is gone, plenty will be said."

"I suppose there will be no wedding now." She ducked her head, embarrassed, watching her feet on the path. "Obviously," she corrected herself. "Is my wrongdoing—was it wrong? Have I . . ?" She did not finish her question.

I walked ahead of her. "I think you will find being a woman is nothing like being a girl. And that grace and justice are sometimes pursued by means less graceful and less just."

Elin frowned. "Life cannot contain such a contradiction."

"Oh, it can," I started, but then hushed. I had the sense of déjà vu, and then I understood why. Up ahead, through the trees, I saw a coach. With royal insignia. And it was headed in the direction of our drive.

"Hurry," I urged Elin.

Up to that point, I had gone through the night as if in a muted kind of stupor. I hadn't fully marveled at the impact of what we had done. To change the course of a kingdom. To alter history. I realized I might die because of it. Would die, if I were found out.

I took the cart over from Elin and we broke into a run. Stayed along the embankment. The cart was horribly noisy, but so was a carriage, and the retinue that accompanied it. We stayed out of sight, slipping back across the road and through the hole in the hedge. I discarded the shovel in the middle of the laurel but kept the cart.

"We won't have time to change," Elin panted, beside me.

"We aren't changing," I told her, veering toward the cellar house. I scrambled inside and grabbed what I needed. Overturned the bushel of apples into the cart. Licked my thumb and used it to wipe the blood from Elin's face.

"Chin up," I told her. I could feel the mud drying on my hands. I took hold of the cart once more. The apples jostled as I moved forward. "We're going to meet the queen."

Sigrid's carriage was first in a long line that stretched down the driveway. She was already alighting from the coach with the help of two gloved footmen when Elin and I pushed our way through the trees. The queen's dress barely fit through the opening of the carriage and the footmen had to reach in to squeeze the hoops of her skirts. She landed in the gravel, took a cautious step forward and looked around with distaste. Behind her, the guards and riders were dismounting. A few courtiers emerged from their own carriages, sniffing the air.

My daughters stood on the front steps, waiting to receive them. They wore the same gray and yellow fine dresses they'd donned to welcome the messenger just a few weeks before. Rosie's hair had been swept into a net. Mathilde had borrowed my stomacher. I couldn't see a trace of the fear they no doubt felt.

All of them turned and saw Elin and I simultaneously. Rosie's eyes widened in alarm. Mathilde winced. But Sigrid's lip curled—perhaps the closest thing to her real smile I had ever seen. I continued forward, the cart ahead of me. "Good morrow, Your Majesty," I called.

Agatha reared her red head then, telling me—demanding—that I drop into supplication. Expressing shock at my mess. Little frissons of disgust and need. But I had had enough of Agatha. I could stand her in my head no longer. I did not sink into a curtsy for my back was already bent with effort to move the wheelbarrow. I called to Sigrid: "Can I please you with an apple?"

I was aware of the full line of guards and courtiers watching me. I paused, straightened, plucked another apple off the tree nearest to me, and tossed it into the cart.

"You're covered in mire," Sigrid observed.

"We were not expecting visitors." I stepped around the wheelbarrow, revealing the extent of the mud on my skirts.

"You've kindled a fire." The queen nodded toward the remnants of the night's flames—a smoldering pile of ash on the lawn.

"A pyre," I said, lightly. "For our house. Our roof fell in." I waved a hand in the air, in the direction of the sky. "Quite a sight if you'd care to see from the rear. Lots of debris to rid ourselves of."

The queen looked back and forth between Elin and I, and to the fire. Sigrid could not make sense of what was in front of her—the mud, the labor. She shook herself, as if she were a dog ridding water, and focused on Elin. "You cannot look like that." The first word came out with venom. *You*—the one betrothed to the prince. *You*—the great Trojan horse.

"The last of the apples must be picked," I told Sigrid.

"Industry is the forge where success is wrought," Elin agreed, clasping her hands like a young girl.

Sigrid glanced back at her long line of courtiers, her guards. The velvet and the jewels looked incongruous in our scrabbly orchard. Following her gaze, I saw, on the back of his horse, Otto. He gave me an almost imperceptible shake of the head, and I looked away.

"We'll go inside," Sigrid announced.

I brushed my hands on my dress. "Girls!" I called to my daughters on the steps. "Tell the kitchens we have . . ." I eyed Sigrid with distaste. "A guest."

IN THE ENTRYWAY, MY SHOES SQUELCHED ON THE FLOOR. SIGRID wasted no time; out of sight of her retinue, she declared: "She clearly cannot spend more time in this household." To Elin, she added: "By gods, get ahold of yourself. Appearing before all of court like a pig in the mud."

"You picked us," I reminded her, leading the way into the great hall, Elin and Sigrid trailing behind me. "Unfortunately, we come with a bit of dirt under our nails."

"A harvest cannot yield gold without a plowman's furrow." Elin settled on a chaise and primly arranged her dirty skirts around her.

Sigrid said: "A girl should not speak!"

I strode across the hall and began to open the window curtains, going down the row. "I do not think you've made the journey so that we can all sit in silence." I used the activity—the time—to try to gather my thoughts and set them in order. If Sigrid was still concerned with Elin's comportment, particularly in front of courtiers, then she assumed Elin would still be marrying her son. She did not yet know that Simeon was missing. (Fists of dirt covering his fine clothes, his well-cut jaw.) It was impossible to guess exactly what Otto had said, or shared, upon his return home, but the safest course of action would be to presume that, in the queen's mind, we had only just come back from successfully blockading the elopement. I had expressly gone against Sigrid's wishes by interfering. She had threatened the future of me and my family, and she would be furious I had dared to test her wrath. But the very fact of her arrival, at Bramley, in person, revealed something else—she still desperately needed Elin. In her own mind, at least.

Confirming my suspicions, Sigrid did not sit, but followed me along the row of windows, protesting like an agitated bird. "Stop that," she commanded. She had probably never opened her own curtains. "I told you," she said, when I turned, "what would happen if you obstructed the wedding."

"So I have done all I can to preserve just that: a wedding!" I dropped the curtain pulls and faced her fully. The trick would be to perform obstinance, but of a much lesser sort than murder. It was easy to cast myself back to the mindset of two days before, easy to start believing, already, my own lies. For they weren't fully lies, but rather truths of an earlier self. The conversation might have been genuine if Simeon had not appeared in the entryway the night before. "Your son may be a prince, but he cannot abduct an unmarried girl on a whim." I fixed her with a stare. "Certainly, we can agree an elopement in a backwater hovel doesn't serve anyone's purpose."

Sigrid pulled herself upward, to her full height, the gesture belying some inner weakness. "I am not concerned with your purpose, and you've explicitly contradicted mine."

"Forgive me, but your purpose, made clear by obfuscations that aid and abet your family members, is to keep good standing in the public eye. Is that not the reason for all this?"

Sigrid, not accustomed to being addressed in such a manner, swelled, ready to spew some venom. But she stopped herself, with great effort—feeling her need of me—and instead turned to look out the window.

Quietly, I added: "And however aligned or misaligned our purposes may be, I'll remind you that your family needs mine behind which to stash your secrets."

"I almost married my cousin," she said, after a minute. "Sibling isn't so different, is it? People make all these rules. It's only the appearance of abiding that makes a difference. They'll forgive anything if it's behind a shut door."

She had almost married a lot of people, by my memory, but I did not think it wise to say as much. "Nevertheless, you wanted Elin to be the door itself. And so she shall. But the door only remains effective if it believably appears to be a door! There must be an actual wedding."

"To have a wedding there must be a groom, and he has not returned."

"Maybe he's taking a few days to nurse his wounds and treat his flea bites."

"You just left him there?" Sigrid cried. "Like a common pauper?"

"We felt confident he could get himself home. After all, he's the one that led the whole expedition in the first place."

"Where is he?" she demanded.

Elin listened, face swiveling back and forth as we spoke.

"I haven't the faintest notion. I'll admit," I continued, beginning to untie the strings of my cloak, "Elin's retrieval was not without some resistance." I took the cloak off, let it fall to the floor. "But Simeon came around. In the end."

Sigrid paled, then turned a shade of green. I looked past her, to the mirror above the mantel, and saw: As I'd expected, my neck was mottled and purple, bruised and welted. The queen put a hand on her own neck, looking faint. I wondered how many times she had felt similarly. How often she'd had to face the unsettling, belly-turning evidence of her son's wrongs. Or maybe that was just it—she'd never had to see any kind of real evidence. Her own point had been that transgressions were much easier to overlook, to ignore, when they were abstract.

"He seems capable of taking care of himself," I added, to fill her silence.

"You will not tell me what happened," she instructed in a whisper. Her face paint had begun to crack about her mouth. The rouge on her cheeks looked violent.

"Only a moment ago, you were insisting upon it."

"He is not a villain," she protested. "Just a boy. Unaware of the force he wields."

"A boy old enough to marry is a man."

The door opened at the far end of the room, pushed by Wenthelen bearing a tray of refreshments. Rosie and Mathilde close behind, faces carefully blank.

Sigrid smoothed her hair, remembering herself, but did not acknowledge them. "Well," she said, "he will return. He will return and we will plan the wedding."

"Certainly," I said, the lie as easy on my tongue as a glug of oil. I turned to the tray, to Wenthelen, to my daughters, as they made their way across the room. "Ah, look—something to eat. But, Your Majesty, I must warn you before you settle in—it really is not safe for you to be here. With the damage to our roof, the structure is not sound. We could not have anything happen to you here."

Sigrid shook her head and regained her haughty composure. "I'm taking my leave," she declared, as if the idea were her own. "It seems your entire household is hanging on by a thread."

"Now, now," I told her, laying a soft hand on her arm. "Let us not resort to insults. If all goes as planned, we will soon be sisters, after all. That is the word you used, is it not?"

"In name only."

"Yes, well." I walked over to the door and held it open so that she might pass. "No one really cares what happens behind closed doors."

THE QUEEN WAS DENIED THE SATISFACTION OF A DRAMATIC EXIT. HER retinue had to vacate the driveway in reverse order of its arrival, and Sigrid's carriage was the last to leave. I did not wait to watch the slow maneuvering, the climbing and turning of horses, the reversal of the carriages, though I could hear the noise—the shouting of men, the hoofbeats, the creaking and jangling of coaches and wagons—as I went up the stairs.

As I was climbing, I heard footsteps behind me. Otto stood in the doorway. He looked back over his shoulder to confirm no one had seen him and then turned to me, brown eyes concerned. I beckoned that he should come upstairs. He followed me and we went down the hall without speaking.

I had taken a gamble, being so impertinent with the queen. But I believed myself to have calculated well. A guilty conscience might have tried to smooth things over, to curry favor, which in turn might eventually have pointed to my guilt. But I felt none, and instead had behaved as a woman with little to hide—and little to lose. Sigrid had been right that our household was hanging on by a thread, but I no longer felt any conviction about what we hung on to. I did not fear a little snip and a fall. It might be better, in the end, than all the clawing upward.

I led Otto to my bedchamber, but no lust or curiosity lit our faces. For on the bed was a box, and inside it lay Lucy. Her feathered body inert, her eyes lifeless. A wing still bent at the wrong angle. A few extra feathers loose, gathered in a corner of the carton.

Otto put a hand on my arm.

I looked at Lucy for a long moment—fruitlessly hoping that she would raise her head, glare at me, and hop onto my glove—before turning to him, my eyes full. His hand stayed on my arm and I raised both of mine to return the gesture, holding him by the elbows. "You shouldn't be here." It did not mean, *I do not want you here.*

He looked me over. Asked questions without words. I knew he saw the bruises on my neck when his pupils widened, his eyes darkening. The hand on my arm tightened. Otto's gaze flicked to the door, as if Simeon might be in the room, or just down the hall. "Where is he?"

"We are all safe now. Except for Lucy."

"I never should have left." His face contorted. He looked me over again, searching for more injuries. "You are covered in mud."

"My natural state." I attempted a smile.

"He will not rest. You will not be safe." He let go of me to rub a hand over his face. "We must get you out of the kingdom."

"Otto—"

"There are routes—"

"Simeon will not be coming home," I told him, voice low.

"You are in danger."

"Simeon will *not* be coming home," I repeated, with more force.

His eyes searched mine. I nodded. And his jaw ticked—understanding. He held his face close to mine, pressed his forehead against my own. "We are in worse danger, then."

"We?" I asked, in surprise. "You were at the palace."

"I should have been here."

"You need to go back outside," I whispered. "To keep yourself above suspicion."

He nodded and then began to speak quickly. "I've told the queen the truth, as far as I knew it. That Simeon acted without honor, taking Elin, lodging with her, without marrying her, and without her family's permission. That I assisted in recovering her, and that I believed her family—you—were within grounds to do so. That we left Simeon there, and that a prince, in the eyes of his kingdom, needs to act with honor or the kingdom will lose respect for him. Sigrid does not know all that I know—not about Simeon's child—for I thought this was the best way to protect you. But maybe if I had told her, maybe, she might have predicted—"

"If you told her, then you would only put yourself in danger without protecting anyone else. You have to go back and pretend all is normal."

"You—" he started, but I cut him off, dropping his arms and giving him a small push toward the door.

"*Go!*"

"Ethel—" he started again.

I could not stop myself. I went to him. Let him hold me a moment. His arms around my shoulders. We did not speak. The words did not feel necessary. "I'll make my way back here," he said, into my hair. He went to the door and with a final look—how all the world can fit in one look—he slipped back out and into the hall.

I watched Otto return to his horse and rejoin the caravan. And stayed at the window until the queen's carriage passed through our broken gates. I knew, but did not fear, that it would be gracing our property for the last time. I could see the future clearly: There would be no more invitations to balls. No more cause for overdone dresses. No more hopes of elevating my girls. Maybe at one point, I might have reached for the coach's receding form. Grasped at all it represented, at what was slipping away from me. But rather than loss, its disappearance brought relief.

We dug another grave that afternoon. A small one. A little burrow carved into the rich earth beneath the oak tree. The excavation was gentle and done with all the care our hands could muster. But it was only my hands that lowered Lucy, wrapped in linen, into the ground.

We took turns dropping shovelfuls of dirt. Saying goodbye. And when everyone had said their part, I knelt on the grass in front of the dark spot of upturned ground and offered my falcon wordless gratitude. For what good are words when you have all of life to express? I had

thought myself Lucy's teacher, showing her, reminding her, of the correct ways of being: loyalty, patience, and fidelity. Except, it had been
she that taught me: Loyalty. Patience. Fidelity. I sank my fingertips into
the dirt and breathed. And Elin and Alice and Rosie and Wenthelen
and Mathilde swayed behind me. Put their hands on my back, on my
shoulders. And in their touch, I felt it: All I had given. All I would take.
Live, live, live. Slender wrists holding up a falling roof.

I did not know what would come next. What time and circumstance
would spit up into our lives. If the events of the night before would
be discovered and spell our end. But I could grasp on to what was in
front of and around me. Elin, still covered in the night's mud. Rosie
and Mathilde, holding one another. Wenthelen and Alice, silhouetted
by the branches of the oak, heads bowed. A bird in the ground that had
saved my life. More than once and in more ways than one.

I looked around at my family. They looked back at me. I nodded,
stood, and we went back into the house together.

EPILOGUE

To HOOD A HAWK REQUIRES PRACTICE—A LIGHT HAND, AND THE ability to watch the bird carefully, and read its signals. The girls all stand with their goshawks in the clearing, practicing.

"Wait until they turn their heads toward your shoulder," I instruct, demonstrating with an imaginary bird in front of me. "The beak needs to pass through the opening, not strike against the side."

"My fingers are lead," complains Rosie. The feathers around her bird's beak are still downy.

"You won't be able to feel it properly with gloves on." Mathilde has already hooded her bird twice.

Goshawks are spooky birds. Pale eyes and huge talons. They kill in thickets, with short, brutal dives off the falconer's fist. They will pursue prey anywhere. They do not need land or air or a manor hall—the benefits of gentility—to hunt.

"Conceal the hood in the palm of your hand," I remind Rosie. "Touch the bird's foot to make it look down."

"There!" Elin marvels at her success. Her gos's head, now covered, swivels, seeing nothing. She cries: "Practice pursued diligently always bestows an abundance of capability!"

"Is that necessary?" Mathilde snaps.

"Sorry." Elin winces. "How much longer until we can fly them properly?"

"Bit by bit." I follow her gaze. We stand in the woods. Not far from where Simeon's body lies decomposing. A year in the ground.

Felon or savior: I have tried to present all to you with an even hand. Goodness is always contextual. I took a finger. I took a life. But stories are made by organizing and reciting details. You can arrange them in so many ways.

When the prince never returned home, the palace sent out parties looking for him. They came through Bramley, barging through our rooms, snuffing about in the cellars as though we might have him tied to a grate. But I do not think they suspected us. Not truly. It didn't fit into Sigrid's understanding of the world. We would not harm him when we had so much to lose. If we were hanging on by just a thread—who would sever those final fibers with their own hand? The queen never thought to search her own lands. And after months of fruitless looking, Hemma was declared the heir.

A few weeks after Simeon went missing, I heard the news from Lavinia. It was a miracle, she said, shaking with the excitement of new gossip. She did not notice my diminished place at the market, or the fact that I had come to sell cider. The queen, she told me, hands in a clawlike grip on my arm, was with child. Her joy in those last two words turned her breath hot.

I did not go into the city or ever see Sigrid's swelled form with my own eyes. She did not interact with my family again. But when the babe was born—as white-blond as Hemma, the criers said—I had enough sense to know for certain what others might only guess at.

Otto oversaw the hunt for Simeon, but really, he told me, to watch what happened with Hemma. After her child's birth, he left the palace for good. He has asked for my hand three times. Three times I've said no. Not to the man, but to the consignment of oneself. He says that is fine, and he will stay by my side anyway. Another set of wrists to hold up our roof. I worried, at first, what people would think. But I've found that, ultimately, I do not care. I can no longer bear passing up an opportunity for happiness.

Alice has grayed, further, with passing time, but is a little bit less stiff. A little bit less grim. Wenthelen has taken on a helper in the kitchen. A new mark for delighted remonstration. The hole in the roof remains, and worsens, but we are saving for repairs. Moussa came back a few months after I sent him away, missing another tooth, and ready to drink us dry. I finally took his advice and started selling our cider. His instinct was right. We do not have enough apples to meet the demand. We buy both meat and sugar.

The girls, for now, are still my own. Their own. Unmarried, with varying feelings about it. Elin works on her trousseau. Rosamund has taken an apprenticeship with a seamstress—her first commission was from the Enright twins. And Mathilde has become my shadow: Making cider. Pestering me about the birds until I relented. But, collectively, I think we've all come to see: Marriage is not a savior. Just a choice. And while the blue dress still sits in paper, it will serve as a witness of, not a cause for, happiness.

Lest you find yourself searching for a neat bundle, nicely tied with a crisp bow, I will remind you: Our futures remain uncertain. All the women are unmarried. A mother lost her child. And a body rots in the ground. You tell me: Is this a happy ending?

High above us, I see a wild hawk hurtling across the sky. "Cover your birds," I instruct, though all the goshawks already have their hoods on. Overhead, the falcon carries a bit of bloodied meat in her foot. Ferrying dinner to some unknown nest. To her children.

"Look," I tell the girls.

They comply. Three upturned faces. Three arms extended afore, birds held aloft. I want to reach for them. Pull them close. But I do not have enough hands to hold them all. So, instead, I watch them. Absorb each detail. Twin sable braids and blond curls. Freckles and scars and mud. Scary, aggressive birds that hint at madness.

I look around, taking in the dappled darkness, the forest. The leaves rotting in layers. The shadows designed to hide. The light playing games, turning branches to claws, twigs to snakes. It is a place to hide or be hidden from. A place for outlaws. Pariahs. A place that should frighten me.

But forget the word *should*.

Over the months, I have thought more about my compendium. My list of things the girls should know. Learned to update my own lessons. My book of maxims—life, distilled—would be short:

You do not need to be afraid. You do not have to be good. You do not need to hide your fleshy interiors behind a carapace of frills and lace. Life is not meant for measurement. There is but one beat to heed. Live like this and you will know with certainty:

You are the scariest thing in the woods.

ACKNOWLEDGMENTS

My profound thanks to all those who brought *Lady Tremaine* to life.

First, to all the Cinderellas that came before. Despite my mother's best efforts, I was enthralled with the folktale as a child. It was only as an adult, and through mothering my own daughters, that I found the need to revisit a tale that, across centuries, languages, and cultures, has continued to tell young women that, if they are beautiful, nice, and follow the rules, they might be lucky enough to be "picked" by a prince. If you've made it this far, you know exactly how I've come to feel about that. Still, I owe a wealth of inspiration to *Cendrillon* and *Grimms' Fairy Tales* and the various fantasies of my girlhood. From the seeds of these old tales—and the realization that we all have the power to write our own endings—grew the desire to reclaim and reshape the narrative that shaped me.

To my brilliant editor, Sarah Cantin: I could not dream of a more seamless partnership. You've gone to bat for Etheldreda since our first conversation, advocating for my vision of this story—and, more importantly, *sharing* that vision—in countless ways. I'm told it's not always this easy. To everyone else at St. Martin's Press—Jennifer Enderlin,

Anne Marie Tallberg, Dori Weintraub, Erica Martirano, Brant Janeway, Alexis Neuville, Kim Ludlam, Tom Thompson, Michael Storrings, Jen Edwards, Layla Yuro, Drue VanDuker, Mary Beth Roche, and others— I am grateful beyond measure. And to Charlotte Mursell and everyone at Orion: Thank you for bringing Lady Tremaine "home," so to speak. I am so lucky to be working with all of you.

To my fairy godmother agent, Alyssa Reuben: You are a partner a decade in the making. Your thoughtful feedback stitched me to your side long before either of us realized it. Thank you, thank you for being my— and Lady Tremaine's—champion. My gratitude also to Hellie Ogden, Laura Bonner, Liza Mullett, Ma'suma Amiri, Hilary Zaitz Michael, and everyone at WME—how lucky I am to have such an indomitable team.

Astute observers will find parallels between Helen Macdonald's masterful writing on falconry and Lucy's journey. *H Is for Hawk* brought to life the crucial hawking details a novice like myself needed, elevating a technical practice to an art form.

To Jennifer Kotlewski: I could not imagine a better set of first eyes for these pages. Your encouragement, close reading, and incredible fireplace were life support when my confidence faltered. To Jena Wolfe, Annie Lenon, and Valerie Gnaedig: Your artistic partnership sustained and nurtured me when I needed it the most. To Kat Collings, Lexi Berard, Sarah Hutcherson, Olivia Austin, and Nicole Elizabeth: I'd go to the moon and back with you all. Love, also, to the extended cast of family and friends, old and new, close and far—my sister Samantha, my brother-in-law, Barbara and Jerry Markowitz, Marisa Markowitz, Craig Hauser, my extended family, Ben and Gabrielle Jacobs, Patrick Hamo, Grace Douglas, Maggie Morris, and so many others—whose support of me and my family was, in turn, support of my writing. I love you all.

I must also thank Olivia Clare Friedman, Susannah Luthi, Mark Richard, Richard Rayner, Helen Schulman, Karen Slade, and all the professors and fellow writers who, once upon a time, believed in my writing. To Ivan Sonier: Thanks for delivering books to my doorstep all the years of my childhood. They're still on my shelf. Thanks also to David Brooks, Sean Berard, and Glennon Doyle for your early advocacy.

This book would not have been possible without childcare—a privilege that should be a right. Brandi Daerr and Naomi Stringer took care of my babies and gave me the peace of mind I needed to focus. You are both such an important part of this story.

Mom, Dad—thanks to you, I know the immeasurable fortune of love, support, and safety. I understand now all you've done for me. My accomplishments belong to you. Wherever you are always has been, and always will be, home.

Most of all: to my little family. Bea and Isabel, when you are old enough to read these words, I hope you'll understand they are all for you. Everything is for you. You are my world.

To Eric, the inspiration, in no small part, for Otto's grumpiness and good heart. This entire book—and its most dramatic scene—would not exist if it were not for you. Marriage is not a guaranteed fairy tale, but I've lucked out with a partner who could not be more encouraging of my endeavors. Since the very beginning, your support of me and my writing has been the purest flame.

ABOUT THE AUTHOR

Cayce Clifford

Rachel Hochhauser grew up in Santa Barbara, California. She attended New York University and earned a master's in professional writing from the University of Southern California. Currently, she lives in Portland, Oregon, with her husband and two daughters. *Lady Tremaine* is her first novel.